Additional works by

J. Eugene Porter

THE NAVAL ODYSSEY OF PROFESSOR JAMES BRAND

U-Boat Scourge

Mission to Britain

Calculated Risk

Night Attack

BRAD BAYLE MYSTERY

The Container Affair

All books available at Amazon.com

BATTLE PLAN

The Naval Odyssey of Professor James Brand

Book V

J. Eugene Porter

Battle Plan:
The Naval Odyssey of Professor James Brand

© J. Eugene Porter, 2021

First Edition

This is a work of fiction. All the characters, names, incidents, organizations, and dialogue in this novel are either the products of the author's imagination or are used fictionally.

ISBN: 9798486243059

Cover Images:
U.S. National Archives and Records Administration

Design: Vivian Freeman Chaffin
vivian.freeman@yellowrosetype.com

Printed in the United States of America

Dedicated to

Kenneth E. Porter
USMC 1938-1941

and the Marine Detachment
aboard the USS Chicago CA-29

Author's Note

To the Reader:

Battle Plan is the fifth book in *The Naval Odyssey of Professor James Brand* series. The book is a work of fiction, but is based upon the historical events of World War II. Some of these events are well known, but many reside on the fringes of history. The fictional characters continue to work on the scientific activities of the war and the often unappreciated story of logistics.

This book begins in late 1942 and ends in May 1943. During these months, fateful decisions will be made by the principal leaders, pushing the war effort toward its ultimate goal of the destruction of the Axis powers. Other decisions will be made by commanders in the field and in the shadows of diplomacy and espionage, many succeeding, but some failing tragically. As readers of the previous books in this series know, the fictional characters are not designed to emulate real individuals from the war. Still, they interact with leaders in Allied government, military, science, and industry, providing the reader with a better understanding of the many issues and challenges facing their nations during the war years.

Conversations and actions of historical figures are based upon reports and official histories of the Allied nations. Much of the information is from the journals and diaries of the participants. Additional information comes from the perspective of current historians and how time has changed the way some are remembered. However, it does not change the management of the war. Nor how these individuals directed their people and, in some cases, how the leaders of two great nations provided leadership to the world.

The book is divided by date. Each chapter begins with daily information about what was happening in the war. My hope is this device will provide additional context for the events unfolding in the book and help the reader better understand the scope and immensity of the war effort.

This daily information comes from two sources:

- *The United States Naval Chronology, World War II,* published on March 17, 1955, by the Naval History Division of the Office of the Chief of Naval Operations.

- *Chronology: 1941-1945*, published on February 21, 1958, by Chronology Section of the Historical Division of the Office of the Chief of Military History, United States Army.

Additional insights were gained by examining the histories of the campaigns initiated right after the war. This includes the seminal work by Rear Admiral Samuel Eliot Morison in his *History of the Naval Operations of World War Two*, and *The United States Army in World War II* by the Office of the Chief of Military History. Additional information comes from the many later studies conducted by the United States Navy, the United States Marine Corps, and the United States Army. Many of the classified documents from the war have been made available to the public, including the United States Naval War College analysis of the campaigns and individual battles covered in this book.

Another declassified source are the *Papers and Minutes of Meetings of the Combined Chiefs of Staff.* Each of the major conferences produced thousands of pages of materials which help explain many of the military and political decisions made during the war. The Naval History and Heritage Command also has extensive materials available online to those who want to find out more about the naval war. Another outstanding source of information comes from the Franklin D. Roosevelt Presidential Library, which includes online access to the daily diary for the president's meetings and communiques.

PART 1

1

14 December 1942
Office of the Chief of Naval Operations
Washington, D.C.

- Guadalcanal--Additional elements of Americal Division arrive.
- New Guinea--Japanese convoy reaches Mambare River mouth early in the morning and unloads without being detected. Allied planes subsequently deliver damaging attacks on troops, supplies, and landing craft.
- Libya--British 8th Army continues to pursue enemy. British 7th Division taking the lead in westward push while New Zealand Division advances rapidly southwest into the desert to get behind the enemy.

Mondays were just like every other day. Everyone worked seven days a week, usually twelve to fourteen hours. A few people noticed the calendar and offered a Merry Christmas to their co-workers—typically met with frowns or impolite non-holiday phrases. Commander Allen was somewhere between in his view of the upcoming holiday. It would be the second Christmas during wartime. Thousands had been killed during the year, and tens of thousands had been wounded, listed as missing, or captured.

Yet, as the father to two young daughters, he needed to be somewhat cheery. His family lived in Washington's outskirts, and as navy "brats," were accustomed to moving around the country. But the city was becoming their permanent home. For the two years the commander served aboard his destroyer in the Atlantic, the family stayed in Washington, where Allen's previous position was with the Bureau of Personnel. After more than three years in the same city, the family began putting down roots and building relationships. The commander hoped his next command would be at sea, which might keep his family in the nation's capital. The only challenge to this bit of Americana was his job. There was still no time to spend with his family, which now played a distant second in his life.

Today's challenge was another new experience for the aide to Admiral Edwards. As the chief of staff to Admiral King, Edwards played a pivotal role in the naval organization and often served as the enforcer of policy and personnel. As Allen sat in the large conference room, he sensed things would not be pleasant, at least for the careers of several officers. Listening intently to determine the direction of the pending formal inquiry, Allen tried to grasp the meaning behind the words.

"Admiral, I appreciate your willingness to conduct this investigation on behalf of the navy. I have assigned Commander Allen as my liaison to you and the members of your team. The commander will provide you access to all records and reports on the battle, as well as the personnel involved."

Admiral Edwards looked over at Commander Allen who returned an ever so slight acknowledging nod. The proceedings of this inquiry could end or seriously damage the career of senior officers. On the positive side, recommendations for the future prosecution of the war would be offered, based upon lessons from the catastrophe at Savo Island. The man who would head this investigation was retired Admiral Arthur J. Hepburn, formerly the Commander in Chief of the United States Fleet. In August, he was named chairman of the General Board of the United States Navy and was both respected and trusted by Admiral King. Seated next to the Hepburn was another retired officer, Rear Admiral James J. Bridges, who had been Judge Advocate General of the Navy before the war. This fearsome duo was now charged with examining the battle of Savo Island. Admiral King wanted to uncover the causes for the defeat and the loss of so many men and ships.

Looking directly at Edwards, Hepburn stated, "Admiral, I hope my efforts to understand the reasons for this defeat will not be to find blame, but rather to build on this loss to expand the knowledge and fighting capabilities of the navy. I have asked Admiral Bridges to conduct interviews. We look to you and Commander Allen to make these individuals available. I have already examined the initial and follow-up reports from Admiral Nimitz dated 7 December. I would like access to every after-action report for the ships in the engagement, as well as intelligence summaries leading up to the battle."

Turning to Admiral Bridges, Hepburn asked, "James, do you have any other requests?"

The old lawyer admiral was well known to Admiral Edwards. The man had been a legend in the pre-war navy and worked hard to remove officers he considered inept, drunkards, or worse, cowards. "Admiral Edwards, if you can make a few recommendations on people who were possibly not in the chain of command but were observers of the battle, perhaps even pre-invasion, this would be helpful."

Edwards knew the two admirals would not whitewash their report but would only make sound recommendations for the future of the navy, and if required, place blame on those who deserved it. He saw a small grin on the face of his aide. Knowing what the man was thinking, Edwards replied.

"Admiral, I know a few men, now in Washington, who could shed a significant amount of light on what happened before the battle and many of the decisions made as the battle occurred."

Speaking to Admiral Bridges, Edwards continued. "Admiral, you know two of these men already, but it's been several months since your introduction."

Bridges didn't quite understand the meaning of the chief of staff's words but quickly raced in his memory back to the first of the year. He had met Nimitz in Hawaii after the man had taken command of the remnants of the American Pacific Fleet. The admiral knew most of the other key players, including Ghormley, Halsey, Spruance, Layton, and many ship captains, but he was unsure of whom Edwards was talking about.

"Do you remember meeting a young, enlisted man in a hospital who had been beaten nearly to death at the San Diego training center?"

The lights went on inside the brain of the former head of the Judge Advocates.

"I recall a very young man who was turned into an officer and then secreted out of town by armed Marines."

"Excellent memory, Admiral. The young man is now a Lieutenant and serves along with Captain Jameson, who was in charge of his rescue back in January."

"I wondered what happened to the young professor. So he's working full-time for you and Admiral King?"

"I wish that was the case, Admiral. It seems Professor Brand is loaned out to the president most of the time, that is, of course, when he isn't working on other super-secret projects, which I'm not allowed to discuss."

Bridges explained the situation to the perplexed Admiral Hepburn. "Admiral, this young man, Professor Brand, is a prodigy and polymath of some significance to the scientific community. He joined the navy right after Pearl Harbor and tried to keep his identity a secret. Still, after an altercation with a sadistic petty officer at the recruit depot, he was discovered and returned to his rightful place in research. But he wanted to stay in the navy and was made an officer. It appears he has done well for himself to be a lieutenant already. Captain Jameson, also a mathematics professor, was an Annapolis graduate who stayed in the reserves. The two of them make quite a pair and must be extremely well thought of by the high command."

Edwards watched as Hepburn made the mental connections. Then with a glance at his aide, he said to the commander, "Allen, fill in the admirals on why they may want to speak to these two men about the Savo battle."

"Admiral Hepburn, Admiral Bridges, both Brand and Jameson were assigned as observers for Operation WATCHTOWER and were with Admiral Turner in the lead-up to the invasion. Three days before the invasion, Captain Jameson joined the Australian cruiser *Canberra* as an observer and was there during the battle. He was severely wounded but heroically helped the executive officer of the ship during its last hours afloat. Lieutenant Brand was on the *McCawley*, supporting Admiral Turner. Both men provided many details of the situation before, during, and after the battle. Additionally, two other officers who serve with Jameson's team were involved in the invasion. Captain, now Major, Flannigan went ashore with the Marine Raiders at Tulagi, and Dr. Feldman went ashore on Guadalcanal with the navy medical team."

Before Bridges could say anything else, Edwards added another comment that enhanced the Science Team's relationship with the senior officers.

"Professor Brand was the first person to recommend an inquiry into the battle. His motives were purely scientific and not focused on setting blame. Lieutenant Brand wants the navy to use scientific methods to understand each battle and, as he would say, "dissect it" to uncover issues, challenges, and opportunities for future improvements. Admiral King wholeheartedly agrees with the professor. We must learn from each encounter with the enemy, whether good or bad. The lieutenant put it best by saying, *we must do this for the living as well as for the dead."

Hepburn looked at his old friend and said, "Bridges, it looks like we need to speak to these two men first. I think it will save us a lot of time and point us in the right direction." Turning to Admiral Edwards, he asked, "Are either of these two men available to meet with us?"

Edwards turned to Allen for the answer. "Admiral Hepburn, Lieutenant Brand and Captain Jameson are working in their offices, and I know at least one of them could meet with you today. I can make a call and get one of them set up for this afternoon, if that would meet your needs."

Admiral Bridges answered for both men. "Commander, if Lieutenant Brand is available, I think he could give us the best starting point for our inquiry. Since he is the one who set this project in motion, we should see what he has to say."

Allen looked at the former head of the navy, wondering what the man was thinking. Hepburn was much older and graduated from the Naval Academy in 1897, then served in the Spanish-American War at the naval battle of Santiago. Now, some forty-five years later, the distinguished officer was being tasked to investigate the defeat of an American force in a battle which lasted only forty-five minutes but ended the lives of over twelve hundred men and the loss of four cruisers. The commander did not envy the admiral but realized the investigation's recommendations would save lives in the future.

James was in his office when he received the call from Commander

Allen. The request was actually an order coming from Admiral Edwards. The professor was in the middle of doing calculations for load factors on the new LSTs, but quickly changed course and left to find the meeting in a conference room near Admiral King's office. With Warrant Officer Jones in tow and closely followed by Sergeant Williams, they left the Logistics Research office and headed for the mysterious meeting. The two Marines acted more like sheepdogs than guards as they maneuvered through the busy building known as Main Navy. Even though the building was one of the most secure facilities in Washington, the two Marines acted like they were back in the jungles of Guadalcanal, searching for snipers and booby traps.

James looked behind him to see Williams checking the perimeter, saying, "Bud, there's no Japs in the building, and I don't think the Nazis have landed either."

Warrant Officer Jones responded quickly before Williams had a chance to say anything dumb, "Lieutenant, we're just doing our job, and it's good practice to keep an eye on these people. There may be a spy in the building."

"Gunny, I doubt there are any spies around, but there are a few individuals who may not like what I do. Thanks for all of your efforts, and Bud, keep an eye out for admirals. We're nearing their compound."

Jones held his laughter as he turned around to see Sergeant Williams scratching his head trying to figure out what the professor was talking about. Warrant Officer Clarence Jones was known as Gunny to everyone in the unit. The long-serving Marine had been promoted to Warrant only a short time ago, but everyone continued calling him Gunny, which Jones considered a superior position to his present rank.

As they moved toward the conference room, Gunny saw a Marine corporal standing guard at the door. As the men approached, the corporal came to attention and looked at the warrant officer.

"Corporal, Lieutenant Brand is here at the request of Admiral Edwards."

The corporal checked Brand's identification card and asked the officer to wait where they were. Opening the door, the Marine walked in and quickly closed it behind him. After no more than fifteen seconds, the door reopened and the corporal said, "Lieutenant, please enter. The other two gentlemen must stay outside."

The request didn't bother the two Marines. James smiled at the corporal and entered the room. He saw Commander Allen rising from his chair and then saw Admiral Edwards and two others, a full admiral and a rear admiral. Slowly, he recognized the rear admiral.

"Admiral Hepburn, Admiral Bridges, may I introduce Lieutenant James Brand." Allen stood next to the long conference table, indicating where James would sit. The professor was now at full attention, and the two seated senior officers stood to greet him. The full admiral smiled at the young officer and said, "At ease, Lieutenant Brand. My name is Hepburn. It is good to meet you. Both Admiral King and Admiral Edwards sing your praises, as does my colleague Admiral Bridges."

Bridges approached the young man he had helped rescue back in January. "Lieutenant Brand, it's good to meet you again, and I'm happy you are doing so well. Quite a difference from those days in the hospital in San Diego."

"Admiral Bridges, it's wonderful to see you again. I never got a chance to properly thank you for all of your help. Admiral Hepburn, sir, it's a privilege to meet you, and I look forward to helping in whatever you need."

The two older officers returned to their seats, and then following Allen's lead, James sat down next to the commander.

"Lieutenant Brand, do you know why you are here?"

"No sir. I was told to come to this conference room. That is all the information I have."

Admiral Bridges looked down at some papers, one of which was the report James had sent after the Battle of Savo Island to Admiral King. As he picked up the documents, the admiral said, "Lieutenant, we are conducting a full inquiry to the events surrounding the Battle of Savo Island. You recommended the navy examine the causes for the losses incurred during the battle and make recommendations for changes to reduce the likelihood of future defeats. Both Admiral Hepburn and I have read your report and several of the recommendations you offered to improve tactics, preparedness, leadership, and communications. Do you recall the specifics of your report?"

Hepburn wondered how the young officer would handle himself and was quickly surprised by the man's assuredness and control of the situation.

9

"Admiral, I can probably recall the majority of the details of the report, but I would need a few minutes to review it to be one hundred percent accurate in my responses."

Bridges recalled the young man's rapid answers, plus the amount of depth his responses entailed.

"No need for complete accuracy, right now. Admiral Hepburn and I are looking first and foremost at the big picture, and since you were with Admiral Turner before and during the battle, your recollections would be of great benefit to our inquiries."

James sensed the two older admirals were sincere in their approach to evaluating the battle. Not smiling but looking directly at Admiral Bridges, James replied, "Admiral, where would you like me to start?"

Hepburn replied to the question by asking an open question. "Lieutenant Brand, where should we start? Based upon your report to Admiral King, you divided the battle into many different parts, starting with Operation WATCHTOWER's overall plan. And one more comment before you reply. I know you have been involved in many operations since the battle, and we would like to know of any operational improvements. We hope that this has been the case, so please provide us with specific examples."

Commander Allen, sensing the two admirals were about to open a massive can of worms, looked at James, who didn't indicate what he was thinking. The man's placid face could be mistaken for someone without any idea of what to say, but Allen knew the professor well. For what seemed an eternity, but in reality was only about thirty seconds, James Brand sat in silence. Finally, looking at the two admirals, he began.

"Admiral Hepburn, I would like to start with what is happening now, based upon what we have learned in a year of war. I will concentrate on naval preparedness, command decision-making, intelligence, communications, and our underestimation of the enemy."

Admiral Bridges smiled and sat back. Admiral Hepburn stared at the young naval officer, a professor and evidently a confidant of the United States President. Then seeing the expression on Bridges face, he sat back as well and said, "Lieutenant Brand, please proceed."

For the next three hours, James enumerated facts, figures, statistics, names, locations, ships, weapons, aircraft, and intelligence, which proceeded the battle followed by a list of future implications. The professor provided a short evaluation of what had been done since the battle to make ships less prone to fires, night battle training, leadership, and continuing failures within the navy and army air forces in fighting the enemy. Both admirals began taking notes, as did Commander Allen. After three broken pencils and hand cramps, Allen was glad James condensed his report. Later that evening, the two admirals were still looking at their notes and wondered how a nineteen-year-old physics professor could summarize the Pacific naval situation so well.

2

16 December 1942
Logistics Research Office
Main Navy, Washington, D.C.

- Guadalcanal--Gen. Patch orders 132nd Infantry, Americal Division, to occupy Mt. Austen.
- New Guinea--Gen. Eichelberger takes command of U.S. 32nd Division after Gen. Byers is wounded observing operations on Urbana front.
- Burma--In Arakan coastal sector, Eastern Army of India Command, under Lt. Gen. N. M. S. Irwin opens limited objective offensive for Akyab at the end of Mayu Peninsula, which is lightly held by the enemy.
- Libya--Enemy, by breaking into small detachments, is able to withdraw from El Agheila positions after hard fighting, but loses twenty tanks and some 500 captured.
- USSR--Red Army opens strong offensive on middle Don against Italian 8th Army, which is forced to give ground. As a result, Germans are forced to abandon efforts to relieve 6th Army on Stalingrad front.

John Meyers sifted through a pile of reports, trying to find a file from early July detailing the number of ships transiting the Panama Canal. Captain Jameson's request was somewhat obscure, and the commanding officer of the Science Team seemed slightly unsure of what the information would be used for, but that was the captain's problem, not his. If his leader wanted information, it must be essential, and no matter what he thought of the request, it was his duty to find it and not to question the reasons. One of the enlisted men working for Chief Presley was pulling files from other departments, and soon the piles of paper were stacked like the Leaning Tower of Pisa.

Captain Jameson seemed to be asking lots of questions since his meeting yesterday with Admiral Hepburn. The captain didn't explain much about the session but advised Meyers to standby for more requests. James was tasked with a similar set of issues, all involving searching reports for facts and figures related to operations in the Pacific since the first of June. The captain examined troop deployments, aircraft deliveries, and tonnage of cargoes unloaded at various islands from Hawaii to Australia. Lieutenant Brand tackled the search like an attorney going through a discovery process before a major trial. Meyers sensed the man was looking more for evidence of activities, or perhaps it was intent on the part of senior officers and ship commanders. Whatever the reason behind the document search, the former Harvard law student knew things would worsen before they got better.

Meyers thoughts were interrupted by Staff Sergeant James McBride carrying a set of files, all stamped TOP SECRET. Eyeing the captain's faithful bodyguard and friend, Meyers asked, "So, Jimmy, what's going on with the captain? Seems we're doing a lot of digging. Any clues from the old man?"

McBride smiled at the young lieutenant, whom had become a good friend over the past few months while working on the invasion plans for North Africa. "Lieutenant, I'm not sure what the situation is, but I know the captain and Mr. Brand have been turning over every file in the building searching for something for some admirals. Not too sure what it's all about, but Commander Allen was in the meetings too, and he is very closed-mouth about what's going on."

The logistics officer knew the sergeant would know more than most of the men about what was happening, but since Brand's meeting two days ago with some mysterious admirals, everything they had been working on came to a screeching stop. Everyone was given new directions and no timetable for what they were doing. Even Major Flannigan met with the admirals, appearing lost in an internal argument when he returned to the office. Dr. Feldman was currently meeting with these same admirals, and the only thing Meyers could think would be the reason for the secrecy was something to do with the early days of Guadalcanal. McBride had told him about the battle and how Captain Jameson had been wounded but still managed to help others on the doomed Australian cruiser. Jimmy wouldn't say much more about the carnage of the battle or the aftermath, but an unbreakable bond was evident between the captain and the Marine sergeant.

After another hour of looking through shipping files, an ensign came into the office and handed Meyers another folder. This one was different because it was all about one man. After he signed for the file, Meyers opened it and saw a photograph of a navy captain named Howard D. Bode. As he examined the officer's fitness reports, all of which were exemplary up to early June, things finally made sense. The man had been the commanding officer of the heavy cruiser *Chicago* until the ship returned to San Francisco for repairs.

The ship had been torpedoed at Savo Island while the officer commanded the southern force during the battle. As Meyers read further, the trained attorney could see where things changed for Captain Bode. He was relieved of command after the ship returned to California. The officer was now posted to the Panama Canal Zone in an administrative position. This meant only one thing—the man had messed up during the battle and was being put out to pasture. The report didn't include details from the action, just personal data and fitness reports. The logistics officer now had a clue as to the mysterious activities. The navy wanted someone to blame.

After he finished reading the report, the lieutenant walked into Captain Jameson's office and stood in front of the man's desk. The commanding officer was not a stickler for military courtesy, especially from his staff. "John, find something for me to look at?"

"Captain, I received this file from BUPERS on a Captain Bode." Saying no more, he handed the file to Jameson. Meyers waited for a reply, hopefully, more than a thank you.

Jameson opened the file and laid it on this desk. Picking up the first page, he studied a photograph of Bode and commented, "At last we finally meet, Captain Bode." Placing the page back inside the file, the captain seemed lost in a bad memory. His momentary silence unnerved the young lieutenant.

Regaining his composure, the captain finally spoke. "John, I guess you and everyone else in the office are wondering what the hell we're doing, and I think you need at least some information. Please close the door and take a seat."

The logistics officer did as he was told and waited.

"John, what I am about to say is, of course, secret and not to be repeated. Is that all right with you?"

"Certainly, sir. I will remain silent about anything you tell me."

Jameson smiled at the man whom in his former life represented clients in a legal capacity. "John, is this part of the attorney-client communication thing, or am I reading too much into this?"

"No sir, there is no need for any lawyer-client confidentiality unless you want me to represent you in a criminal proceeding. I just want to know more about what I'm looking for, which may help everyone improve their search parameters."

"John, the Savo Island battle was a catastrophe for the navy, and recommendations were made by many individuals urging an investigation of the causes for the defeat and ways to eliminate mistakes made in the battle. Lieutenant Brand was one of the first officers to recommend an analysis of the battle, and as you know, the senior officers around here take notice whenever James makes a request."

Looking at the photograph of the cruiser captain, Jameson continued. "Captain Bode was the commanding officer of the *Chicago* and has been singled out for numerous command failures. The biggest one is his failure to notify anyone about the attack on his ships. The *Canberra*, which I was on, was burning furiously and out of control. The *Chicago*, which was right behind the Australian cruiser, received a torpedo hit to the bow and turned away from the engagement. No attempt to notify the ships of the northern force or the senior admirals was given. You know the rest of the story, but many people are beginning to lay blame on Bode for the disaster."

"The admirals I met with are not just looking for a scapegoat, but rather want to learn all aspects of the battle so we can be better prepared to fight the enemy in the future. Many of Lieutenant Brand's comments are already being initiated within the navy to reduce the fire hazards on-board our ships and improve night fighting capabilities. All of these things will improve our ability to defeat the enemy and reduce our casualties."

Meyers thought for a moment about what he heard. The severe losses at Savo Island had come as a shock to the navy and to the public. America had lost thousands of men so far in the Guadalcanal campaign. Dozens of warships, including two carriers, had been sunk with dozens of other ships seriously damaged and out of action for months. John Meyers knew enough about what was going on in the navy to understand the significance of these investigations. If individuals fail to perform their jobs, whether it is the captain of a ship or a gunner's mate loading ammunition, many men could die, and battles lost.

"Sir, what else do you want me to research on the battle? Now, I know more of the direction of the investigation, I could probably help sharpen our focus on what you need."

"Meyers, dig deeper into the after-action reports on every surviving ship and those which were sunk. Somewhere in all of these papers, we should be able to find more facts to help the admirals in their search."

Meyers now understood the project and his role in it. To him, it was like going back to law school and searching old cases to make his current case. This time, however, people's lives depended on the outcome. For the next two days, he and most of the Science Team members would search the records and summarize their findings. Captain Jameson would then forward the information to Admiral Hepburn, giving him a starting point for his formal inquiry.

3

18 December 1942
CINCPAC Headquarters
Pearl Harbor, Territory of Hawaii

- United States--Combined Chiefs of Staff authorize occupation of Amchitka, less than 100 miles from Kiska, provided it is suitable for an advanced airbase from which Kiska can be attacked.
- Guadalcanal--3rd Battalion, 132nd Infantry, advanced up northwest slope of Mt. Austen to Hill 35, where enemy fire is encountered.
- New Guinea--Australian 39th Battalion, which has been joined by elements of 2/14th Battalion, has reduced enemy strength at Napapo to about half and is being relieved for action on Sanananda front by Australian 2/16th Battalion and 2/27th Battalion.
- Libya--Continuing pursuit of enemy, New Zealand 2nd Division of British 8th Army clashes sharply with rearguards at Nofilia. After the action, pursuit is largely abandoned for administrative reasons.
- Japanese naval vessel sunk: Light cruiser **Tenryu**, by submarine **Albacore** (SS-218), Bismarck Sea.

Things were looking better on Guadalcanal, with more army units being deployed along with additional detachments from the Second Marine Division. The Americans now outnumbered the Japanese forces on the island. With the lack of supplies, the Japanese were losing more men to disease and starvation than American attacks. Admiral Tanaka's destroyers were now trying to rush in supplies packaged in oil drums and then strapped to the warships' decks. When the ships got close to the beach, the drums were jettisoned with the hope they would float ashore.

The Japanese destroyers couldn't wait for the men on the island to meet them and offload the supplies for fear of American aircraft taking off before first light for their routine patrol of the beaches and shooting up anything resembling supplies. Other planes would search toward Rabaul, looking for the Japanese destroyers, and relentlessly attack them until the ships got out of range of the vengeful pilots. The enemy prayed for gray skies, thunderstorms, and any other sort of bad weather to mask their movements. Their worst fears were for clear blue skies, which allowed good hunting conditions for American bombers.

Commander Layton read Admiral Halsey's newest report, which started with the previous day's casualties, land battles, aircraft losses, enemy sightings, and the current supply situation on the island. At last, ships were getting through in large numbers, bringing more fuel, food, and ammunition. Aircraft maintenance items were top priority, and the daily listing of available aircraft was a critical factor in the campaign's ongoing success. The days of only twenty planes capable of flying were long over. Now, over one hundred aircraft of all types were on the island. With an additional Seabee unit, infrastructure of the base was quickly improving. The landing strip was being extended for larger planes with plans for another fighter strip nearby since supplies of Marston mat were no longer a problem.

Things had changed since the dark days of September, but Commander Layton didn't have the luxury of relishing the improved outlook. The enemy had pulled back its major fleet units, and so far, Japanese carrier forces had not attempted to intervene in the American buildup in the Solomons. Intelligence worked to decipher the newest changes in the Japanese code. However, a large amount of information still had to be gleaned through communications analysis and long-range reconnaissance, either by plane or submarine. MacArthur's bombers spent much of the last month making small raids on the principal enemy base of Rabaul, but from everything Layton saw, they had accomplished very little. More planes, including the new ones heading to Guadalcanal, would be needed before significant damage could be done to the essential Japanese base. Over 100,000 enemy soldiers, sailors and airmen were based in and around Rabaul. Hundreds of planes defended one of the best anchorages in the Pacific, and all this belonged to the enemy.

As the intelligence officer looked at Admiral Halsey's newest report, he could see the importance of the airfield on Guadalcanal and how the Cactus Air Force's expanding size was making life more difficult for the Japanese. The enemy was trying to build new bases on Munda Island, which would allow them to easily attack Guadalcanal. Still, Halsey's flyers attacked the island almost daily, hampering construction and destroying more enemy aircraft on the ground. Admiral Nimitz had urged Halsey to step up his attacks on these bases as a way to keep the enemy engaged and reduce the Japanese air forces. Evidently, the ever aggressive Halsey was doing his best to oblige.

Glancing to his right, Layton saw Admiral Spruance's aide, Lieutenant Robert Oliver, sifting through Guadalcanal's newest intelligence reports. The officer had been sitting quietly at the conference table covered with maps, charts, and files. "Mr. Oliver, have you found what you're looking for, yet?"

Smiling back at Commander Layton, the efficient admiral's aide replied, "No, Commander. The admiral asked me to find a situation report from the new army commander, General Patch, on his men's progress in taking Mt. Austen. I know things were not going as planned, but the admiral wanted an update."

Layton replied, "Yesterday's update suggested some progress, but the enemy was reluctant to leave their positions. I think General Patch is getting a good education on how the Japanese defend their territory. If it helps, I can have one of my assistants dig into today's newest message traffic."

"Thanks, Commander. If one of your men can locate anything resembling an update, I would be most appreciative."

The commander's attention was broken by one of his assistants bearing a message from Washington. Barely acknowledging the messenger, Layton opened the sealed envelope. Everything sent to Layton was TOP SECRET, and this one had the usual stamps telling everyone the message was not to be opened by anyone but the intelligence officer. The commander always thought the practice silly, especially in the headquarters of the commander in chief of the Pacific Ocean Area. But the navy loved to stamp and date everything, so he let it slide. Opening the communication, he smiled at the sender's name and began taking notes.

TOP SECRET—No Duplication Allowed

Commander E. T. Layton—CINCPAC

18 December 1942

Washington, D.C.—Office of the Chief of Staff

Please advise this office as to the following on or before 20 December:

1. *Current strength of CACTUS air units by type of aircraft.*
2. *Number of CACTUS pilots available for duty.*
3. *Present supply situation for aviation fuel and spare parts, CACTUS, and support bases.*
4. *Operational strength of Army and Marine units at CACTUS.*
5. *Available reinforcements for CACTUS by unit, battalion or larger.*
6. *Current fleet units available in SOPAC.*
7. *Current fleet units available at Pearl Harbor, Aleutians, and in support of SWPA.*

Operational update: Please inform Nimitz of the following and update how these units will be employed.

Task Force 13 will be underway to CINCPAC shortly with an ETA of 13 January. Escort carriers including Chenango, Suwannee, *and* Sangamon, *plus escorting destroyers from recent TORCH operation will be part of this movement. Will advise of other reinforcements shortly.*

The professor says to expect a particular British support unit coming soon after refitting at Newport. CNO approved a temporary assignment. Updates to follow.

Rear Admiral R. S. Edwards

"Well, I'll be damned, the kid did it!" The commander's outburst startled Lieutenant Oliver, who quickly asked what was happening.

"Sir, what kid did what, sir?"

Still holding onto the secret message, he looked at Spruance's aide saying, "Remember Lieutenant Brand, the kid professor who works for Captain Jameson?"

"Sure do. One smart guy who's really connected to the top brass."

"It appears the professor helped move not only a few mountains but some huge egos in the highest of holy places. Lieutenant Brand gave Admiral Halsey and Nimitz an idea to help us out of our carrier problem by borrowing one until the new *Essex* class ships are available. I think the kid worked the official channels but went over the heads of just about everyone, so it looks like our cousins are going to let us borrow one of their carriers."

Oliver looked strangely at the intelligence officer, and then the lights came on in his mind. "You mean the British are giving us one of their carriers? How will this work from an operations standpoint? I'm sure the Brits do things differently and have different types of planes, and communications systems and God knows what else."

Layton put the message down and then quietly answered. "Oliver, you have some outstanding questions. I'm certain that someone, somewhere, is going to sort through all of them but for right now, I know Admiral Halsey wouldn't care if the Brits were flying Messerschmitts from their ships. You know as well as I do, we're in big trouble with only the *Saratoga* and a patched up *Enterprise*. If the Japanese want to bring their carriers out for a battle, we would be hard-pressed to match them."

Oliver thought about what he had just heard and then asked another question. "Commander, do you expect any more help besides the British ship?"

"The message I received telling me about the British carrier also reported that we will soon get three new escort carriers along with their aircrews. These ships all participated in the TORCH landings in Africa, so they have some experience. Right now, I'd take anything that floats and can carry a plane. Maybe we'll be out of the woods soon, but until the new ships start coming this way, we'll just have to get by with what we have."

Oliver looked at the overworked intelligence officer, a key person in the operations of the entire Pacific theater of war, and wondered what kept the man going. Admiral Spruance's aide also thought about what he had heard about the young professor. Lieutenant Brand was getting the U.S. Navy and the governments of two countries to agree on taking a ship from somewhere in the North Atlantic and moving it around the world to fight a different enemy. He made a mental note to get to know the professor whenever he returned to Hawaii.

The assistant chief of staff for War Plans worked hard to keep up with the young man seated across from him. Rear Admiral Charles M. Cooke had replaced Admiral Turner as the head of the navy's War Planning department in June and was exceptionally well versed in logistics. Still, he was now receiving a short course in advanced logistics management. Cooke had met the young officer on several occasions, but this was the first time he had been subjected to a full mental onslaught of facts and figures from the professor.

"Admiral, as you can see from this chart, we are falling further behind in the production of landing craft. Without these ships and trained crews, many of the planned operations will have to be delayed. In particular, any further actions in the Mediterranean will have to be postponed by at least four months."

The admiral scrutinized the scheduled delivery chart for a wide variety of landing craft. The first item listed was the LST (Landing Ship Tank), which was necessary for any large-scale seaborne invasion. The other landing boats included the LCI (Landing Craft Infantry), LCT (Landing Craft Tank), the large LSD (Landing Ship Dock), and the small but most important Higgins Boat or LCVP (Landing Craft Vehicle and Personnel). Orders were placed for thousands of these boats and ships. New shipyards and inexperienced ship workers struggled to build these vessels along the country's major rivers and coastal areas.

Cooke knew every one of these boats competed with the navy's other shipbuilding priorities. The Destroyer Escort program had been deemed essential, and these ships were now being launched with the first ship in the class, *Evarts* (DE-5), scheduled for commissioning on January 20, 1943. This ship was the first of ninety-seven to be delivered to both the American and British navies. Several hundred more of these ships were planned for the coming two years, as were thousands of other warships and cargo vessels.

Knowing the situation well, but not armed with all of the statistics the young man was using, Cooke stated, "Lieutenant Brand, I understand the issue of getting more landing craft and how they serve as an integral part of our planning process. I'm afraid about how we can change priorities in mid-stream. The DE program is a commitment set by the president, and Admiral King has told me nothing will interfere with its top priority."

Looking back at the head of Plans for the CNO, James grinned at the man and then replied. "Sir, I realize the priority of the escort vessels. I worked very hard to get this established as a priority back in March. I have an idea on how we can keep the production on target and at the same time expand the production of the landing craft. It revolves around the problem of distribution of work and materials. With your permission, may I explain the concept?"

Admiral Cooke smiled back at the professor, knowing he had been hoodwinked by the younger man. The mature officer now knew he had been set up with many facts and figures and requests for changes that did not fit his current views on production. The professor had planned his attack well, and now the admiral awaited the solution to the problem, which he had said was unsolvable a few moments ago.

"Go ahead, Professor Brand. I think I've been had, but I was warned by Admiral Edwards about how you work and failed to plan accordingly."

"Thank you, Admiral. Let me show you how we redistribute the work on several projects around the country and how this will meet all production goals and at the same time utilize workforces which are underutilized."

The admiral sat back in this chair and examined a series of charts, accompanied by several maps of the country, some denoting primary work locations, subcontractors, railroads, major roads, and navigable waterways. The professor had a letter from Andrew Higgins, the designer of the LCVP and owner of Higgins Industries, with the man's plans for expanding his operation in New Orleans. The creative genius behind the boat's design had already drawn up plans for expanding his operation and was recommending using several subcontractors to expedite parts of the construction process. Higgins also addressed the issue of adding personnel to his operation by hiring racially integrated work teams and women. The letter stated unequivocally that Higgins Industries could produce twenty thousand of the landing craft within two years and employ over eighty-five thousand people doing it. In addition to the landing boats, his company was also making PT boats and other support craft for the navy.

Lieutenant Brand handed the admiral a set of charts showing the monthly quota for all landing craft to meet the war's next twenty-four months. As Cooke scanned the chart, he noticed an item that piqued his curiosity. "Lieutenant, what is the reason for the increase in the 1944 production?"

"Sir, I think by that time, we will be ready to mount an invasion of Europe, and I think we will need thousands of these ships for that event. I also have a chart on the delivery schedule for the assembled landing craft to Britain starting next year."

Admiral Cooke looked at the chart and then examined the face of the professor. He was looking intently at what might be going on in the man's mind, which allowed him to peer in the future.

The conversation was one way. Except for an affirmative answer indicating the order was understood, replies were not necessary. The man doing the speaking was Admiral Edwards. The man doing the listening was Major Flannigan.

"Captain Jameson is aware of this order and agrees as to the need for another officer to join the command. You and your unit have been under heavy pressure in the last few months, and Admiral King wants you to have an assistant."

Edwards could see the Marine officer on the opposite side of the desk was not happy having to add another man to his unit. Referring to the naval officer next to Flannigan, he continued. "Commander Allen will secure a list of recommended officers unless, of course, you have someone in mind."

Flannigan was not convinced he needed a second in command. Warrant Officer Jones was doing just fine in supporting him, but the man was more of a father figure to James Brand than an executive officer. Yet, after the Guadalcanal experiences and the continued increase in the unit's operational tempo, perhaps it would be a good idea.

"Admiral, if Captain Jameson thinks it would be advisable to get another Marine officer in the unit, I have no problem with the addition.

I do have a question as to what you believe would be the qualifications for the position."

Edwards thought the question was valid and was quick in his reply. "Major, I think you need a man with some solid field experience, combat would be best, and a proven ability to work under pressure. Do you have a candidate?"

Flannigan was already working his way through men he had known in his career, starting with his classmates at Annapolis. Many of them would have been assigned to combat units early in the war and probably promoted to first lieutenants or maybe captains by now. No names came to mind, but suddenly he recalled his more recent experiences on Guadalcanal and one man jumped to the top of his mind.

"Sir, there was a man I served with during the invasion of Tulagi who impressed me. I recommended him for a field promotion, and I understand he later played a key role in the defense of Bloody Ridge in late September. As I recall from my conversation with Colonel Edson, the man was recommended for the Navy Cross for his bravery."

The admiral figured any man the major recommended would have the kind of experience and courage to match his own. "Major, if you think this man could do the job, give Commander Allen his name, and we will find him and transfer him to your command."

The admiral's aide asked Flannigan, "What's the man's name and unit?"

The Marine's smile faded. "The name is Bill Waverly, and he was a second lieutenant in the First Raiders. They were taken off the island in early October, and if I recall what Colonel Edson told me, less than two hundred of the original eight hundred were able to walk off the island. I have no idea where they went or what Lieutenant Waverly is doing now."

Being a former officer from the Bureau of Personnel (BUPERS), Allen knew the navy bureaucracy could find anyone, anywhere. It just took time. "Major, I'll get someone working on this immediately. Hopefully, it shouldn't take too long."

As Flannigan and Allen were dismissed, the two men had a quick conversation.

"Major, do you know if this Waverly fellow was wounded during the battle? It would make our job easier if we had a place to start."

"Sorry, Commander, but I didn't get any information from Colonel

Edson besides how the lieutenant was being recommended for the medal. I assume he survived and left with the remnants of the Raiders, but I just don't have any idea as to where the unit went or, for that matter, if the First Raiders still exist."

"Don't worry, Major, we'll find him, and if he is fit for duty, I will let you know."

Both men knew what this meant. The war was getting hotter, and with each day, more and more casualty reports came in. Men who served in the Pacific were often hospitalized for medical reasons beyond combat wounds, with some being fatal.

4

20 December 1942
Calcutta, India

- Guadalcanal--Enemy riflemen harass flanks and rear of 132nd Infantry on northwest slopes of Mt. Austen. 1st Battalion attempts unsuccessfully to locate enemy's east flank. U.S. engineers complete construction of jeep road to Hill 35.
- New Guinea--Australians on Sanananda front continue to reduce enemy positions beyond track junction.
- Japan--Submarine **Trigger** (SS-237) lays mines in Japanese home waters.

The party was getting louder if that was possible. The local band did a fair job of the dance music but was pitiful when it came to anything remotely resembling the Glenn Miller Orchestra. Robert Beck wasn't listening to the music or even looking at the few British women dancing with the officers. Instead, he was trying to make sense of the nearly incoherent voice of an American staff officer of the Tenth Air Force. The navy lieutenant had been buying rounds of drinks for his new American friend, as he and his business partner Major Smythe-Jones tried to learn as much as possible about future shipments of supplies for the buildup of the Allied forces in the China-Burma-India (CBI) front. Beck was wishing he didn't have to contend with the loud local band's off tune playing, but it was probably best to have this conversation in the crowded American Flying Club.

"Well, you know General Bissell hates Chenault and even arranged to have his date of promotion one day earlier than the famous Flying Tiger. Something about their early days flying biplanes or something. No matter, the two men are always sniping at each other."

This was useful information for Beck and his British business partner. Two commanders at odds with each other provided better cover for their future dealings. The navy lieutenant continued questioning the inebriated staff officer.

"William, my new friend, you told me the general was making more requests for large numbers of vehicles for his command. It would be beneficial for me to understand the size of these requests so I can plan for priority handling and delivery from the docks."

Beck smiled at the man, who smiled back, even though he wasn't looking directly at him. The man's gaze was distracted by a large brunette walking by in the company of an American pilot. The club was founded earlier in the war when the first American aviation units were sent to help the British after the fall of Java in March 1942. Slowly, the command expanded and now numbered more than fourteen hundred officers and eleven thousand enlisted men. The Air Transport Command was also growing in size, including three hundred officers and fourteen hundred enlisted men.

These two aviation units were just part of the growing American commitment to the CBI. Lieutenant General Joseph Stillwell, the overall American commander in the theater, was adding more men each day to support the Nationalist government of Chiang Kai-shek. This support's key component was Brigadier General Claire Chenault's former American Volunteer Group (AVG), which was now expanding to become the Fourteenth Air Force. The mission of Bissel's Tenth Air Force was to support Allied operations in India and Burma. There were not enough planes or pilots to plan large strikes against the Japanese, but a few missions were made on Rangoon in Burma and northern Malaya. Being on the end of the longest supply line in the American war effort meant the CBI men were the last to get anything.

William, the drunken army air force supply officer, was now nearing the end of his ability to communicate. Beck tried one more trick to get the information he was searching for.

"Tell me about the request you saw for more trucks. It would help me plan for the delivery and shipment to the forward bases."

Slowly the drunken officer reached for his glass, now held beyond his grasp by the British major. Smythe-Jones—who described himself as a professional drunk and could out drink anyone he met and remain lucid—continued the interrogation, "William, how many trucks are being ordered for your command? It would help both Lieutenant Beck and me to know so we can make plans for their arrival."

William's gaze fixed on the glass resting in the hands of the British officer. "The general demanded more transportation in his last meeting with my colonel, who is the head of supply. I think the request was something like two hundred fifty trucks, three hundred more jeeps, seventy-five sedans and ambulances, and something else." The man's eyes were rapidly glazing as he tried to remember the rest of the requisition. The supply officer stared longingly at the glass of gin held by the major, muttered something unintelligible about tractors or something the two men could not quite understand before his head slowly dropped to the table into a drunken sleep.

"Sorry about that, Robert, but it seems our new young friend cannot hold his liquor. I think we have at least a good idea about what the general is trying to get for his command."

Beck looked at his business partner and smiled. Peter Smythe-Jones had known the young American air force captain for a few months. They had been learning about the Tenth Air Force's operation as part of his regular position as the British army supply liaison for Calcutta. Since meeting Robert Beck, his interests in all things American had increased substantially. His new friend and business associate promised a significant income from redirecting Allied supplies to cash-paying customers throughout the subcontinent. This large shipment of vehicles promised quite a payday if managed correctly.

"Peter, don't push our drunken friend for any information for at least a week. Let him think we were drunk as well. Then, you can make more inquiries for the sake of Allied cooperation."

Both men smiled and picked up their drinks, toasting the newest intelligence. Beck pulled out a small notebook, and at the back wrote down the number of vehicles being requisitioned and the probable dates for delivery. It would take months to make the trip from the United States to India, but having any prior knowledge would make it a much safer and more successful operation for the two men.

Beck looked at the numbers and then told the British major about the size of the order. "It would be somewhere near five thousand shipping tons to get that amount of equipment to India. I figure it will be sent in two or three convoys with the jeeps stored in the hold and the big trucks on the deck. At the earliest, we could see some deliveries in March. If, we arrange for some diversions on the roads north of the city, I think we could acquire a dozen or more trucks and the same number of jeeps."

Smythe-Jones sipped on his gin then added to the plan. "What say you if we could arrange for these trucks to be delayed in transit? If someone, such as a bored clerk, requested these vehicles to pick up additional supplies before heading north, would this be worth our time?"

Beck enjoyed the malevolent nature of his British partner's thought process. If one was going to steal, do it in a big way. "Peter, that is an excellent idea, and if we could make these supplies of a high value, such as tires, fuel, or food, perhaps we could increase our profit."

Peter picked up his glass to down the last drop of gin, but more serious activities interrupted his celebration. Outside the window searchlights glared through the clouds as air raid sirens wailed. A split second later, both men responded to the sound of antiaircraft guns firing into the surrounding sky.

"What the hell is happening?" Beck's eyes widened as he stared out the window. Fear was evident in the face of the man who lied about his whereabouts when the Japanese attacked Pearl Harbor the year before. He liked to tell people that he was near the docks when his ship, the *West Virginia,* was struck by the enemy bombers, but instead he was a great distance from his ship hiding under his bed after being hospitalized for the flu.

"Looks like the Japanese are attacking," the English major calmly stated. The man was not a coward, simply a drunk who had sold out his honor many years ago. Now, as he stared out the window, the sounds of bombs blasting the nearby Kiddespore docks became louder. The American Flying Club was nearby, across the Hooghly river, and the bombing was coming closer.

"I think we should find refuge from the bombs. Never know where one is going to land." Peter's demeanor was increasingly calm as he grabbed the drunken American supply officer passed out on the table and yelled for Beck to help him. "Grab the bloody captain's arm and help me get him downstairs."

Beck slowly complied and grabbed the man's arm. With Peter on the other arm, both men dragged the sleeping captain down the stairs. Before they got to the bottom of the first-floor landing, a bomb exploded across the street. The explosion's force knocked the men off their feet and part of the building's wall collapsed. Luckily, they were in the stairwell and spared from the falling debris. They quickly dusted themselves off and moved into the main lobby of the building where they saw people holding onto one another, many covered with plaster or bricks, some bleeding from flying glass.

The bombs continued to fall but were beyond their building. Smythe-Jones let the drunken Yank down, going to the aid of a nearby woman who was covered with bricks and bleeding from cuts to her head. Beck remained beside the supply officer and began to tremble with panic. Lieutenant Beck's urge to run was overwhelming. He saw his business partner, with assistance from another officer, pull bricks and fragments of wood off the injured woman. Consumed by fear, Beck bolted for the door, leaving the American supply officer sleeping peacefully, completely unaware of what was happening around him.

As Beck left the room, he yelled out to Peter, "I'm going to find help!"

The British major heard the man's shouting but didn't bother to look at him. Peter was a drunk and a disgrace to the British army, but he still expected more of himself in a crisis. Even through his own flaws he could recognize fear and cowardice in others and now knew his business partner would have to be closely observed in the future.

The order was sent to find the lieutenant and have him report immediately to the commanding general's office. A sergeant searched several offices to find the man in question. The company commander was not in his office, nor was his first sergeant. The lieutenant was not in his quarters and no one seemed to know his whereabouts. Finally, a clerk said the battalion was engaged in a field exercise on the other side of the base. The dutiful sergeant got in his small truck and drove over Camp Pendleton's hills and finally located the unit at a firing range. Finding the company commander, the sergeant was directed to the lieutenant laying in a prone position firing at targets down range.

"Men, think of your rifle as your best friend, your girl, your mother, whatever works for you. Never let me find you dragging it around in the dirt. It should always be clean, ready to fire, and above all else next to you." The officer looked up at the squad of men assembled around him, took aim and fired three rounds.

As the officer stood, he asked, "Who would like to be next on the firing line?"

Before he received an answer from the squad members, the sergeant from HQ stepped forward and came to attention.

"Sir, the commanding general wants to see you immediately."

Second Lieutenant Waverly looked at the clean and perfectly dressed sergeant and asked, "What does the general want with me?"

"Sir, I was told to find you and bring you immediately to his office. That's all I know."

"All right, Sergeant, I guess I will go advise the general on the war situation."

The squad's men began laughing at the comment as the officer handed the M-1 to a corporal. "Take care of that weapon. I want it back later."

The sergeant and the lieutenant sped off to see Major General Barrett, commanding officer of the new Third Marine Division. There was no time to change into a new uniform or clean up from the muddy training class.

The lieutenant waited in a chair outside the commanding general's office for twenty minutes. Watching a half a dozen senior officers come and go, including his battalion commander followed by the regiment's commanding officer. Each time these men left the general's office, passing the waiting lieutenant, no one spoke a word to Bill Waverly. Usually, the officers were cordial to him, with many of the older men knowing the mustang lieutenant from previous assignments, but now, everyone gave him the cold shoulder. Waverly was becoming more concerned about the situation. *Did something happen early in my career which was deemed detrimental to the good order of the Corps?* He couldn't think of anything, but the worries persisted. Finally, he was called into the office.

As he came to attention in front of the general, he noticed the assistant division commander, Brigadier Allen Turnage, standing next to the desk.

"Lieutenant Waverly, reporting as ordered."

The general had met Waverly on several occasions and knew of the man's combat record. The lieutenant was in a dirty uniform, evidently coming directly from some training exercise being conducted on the sprawling new base.

"At ease, Lieutenant. You know General Turnage, so I'll spare the introductions." Looking down at the file in front of him and a teletype message next to it, he asked, "Waverly, who the hell do you know in Washington? Specifically in Admiral King's office?"

Waverly didn't have a clue about anyone in the nation's capital knowing him, let alone in the office of the chief of Naval Operations. "Sir, I don't know anyone in Admiral King's office and I haven't been in Washington since I served at Marine Barracks in 1936."

"Didn't think you did, Lieutenant, but when I get an order from the chief of Naval Operations, I get concerned." Picking up the Marine's file and handing it to the General Turnage, he continued. "Lieutenant, you have a good record, especially in leading men in combat. You have been awarded the Navy Cross, Silver Star, and the Purple Heart. You were wounded at the Battle of Bloody Ridge, and Colonel Edson thinks highly of you. I hate to lose you, but you have been ordered to Washington. You have priority transportation and I have been told to get you on a plane out of San Diego no later than tomorrow. You will not have any leave granted, nor will you have time to get much more than your personal gear ready. I have no idea why they want you, but you are to report to Admiral Edwards, who is King's chief of staff."

Waverly didn't understand. He was pleased in his new billet and training his new platoon for deployment. Most of the men were young, and except for one sergeant, no one had combat experience. Everyone in his regiment looked at the former Raider as the god of war.

Many had heard of his bravery on Guadalcanal. How he had

been wounded, saving the life of a machine gun crew which were being overrun by the Japanese in a ferocious nighttime assault at a place called Bloody Ridge. The lieutenant had killed several of the enemy and dragged the wounded machine gunners to safety, going back three times to pull each man out of the position to the temporary safety of American lines. His wounds were so severe he was airlifted to Noumea. After being stabilized, they sent him to the naval hospital at Mare Island in San Francisco. His injuries slowly healed. He was then placed on limited duty and assigned to the new Third Division in late November as a temporary training officer.

"General, I would like to stay here and help the men of the Third Division. We all know the men of this command need a few old hands to help them get ready for the war."

The general smiled and appreciated the commitment to his new command, but there would be no changing an order coming from the head of the United States Navy.

"Lieutenant, as much as General Turnage and I would like to keep you here at Pendleton to help train our Marines, the CNO wants you for some reason, which must be crucial to the war effort. I will have my sergeant help you get your gear packed and arrange your transportation. My personnel officer will get your records ready and arrange for your pay to catch up to you in Washington. Any questions?"

Bill Waverly knew his commanding general had received an order and it would be carried out. "No sir. General, I would like to thank you for your help, and I look forward to serving with you again." The lieutenant went to attention and executed a perfect about-face before walking out of the office.

General Turnage sat down in front of the commanding general's desk and asked, "Charles, do you have any idea what Admiral King wants with a mustang lieutenant like Waverly?"

"I don't have a clue, Allen. I got the order this morning, and it was one of those you don't question. I've been around King several times in my career and you don't want to cross him or question his commands. So whatever they want the lieutenant for must be important."

"I looked through his record and besides his combat experiences with the Raiders, I didn't see anything spectacular that jumped out at me."

"Allen, I agree, there is nothing in his file which tells me what he has done over his years in the Corps that would make him of interest to the admiral. But evidently, his experiences on Guadalcanal must have something to do with it."

Turning his gaze to another set of files on his desk, he asked, "Do we have anybody with combat experience to replace him in the training group?"

"No sir. The First Division's experienced men are regrouping in Australia, and except for wounded men like Waverly, very few men are being sent back to the States. I guess we have to work with what we have and hope for the best."

The Third Division commander took note of his trusted assistant's comment, then added, "We must go to war with whatever we have and hope the men learn fast."

5

23 December 1942
Office of Admiral Edwards
Washington, D.C.

- New Guinea--Virtual stalemate exists on Sanananda front, where the Japanese stubbornly defend well-organized positions.
- Tunisia--Three day period of torrential rain begins. Elements of RCT 18, U.S. 1st Division, relieve 2nd Coldstream Guards at Djebel el Ahmera and are forced to withdraw under German counterattack.

It was late afternoon when the haggard-looking Marine lieutenant arrived at the office of Admiral Edwards. It had taken three plane rides, two of them in new B-25s, to make it to the nation's capital. The man was met at the National Airport by a petty officer from Main Navy's motor pool and taken directly to headquarters. Upon arrival at HQ, the petty officer walked the lieutenant to the security office. A bored-looking ensign checked out his identification and verified the man's reason for being in the building. The ensign searched the daily roster for incoming personnel and found the name, Waverly. As his finger moved from left to right, he immediately became alert when he saw the Marine was to be taken to Admiral Edwards' office upon arrival. Picking up the phone, the ensign called the admiral's office alerting him of the new arrival.

"Sir, there is a Marine Lieutenant Waverly at security. Do you…"

Before the ensign could say another word, a voice on the other end of the telephone told the befuddled officer to immediately have someone escort the lieutenant to the admiral's office. The connection broke before the ensign could reply. Looking at the Marine, who was much older than most lieutenants, he ordered one of the men to watch his desk while he personally accompanied the officer to Admiral Edwards' office.

"Lieutenant, if you'll follow me, I will escort you to the Admiral's office."

Waverly replied, "All right, Ensign, I'm right behind you."

The two men walked past the security personnel and entered the long corridors, which would take a newcomer weeks to learn. After climbing two flights of stairs and down another hall, the men came to an office full of enlisted men and officers looking at reports or filing them away in temporary boxes. Waverly had never seen so much paper in his life, but kept his comments to himself. The two men then passed into a second office, with about a dozen officers and a few senior petty officers. Most were lieutenants and above, including many commanders and a few captains standing in small groups discussing something of obvious importance. At least, that is what the lieutenant thought. Finally, entering a third office, Waverly encountered three officers and a chief petty officer seated next to an imposing door that had no name. As the two men entered, the lieutenant went to the chief's desk and stated his business.

"Chief, this is Lieutenant Waverly."

The chief looked up at the ensign and then the older looking Marine officer before pointing to the desk to his left and stating, "Commander, Lieutenant Waverly is here."

Waverly and the ensign escort moved to the desk of a navy commander and stood at attention.

"Commander, Second Lieutenant Waverly, reporting as ordered."

Allen looked up from his desk and saw the two officers standing before him. The ensign was a young-looking reservist, who appeared small and weak next to the Marine officer's imposing figure. He was impressed by what he saw. Waverly was a self-confident man in his early thirties who knew what he was doing. Now, he understood what Flannigan had seen in the man.

Standing and moving to the front of his desk, the admiral's aide said, "Lieutenant Waverly, welcome to Main Navy." Allen shook the Marine's hand then dismissed the ensign.

"Sit down, Waverly. I'm certain you have lots of questions."

Bill Waverly sat down and saw in the commander another warrior. Noticing the various awards and ribbons on the man's uniform, the Marine knew the man seated in front of him was not an ordinary staff officer, which, at least to him, made all the difference in the world.

"Waverly, you have a distinguished combat record and made a big impression on an officer who is highly regarded by Admiral King. Admiral Edwards will explain all of this in a few minutes. I told him you were in the building, and he wants to personally brief you on your assignment. Let me check if he's ready to meet you."

The Marine was hoping for information on the situation from the commander, but would be thrown into the lion's den instead. As he waited, he looked around the room and saw a navy captain speaking loudly on the phone, and next to him a lieutenant commander staring at a report. The chief petty officer was on the phone speaking softly to avoid being overheard by anyone in the office. The navy commander named Allen appeared at the admiral's door and signaled for Waverly to join him. The two officers walked into the office and came to attention in front of the chief of staff.

"Admiral, may I present Second Lieutenant William Waverly." The commander did not smile, nor did he offer other comments.

The chief of staff stood up and walked in front of the two officers and then said, "At ease, gentlemen." Extending his hand in welcome, the admiral said, "Welcome to Washington, Lieutenant. I have heard only good things about you from a friend of yours."

Waverly shook the admiral's hand and then was directed to a conference table and told to sit down. Allen sat next to him while the Admiral went to his desk, grabbing a file. Joining the two men at the table, Edwards scanned the file and then turned his attention to the man seated in front of him. "Lieutenant, you must have a lot of questions about why you're here. I'm certain you will have many more questions that Commander Allen should help you with after my briefing. You will meet your new commanding officers in a few minutes, who will provide additional details on your new assignment. But first, let me explain that you have an important mission critical to the war effort requiring a great deal of secrecy. You have proven yourself in combat and in your ability to lead men—two qualities Admiral King and I find most important in this war. Your last assignment training men in the new Third Division demonstrated your ability to communicate the lessons you learned on Guadalcanal and in your years in the Marines."

Pulling out a recent medical evaluation from Waverly's file, Edwards continued. "It seems the navy's medical professionals think you should be on limited duty status for the duration."

Seeing the lieutenant about to speak, the admiral held up his hand. "Waverly, the doctors report you suffered severe wounds which should have killed you. You lost a significant amount of blood, suffered a major wound to your right lung, took shrapnel to your back and legs, had two bullets removed from your shoulder, had a broken clavicle bone from one of the bullets they pulled from you, and had a serious concussion. Your leg wounds indicate severe damage to the calf muscles and damage to your knee. How you were able to pull three wounded men from their machine gun position is truly remarkable."

Looking directly at the Marine, Edwards asked, "What made you go back three separate times to pull those men from their position, especially after being wounded so severely?" Knowing what was in the file, the admiral wanted to comprehend why a man risked death three separate times to save his men.

"Admiral, it's what had to be done. It was pitch black, and the Japs were swarming our positions on the ridge. The machine gun position was being outflanked. The five men in the pillbox were doing their best to mow the bastards down. There were just too many of them attacking at one time. I ordered a squad to follow me to break up their attack, but we were beaten back. I think I lost two men, but I'm not sure. I saw the gun firing, so I knew someone was still alive, so I ran forward. Seeing two men down, I pulled one back and returned for the next one, but another man had been hit, so I did it two more times. They were my men, and I had to take care of them."

Edwards looked at the Navy Cross citation the man had received. "Waverly, I'm glad we have men like you in the Corps, and now I know why Major Flannigan asked for you."

The look on the lieutenant's face was priceless. Allen thought he could see the man's brain reviewing his past to find a man named Flannigan, but nothing came to mind. A lot had happened on Tulagi and then Guadalcanal. Men moved in and out of the Raiders then the survivors of the Raiders were consolidated with the Parachute Battalion to support Edson's Fifth Marines at Bloody Ridge. Finally, it hit him. He recalled a Captain Flannigan on Tulagi who took over for the wounded platoon lieutenant and how the man had worked with him to wipe out Japanese positions in caves.

"Admiral, I remember a Captain Flannigan. Is this the same man?"

"Yes, Lieutenant, Major Flannigan asked specifically for you. He thought you were one hell of a Marine."

"Sir, it would be good to serve with the major again. He was a good leader on Tulagi, but I never heard what happened to him once he went over to Guadalcanal."

Edwards closed the file and said, "Lieutenant, you will get a chance soon to visit with the major, but first, you need to meet the commanding officer of the unit and be informed of your new duties." Commander Allen knew the drill, standing and exiting the room. In another few minutes, he returned with a navy captain and a familiar-looking Marine major.

The two officers came to attention in front of Admiral Edwards and were immediately told to be "at ease" and meet Lieutenant Waverly. Jameson shook the Marine's hand and noticed the steely look in the man's eye, noting how he was not afraid to focus directly on the superior officer. "Lieutenant, it's good to meet you. The major has spoken highly of you."

"Sir, it is good to meet you, and I look forward to being in your command."

Flannigan flashed the man a smile and shook his hand with a firmness that helped connect the two professionals. "Waverly, it's good to see you again."

Before the two men could say anything else, Edwards directed the men to take a seat.

"Lieutenant Waverly, you are being assigned to Major Flannigan as second in command of the security team for Captain Jameson's organization. The captain's unit is known as the Science Team and reports to

Admiral King. The men in this unit are charged with important projects concerning the war effort. Captain Jameson and Major Flannigan will provide you with additional details concerning the team's activities. You will have a small security detachment of NCOs who were hand-selected for this mission. Everything associated with this team is top secret and will be guarded at all costs. Do you understand the meaning of my words, Lieutenant Waverly?"

The Marine lieutenant, surrounded by four senior officers, knew full well what *all costs* meant to a warrior. No quarter will be given and death is the only way out. Looking at the admiral, he replied, "Sir, I understand the order and will fight to the death if required to fulfill my duty."

Edwards eyed the man seated across the table and knew he was telling the truth. A professional who had already met the enemy and survived. A Marine who saved the lives of his own men at the expense of nearly losing his own life. Yes, the admiral thought, this man would die doing his duty.

"Excellent, Lieutenant. Captain Jameson will provide more details of your mission, but I want to make sure of one thing. There is one man who is key to the operation's success, and his name is Lieutenant Brand. Everyone in the team knows how important Mr. Brand is to the war effort, and he will be your primary responsibility. Nothing is to interfere with his accomplishing his tasks." Edwards stern look was directed at the lieutenant as he spoke. As the admiral thought for a moment, no one said a word. A small grin crossed the senior officer's face and he resumed talking. "One more thing, Waverly, as of today, you are promoted to First Lieutenant. Congratulations."

Waverly was still trying to understand the significance of being responsible for an officer named Brand and didn't hear the last words of the chief of staff. Suddenly he was being congratulated by the officers around the table. Flannigan was first saying, "Well deserved promotion, Bill."

Edwards stood, approached the Marine, and shook his hand, saying, "Well done, Lieutenant Waverly. I expect you will be a captain very soon. Keep up the good work and follow the instructions Captain Jameson gives you."

All of the officers came to attention and left the office. Commander Allen escorted them to his desk and handed a set of new silver bars to Waverly. Shaking the man's hand, he whispered, "Good luck, Lieutenant, you're going to have your hands full."

Later that evening, after meeting the officers and men in the Logistics Research Department, Bill Waverly received a briefing by Flannigan and Warrant Officer "Gunny" Jones about his role and the challenges of protecting James Brand. Both men stressed the importance of the mission and the critical nature of the intelligence he would be charged with safeguarding. Gunny told him the learning curve was steep but knew the Science Team's newest member was up to the challenge. Waverly hoped that was true but was still unsure of his role. In the next few days, the new security officer would meet the professor and learn how much of a challenge it would be to keep James Brand safe.

6

24 December 1942
The White House
Washington, D.C.

- Guadalcanal--3rd Battalion of 132nd Infantry,
  followed by 1st Battalion in reserve, moves west
  without incident to Hill 31, west of Mt. Austen; upon
  attacking toward Hill 27, is stopped by fire from
  enemy strongpoint, called Gifu. The Gifu position is
  held by about 500 Japanese.
- New Guinea--After artillery preparation, Urbana
  Force, employing 127th Infantry, begins drive
  toward the sea, through Government Gardens,
  where enemy defenses are organized in-depth and
  concealed with high kunai grass.
- Algeria--French Adm. Darlan is assassinated in
  Algiers.
- Tunisia--Decision is made at conference between
  Gen. Eisenhower and Gen. K. A. N. Anderson to
  abandon the attack on Tunis until after the rainy
  season.

Admiral Leahy had spent most of the morning going over changes to the budget for 1943 military production. This budget included everything from clothing and boots to ships and airplanes. Food, fuel, tires, bullets, and beans were all necessary to win the war, and the production war would be the key ingredient to the eventual success of the American military. Leahy mulled over the task at hand. *Both the navy and the army fight like small dogs over every item on the list. Which service got priority on each item. High octane aircraft fuel is needed not by gallons but by thousands of tons. But if the flyers get their wishes, what would the army get for their thousands of tanks and trucks? And what about the fuel oil consumed by the navy? Each service demands everything, all at the same time, and they want it now.*

President Roosevelt's War Production Board had been chartered to deliver these items in ever-increasing quantities to the services, but changing American production lines from washing machines to tanks and from cars to bombers took time, tooling, and training. The man in charge of this task was Donald Nelson, the former chairman of Sears, Roebuck and Company. Nelson knew the world of manufacturing and the tenuous nature of something called the supply chain. Now, the former retailer was trying to build new industries out of nothing. In particular, was the need for rubber.

The supplies of natural rubber were mostly now in the hands of the Japanese. The Brazilian capability could not match those of Malaya, and now the need for the commodity had quadrupled. American industry was building a synthetic rubber industry from scratch, but it was still building plants and improving its technology. Trucks needed rubber for tires, as did airplanes and thousands of other rubber items required for the war effort. And rubber was only one of the essential products needed by the military and the hundred and thirty million American civilians, plus supporting the Allies. The Arsenal of Democracy was growing, but like all living things, it took time to mature. Admiral Leahy knew full well that America didn't have the time to wait.

Added to the list of challenges of meeting the wartime production goals were graft and corruption. The admiral was kept informed about the Truman Committee's activities, which had been established in 1941 to investigate waste, corruption, and mismanagement by industry in military contracts. The committee was bipartisan and worked well with the president by providing advance notice of any significant problem uncovered by their work. Senator Harry Truman had started looking into contract problems in early 1941 when he traveled around his home state looking into allegations about shoddy work and price gouging at the Camp Leonard Wood installation being built in Missouri. His report contained proof of overcharging and waste allegations and led to establishing a Senate committee to investigate other examples across the country. The senator from Missouri was performing excellent service to the country by keeping contractors tied to the terms of their contracts.

As chief of staff to the president, Leahy was the conduit of these reports and kept Roosevelt informed of significant allegations which might be controversial or damaging. Every statement angered the admiral, not for publicity issues but for the knowledge that fellow Americans were damaging the war effort through greed, stupidity, or outright lies. Senator Truman was making a good name for himself and apparently without taking credit for his work. The man seemed honest in his wanting to ensure the American taxpayer got their money's worth from every contract, and no serviceman died because of poor workmanship. But today, there were no recent reports from the senator. Perhaps the best thing about the Christmas season was not the concept of "goodwill to men," but that many people were not working, especially politicians.

But everyone in a uniform was working. The war didn't stop for a religious or secular holiday. Men were fighting and dying across the world in remote villages, windswept deserts, and raging cold seas. The admiral saw the casualty reports and knew Americans were dying at an increasing rate. The estimates for 1942 showed more than thirty-five thousand Americans would die by the end of the year, which was only the first full year of the war. The planning staffs of both the navy and army estimated another four hundred thousand to six hundred thousand men would die before the Axis was defeated. The wounded would easily double the number killed, and the war's human cost would affect every family in the country. These sobering numbers were constantly rumbling around in his brain, and every decision made by him and the American Chiefs of Staff affected someone's life. Leahy vowed to make every decision count and minimize the number of casualties, not just for the public but also for his own conscience.

As he examined the latest report on the Tunisian front's lack of progress, his military aide walked in to announce a visitor.

"Admiral, Field Marshal Dill asked if he could speak with you. He's standing in my office."

"Yes, of course. Bring Sir John in and I may want you to bring us some coffee."

The army captain turned and went to the outer office to bring in the British officer.

Leahy stood and adjusted his uniform, waiting for the military representative of His Majesty's government. The field marshal entered and shook the hand of President Roosevelt's chief of staff saying, "Admiral, so good of you to see me. I promise not to take you away from your many duties."

"Sir John, you are welcome anytime. I didn't know you were in the building; otherwise, I would have met you earlier."

"Seems to be a cockup on communications today between my office and the president. I have a private communication from the prime minister for him. Seems he is doing a reception for the staff this morning, so I must wait."

Leahy was immediately interested in any private communication from the British prime minister, so he asked the note's nature.

"Sir John, if I had known you were coming, I would have arranged the president's schedule, but from what I know of his reception, this should be over by 11:30 because he has a meeting with Sir Girija Bajpai, the Agent-General for India."

The admiral thought the private note from the prime minister might be tied to the meeting with the Indian diplomat. India was the most important part of the British Empire. Still, the subcontinent politics were such that additional autonomy was not being granted to the three hundred million inhabitants of the largest part of the Empire.

"Yes, I knew Sir Girija was coming over for a meeting. I think he has Sir Zafarullah Khan, the Agent-General of India to China with him. Both perfect gentlemen and well thought of by Mr. Churchill." Thinking for a moment at the possible motive for a meeting with India's two representatives, Sir John quickly answered the question in the mind of the chief of staff.

"Admiral, the note I am delivering has nothing to do with India or the meeting with these two gentlemen. I know your president has strong views on Indian independence, but the communication is on a different subject." The British military representative continued looking at the passive-looking admiral, known as both a naval professional and a discrete diplomat.

"Actually, the note makes a few recommendations for the meeting in Morocco. Seems the prime minister has some ideas on an excursion to Marrakech. Mr. Churchill loves to talk about the beauty of the Atlas Mountains at sunset. I'm certain there are other motivations for the two men to be alone, but I have not been so informed. Also, there is a recommendation which affects both countries, which I believe would help develop stronger relations going forward."

Leahy was now all ears, especially thinking of the president and the prime minister stealing off to the Atlas Mountains to look at a sunset. No doubt the British leader would lavish praise on his American partner and then suggest some wild scheme with little to no relevance to the war effort. He was interested in the other item Sir John had broached.

"Sir John, what is this idea? I hope it doesn't involve our invading Turkey or Spain?"

The British officer smiled and casually stated, "No, nothing so serious. The prime minister and General Brooke are recommending we provide a liaison to assist Professor Brand. I think it's a good idea as well, because of many activities the professor is engaged in which affect our joint efforts and ongoing technological developments."

Leahy was immediately suspicious. Was Churchill enacting his own idiom of *"If the camel once gets his nose in the tent, his body soon follows."*

Being a keen observer of leadership, the admiral knew Sir John didn't have personal interest in this idea. Still, thinking further about the professor and the man's many activities, perhaps another person could be of assistance.

"Seems that the professor is garnering more attention each day, by not only our people but by our Allies. Do you have a recommendation for this liaison?"

Sensing the admiral could be in agreement with the British plan, the field marshal provided some details.

"We have a young man with impeccable qualifications from not only a scientific background but also a military one. The man's name is Duncan Clark, and he is a lieutenant in the Royal Naval Volunteer Reserve and a pilot with the Fleet Air Arm. As I recall, the officer is a graduate of Oxford with a degree in chemistry and fought valiantly in the Battle of Britain when seconded to the RAF. After this experience, he joined the *Ark Royal* in the Mediterranean. I think he has over seven victories, including two Germans shot down over Britain. I believe he was shot down and wounded over Malta, and upon his recuperation was sent to work with your Grumman company on testing your new Hellcat. I don't have his complete file, but was provided a glowing review by both the RAF and Royal Navy people here in Washington."

Admiral Leahy thought Sir John probably knew a lot more about the officer but did not press the issue. Understanding the political challenges of an appointment such as this, especially with the many top-secret activities Professor Brand was involved with, only the president could decide and then force Admiral King to agree with the arrangement. Thinking it might be a good idea to accompany the British military representative in the quick meeting with Roosevelt, Leahy stood up and said, "Do you mind if I join you in meeting with the president?"

Smiling and gracious as usual and knowing the chief of staff was now on board with the recommendation, Sir John said, "Of course, Admiral, I would enjoy your company. I think the president will be happy to further cement our two countries' scientific relationship."

The two men walked down the hall and waited to be summoned into the office to speak with Franklin D. Roosevelt. After only a few minutes, the two senior officers left. Both made phone calls to get things moving, but Admiral Leahy's was the unpleasant one.

7

29 December 1942
Office of Admiral Edwards
Washington, D.C.

- New Georgia--Enemy completes airfield at Munda despite frequent Allied air attacks.
- Guadalcanal--At a conference at Gen. Patch's CP, the decision is made to continue attack on Mt. Austen.
- New Guinea--Japanese Gen. Yamagata, charged with rescue of Buna garrison, arrives at Giruawa.
- Libya--Advance elements of the British 8th Army come to a halt just west of enemy's Buerat position.
- USSR--Kotelnikov, southwest of Stalingrad, falls to Red Army.
- United States naval vessel sunk: High-speed minesweeper **Wasmuth** (DMS-15) by explosion of two of her own depth charges, during a gale in Aleutian island area.

Looking at the latest ship construction report, the officer wanted to pick one of the new destroyers for his own. *Yes,* he thought, *a new* Fletcher-*class ship would be just the right command to take me away from Wash-*

ington's political battles. But as he examined the details of the most recent builds, Commander Allen knew none of them would be skippered by him anytime soon. As a trusted aide to Admiral Edwards, who served as chief of staff to the chief of Naval Operations, his only command would be the desk he currently occupied. Yet, the thought of conning a fast destroyer was his destiny, and with each day, he hoped his transfer would be approved. But today was not going to be the day.

When the door opened to the admiral's office, a very stern-looking Marine general walked out without speaking to the lowly commander. The senior officer was almost through the outer door before Allen could come to attention. Quickly sitting down again, he was interrupted by a phone call.

"Commander Allen speaking."

"Commander, this is Jameson. How are you today? Any battles being fought in the admiral's office?"

Smiling at the familiar voice, he replied, "No, Captain, just the same angry-looking generals and admirals who want something yesterday. How can I be of service, sir?"

"Does the admiral have time to meet the new British liaison officer?"

Allen was aware of the latest addition to the Science Team and recalled the loud voices coming out of the office when it was announced the president approved the idea without discussing it first with Admiral King. "Sir, if the British lieutenant would like to be sacrificed on the altar of Allied cooperation, I think the admiral will be ready to meet in fifteen minutes."

"Very good, Allen, let me set the stage for the lieutenant to ensure his survival. Anything we should not discuss around Admiral Edwards?"

"If you could stay away from discussions about North Africa, that would be wise. I think Admiral King believes he is going to be sucked into a British scheme in the Mediterranean which would require more ships being sent to help our cousins."

Hearing a chuckle from Captain Jameson, Allen continued. "Admiral Edwards has an open mind, so keep the Brit in check. Only positive things should be said, and make sure he's diplomatic in his approach to the boss."

Jameson thanked the commander, hung up the phone, and turned his attention to Lieutenant Clark. "Well, this is going to be a fascinating meeting. Let's take a walk to see the admiral."

After being shown into Admiral Edwards' office, one American officer and one British were asked to sit at the conference table. Commander Allen was told to stay as an observer—standard procedure for many of the chief of staff's meetings with his subordinates.

Edwards opened a file in front of him. Sent over by Field Marshal Dill, the documents provided a summary of the officer's record. Everything was positive, demonstrating superior performance in battle and all aspects of the man's career.

Noticing burn scars on the British officer's hands and forehead, Edwards began the discussion. "Lieutenant Clark, it is good to meet you. From examining the file sent to me by Field Marshal Dill, it appears you have demonstrated not only your bravery but also your intelligence." Referring to the file, Edwards asked his first of many questions. "Lieutenant, what would you rather be doing instead of sitting in an office talking to an American admiral?"

Taken back by the comment, the Oxford-educated flyer was quick witted and enjoyed the challenge. In his best Scottish accent, he replied, "Sir, I would rather be in an airplane fighting the Germans than in this office. No disrespect, sir, but I think of myself as a pilot, not a staff officer."

Jameson smiled at the comment and wondered about the man's frame of mind being pulled into the Science Team. The captain had examined the file earlier and knew from his telephone conversation with Sir John that Clark was well qualified to work with his command but would much rather be doing anything else, reminding him of a certain navy lieutenant under his command who would also prefer flying a plane against the enemy.

Edwards caught the grin on the face of Captain Jameson. Lieutenant Clark was twenty-five years of age, with a degree from Oxford in chemistry. The academic credentials were impeccable, and the man had graduated with top honors at the Magdalen College with a secondary emphasis in mathematics. The officer's military record was extraordinary. Deciding to get more details on the man's accomplishments and to see how he handled the pressure, the admiral asked a series of questions.

"Lieutenant, it seems you learned to fly while at Oxford and then in

your last year joined the Royal Navy Voluntary Reserve. After graduation in 1939, you went to flight school to learn the Fleet Air Arm's flying
system. Did you find that redundant?"

"Sir, it was good to learn the navy's way of doing things. Seems the
senior service in Britain believes in making a man do all the basics again
no matter what you already know."

"After completing flight training, you were assigned to a land-
based squadron when the war broke out. What were you flying then?"

"Admiral, they had me in a Sea Gladiator, which was a biplane fighter. The thing was a death trap to any man who flew against the Germans."

Thinking any man who would have to fly a biplane against the
Luftwaffe must be incredibly brave or foolish, the admiral moved on in
his discussion.

"Your records show you were flying something called a Skua and
attacked German ships in the Norway campaign. Can you tell me what
you did during this time?"

"Admiral, the Blackburn Skua is a slow single-wing fighter bomber
which would easily get you killed. It is no longer in service, but it was the
only thing we had. I was flying out of the Orkney Islands when we got
the word the Germans were off Norway's coast. We were fortunate and
sighted the *Konigsberg* in Bergen harbor and successfully attacked the
cruiser. Later efforts against other German ships were not as successful,
and many of my squadron mates failed to return."

Jameson noticed the man avoided embellishing his experiences but
was quick and precise with his answers. Clark had been in many battles,
and there had to be mental scars attached to these deeds.

"How did you get seconded to the RAF?" The admiral looked up
at the British officer to see the man looking directly at him, showing no
expression.

"Admiral, after the Norway mess, my squadron was down by half
and a few men had been wounded as well. The Germans took quite a toll
on our squadrons in France and more planes were lost in the Dunkirk
operation. I think it was the middle of June when the base commander
asked for volunteers to help the RAF. They needed trained pilots and
were rounding up every man who could fly a plane. I was ready to get out
of flying the Skua, so I was sent to a base near Manchester to learn about
the Hurricane. Quite a jump up from the Skua, if I may say."

"The file says you shot down two enemy aircraft and were shot down as well. Tell me about your experiences with the RAF."

Clark was still quite stoic and didn't appear ruffled by the questions. Jameson was growing to appreciate the man's demeanor and ability to deal with senior-level officers. This trait would serve the Science Team well.

"I joined a reserve squadron in late July and flew my first heads-up mission in early August. We were at a fighter station near Andover, north of Southampton. The Germans were hitting our Kent bases hard, so our squadron went on a sweep from the west toward Kent. We had only a few tussles in early August, but we were flying three to five times each day by the middle of the month. Sometimes we were attacking the bombers that were hitting the Southampton docks; other times we were sent to intercept the Germans coming toward Croydon. I shot down my first Heinkel bomber on the twelfth, and my second bomber was a Dornier on the fifteenth. A few days later, I was making a pass on another Heinkel when I got a Messerschmidt on my tail and found out the Hurricane is made of wood and paper. The bloody thing burns quite well."

With a smile on his face and not looking at the burn marks on his hands, Clark continued. "I bailed out near Redhill after discovering my engine was on fire, and so was part of my right-wing. I got a few burns getting out and then sprained my bloody ankle hitting the ground."

"How long were you on recovery leave, Lieutenant?"

"They gave me some time off and put a cast on the ankle. I think I was back in a new plane around September 7, when I was put on duty with the Midlands Group 12, but I quickly found myself working far down south again with Group 11. I shot down another Heinkel 111 and a Junkers before I encountered a lucky German, who got on my tail and put me out of action."

Picking up the file, Edwards read from the report on Clark's performance. "The official report states you were attacking a German bomber when two ME-109s attacked you and severely damaged your aircraft. You lost all power to your engine and began a dive before you could gain control and then brought the plane to a wheels-up landing in a plowed field near Dover. Why did you stay with the plane?"

With a bit of a smile on his face, Clark replied, "Admiral, I didn't want to jump out of another airplane. The first time was enough for me to know you can get hurt, and I thought the Hurricane could make it down safely."

"You were awarded the Distinguished Flying Cross for your efforts and were back in the air the next day. Is that correct, Lieutenant?"

"Yes sir. I had not much else to do, so I thought the boys could use my help."

Jameson was now grinning broadly. The man's demeanor coupled with the Scottish accent was terrific. Commander Allen also smiled at the flyer's responses and wondered if he had the guts to do the same thing.

"Lieutenant, you continued your RAF posting for another two months and ended up with six confirmed kills. You were posted back to the Fleet Air Arm in December and joined the HMS *Ark Royal* in the Mediterranean. What were you flying off the carrier?"

"Admiral, we still didn't have any of your Wildcats yet, and the best fighter we had for shipboard duty was the Fairey Fulmar. Far superior to the Skua, but it could not keep up with the German fighters. We could do a lot of damage to Italian planes, but if we ran into a Messerschmitt, we were in trouble."

"Were you aboard the *Ark Royal* when it was lost?"

"Yes sir, that was in November of last year. A U-boat got in close and torpedoed the ship on our way back from delivering planes to Malta. I was able to get off the boat early and watched her go down. Following the loss, the carrier's squadrons were sent to Egypt, and finally, in March, I made it to Malta—again flying the Fulmar. We had some Hurricanes and a few Spitfires, but the Italians and Germans came just about every day and blasted the island."

"At Malta, you shot down two Italians and one Stuka, is that correct?"

"Yes sir. If the Fulmar could get support from the Hurricanes or Spits, we attacked the bombers. The Fulmar packs a lot of firepower, and most of the Italian bombers were slow and not well-armed. The best Italian plane was the Caproni which was a bit faster but not very agile."

Looking directly at the British flyer, Edwards continued. "Lieutenant, you were shot down again off Malta and rescued a day later by a Royal Navy torpedo boat. What happened?"

"Admiral, we were on a mission to break up a major German attack, and the Heinkel bombers were well protected by fighters. The Spits broke up the escort, and a few Hurricanes and the three remaining Fulmars went after the bombers. I'm not sure what got me, but my engine stopped mid-flight, which is never a good thing. Oil was flowing out all over the windscreen, and it was only a minute away from catching on fire. I flipped the plane over on its back and bailed out. Once I hit the water, one of my squadron mates flew low over my position, so I knew at least someone had seen me. I spent the evening in the blue waters of the Mediterranean. The next morning the navy found me, and I got a good brace of whiskey once I returned to land."

Knowing the details omitted from the lieutenant's explanation, Edwards began reading from Clark's file. "Lieutenant Clark shot down a German HE-111 and began attacking another plane in the formation when he was attacked by an enemy fighter. Taking several hits in the engine, the plane began an uncontrollable descent into the sea. Even though wounded in the arm and the shoulder, Lieutenant Clark escaped the aircraft and parachuted to the sea. Enduring a long night alone on a small life raft, Clark bandaged his wounds and waited for rescue."

Seeing the American officers serious expressions, Edwards continued. "Lieutenant Clark was awarded his second Distinguished Flying Cross and a Mention in Dispatches for his heroic efforts in the defense of Malta." Completing his reading from Clark's file, the chief of staff returned to his questions. "Tell me, Lieutenant, why were you sent to the United States?"

"Admiral, I spent a week in a Maltese hospital, which is not a good place to recuperate. The crowded conditions and daily bombing by the Germans or Italians caused a lot of dust, which made for an unpleasant experience. I was able to get to Egypt and spent another month in Alexandria before I was in good shape and sent packing to the Admiralty Building in London."

"I see you were given a thirty-day leave and reported to the Admiralty in late May. What were you doing at the Admiralty?"

"Sir, they had me working on operations manuals for the new carriers, specifically what you call escort carriers. Knowing I had seen many aspects of the enemy's capabilities, the senior planning officer wanted someone with recent experience to review the proposed procedures."

"Did you have any changes to offer?" Field Marshal Dill had briefed Edwards on Clark's experiences with administrative procedures.

"Admiral, the bloody fools did not understand anything about flight operations on a carrier, especially a wee one like the escort models. Their experts proposed putting on too many planes, the wrong mix of aircraft types, and their ideas on how many planes could be flown off in a short timeframe didn't take into consideration the slowness of the ship and the mandatory use of catapults for large aircraft like your splendid Wildcat."

Jameson and Allen suppressed the grins forming on their faces. They now saw a man who would not shy away from expressing an opinion based upon fact and experience. Both men noticed how Edwards seemed to appreciate the comments coming from the British officer, and at that moment knew the Scot would be an excellent addition to the Science Team.

"I would think that your candidness helped you return to limited flying duty?"

"Sir, I believe it was my ability to show my distinguished colleagues the difference between fact and fiction that allowed me to get out of the staff job and sent to America."

Edwards almost laughed but quickly composed himself as he focused on the file and moved on. "How were you chosen to come to America to work on the selection process for new aircraft for the Royal Navy?"

"After my short time at the Admiralty, I was sent to train new pilots in Scotland, which was not at all bad. The flight surgeons were still not letting me go on full combat duty, but I was put on a limited flight schedule. After about a month, I was asked if I would join a small team of officers going to America to check out the new Grumman Hellcat. Sir, I jumped at the chance to fly the new plane and to see your country."

"And what do you think of the Hellcat?" Edwards had spent part of the previous day working on the Grumman's final contract and making sure the plane would be operational with the fleet no later than March.

"Admiral, the plane is a beauty! Great speed, at least seventy miles per hour faster than the Martlet, your Wildcat. Much faster to altitude and turns quicker, which will be a big help if you run into a Messerschmitt. I was hoping to get a chance to fly the Corsair as well, but perhaps that can be arranged later."

"That might be possible in the future, Lieutenant, but for now, you are going to join Captain Jameson's command and assist in many aspects of the war effort. I understand Field Marshal Dill provided you an overview of what you are going to be doing?"

"Admiral, the field marshal explained the roles and responsibilities of Captain Jameson's Science Team and how it was vital to the Allied war effort. He also stressed the need for the utmost secrecy in everything this group is involved in and how it will be part of my duties to provide whatever assistance I can on behalf of Great Britain."

"Well said, Lieutenant, I think I will leave the details of your duties to Captain Jameson. I think you have already met Major Flannigan about the team's security, so I will not belabor this topic further. You have not met Lieutenant Brand, is that correct?"

"No sir. I have not had the privilege, but the field marshal is very impressed with the man's abilities and importance to the Allied cause."

Edwards came to his final question. "Did Sir John tell you much about what Lieutenant Brand does for the war effort?"

"No sir. The field marshal instructed me to follow Captain Jameson's lead on all interactions with Lieutenant Brand and be ready to support him in any way possible."

"I'm certain you will have a most enjoyable experience working with Captain Jameson's team and I look forward to seeing you whenever you're in Washington."

Clark immediately wondered what the admiral had meant by the last comment. He would ask Captain Jameson about this statement later. The Scotsman hoped he would be given a chance to travel around the country but didn't have a clue as to what he would be asked to do in the future.

Later that evening, Lieutenant Duncan Clark, RNVR, was getting situated in his new quarters at the Bethesda residence of Captain Jameson. Having come from an upper-middle-class background in Kirkcaldy, a mid-size town eighteen miles north of Edinburgh, Clark had lived in a modest house with his parents and three sisters. Being the oldest of the four Clark children, he was given a stern upbringing by his conservative Presbyterian parents. Now, he found himself in what he considered the lap of luxury. He was even given his own room, albeit very small, but it was his alone. The other officers, except for Captain Jameson and Lieutenant Brand, shared rooms.

He was further amazed by the exceptional dinner at the house and the inclusion of the enlisted men in the dining room. The Scot's American experience had demonstrated the lack of significant class distinctions, and now this small group of sailors and Marines furthered his appreciation for how the former British colony had become more democratic. After dinner, Clark was invited to have a drink with a few of the officers. Major Flannigan was impressed since his initial meeting with the British naval officer and thought he was a fighter first and a scholar second. The man had proven his bravery on numerous occasions and bore the marks of serious wounds. Dr. Feldman was intrigued by the redheaded Scotsman or, as the Brits called them, "gingers." He found the Scot quick with his answers, which were always precise. Later in the evening, the men, along with Lieutenant Stevens and Lieutenant Meyers, sat around the dining room table at the Bethesda house drinking the contents of a bottle of Dr. Feldman's best Scotch.

Only after the third or fourth round did the Scotsman open up. He told them of learning to fly while still a student at Oxford and getting into the Royal Naval Air Arm instead of the RAF because of less than perfect eyesight. It was good enough for the Royal Navy, and they quickly used his previous flight training to make him an instructor for new pilots in late 1939. Clark brushed over his aerial victories, and no one asked about being shot down. As the Scot took one more sip, he let his wishes be known to all. "I think I will never get a chance to fly a Hellcat against the enemy, but I follow orders, and now I'm a prisoner of some secret Yank organization for the duration." Clark smiled and then commented, "At least you have the best supply of whiskey I have seen since I was a wee lad in Kirkcaldy."

Looking a bit worn but still in good form, Clark asked his new comrades, "So, when do I get to meet Lieutenant Brand? From all I have been told, he must be important to your leadership."

Flannigan decided to end the late-night gathering by answering the newcomer's question.

"Lieutenant, the professor is in Boston, along with four members of our team. I think he is at the Massachusetts Institute of Technology consulting on new radar systems."

Clark grinned and knew the party was over, at least for him, but as he stood, he added, "The professor sounds like a most interesting person.

I look forward to meeting him. Now I must sleep before the good doctor pours me any more of the lovely malt from my homeland."

With his last words, he turned and walked toward his new room. The Americans continued to sip their whiskey, noting the young pilot had consumed three times more than any of them. Dr. Feldman made a mental note about the cost of war and wondered about what the young man had seen and done since the opening days of Britain's war in 1939.

8

30 December 1942
Massachusetts Institute of Technology
Radiation Laboratory

- Guadalcanal--In preparation for renewing attack on Hill 27, 2nd Battalion of 132nd Infantry begins movement to forward positions.
- New Guinea--Urbana Force maintains pressure against Buna Mission from southeast and prepares to envelop it by attacking eastward from Buna Village and Musita Island.
- Netherlands East Indies--Submarine **Searaven** (SS-196) lands agents on south coast of Ceram Island.

Bill Waverly paced up and down the hallway trying to stay awake. Warrant Officer Jones had already given the lieutenant a hard time for being unable to sit still. Both men watched as Sergeant Harold Dillard stood outside the door, barring people from entering the conference room unless they were on the list of attendees. The gunny had dispatched Sergeant Timothy Pride to buy more coffee for all four men. Their job was to maintain security for the professor and the job was proving to be more boring than usual. The only Marine content in the day's duty was Jones because he knew exactly where Brand was located and not chasing Japanese planes.

The meetings at what Lieutenant Brand called the "Rad Lab" had been going on for two days, and all four members of the security team looked forward to leaving cold and snowy Boston. James promised the meetings would be over by early afternoon, and then they could catch the train back to Washington. The gunny knew the reason for the departure was a New Year's Eve date with an English lady who was now the professor's fiancée. There would be no greater disaster than to miss an evening with Lady Margret. Every man in the security detail thought highly of not only her beauty but the woman's charm and kindness. The most recent team member had yet to meet the lady but had been told all about the courtship's trials, tribulations, and now engagement.

Inside the meeting room, the attendees were going over the final development plans for improvements to the SCR-584 and the SCR-720. The first unit was the targeting radar which had undergone constant improvements, including reducing the unit's size and improving the operator's screen layout. The SCR-720 was designed for the airborne interception role in night fighters. The new system was a significant improvement from previous versions. It integrated many of the developments used in the air to surface radar systems, which were proving deadly to the U-boats. Each new iteration of these units reduced the size, enhanced field maintenance, improved the ease of use for operators, and most importantly, expanded the system's range. James had been in discussion with Lee DuBridge on how to speed up the manufacturing process when Lee looked at his watch and asked, "James, don't you have a train to catch?"

Looking at his own timepiece, Brand blurted out, "Damn! I've got to get out of here, or my fiancée will kill me."

DuBridge, the Radiation Lab director at MIT, smiled and replied to the young officer, "James, we can finish these last details without you and send you a summary of each project."

James started to say something but was stopped. "Get out of here, James. I've been married a long time, and you should not start missing important dates now. That comes later, but for now, go."

The professor thanked his colleague, said goodbye to the other participants, and exited the room. As the door closed, DuBridge noted,

"For a brilliant man, he seems to forget the important things of life." Everyone around the table laughed in agreement and then began discussing the need for more skilled workers for the assembly of the next version of the radar system.

As the team hurried to the train station, James scanned his reports and occasionally gazed out the window to make sure Sergeant Dillard was going in the right direction. "Harold, turn right at the next street and then look for Atlantic Avenue. The South Station is on Atlantic at Summer Street. Shouldn't be too far."

Lieutenant Waverly was seated next to the professor alongside Warrant Jones. The men had a train to catch precisely at 1500 hours and needed to be there early to drop off the car at the navy motor pool next to the station. As the Marine looked at his watch, he wondered if they would make it in time. Still unsure of his situation in the closely-knit group, he asked , "Gunny, what happens if we miss the train? Is there another one later tonight?"

The old Marine looked at the new lieutenant, who he had already counseled about acting more like an officer and less like a sergeant, and said, "Don't worry, Bill, we'll make it with plenty of time to spare." With a smile on his face, he moved closer to Waverly and whispered, "I made a phone call this morning to alert Washington we might be cutting it close. Commander Allen told me not to worry; the train would be held for us."

The look on Waverly's face was priceless. He wanted to blurt out a few four-letter expletives but had the good sense to keep quiet. Evidently, the unit he was assigned to was more important than even the admiral had told him. He looked out the frosty pane of glass on the 1939 Dodge staff car and saw they were approaching the station. Looking down at his watch, he saw they were fifteen minutes late, but it seemed that was not going to be a problem.

The men jumped out of the car, and Dillard raced to the office and turned in the keys. No one asked him to sign anything, nor did anyone say a word. Earlier in the day, a phone call told them to facilitate the departure of the men from the chief of staff's office and ensure they got on their train. A chief petty officer was waiting for the car and took charge to get them to their train. As the men walked quickly through the station, two Shore Patrolmen cleared the way. As they arrived at their assigned first-class car, the train's conductor was waiting for them.

The man in the train uniform had seen lots of VIPs in his life, but the phone call he received from the head dispatcher told him in no uncertain terms the train would wait for a critical group of people. Once the train left the station, other orders were sent to help ease the train's passage to New York and then onto Washington.

The youngest member of the team, a navy lieutenant, thanked the chief petty officer and wished him a Happy New Year. As the officer boarded the train, the conductor signaled the engine to leave the station. He followed the five men on board and showed them their separate cabin. It was designed for four, but a fifth man would fit snuggly. The conductor thanked the men for being on board his train and knew enough not to ask questions. He noticed the one navy officer was carrying a briefcase and an old Marine had another one, which was so full it looked like it was going to explode. He also noticed the Marines carried sidearms and were constantly surveying their surroundings. Whoever these men were, they were earnest and protective of the young navy officer.

As the train picked up speed, Waverly looked at his watch. The train had been held for twenty minutes, which further amazed him. The gunny caught his expression and smiled once more. "Lieutenant Waverly, things are going very smoothly today. Sometime soon, things won't be so easy. Enjoy the little things."

Dillard looked at the new lieutenant, who he was growing to like. Being around a proven professional was a good thing. The man had served with Major Flannigan at Tulagi and impressed him enough to recommend Waverly for a battlefield commission. If the lieutenant was good enough for the major, he was good enough for him.

"Lieutenant, I will go find the head and do a quick sweep toward the dining car. Does anybody want anything?"

"Good idea, Sergeant. I'm okay for right now, but the professor might want a Coca-Cola."

Hearing his title, James looked up at the now standing Dillard and nodded his head in agreement. "Thanks, Harold, a cold drink would do me good. Anybody else?"

Gunny asked for a coffee, as did Sergeant Pride. Waverly passed but instructed Dillard to take his time to see how packed the train was. "Look out for the number of troops on board. If you sense anything which makes you uneasy, let me know."

After Dillard left the cabin, James started writing up a report and pulled out his slide rule to do calculations on producing the latest versions of the radar systems. He had promised the researchers more help in securing workers for the ongoing production of the systems. The Rad Lab had over two thousand people already, and James estimated another two thousand would be required by the end of 1944 to meet production targets. Finding the thousands of components, wiring, and vacuum tubes would be even more complicated. Radios of all types required many of the same parts, and the fight over limited production meant someone would have to make hard decisions on priorities.

Later that night, when the only man awake was Sergeant Pride, who was on duty guarding Brand, James reviewed a letter from Professor John von Neumann from Princeton University. The Hungarian-American was one of his idols and was now working on the Manhattan Project. The letter was in reply to an earlier communication on the utility of shaped charges and how this might be an answer to the detonation of an atomic weapon. The wording in the letter never mentioned the word atomic or anything about the project but suggested how the mathematics involved in shock waves could enhance the effects of an explosion. James had been one of the earlier supporters of the concept, and since von Neumann was considered the greatest mathematician in the world, it had been an honor to assist with its validation. The other key scientists in the project, including Edward Teller, thought the idea would work as well. Since the possible amount of fissionable material available would be limited, any method to amplify the detonation would be of great importance.

James put the letter back in his briefcase and wrote a note to send the information to Vannevar Bush for additional validation and support. Brand watched Sergeant Pride gaze out the window on the cabin door. The other men were slumped in their chairs sleeping away the long night before they arrived back in Washington the next day. Pulling another report out of his briefcase, James began reading about delays in the B-29 program. The first pressurized bomber was proving itself difficult. The engines on the first prototype, huge Wright R-3350 Duplex Cyclones, with eighteen cylinders in two rows, were being temperamental. Overheating, fires, loss of power were only a few of the maladies plaguing the engine.

The bomber prototype had flown for the first time in September, and with each flight, more problems were discovered. General Arnold sent the professor a detailed report on the plane's challenges and asked for his suggestions. The plane was way behind schedule and eating up resources at an alarming rate. James took notes and then began to get sleepy. He would revisit the Boeing problems later. For now, he needed some sleep. New Year's Eve held great promise for something entirely different than differential equations and wavelength analysis.

9

31 December 1942
Willard Hotel, Washington, D.C.

- Guadalcanal--2nd Battalion of 132nd Infantry reaches Hill 11, east of the Gifu strongpoint, line of departure for enveloping movement.
- New Guinea--Urbana Force begins envelopment of Buna Mission. Other elements of Urbana Force maintain pressure on the enemy from the southeast and finish clearing Government Gardens, but enemy retains positions in swamp north of gardens.
- North Atlantic--Enemy naval force engaging USSR-bound convoy sustains damage to one cruiser and at least three destroyers.
- United States--Carrier **Essex** (CV-9) is commissioned at Portsmouth, Virginia.

It was a tough fight. A frontal assault was the only option, so with the officer in front and the ladies bringing up the rear, the group maneuvered their way through the grand lobby of the Willard Hotel. This was only the beginning phase of the battle. Next, a scout was sent forth to find the most direct route to the planned objective. With a report in hand, the group fought their way into the Round Robin Bar. The place was packed, but it was New Year's Eve, so everyone who could afford the tariff was present and working their way to the bartender. Luckily, the commando training had paid off, and the advance team of Lieutenant Meyers and Lieutenant Clark had secured a table and held it from all enemies.

"Great job! Thanks for getting here early." Major Flannigan looked around the room and raised his hand to wave the rest of the group over. First Lieutenant Waverly and Lieutenant Stevens bulled their way through the dense crowd, upsetting many of the people packed into the room. Stevens and his date, Barbara Ann Warren, slid into the booth, followed by James Brand and Lady Margret. Wanda Jackson held tightly to Flannigan, and everyone pushed tightly into the seating area designed for five at the most.

The ladies were introduced to the redheaded Scot. Questions were asked of Meyers about what happened to his date.

"Seems the lady found a higher rank to go out with this evening, so I will have to do some reconnaissance of the area to find some company."

Barbara Ann raised her voice to be heard. "Looks like lots of talent at the bar!"

Meyers, Waverly, and the newest member of the team, Clark, looked in the bar's direction and quickly agreed they needed to secure a drink. They excused themselves and went to join the party at the bar.

Margret turned to James, saying, "Lieutenant Clark seems to be a capable man. Do you know much about him?"

Looking at his fiancée, whose eyes sparkled from the candlelight in the room, Brand replied, "I just met him this morning, but he's full of ideas and ready to work. Clark has a great flying record and is an ace as well."

Lady Margret knew not to ask much more and then posed a question to Flannigan. "Major, where are Dr. Feldman and Warrant Jones?"

"Margret, please call me Robert. James is required to recognize my rank, not you."

Everyone at the table, including Brand, laughed at the comment. "The good doctor is working tonight at Bethesda. I don't think he wanted to be with a lot of people tonight, and is covering for other doctors who wanted the night off. As to the gunny, he's at the house. He told me he wasn't interested in going to a party."

Before Margret could ask something else, Flannigan continued.

"Captain Jameson is at a certain hospital in West Virginia and will be back in two days. Any more questions?"

"No, Robert, I think everyone is accounted for, so now we can all enjoy a drink."

Lieutenant Waverly watched the three couples talk as he slowly sipped on a beer. Meyers and the Scot were drinking Scotch, of course, but Waverly was officially on duty. He did not have his regulation M1911 .45 pistol, but he did carry a .38 snub-nose revolver in a shoulder holster. Sergeants Dean and Williams were outside in the staff car, watching the entrance of the building. Before he left for his trip to West Virginia to see Major Carol Robinson, Captain Jameson gave the lieutenant standing orders for the planned New Year's Eve event being attended by the professor.

"Lieutenant, you will go to any party which Brand attends. Have two men with you and be armed. I'm sorry to spoil your plans, but we need to make sure the professor is secure. I will let you use your discretion in activities involving Lady Margret, but you need to be sure of Brand's whereabouts at all times."

Waverly understood his orders, which were specific and like those he had received from Admiral Edwards when assigned to this mission. The Marine hated to be a babysitter for a love-struck kid, but his job was to keep the professor safe. He held himself to only one beer every other hour and then perhaps only water. "Damn," he said to Meyers, "I guess it will be a very lonely night for me."

Meyers, knowing the rules surrounding James Brand, commiserated as best he could.

"Bill, a hell of a job, but once we get the boy home, I'll buy you a bottle, and we can drink the whole damn thing." Moving closer, he whispered, "Just don't tell the Scotsman we have a bottle; it would disappear in five minutes. The man can really drink!"

As the three men checked out the young women at the bar who were trying to look sophisticated, an RAF officer approached Clark and asked for a light.

"Lieutenant, would you have a light for a fellow soldier of the Crown?"

Clark turned to see the thin man holding a cigarette and pulled out his lighter. "Here you go, Flight Lieutenant. Good to see the junior service is still capable of walking around a bar."

The man puffed on his cigarette and said, "Thank you for the assistance. It would appear we are not the only brave pilots in this bar. The Yanks seem to have all the ladies surrounded, and I doubt they would lend us any of them."

The pilot put out his hand saying, "The name is Dahl, Roald Dahl. And you are?"

Clark smiled replying, "Duncan Clark from Fife. What is your mission in this corner of the world, Roald?"

Dahl inhaled once again and sipped on the beer he held with his left hand stating, "I came over in the spring as assistant air attaché, helping out with the lend-lease effort. What brings you to Washington?"

"I came over during the summer to do technical evaluations for the Grumman aircraft to be used by the Fleet Air Arm. Now I have been seconded to an American command for additional research and supply issues for the Royal Navy."

Moving close to the Scotsman's ear, Dahl whispered, "Glad to have you here. I'll be your contact if there are any problems. Sir John brought me into the game, so be careful."

Clark said nothing, nor did he acknowledge the comment. Turning to see his two American friends still searching the bar for any unattached ladies, Duncan pulled back and then said, "Let me introduce you to my Yank friends."

Knowing the contact had been acknowledged, Dahl put on his best charm. The two Americans were introduced to the RAF officer, and for the next ten minutes, Roald told the men a few war stories about his poor flying prowess. Clark enjoyed how the British officer told his tale and recognized the story from the *Saturday Evening Post* article entitled, "Shot Down Over Libya." The Scot would ask later about the background of the story, but it seemed plausible.

The four officers had another drink and then meandered over to the table where the team's other three officers and their ladies were seated. After being introduced to everyone, Dahl told more stories which entranced the audience. He discussed the phenomena British pilots discovered flying bombers over Germany. "Seems the Huns have small little devils called gremlins, who eat our wings, puncture our tires and foul our windscreens. Damn, Hitler never ceases the cruelty!"

His audience roared with laughter and thought his description of some sort of little animal chewing on wings was hilarious. Lady Margret asked if he was going to write the story down. "Lady Margret, the Walt Disney Company, is working up the story for me, and I have already been working with a publisher on a children's book. I do hope you read it once it's ready."

Later, the gremlins would be seen in cartoons in movie theaters worldwide, but for now, Dahl wished everyone a good evening and told them he would see them again soon. He had a room at the Willard as did many other members of the British military liaison staff. As the man walked out of the room, Clark observed, "Not a bad bloke for someone from Wales."

No one took notice of the interaction, which was precisely what Dahl had wanted. He was now a known figure to the Science Team members and could move with ease whenever he needed access to Clark. The British pilot was no longer able to fly, but his personality and comfort with new people had attracted him to the intelligence service. The air attaché appointment allowed easy movement within Washington and proved vital in swaying American opinion to the British viewpoint. Clark would serve as an information source for the activities of Professor Brand. Whenever possible, the Scot would try to influence the man's views to match the objectives of His Majesty's government. Duncan enjoyed his association with the Americans and looked forward to learning more of the team's mission but was unsure of his actions which some could say was spying on an Allied government. Sir John told him how important it was to keep America on track and one way to do this was to be on the inside with individuals who could sway the opinion of the top leadership. James Brand was one of those people.

10

1 January 1943
Naval Station Norfolk
Norfolk, Virginia

- Northwest Africa--Gen. Eisenhower places Gen. Fredendall in command of the U.S. II Corps, which is planning for Operation Satin, the capture of Sfax, Tunisia, to prevent the junction of Axis Armies.
- USSR--Encircled German 6th Army on Stalingrad front, now compressed into area some 25 by 40 miles, remains under attack from all sides.
- Solomon Islands--Submarine **Nautilus** (SS-168) evacuates 29 civilians from Teop Island.

The aircraft carrier looked odd to everyone at the base, except for Lieutenant Clark. HMS *Victorious* arrived the day before and was now tied up alongside a large dock filled with piles of supplies and men milling about trying to make sense of the situation. Captain Jameson was tasked with going down to meet the captain of the ship. The professor and Lieutenant Clark came along to begin the conversion process. The armored carrier would need to be modified to make it compatible with the American way of warfighting.

Jameson had met with Commander Samuel G. Mitchell a week earlier to get his views on the operational changes required for the ship to function with the Pacific fleet. Admiral King decided the British would follow U.S. Navy methodologies in everything from signals, flight patterns, and fleet tactics. The Admiralty had reluctantly agreed, but now the time had come to get everyone on the same page.

Mitchell had been the commanding officer of VF-8 on board the *Hornet* until it was sunk in October. He would become the American liaison with the British and serve as an advisor to the ship's captain R. L. Mackintosh. An additional thirty-five Americans—officers and ratings—would be assigned to the vessel to deploy to the Pacific. A few would be working the secret coding systems which would be installed, while others would be technical experts on the new American-made radar systems, aircraft, and other operational requirements new to the Royal Navy.

The following month would be filled with installing systems such as the coding machines. The ship would be fitted with new firefighting systems, the Talk-Between-Ship (TBS) radio system, nineteen new Oerlikon 20mm antiaircraft guns, a new vertical plot for the Fighter Direction Office (FDO), removal of searchlights and extending the flight deck to accommodate more aircraft. While the ship was besieged by workmen performing all of the modifications, the fighter pilots would be given the latest model of the Wildcat. At the same time, the British Albacore bombers were replaced with Grumman Avengers. The pilots would also have to be trained in the American landing system, which would require them to do qualification flights on the training carrier *Charger* operating in the Chesapeake Bay. All of this would take time and negotiation.

After Jameson and his men finished their tour, Captain Mackintosh escorted them to his quarters for a private conversation. The man was optimistic about the mission and, along with his pilots, looked forward to operating with the Pacific Fleet against Japan.

"Captain Jameson, I think this endeavor will help our two countries in ways we do not yet comprehend. I had the opportunity to work with American battleships on missions out of Scapa Flow, but this will be the first time to coordinate with one of your carriers."

The man was in good form. He seated his visitors at a conference table in the spacious cabin then pulled a bottle of Scotch from a credenza next to the desk. There were already several glasses arranged around the table, and he quickly served up a healthy pour of the golden elixir. Raising his drink, he looked at Jameson, stating, "To President Roosevelt and the United States Navy."

Each man, including James Brand, raised his glass and then took a sip. The warmth of the whiskey was welcome on a cold and dreary January afternoon. Jameson immediately returned the toast saying, "To the King and the Royal Navy. We look forward to your help in the Pacific and ultimate victory."

Again, each man took another sip. James was starting to like Scotch and would have to tell Dr. Feldman about this bottle. He was trying to make out the label when the British captain spoke. "Lieutenant Brand, I was told by the Admiralty about your contributions to the anti-submarine effort. I see you are also a pilot. Have you seen combat?"

"Sir, thank you for your kind comments about our activities on nullifying the U-boats. But I have to say I learned far more about anti-submarine efforts from your nation's success than we could have hoped to achieve on our own. As to flying, I have had some experience flying against the Japanese. Commander Mitchell is the real expert on fighting them and was at the Battle of Midway and then Guadalcanal."

Turning to the commander, Mackintosh queried, "So, what is your opinion of the enemy?"

The American fighter pilot put his glass down and calmly replied, "Sir, the Japanese are proficient in aerial combat. They specialize in aerobatics and have no fear of closing with us. Their Zero fighter is extremely nimble, and we learned the hard way not to get into dogfights. The Wildcat is superior in diving speed and can take significant punishment and continue flying. The Zero cannot. We have had the chance to do some technical analysis on some of their downed aircraft, and the planes are very light, which gives them great range and speed, but the enemy's planes do not have self-sealing fuel tanks and when hit, they quickly burn."

The British captain mulled over the information. The Admiralty provided a briefing about what he would encounter in the Pacific, but these men were the first people who had actually fought the enemy. His experience against the Italians and Germans had provided him with many sleepless nights. Now, he would take his ship to the other side of the world and fight a new enemy. Mackintosh was grateful to have Commander Mitchell assigned to his ship.

"Captain Jameson, what else can you tell me of my mission?"

"Captain Mackintosh, as you know, the situation in the Pacific is dire. We have the *Saratoga* and some escort carriers supporting the ground units in the Solomon Islands. The Japanese have not made any major movements against us since November. Our intelligence suggests they have two large carriers at Truk and are trying to reinforce their air and ground units at Rabaul and New Guinea. We have repositioned several new major units, including battleships and cruisers to the area, but there are no other carriers. The *Enterprise* is still undergoing repairs which will last another two months. That is why your help is needed. Our first new carrier, the *Essex,* was commissioned only two days ago and now must go through testing and evaluation before heading into the war. We estimate May or later before it can be on station with the fleet."

Mackintosh sipped his whiskey as he evaluated this new information. His ship was worn out and had been in constant use since the early part of the war. His crew was tired but well-seasoned. The pilots were good and looking forward to new planes and working with the Americans. There would be a lot of work to prepare the ship for the war in the Pacific.

Turning his attention to the Fleet Air Arm pilot who had accompanied Jameson on the trip, Mackintosh asked, "Lieutenant, what is your role in this endeavor?"

Jameson responded for the Scotsman, "Captain, the lieutenant was assigned to my command to assist in inter-Allied planning. As a pilot, he brings significant expertise to our understanding of the British war effort."

Smiling at the political answer, the aircraft carrier captain reworded his question. "Thank you, Captain Jameson, for the information. I was wondering what an experienced pilot was doing on this side of the Atlantic."

Clark answered quickly. "Captain, I have been attached to Captain Jameson's command to assist in aircraft technology and tactical operations. I have been working with Grumman for the past few months doing technical analysis of the new Hellcat fighter. I had hoped to go back to an operational squadron, but it seems the government thought this assignment was a better use of my talents."

Captain Mackintosh raised his glass to the flying Scotsman saying, "Well said and a most diplomatic response. I will not ask any more questions, but I hope you will be able to help us in the transition to the American navy."

Everyone laughed and Jameson raised his glass once more. "Captain, on behalf of the United States Navy, we welcome His Majesty's Ship *Victorious* to America. I think the code name for your vessel is appropriate and we thank you for the gift of your service."

As the men sipped the last of their whiskey, they knew there was a large job ahead to get the British carrier ready for the war in the Pacific. The ship's code name was a tongue-in-cheek comment about the British having more carriers than the Americans, and lending one to their poor American cousins seemed the correct thing for them to do. The ship would be known as the USS *Robin* as in the legend of Robin Hood.

Traveling by train is strictly overrated. The journey provided hours of tedium, interspersed with complete boredom while waiting on sidings for other trains to pass or pacing about on station platforms, waiting for the connecting train. Four days had passed since leaving Hamburg. Still grumbling about the new assignment, but nevertheless, following his orders, the officer knew he would never be given another sea command, nor would he be given a good staff position. Naval headquarters wanted officers who were submariners, not line officers from the dwindling number of large ships still existing in the Kreigsmarine. Looking at his constant companion, a dark wooden cane with a shiny brass head embossed with an eagle and anchor, Kapitanleutanant Gebhardt Wagener knew he was lucky to have a job.

This new position was never part of his career plan. He was looking forward to becoming the captain of a destroyer, one of the large Z class destroyers, or perhaps one of the T class torpedo boats, which were similar in size to the British corvettes. These dreams came to an end while serving on the battlecruiser *Scharnhorst* anchored in Brest, France. The irony of his injuries still amused him. Gebhardt served as an assistant gunnery officer on the ship and participated in its last cruise in the Atlantic, ending March 1941. Ever since, the ship waited in the harbor along with its sister ship *Gneisenau* for oil and orders to resume the war.

British bombing attacks were persistent, and the warship had been damaged several times, nothing severe, but enough to keep the two German battlecruisers bottled up in the French harbor. Early in February 1942, the ship's crew had planned a reckless high-speed run straight up the English channel, directly across from the British defenses. The young officer had spent weeks getting his men trained for the mission, but two weeks before the February 11 departure, he was on the receiving end of a British bombing attack on Brest. Wagener attended a party for two officers who were being transferred to Norway when the bombers flew overhead, dropping their bombs on the men huddling in an air raid shelter. A lucky hit by a thousand-pound bomb struck the building above the shelter and penetrated into the old brick basement where the men had sought safety.

Thirty-five men were killed, and another twenty were seriously wounded. Luckily, Gebhardt survived but with crippling injuries. The doctors in Brest wanted to amputate his leg, but the naval officer begged for a few more days before they had no more options. Luckily, the leg got better and the infections slowly subsided. Yet, with compound fractures to both legs, a set of broken bones in his foot and right ankle, multiple lacerations to his chest, significant loss of blood, plus damage to his left eye, the man should have been retired from the service. But he persevered enough to request any job the navy thought he could handle. After many months of recuperation and therapy, he secured a meeting with a former commanding officer, a captain (Kapitan sur See), based in Berlin. The captain was a good judge of character and knew the navy needed good men perhaps in different positions, especially highly educated officers like Kapitanleutanant Gebhardt Wagener.

The captain had examined the young officer's personnel file and noted his educational achievements before the war. The officer had received a degree in chemical engineering from the University of Leipzig and worked on research projects when he was called up by the German state in 1938. Gebhardt joined the navy and served on destroyers in the early part of the war, and was a survivor of the Battle of Narvik in April 1940. The destroyer he was serving on was sunk, one of eight destroyed that day by the British fleet. Escaping the sinking ship, he made it to land and fought with the army until the British were eventually defeated in June. Returning to Germany, he was promoted and then assigned to the *Scharnhorst* until his near-death experience. Now, the man who needed a cane to walk and had blurred vision in his left eye wanted to help the navy.

The captain listened to Gebhardt's story and arranged a meeting with a senior officer who could use the man's intellect. The next day, Kapitanleutanant Gebhardt Wagener met with Rear Admiral (Konteradmiral) Wilhelm Canaris, the chief of German military intelligence, the Abwehr. The young kapitanleutanant was unsure of what kind of job he could do in intelligence, but the admiral quickly told him what he needed.

"Herr Wagener, you come highly recommended by my old friend Hans, and he knew I was looking for someone with your scientific background. I see you had an illustrious career in the navy and were awarded the Iron Cross for your courage at Narvik. You served with distinction on the *Scharnhorst*, but then a British bomb found you in Brest. So, tell me, Herr Wagener, why do you want to continue to serve the Fatherland?"

The junior officer was ready for the question and offered a simple explanation. "Admiral, if I stay at home, I will go crazy, and the state would put me in a factory doing some kind of paperwork, which would be boring."

Canaris laughed at the explanation. He replied, "Well said, Herr Wagener. I think I would rather do anything than sit behind a desk at some factory waiting for the British or Americans to bomb it." Looking at the man's file, the admiral continued.

"What I have to offer is unique. It will require you to use your chemical engineering training and your naval experiences. We need a man like you to work on improving our supply of wolfram. I am sure you could tell me all about wolfram's scientific properties, but I do not need to know anything more about the material, except Germany needs it for the war effort. How familiar are you with this element?"

Gebhardt knew about wolfram, commonly known as tungsten. It was rare and found most often in wolframite and required significant processing to become pure enough for industrial use. Yet, tungsten alloy properties allowed for incredible strength and light weight, all needed in building weapons of war. "Admiral, I am familiar with the processes required to refine the feed materials into the base material. If given a few days, I am certain I could be quite conversant in the mining and processing of the mineral."

Smiling at the young officer, Canaris said, "I will instruct my aide to provide you with the background you need on our current supply situation, plus some training in dealing with the secrecy of your critical mission."

The young naval officer suddenly felt confused. He knew the role of intelligence, but it was beginning to sound like some sort of spying was required in this assignment. Before he could say much more, the admiral finished his comments.

"Once you have received some training in dealing with enemy agents and the peculiarities of neutral countries, you will be assigned as assistant naval attaché in Lisbon, Portugal. There you will work with the embassy staff to secure more wolfram for the Fatherland."

The admiral looked at the young officer and then asked one more question, which Gebhardt thought peculiar. "Herr Wagener, I do not see anything in your record which indicates membership in the party. Is there any reason you have not joined?"

The junior officer knew why he didn't join the Nazi party, but was afraid of discussing it with anyone, including close friends. Now the German head of intelligence was asking the question. He decided to tell the truth, fearing any subterfuge would be found out later. "Admiral, I declined membership because of my religious beliefs. I do not believe in putting anyone above the Almighty."

The admiral didn't say anything but wrote a note on a piece of paper next to the file and said, "Welcome to the Abwehr."

With these final comments, the admiral stood and walked Gebhardt out of his office and into the waiting arms of Oberst Fromm of the German Army who would get him oriented to his new world. After two months of training and research, Kapitanleutanant Gebhardt Wagener arrived at his new home, Portugal's neutral and spy-infested capital, Lisbon.

11

4 January 1943
Logistics Research Office
Washington, D.C.

- North Pacific--Adm. Nimitz replaces Adm. Theobald with Adm. Kinkaid as commander, Task Force 8.
- Guadalcanal--Japanese are ordered to withdraw from Guadalcanal to New Georgia Island.
- New Georgia--U.S. cruiser and destroyer force bombards Munda airfield.
- New Guinea--Japanese overrun outpost near Tarakena, forcing patrol to swim for Siwori Village. With Tarakena in their possession, Japanese are able to rescue some of the survivors of Buna garrison.
- Libya--Severe two-day storm begins, sharply decreasing the capacity of Benghazi port and forcing British 8th Army to make greater use of more distant port of Tobruk.

The officers examined reports while some of the senior enlisted men searched boxes and file cabinets for information being sought by Captain Jameson. Except for James Brand and Duncan Clark, everyone worked on position papers, strategy assessments, summaries of ship and airplane construction, and manpower estimates. The two flyers were in the professor's office looking at intelligence estimates of enemy aircraft production. Everyone was working toward the goal of meeting a January 6 deadline. On this date, Jameson and Brand would provide the team's assessment of American military capabilities to Admiral Leahy and the Chiefs of Staff. This report would be matched to the staff reports from the army, navy, and army air force. The end product would form the basis for the American strategy to be presented at the Casablanca Conference, code named SYMBOL. It had been decided early on that the Science Team would travel to North Africa to support the American leadership at the conference.

The professor had worked on the plan since Christmas, incorporating input from American and Allied intelligence. The biggest challenge facing him were the inconsistencies found in many of the reports and what he called "large holes" in the intelligence materials. Knowing much of what was in the ULTRA and MAGIC intercepts, James was able to piece together a more precise estimate of enemy intentions. The most significant gap in the knowledge was the Russian viewpoint. The Japanese and Soviets had a non-aggression pact which benefited both countries. Neither wanted to fight a new war, but each eyed the other with increased suspicion. The German activities on the Eastern Front were more of a concern. Usually, only after a victorious battle did the Russians inform their allies about the situation, often in minimal detail. The British and Americans were learning more from ULTRA than they did from their Soviet ally.

James knew the Soviets had surrounded the German Sixth Army at Stalingrad and had mauled the Nazi relief forces sent to rescue them. Hitler had refused a request from the German commander, General Paulus, to break out and now the end was near for the freezing and starving survivors. The Germans were also forced back from their incursion in the Caucasus region, and in the north, the city of Leningrad still held out. The Allied assessment of German losses since the invasion of Russia in June 1941 stood at a million casualties, with their vassal states of

Romania, Hungary, Finland, and Italy all losing large numbers of men alongside the Germans. The professor knew these numbers could not be replaced by new conscripts reaching military age. The Germans were losing their most experienced men, and with each loss, their effectiveness decreased.

Duncan Clark looked at the professor's conclusions and agreed. "James, the Germans are losing too many experienced men. I think you told me about the drop in quality in the Japanese pilots and I observed some of this in my last flights from Malta. These were not the same men I flew against over Britain in 1940."

Clark beamed at his new American friend. "Now that does not mean the bloody Germans have lost all of their best pilots. I think one of them shot my arse down over the Med because it could not have been a new pilot."

James came to the Scotsman's rescue replying, "Duncan, I think you're one hell of a pilot, and a good pilot is one that survives to tell his stories." Now laughing, Brand continued with his train of thought.

"Duncan, how long does it take to make a good fighter pilot? Not just one who can land and take off without smashing the plane into bits."

"James, that's a good question. First of all, you have to find someone stupid enough to want to get into a machine built by hundreds of workmen who may have missed a few bolts that hold the engine to the frame. You have to learn how to fly by the book, which requires hundreds of ground school hours and then primary flight school. Finally, you get a fighter and learn to fly it way past its edge of safety. Then you get to join a squadron and hope like hell your wingman has more experience than you."

"So how long does it take in Britain to be qualified to fly?"

The Scotsman gazed at the ceiling and tapped a finger against his chin as he made mental calculations, then recited the information to James. "You need eight weeks of initial training, what you call ground school. Then you have ten weeks of elementary flight training, usually in Tiger Moths. Next, you have sixteen weeks of service training school. This is where you are trained in what we call the Harvard, your North American Texan. Then you get your wings and move to an operational training unit, where you fly the specific model you will be assigned. When you leave this training, you are assigned an active squadron and, hopefully, live more than two weeks. So all told, figure it takes eight months to get a pilot from ground school to a fighter squadron. Most of the early pilots had no more than one hundred fifty flight hours before they joined their unit. I think it's taking more time now because of what we learned in the first few years. Most of the new men have two hundred to three hundred flight hours, so this could be nearly a year in training."

James listened intently to the description, which paralleled much of the American training. Searching his desk, he opened a file and found the information on the Luftwaffe. "Duncan, your military intelligence boys have done a splendid job by doing detailed interrogations of captured German pilots. It appears the German system is beginning to crack under the pressure of the war. One of the pilots shot down in 1941 over North Africa stated he had over two hundred hours of experience in his Messerschmidt before joining his squadron and over a year of training in all aspects of flying. Another pilot your people shot down over Britain earlier this year commented he had been flying for a month with his squadron and had about one hundred fifty hours in his Heinkel, and his basic course had been cut in half due to lack of fuel and instructors. Seems the trainers were sent to Russia to fly supplies to the front."

As James put the paper back into the file, he asked Duncan. "Based upon this intelligence, what does that tell you about the German's ability to sustain air operations?"

Clark connected the dots. "James, it would seem the Luftwaffe is running out of pilots, and the new ones will be of lesser quality with each passing month while our people grow stronger."

"This is good news, but the question remains, how long before the quality of the Luftwaffe drops to a level of inexperienced pilots and shoddy equipment?"

The Scotsman liked the process the professor used to elicit information from people in meetings. Ask a question and then ask a follow-up which digs deeper. This requires more profound thought and more facts. Sometimes, the facts are no longer evident, requiring building new lines of questions and answers to construct a hypothesis of what was possible and what was probable. Clark replied, "James, we don't have the information to answer the question. I suppose we could do some work on German training programs and tie this to plane production. I know the intelligence community is building a list of factories, airfields, even training bases. If we can get access to this information, I think we can come up with a set of assumptions which would be accurate enough for our purposes."

Brand grinned and asked his third question. "So what would we do with this information?"

Clark smiled back and, in his best Scottish accent stated, "We build a bloody map of Germany and bomb the hell out of them!"

Both men laughed, knowing much of this bombing was already underway. James had access to the target lists for the Allied bombing program. The American Eighth Air Force's responsibility was to pursue a daylight precision program of targeting industry. The British went after the cities at night using a simple but direct method of destroying the manufacturing plants and its workers. The leader of RAF Bomber Command was Air Marshal Sir Arthur Harris. He had been given the Area Bombing Directive by the War Cabinet in 1942 and was an ardent believer that massive bombing would win the war.

All he needed to accomplish this goal was thousands of planes, crews, and bombs. He had the approval, and now he planned to prove his theory. The challenge was finding the target at night and not losing too many planes and crews. A five percent loss was deemed acceptable, but some of the missions were now sustaining ten percent losses.

The American effort led by General Ira Eaker had been bombing since the summer. Now the Eighth Air Force had five hundred B-17s available and ready for deep-penetration missions into Germany. Their earlier missions had been short runs into German-occupied France and targets on the periphery of the Nazi homeland. The belief was the Boeing Flying Fortresses would get through to its target. Most of the early raids had been accompanied by fighter escorts, but any deep attacks would be beyond the range of Spitfires and P-47s. James was aware of the plans for approving a massive round-the-clock bombing campaign which was to be presented at the Casablanca Conference. Both Clark and Brand felt uncertain about the program because even with the weakened Luftwaffe, the enemy's reaction would be quick and brutal. James did not believe the B-17s would get through the enemy's defenses, accurately bomb the target, and then fly back to their bases with minimal casualties. Yet, the professor knew about Churchill's push to pursue massive attacks against the heartland of the Reich, even if the losses were high.

Putting down the report, James turned to his new friend. "Duncan, we should table this discussion for later. Right now, I think we should check in with the captain to see if he has any final questions on the report to the Chiefs of Staff." The two men picked up their files and walked to Jameson's office, hoping the situation was well in hand and their assistance was not needed. As usual, their prayers went unanswered.

"James, Lieutenant Clark, glad to have your help. We need to double check our assessments on landing craft construction, escort ship availability and the number of long range B-24s available to both us and the British Coastal Defense Force. Also, if you can take a look at the construction of oilers, that would be helpful."

The young officers couldn't help but smile learning the free time they had hoped for was now filled. Brand replied, "Yes sir. Do you know where the reports are located?"

Jameson was exhausted, but maintained a smile, "Hell, I'm not sure where anything is located. Meyers and Stevens are trying to pull everything together, so you need to ask them."

As the two pilots left the captain's office, Gunny picked up another box of files and placed them on Jameson's desk. "Captain, I think those two are hitting it off well. Now, if they can find the information we need, maybe we can get out of here by midnight."

Jameson agreed with the old Marine. The two pilots were similar in many ways. Clark was brilliant and his engineering background blended well with Brand. Perhaps this new partnership would benefit both nations or at least the work of the Science Team.

12

7 January 1943
Office of the Chief of Naval Operations
Washington, D.C.

- Guadalcanal--In preparation for offensive on
  10 January, 35th Infantry of 25th Division leaves
  Lunga Perimeter for Mt. Austen. About 50,000 Allied
  air, ground and naval forces are in the Guadalcanal
  area.
- New Guinea--127th Infantry continues toward
  Tarakena. Japanese convoy with reinforcements
  reaches Lae despite efforts of Allied aircraft to turn
  it back.
- Iraq--Americans take exclusive jurisdiction over the
  port of Khorramshahr, where the first U.S. Troops
  arrived in December 1942.

Admiral Edwards had just left Admiral King's office with a new set of
orders. The boss would be flying out to the Casablanca Conference tomorrow along with Marshall and Arnold. Additional staff officers would go
along on this trip, including Rear Admiral Cooke, the navy's head of war
planning. Lieutenant General Somervell, Brigadier General Wedemeyer,

and Ambassador Harriman would accompany Generals Marshall and Arnold. Field Marshal Dill was coming along as the special guest of General Marshall. The senior British officer worked well with the Americans and helped the Allies soothe over many strategic differences. Even Admiral King liked him, which was a proper credit to the man's diplomacy and tact.

The army had worked up quite a security plan along with the Secret Service. Advance teams were already on the scene making final adjustments to the operation. General Patton had overall command of the Morocco area and worked for weeks to secure the Anfa Hotel located in the outskirts of Casablanca. Barbed wire barriers had been erected, anti-aircraft cannons were set up, and thousands of American soldiers patrolled the perimeter. American fighter planes were aloft from morning to night, searching for enemy aircraft. The hotel had several spacious villas that would serve as the president's and British prime minister's accommodations. Conference rooms were established for the Combined Chiefs of Staff's meetings and private meetings for the two Allied leaders. Everything appeared on track for a successful conference, but Edwards knew things could and would go wrong, no matter how much planning had been accomplished.

King's chief of staff had sat in the meeting where Captain Jameson and the professor briefed the American Chiefs of Staff on future war strategy. The two men were efficient in using words and brought only two large maps, showing the two main theaters of war—the Pacific and the European. In less than an hour, the two scholars compressed the American war plans into a list of issues, challenges, and possible solutions. Each item was listed in terms of how the British would or would not agree to the American assessment. Brand discussed the probable British reaction to these plans and offered a set of scenarios on how to proceed.

Several of the staff officers, who would be attending the Casablanca meetings, were skeptical of the brash professor's recommendations. Still, General Marshall thought Brand had examined the situation fairly and without prejudice to American ideas. As the meeting broke up, Marshall and King quickly discussed the probability their Allies were well prepared for the joint meeting with all sorts of position papers, facts, and figures, which would be used to their advantage. Brand had told Jameson the same thing. The Americans were not, as of yet, well versed in war planning.

Upon his return, King pulled Admiral Cooke into his office along with Edwards, and in his usual angry demeanor stated, "The Brits are going to eat our lunch again. I think the navy has a good grip on what's going on, but Marshall and Arnold aren't ready yet for the big leagues. Make sure Brand stays close by in Casablanca. We may need some quick ideas on how to counter our cousins."

Edwards pulled Jameson into his confidence, asking him to keep Brand on a short leash while in North Africa. King would need help, and if what Brand reported was true, the Americans would be cornered into things they did not want to do. The only good thing King reported from the briefing was Brand's analysis of American participation on each front. The British provided the majority of the troops in North Africa. The Americans would have five or more divisions by the spring, but this was a fraction of what the British had in Montgomery's Eighth Army or Anderson's First Army. The British navy provided the vast majority of ships in the Mediterranean as well as in the Atlantic. The same could be said for the air forces.

The United States was ramping up, but was still nowhere near parity in the European theater of operations. Only in the Pacific—a *de facto* American campaign—were the Yanks in the majority. The professor stated the American Pacific campaign was only receiving fifteen percent of American industrial output. The number of personnel in each theater would change little in the early months of 1943. Still, so much production was going to the European theater in Lend-Lease and support for British industry, the professor told King he should fight for a higher percentage of American production, if not manpower. This fact made King ecstatic, and he would not hesitate to use this information if and when needed.

For the moment, Edwards needed to finalize everything for Admiral King's departure. Two new C-54s were readied to take the American contingent to Morocco. Each plane was double-checked then checked again to ensure safety. The aircraft would fly across the Atlantic using the southern route through Brazil to Accra in the Gold Coast and then north to Casablanca. The four-engine Douglas transport could fly much further than the twin-engine DC-3 and with a much bigger payload. Twenty-six passengers could be accommodated in the early models with a range of three-thousand miles, thereby allowing it to fly over the

Atlantic without stopping to refuel. Each plane would be at maximum capacity with staff members, security, and thousands of pounds of paper reports, maps, and baggage. Two additional aircraft would carry additional staff, including Captain Jameson and most of the Science Team.

The president and Admiral Leahy would be flying separately in a Boeing 314 Clipper seaplane. A second Clipper would be used to transport other members of the White House party and would serve as a backup aircraft. James Brand, Lieutenant Waverly, Warrant Officer Jones, and Dr. Feldman would fly in the second aircraft. The four Science Team members would meet the presidential party in Miami on January 11 and begin their journey on the Boeing seaplanes, much larger and spacious than the new C-54s but also much slower. As a precaution, navy ships were pre-positioned in the Caribbean and the Atlantic in case of an emergency. Having two planes flying the same route was another safety measure. FDR's trip was the first time a president had left the country in wartime. The two Clippers provided a great deal of safety and space for the president to get plenty of rest on the three-day journey.

Roosevelt would leave the White House in secret on the night of January 9 and travel through the night on the presidential train to Miami, boarding the Boeing seaplane early on the morning of January 11 for the first leg of the journey, a flight to Trinidad. From the American base on the island, the planes would fly on to Belem, Brazil, then to Bathurst, Gambia, where they would switch to two C-54s for the flight onward to Casablanca, arriving on January 14. The entire journey would total 7287 miles and impact the lives of millions.

Admiral Edwards was concerned about the entire operation. Secrecy was paramount and few people knew of the plan. The press was totally in the dark and would remain so until after the conference. A news blackout was ordered. A few reporters would be allowed to be in Casablanca for some event, but none of them knew the details of what or who would be involved. The last thing reporters expected was a meeting of the two Allied leaders in the middle of the North African desert. The admiral would have preferred a conference in the United States, but the president thought it would boost morale and show the Nazis that the Allies were closing in on their empire.

Commander Allen took down the list of items the admiral wanted to check before King and the Science Team's departure but was interrupted by Edwards changing course mid-sentence. "Inform the professor and his group flying on the Clipper about security plans for the trip. I'm not sure if they are aware of the overnight stops and the people they will meet along the way. I want to make sure Brand keeps out of trouble and away from people asking questions about what the hell he's doing on this trip. Have a quick word with Gunny about it. He has more influence on the professor than anyone else."

"Anything else, sir?" Allen had a long list of items to double-check in the next few hours before people started to leave town, so he needed to get moving.

"No, Commander, that should be it. It looks like Brand and his small group will be on the second plane and not with the president. I would hate to have our boy spending several days alone with the commander in chief."

Allen acknowledged the order and left the chief of staff's office. As soon as he got to his desk, he called Lieutenant Stevens to find Warrant Officer Jones. This was probably more important than checking on transportation to Africa because the ramifications of a confident young navy lieutenant having unfettered access to America's leader could have enormous consequences. As the commander dialed the number for the head of the Logistics Research Department, he started to smile. Perhaps having the professor spend a few days alone with the president would be a perfect idea.

13

10 January 1943
The Saturday Club, Calcutta, India

- Guadalcanal---25th Division, reinforced, begins largest and final offensive to clear Guadalcanal, immediate objectives being Galloping Horse, Sea Horse and Gifu strongpoint.
- Libya--Gen. Montgomery briefs assault forces of British 8th Army on projected drive through Buerat line to Tripoli, which must be accomplished within 10 days to avoid supply difficulties.
- USSR--Since the ultimatum of 8 January has not brought about the surrender of the German 6th Army at Stalingrad, Soviet forces with strong artillery and mortar support are attacking to destroy it.
- Unites States naval vessel sunk: Submarine **Argonaut** (APS-1) in an attack on convoy southeast of New Britain.

The place looked old and right out of some design book for what an English gentlemen's club should look like. But this was India and it also had some of the tell-tale elements of British Raj architecture. Standing as a

90

testimony to the power of Great Britain, the white façade would fit in well anywhere the British flag flew in the world. The building reminded many of the grand hotel Raffles in Singapore with its bright white brickwork challenging the heat of the Indian sun. In 1875, the club was established by the Calcutta Light Horse Regiment officers and moved to the new location at 7 Wood Street in 1900. Since it was a member's only club, one had to have an invitation to enter, which Lieutenant Robert Beck received from club member and his business partner, Major Peter Smythe-Jones of the British Army.

The major had been hunting for information the past few weeks on shipments from Calcutta's port to points north. This intelligence provided the American naval officer with possible points of attack. Not the kind involving weapons, but places along a route where a truck could disappear or a shipment could be misplaced. So far, the major's services resulted in a dozen shipments being "lost" to the Allied cause. Trucks were highly sought after by those who could afford them, but usually, the vehicle was stripped of its parts and even the bare frame would be used to construct some sort of new vehicle. Military trucks were plentiful but stuck out like a sore thumb to the police, while a non-descript transport chugging down the road on what appeared to be new tires didn't raise an eyebrow of the local constabulary. The business proved to be good, but the American was looking for bigger fish to ensnarl in his net of deception.

Smythe-Jones and Beck occupied a table in the back part of the club. Most of the old-time members acknowledged the newcomer, and as an American officer, he was welcome to utilize the bar but had to pay in cash, no credit for non-members. Beck had arrived with the major and waited for their new friend, Colonel Edmund Granger, DSO, of the Calcutta Light Horse.

The British major had explained the situation to Beck the previous day. Granger was a retired officer of the Indian Army, serving in the Boer War and in Palestine during the Great War and now, as a sixty-six-year-old retired colonel, watched the world moving on without him. Granger had lost both of his sons to a cholera epidemic in Calcutta in the 1920s, and soon after that, his wife of twenty years left him for a low-level Spanish diplomat. The man was bitter and an alcoholic. His complexion was blotchy and red, his nose enlarged and pocked by the ravages of diseases encountered while serving with Allenby's army fighting the Turks. The man nearly died from wounds suffered at the third battle of Gaza in 1917. Soon after, his military career foundered, and eventually, he returned to a job in a Calcutta bank. He had stayed in the Light Horse reserve unit and found the comradery the only thing holding him together. Many nights found him slumped in a chair and carried by the house boys to a cot where the man would sleep it off and awaken to a new round of headaches requiring more gin.

As long as Granger could stand or sit without falling, he was full of information and opinions. The man loathed anyone who would dare speak of Indian independence or the possibility of the British empire in decline. His attitude toward Americans was indifferent, but as fellow fighters against the Huns or the Japanese, the colonials were tolerated. His weakness for liquor was his undoing, and he had lost many friends in the past years for breaching someone's trust. Yet, the old colonel retained many friends, and most of his banking connections were strong as ever. This is one of the things Beck needed. If plans to become wealthy from his ventures were to succeed, he needed help to safely move money. Smythe-Jones reminded him to keep the conversation at a high level and from one of interest in how things got done in India, especially within the banking sector.

The colonel arrived late but was in good form. After introducing the American, Smythe-Jones caught the eye of a waiter. "Two more whiskeys and another gin for the colonel," Jones told the bar waiter and passed the man a few coins to keep the alcohol flowing.

"Thank you, Smythe-Jones, for your kindness, and it is good to finally meet your American friend."

"Colonel, it is terrific to meet you as well. The major has sung your praises for some time and told me you would be the best person to give an overview of the banking sector in India." The men were served their drinks, and the ever-thirsty colonel immediately started sipping his beverage while Beck continued.

"As Major Smythe-Jones told you, my position with the American forces in India is to get the supplies through to the front line forces fighting the enemy. As part of this process, I have realized I know very little about the financial requirements to get things done. My superiors are concerned about rumors of graft and corruption prevalent in Indian society and ordered me to find out how to move supplies around the country with the least pilferage. Also, my commanders wanted information about banking in the country because of the large number of contractors we need to perform our mission. I have had some information from members of the senior command in Delhi, but I think I am not getting a full picture. Would it be possible for you to fill in the holes on how things really work around here?"

Having already downed half the glass by the end of Beck's question, the colonel moved forward in his chair. "My new friend, I think you colonials are in for a hell of an education on how the world really works." Leaning back and again taking a sip from the glass of liquor, he continued. "Money is the grease that gets things done in India. It was the same way when Alexander the Great came calling in 326 B.C. and will be the same way in another two thousand years. Yes, my young American, India either invented corruption or was one of its early disciples. It is good the empire came to save them from themselves. Otherwise, the Maharajas would have stolen everything and the bloody natives would have all starved. But then again, most of the natives are of strong character and hard workers."

His empty glass was immediately replaced with a full drink by the ever-vigilant waiter. After taking another sip of the clear liquid, Granger continued. "Now, what we introduced here some two hundred years ago brought some rule of law, but the barter system still reigns supreme. You have banks and other lenders of record, but the rules are often loose and only during the war years has the government been active in examining the books. Extra sets of ledgers are famous around major cities like Calcutta and Delhi, but Bombay's bankers are notorious fraudsters. If you want to hide money, you simply make a visit to Goa."

Beck's eyes brightened. He knew of Goa, the Portuguese enclave had existed for over four hundred years, far earlier than the British East India Company. Yet, his knowledge of the present-day colony was minimal. "Colonel, what did you say about Goa? All I know of it is it's a Portuguese colony."

"Yes, Lieutenant, it is a tiny piece of Portugal sitting on the coast of India. The Portuguese have always been good traders and got here far earlier than anyone else. The enclave is not very big but possesses an excellent harbor. The Portuguese are neutral in this war, but I believe they lean toward our side more than the Germans." Sweating profusely in the tan suit with his tie askew, the old man reached for his drink, downed another sip and continued his tutorial.

"Portugal is neutral, but even before the war, they were quite opportunistic about the comings and goings of valuables from India. I'm not saying I have any direct knowledge of anything sordid, but if an individual were to take some ill-gotten gains to Goa, it could disappear from sight in numerous ways. I know many of my former banking clients who would take holidays in Goa to soak up the excellent food, stay in their excellent hotels, lounge about on the beach and drop gold off at a Lisbon-based bank. From Goa, it could be sent on their flagged vessel to another colony or all the way to Lisbon, where it could again just disappear. But, again, I have heard only rumors of this behavior. I am certain this activity does not occur." The colonel leaned back in his chair, put his finger to his nose, and then moved it away rapidly above his head and smiled.

"Colonel, do you believe individuals who were trying to skirt the law would use this tactic in wartime?"

"Now, Lieutenant, I know you are a man of the world. I see you possess a class ring from your American naval academy, and as an educated man, you are sensing that I may be telling you the truth. Far be it from me to keep you in the dark, but I would believe things happen during a war where fortunes are lost and sometimes found by those who skirt the rules."

Again, the old man took a sip of his drink and noticed the attentive waiter stood nearby with another refill. The two men asking questions had only finished half of their original whiskeys, but the old colonel did not mind. Here were two men willing to pay for his drinks, and perhaps more would be offered for his consulting services. Sensing the British major and American lieutenant were not as patriotic as they pretended, the colonel knew a partnership was about to blossom.

Beck sipped his drink while glancing at his partner, Major Smythe-Jones. An ever so slight nod in Beck's direction brought a smile. Raising his glass, Beck offered a toast. "To Colonel Granger, a man of great knowledge and proven courage. We look forward to many more opportunities to learn and perhaps earn."

The three men drank heartily, with the old man taking more than one large gulp. He was about ready for his fourth drink, aware his new students would happily purchase his fill. Granger was unsure of what the two men were up to, but felt it was not his concern. He had learned much in his sixty-six years, and knew his life would be short. In whatever time he had left, he wanted to enjoy it to the utmost, and if these two gentlemen were up to some nefarious enterprise, he didn't care.

Beck stopped smiling and began plotting his next move. Goa could be the answer for moving money out of the country without suspicion. Secrecy was the key, and if a neutral country could be used to hide his growing wealth, so much the better. Now, he needed a plan and a reason to visit the Portuguese colony. His position offered the cover for traveling around the country, and a visit to Bombay, north of Goa, could easily be arranged. A plane trip would be the easiest way to get there. Otherwise, a thousand-mile train journey across the subcontinent would be the only alternative. Major Smythe-Jones would help him as well as his other partner, Rolle Cavendish. Both men possessed good contacts throughout India and could help set up an exploratory trip. This would have to be in the next month because his small safe was filling up with his portion of the profits. It would be best if he did not have large sums of cash, gold and precious stones sitting about his apartment.

PART 2

14

12 January 1942
Naval Air Station
Trinidad, British West Indies

- Aleutian Islands--Small U.S. Army force under the command of Brig. Gen. Lloyd E. Jones lands on Amchitka without opposition.
  - United States naval vessel sunk: Destroyer **Worden** (DD-352), by grounding, Amchitka, Aleutian Islands.
- Guadalcanal--27th Infantry Regiment, 25th Division, continues attack on Galloping Horse, replacing 3rd Battalion and makes limited progress toward Hill 53.
- New Guinea--After artillery preparation, two battalions of Australian 18th Brigade with tank support, attack enemy positions at the trail junction. Japanese artillery fire disables tanks; Australians continue battle, progressing slowly at great cost.
- USSR--Soviet forces of Leningrad and Volkhov Fronts launch a limited offensive, supported by air and artillery, to raise siege of Leningrad.

The flight from Miami to Trinidad was pleasant, especially in the big Boeing Clipper. Brand's plane followed the president's Clipper by fifteen minutes but quickly closed the distance in case of emergency. The number one plane carrying the president also included Admiral Leahy and Harry Hopkins, plus Roosevelt's physician, Admiral McIntire, and naval aide, Captain John McCrea. Other staff members were on board along with the president's Secret Service detail. Landing January 11 at 4:25 in the afternoon, the passengers were met by Rear Admiral Jesse Oldendorf, the Naval Operating Base commander, Trinidad, and Major General Henry C. Pratt, commanding general, Trinidad Base Command. The president and his senior advisors had a private dinner with the two local commanders and then were taken to their rooms for a short but sound sleep. It was during this late evening period that James received an abrupt wake-up call from Captain McCrea.

The professor was informed of a change in plans. Admiral Leahy had become ill on the trip down. Admiral McIntire advised Leahy to stay in Trinidad to recover from a profound chest cold the doctor feared would turn into pneumonia. The president's physician had also discussed his concerns with Dr. Feldman earlier. Both men were in complete agreement. With this abrupt change, the president wanted James to fly in plane number one. There was ample room for Gunny, Dr. Feldman, and Waverly on the plane, so with a bit of baggage juggling, the men joined the president's party for the flight onward to Belem. Leaving at dawn and skirting South America's coastline, the plane slowly climbed to an altitude of nine thousand feet, and with puffy clouds, the ride was amazingly smooth.

The smooth ride was in contrast to the present condition of First Lieutenant Waverly. Seeing Roosevelt from a distance when the two planes arrived at Trinidad and watching as the commander in chief was placed into a wheelchair and then a car for a short tour of the island base was a shock. The Marine had never seen the president before today, except in the newspapers and newsreels. Knowing FDR had polio was different from seeing the leader of his country picked up by a powerful Secret Service agent and placed in a wheelchair. Now, he was only a few feet away from the president and was afraid to even look toward the front of the plane to see him, but couldn't help himself.

Seeing Waverly in distress, Dr. Feldman intervened. "Bill, have you met the president? He doesn't bite."

The lieutenant looked at the smiling doctor, who was trusted by everyone on the team. "Sorry, Doc, I just don't know what to say or do. I didn't know the seriousness of his condition. I always see him either standing or sitting, and had no idea of the true situation."

Feldman got closer to Waverly's face and whispered, "Put it out of your mind. You don't share what you know or think you know about the president's condition. Remember, he is your commander in chief." As he pulled away and sat back in his chair, Feldman continued, "I'll ask James to have you go forward and have a chat with Mr. Roosevelt. I think that will clear up any misgivings you have."

Waverly was uncertain of how he should respond. He was a combat Marine sergeant, now an officer, who knew he was not well educated or sophisticated, but now Bill Waverly sat twenty-five feet away from the most powerful man in the world, heading to Africa to meet Prime Minister Churchill to plan the rest of the war. Experiencing a different kind of fear than he had ever known made him unaware of the two men standing in front of him.

"Mr. Hopkins, I'd like you to meet the newest member of the team, First Lieutenant Bill Waverly." James looked at Waverly saying, "Bill, say hello to Mr. Hopkins."

The Marine came out of his stupor and jumped up like a brand new recruit. "Sir, it's an honor to meet you, sir." That was about all Waverly could say, and it came out in a torrent.

Sensing the man's unease, Harry put out his hand and said, "Good to meet you, Lieutenant. I understand you did a hell of a job on Guadalcanal and that Major Flannigan thinks you are a great addition to the security of the professor."

As the two men shook hands, the ease and familiar touch of Hopkins relaxed Waverly. Harry sat down and asked if anyone had a cigarette. Immediately, several appeared, and after it was lit, a new conversation began.

"Can I call you Bill, Lieutenant Waverly? It would make it easier on everyone on this plane."

"Certainly, Mr. Hopkins." Not knowing what else to say, the lieutenant waited.

"Well, Bill, if you want, you can call me Harry. The president calls me that plus a few other names on occasion, but you don't want to hear bad words. It would be hard on morale." Smiling as he spoke, the presidential advisor noticed Dr. Feldman smiling as well as Warrant Jones.

"Tell me, Bill, what do you think of this plane? Pretty nice, huh?"

"Sir, I mean Harry, it's a much better ride than spending six or so weeks on a troopship slowly pounding across the Pacific." Waverly was beginning to relax and feel at ease with the man in the ill-fitting suit.

"Well, I can't promise you this kind of treatment all the time, but if you keep the professor out of trouble, I know you will enjoy your travels in the future. Now, have you ever met the president?"

Not sure of what to say, Waverly replied, "No sir. I have seen him only in the newspapers."

"Well, Bill, you're in for a treat. I think the president wants to talk to you about your experiences in the Pacific and how you and the professor are getting along. Let me check to see if he's got some time."

Hopkins got up and walked forward to where the president was talking to Admiral McIntire. After a few minutes, the president's advisor returned and said, "Bill, the president would love to talk to you and the professor. Let me introduce you to the boss."

The two men followed Hopkins up the large plane's aisle, and both men came to attention in front of the president. The admiral relinquished his seat to the two junior officers. As both men sat down, Hopkins introduced the Marine saying, "Mr. President, Lieutenant Waverly is the new security officer for the professor and his team. He has a distinguished record fighting at Bloody Ridge in Guadalcanal where he was severely wounded while saving the lives of several men."

The president was in an excellent mood and shook Waverly's hand with his strong vise-like grip and showed his familiar toothy smile. "Good to have you aboard, Lieutenant. You know my son is a Raider, and as I recall, you were with the First Raiders. Tell me about your experiences on Guadalcanal."

For the next thirty minutes, Bill Waverly told the story of the campaign for Tulagi and the vicious struggle for Bloody Ridge. FDR interrupted from time to time, asking for additional details and how the Marines dealt with the diseases, supply problems, and the enemy. Later that day, after the plane had arrived at Belem, Brazil, Waverly sat down with Dr. Feldman, describing the conversation and how it affected him.

"At first I was nervous sitting down with President Roosevelt and answering his questions, but after a while, it was like talking to a favorite uncle back home." He recalled facts much quicker than any time before and felt relief at letting go of his demons from the night on Bloody Ridge.

"Bill, being open like you were with the president can help a person deal with horrific events. I hope you'll feel free to talk with anyone of the team members about your experiences." Feldman listened and acknowledged the man's openness and how it helped in dealing with a terrible experience. The navy doctor thought this would be a good thing for him to do as well. His demons were always nearby, prowling the blood-filled rooms and corridors of the cruiser *San Francisco* during a long night in November.

The man paced back and forth waiting for an answer, which was slow in coming. Hearing the explanation for the series of mistakes, the general stopped and stared at the major standing at attention. The response was not what the senior officer wanted to hear.

"Damn it to hell! What kind of outfit are you running, Major? Is this some sort of social club, or is it the United States Army? Which one is it?"

"General, sir, sorry, sir. The men ran out of barbed wire, and we don't seem to have any left to finish the cordon around the hotel." The major in charge of the Military Police, a reservist with many years in the Baltimore police department force, failed to supply the correct answer, which was when, not if, the barbed wire would be found and installed.

"What the hell did you do in civilian life, Major? Run a bordello, or was it some sort of vaudeville troop?"

"General, sir, I was a captain in the Baltimore Police Department."

"I'm sure you were a good cop back in Baltimore, but if you can't find me some more wire, I will make sure you go back to Baltimore as a private."

Another officer spoke up, which usually annoyed General Patton, but he knew the man as a good source of information and common sense.

"General, if I may make a suggestion?"

"Go ahead, Captain, what do you have to offer?"

"Sir, when we occupied Casablanca back in November, we developed a good relationship with the port authorities and the French navy.

I recall seeing lots of barbed wire in their supply area near the harbor office. I think we could find it and get it for the major."

Looking at the captain and then the major, Patton stated, "Now, Major, it takes the damn navy to come up with a good idea. Captain Jameson has been in town less than forty-eight hours and has come up with more ideas than you have since you were born."

Turning to Jameson, Patton calmly said, "Jameson, do you think one of your men could find the major any French wire and get it to the hotel complex by tonight?"

"General, my aide, Lieutenant Meyers, can make inquiries as to the location of spare wire. I will arrange for any French transaction fee required."

Hearing the last few words, Patton exploded in laughter. "Damn it, Jameson, I like your style. Whatever it takes, you have the keys to the candy store. Just get me more wire."

Jameson smiled and pulled Meyers close to him and pointed at the major, saying, "See if we can get our *gendarme* Paul on this. I think a finder's fee would be appropriate. Take the major with a couple of trucks to the docks and make a deal."

The lieutenant didn't say a word but made a motion to the major, standing at attention to exit the room. Jameson interceded on the man's behalf.

"General, if you can see fit to let Lieutenant Meyers borrow the major and a few of his men and trucks, I think we can get the wire to the Anfa Hotel by this evening."

Patton's icy stare echoed his disdain for the Military Police officer, "Major, you are dismissed. Do not come back to this command without that damn wire."

The major saluted, and when it was returned by the general, the major executed a perfect about-face and walked out of the office, following a navy lieutenant named Meyers. Once the door was closed, Patton, still pacing the room, asked Jameson, "Tell me, Captain, how did you find such a resourceful man like the lieutenant? I have a good aide and a few other men who are independent thinkers, but most everyone waits to be told what the hell to do, and I don't have time to hold everyone's hand."

The navy officer standing near the general's ornate desk replied, "General, I look for men with the ability to think first and ask questions later. The other members of my team, including the Marine security sergeants, are all of the same cloth."

The general understood the type of man Captain Jameson described then asked. "So what is your Lieutenant Brand, the professor, going to be doing here with the president?"

"General, the president requested my team, including the professor, to be available during the conference. As to what that means, I don't know."

"Come on, Captain, you and Brand are as thick as thieves with the Chiefs and the president. What can you tell me about what's going to happen at this meeting with Churchill."

Jameson was now in a difficult position. His orders were clear as to what he was expected to do once he arrived in Casablanca. Admiral King told him to investigate the situation from the security aspect of the location and what the British were going to suggest. Already, Jameson had found out the British were in town in much larger numbers than the Americans. A converted passenger vessel, the HMS *Bulolo*, had docked in the city loaded with maps, documents, and position papers, along with experts from every department in the British government and military. These resources would provide additional backup to the British generals and admirals attending the meeting. Once again, the Americans would be outmaneuvered, outclassed, and hard-pressed to counter the British strategic vision. Turning to answer the general's question, Jameson could only offer a politically neutral observation.

"Sir, you know I can't go into any details, but I think the president, General Marshall and Admiral King are very concerned about what the British want to do going forward. I think having Professor Brand available will be of some value to any future plans on behalf of the Allied governments."

Patton walked over to the window, looked down at the street filled with American vehicles and soldiers and then turned back to face the navy captain. "Damn good political answer, Jameson. You didn't tell me much, but I think I get the general idea. Our side isn't ready for the big leagues yet, and General Marshall is afraid of getting run over by Churchill wanting to do some wild ass scheme in the Aegean. I will not ask any more questions about the conference." Now smiling, the general asked, "What else can you tell me about the situation we're facing in North Africa?"

"General, you are aware of most of the things going on with General Eisenhower's command and the lack of troops and good weather in Tunisia. Montgomery is moving up to the Mareth Line on the border of Libya and Tunisia and is bringing up supplies. His situation, like ours, is tied to a long and tenuous logistics train. Montgomery's supply train stretches back to Egypt on one road, with the Royal Navy still working to clear the ports in Tripoli and Benghazi. Until then, every supply item must be taken by truck from Alexandria to the front line. The air situation is still tenuous as well, with the Luftwaffe making a major investment in new bases in Tunisia and Sicily. Estimates are all over the place. We think there are over a thousand German planes within reach of our lines in Tunisia. The good news is the Royal Navy is making a serious dent on the German's supply situation, and if this continues as planned, the Nazis will run out of food and fuel by summer."

The general crossed the room, stopping at the large wall map and motioned for the captain to join him. Pointing toward the northern part of Tunisia, he spoke. "Jameson, here's the situation Ike's in. He has Anderson with the First British Army sitting along the northern part of these Tunisian mountains within a hundred miles of Bizerte and Tunis. He can't move forward with the rainy conditions, and the Germans have the high ground. In the middle, II Corps under Fredendall has three divisions scattered about the Eastern Dorsal of the Atlas mountains waiting for something to happen. Lloyd knows better than this, but he must be under General Anderson's orders to sit out the bad weather. South of our troops are a bunch of French troops, colonials mainly, plus some regulars without heavy equipment. There isn't much past this center line except desert and mountains, so the French are doing some patrols to make sure the Germans are staying put behind their side of the mountains."

Using his hand to indicate the southern part of Tunisia, Patton continued his assessment. "Montgomery is pulling up his Eighth Army along the Mareth line. Evidently, the French created some nice fortifications, tank traps, pillboxes, and some observation posts along the border with Libya back in '39. The Germans must not be pleased with the French engineering because they have made several improvements which will cause anyone doing a frontal attack a lot of problems.

"What we think the Germans are planning is still a mystery, but they have added tanks, infantry, and artillery along the southern border and along this Eastern Dorsal. What worries Ike is that our intelligence says the bastards have added a lot of experienced fighters pulled from Russia. Hitler putting more people in Tunisia is stupid. He should pull out and fight in Italy or France." Looking at the map again, Patton quietly said, "Our boys are fresh and willing to fight, but I don't think some of our commanders have put in the hours training our people to deal with hardened troops who know how to defend positions to the death."

Jameson watched as the general looked closely at the map and then pulled back with a smile on his face. "Captain, what this war needs is me. I think I could come up with a hell of a plan to beat the Germans at their own game and close down this front in two weeks. But I'm stuck in Morocco waiting to be nursemaid for a bunch of politicians." After another moment of silence as he pondered the German's next move, the spit and polish general commented about the American forces.

"Captain, I've met with your Major Flannigan, and he impresses the hell out of me. I think he has seen more combat than any American in this command. He gave me the unvarnished truth of what he experienced fighting the Japanese. Knowing the Germans and how they have fought the British and the Russians, we'll have a rough time. I was wondering if I could borrow him to brief some of my battalion commanders about what to expect when they go head to head with the enemy?"

"Sir, I don't think that would be a problem at all. As long as we are in your command and don't have conflicting orders from Admiral King, I am certain the major could provide some good insight into small unit tactics, especially against fixed fortifications. He did something similar for General MacArthur in Australia with one of the regiments now fighting in New Guinea."

"Excellent, I will get my aide to pull together some of the officers from my divisions to participate. Perhaps one of your sergeants could accompany him and spend some time with the senior NCOs as well."

"Certainly, sir. I think two of his sergeants did the same thing in Australia, and it was well-received. All of the men went through the British commando school in Scotland and then worked with the Marine Raider battalions."

"Better than I had hoped. Your men would be a great addition to our efforts. Perhaps I can get them transferred to the army, but I don't think Admiral King would agree." The general was now smiling because he liked being with warriors, and Flannigan and his men were all veterans and highly trained in the art of war. He wished more of his men were as well prepared as the Marines.

"All right, Captain, let's get back to the final review of the security of the hotel complex, and then we can get with the Secret Service agents to make sure they agree with our plans. I'm quite sure your lieutenant will find the needed wire and provide the Military Police major some training in clandestine operations."

⁂

The Military Police major was not a happy man. His name was O'Rourke, and he had spent fifteen years with the Baltimore police and moved up the chain of command based upon his handling of criminals and politicians. Now, he was being lectured by some young navy lieutenant who was an aide to some highly placed officer working with General Patton. Evidently, the navy knew where more wire was located and now he looked like a fool for not finding it through normal channels. He was embarrassed and angry, but smart enough not to show it. Perhaps the young officer could help him recover from this foul-up. They drove through the city, going down small streets barely usable by the three two-and-a-half-ton trucks known as six-by-sixes or simply deuces, carrying four men each to help load and unload the wire, if and when they found it. The two officers were in a jeep accompanied by a *gendarme* named Paul, and a young private driving the vehicle.

"Lieutenant, how do you know there is wire at the port? I asked around, including the navy supply people, and they told me they had provided us with the last roll in the whole of Morocco."

Meyers didn't reply to the older man, who he figured to be thirty-five or so, but directed the driver instead. "Turn right at the next street, then go slowly down for about a quarter of a mile." Addressing the major, he said, "Sorry, sir, needed to tell the private where to go; otherwise, we would get the trucks stuck in some alley. To answer your question, Major, when I was here in November, the day the French signed the armistice, I found all sorts of interesting items which could be useful to our mission. These things, according to my good friend Paul, still exist, so all we need to do is set up the conditions for a mutually beneficial arrangement."

The major looked strangely at the navy officer, and then he fig-

108

ured out what was happening. As an officer in the Military Police, he was responsible for the legal use of United States government property, including supplies, weapons, and the individuals using these items. As he pondered what he had just heard, he now understood the situation. The major was about to follow a direct and lawful command of a senior officer to do something contrary to the rules and regulations regarding the use of military property.

The navy officer knew the major was a former civilian police officer and realized the situation. Coming to the man's rescue, he said, "Major, we are about to reach an agreement with the commander of an Allied power to secure supplies for the common defense of both nations. By doing this, we are engaging in a transaction that will provide both parties something needed to fulfill the mission—theirs and ours. I am certain our commanding general understands and agrees to whatever terms are reached in the upcoming discussions. Please allow me to conduct these negotiations as that is part of my job and training."

Major O'Rourke knew he was skating on thin ice, even in the deserts of Morocco. Realizing he had no choice but to go along with Meyers, he nodded in agreement. This way, he could always testify that he never verbally agreed to the situation. The navy lieutenant spoke in French to Paul about the next set of turns and then informed O'Rourke of his role when they met the French.

"Major, I will be speaking French. Since you said you know a few words and phrases, I'll be doing the talking. I don't know how much English these people know, so if I speak to you or ask you a question, go along with whatever I say. Hopefully, we will have enough to trade in the back of the trucks. If I start to get angry and raise my voice, then point to the jeep, I want you to walk toward the jeep and get in the front seat, then cross your arms and look straight ahead. Don't worry, this will only be a way to quickly seal the deal. I don't think it will take much to get your wire."

O'Rourke agreed and wondered what would happen next. He knew each truck carried some sort of American supplies but was uncertain about what the navy lieutenant had requisitioned. This lack of knowledge on his part was a good thing. If things went south, he could point his finger at the navy and honestly state he was unaware of what was happening. It took only another five minutes until the jeep and the trucks came to a stop in front of a warehouse on the French naval base. Looking to his left, O'Rourke could see the French battleship *Jean Bart*, with its massive cannons pointing seaward. The ship was low in the water, and the French navy was slowly trying to make the vessel seaworthy and hoped the warship could be sent to the United States to complete the repair work which could not be accomplished in Casablanca.

The enterprising *gendarme*, Paul, went inside the building, and in a few minutes, a haggard-looking French navy commander walked out, along with four junior officers, each equipped with holstered pistols, looking none too happy to be in the company of Americans. Paul introduced the commander, Capitaine de fregate Antoine Bachand, to Meyers and Major O'Rourke and then left the discussion to the resourceful American navy officer.

Speaking in flawless French and using his hands like he was in Paris, Meyers said, "Capitaine, thank you for allowing the major and I to speak with you. We come on a mission of some importance to the American commanding general."

The French commander didn't say much more than to continue and shrugged his shoulders, showing whatever the American commanding general desired was not important. Meyers continued his speech. "It is our understanding that you have a large quantity of barbed wire in your warehouse, and we need some additional stocks to complete a major defensive position nearby. I hoped that we could borrow some of your stock in the spirit of our friendship with the French people. We would, of course, resupply you once our next shipment arrives from America."

The commander maintained his stoic persona and gave nothing away, which told Meyers the French officer was unsure of his position. Not wanting to lose face in front of his junior officers, he needed to say no to the Americans, who only a few months ago had shelled the base and killed a few hundred sailors.

"Lieutenant, I do not think we have any to spare at this time. Perhaps in a few weeks, we could make some sort of addition to your supply, but for right now, I am ordered to maintain what we have in stock. I am sorry."

Expecting an opening move, the American replied without smiling but not looking very distressed either. "Sir, I understand your position fully. You and your brave men have had a difficult few months, and as someone who was here during those dark days in November where our two sides were fighting each other, I recognize the reluctance to be of help. But perhaps we can make some sort of temporary accommodation to make this transaction possible."

Commander Bachand now understood the Americans needed barbed wire and were willing to provide some sort of incentive to make this deal happen. "Lieutenant, perhaps we were interested in some sort of, as you say, accommodation. What would you propose?"

Meyers asked the commander to walk with him but keep his four young officers back with the *gendarme* and the major. As the two men walked to the first truck, Meyers jumped up on the back and opened the flap. Inside were one hundred pound bags of rice and beans. The American said, "There are fifty bags in this truck, and I know your rations have been minimal, so this might be of great help to you and your men."

The French officer nodded his head and said, "This would be a welcome addition to our supply of food. You said fifty bags, correct?"

"Yes, Capitaine, plus in the truck behind me, I have brought fifty cases of canned meat, which we call Spam. I think your men would appreciate some meat, would they not?"

"I am sure this would be a great addition to our kitchen. Now, how many rolls of wire were you looking to get?"

"As many as you can fit in my trucks, Capitaine, and if we could do this soon, I need to get back to our headquarters and tell them of your great support for our efforts to rid France of the Boche."

The French officer was still unsure of the deal and crossed his arms to signal he wanted more in return for his wire. Meyers had anticipated this and now went to the big army truck's passenger door and asked the private sitting in the seat to hand him the duffel bag which the man had been entrusted with on the journey to the port.

Holding the large green bag, the lieutenant walked back to the French commander and put the bag on the ground. The French officer said nothing, but as the American opened the bag, Bachand became very interested indeed. Inside the bag were dozens of cartons of cigarettes. Signaling the American to quickly close the bag, the French officer turned and yelled to his officers to get a dozen men to help load barbed wire on the American trucks. Shaking Meyers' hand, he said, "Lieutenant, please let me know what we can do for you and the American army anytime. Perhaps we can share dinner soon together, and you can tell me more of your supply challenges."

Meyers passed the duffel bag to the French officer and then asked the truck drivers to move the trucks to the warehouse entrance to begin unloading the American foodstuffs and load the French barbed wire. On the journey back to the American headquarters, Major O'Rourke complemented the navy officer for being resourceful.

"Lieutenant, you did a good job back there. I'm unsure of the value of what we gave the French, but we needed the wire."

Meyers looked at the major replying, "Sir, I think we got five dollars of wire for every dollar of rice, beans, and Spam traded. The cigarettes were old, probably came over during the invasion, but the French would smoke old rope right now, so I think we got our money's worth."

Smiling back at Meyers, O'Rourke now asked another question that had bothered him for several weeks. "Do you know what all the fuss is about concerning this meeting at the hotel? Is Eisenhower coming down from Algiers, or maybe Montgomery is coming to meet with Patton?"

Meyers didn't smile but calmly said, "Sorry, sir. I can't help you with any of that information. I'm just a simple supply officer in the navy."

The major started to laugh and then held on as the jeep came to a quick stop behind an old truck turning onto the road leading out of the city. "Lieutenant, if you're just a simple supply officer in the navy, I'll eat my boots."

Meyers smiled back then turned his focus forward as the driver headed down the road to the commanding general's office. Hopefully, Captain Jameson would get him involved in something more important than finding barbed wire to ring around the Anfa Hotel.

15

14 January 1943
Casablanca, Morocco

- Guadalcanal--In the coastal sector, 8th Marines
  of 2nd Marine Division is still unable to advance
  because of fire from ravine west of Hills 80 and 81.
  Japanese land about 600 replacements near Cape
  Esperance to cover the withdrawal of forces from
  Guadalcanal.
- New Guinea--Gen. Vasey, Australian 7th Division
  commanding general, launches offensive to
  intercept enemy withdrawal from trail junction.
- Libya--30 Corps, British 8th Army, moves forward
  in preparation for assault on Buerat line and drive
  on Tripoli.
- Philippine Islands--Submarine **Gudgeon** (SS-211)
  lands personnel and equipment near Catmon Point,
  Negros Island.

The men were happy to have Brand and his three traveling companions
safely arrive in Casablanca. The men were billeted in Anfa Hotel's older
wing, close to the chaos now enveloping the complex. Senior officers, diplomats, bureaucrats, security personnel, and military aides moved about

as if thrown together by waves. The army had cordoned off the entire site with barbed wire. Passes were required of anyone entering the complex, and soldiers were stationed at every building entrance. The Science Team had a group of rooms with four men to a room, except for Captain Jameson and James Brand sharing one room. Late into the night, the two men talked about James's trip with Roosevelt, specifically, the strategy discussions the professor had with the president and Harry Hopkins.

Once Jameson knew about Admiral Leahy being left behind on Trinidad because of health reasons, it became apparent that James was serving as the admiral's replacement. The professor didn't provide a complete analysis of his discussions but gave his commanding officer a review of the situation.

"Sir, there are several topics that will be discussed in this conference. Most focus on the strategic direction of the war for 1943 and beyond, plus making decisions to solve immediate tactical problems facing the Allies. The first problem, which I reinforced to the president, was the war against the U-boat. If we can't defeat or slow the German attacks on our merchant fleets, all other plans are impossible. Without shipping, there will be no second front. Without a continuous supply of oil, there will be no bombing offensive against the German war industry. The president agreed with my ideas on focusing our efforts to curtail the enemy's submarine attacks first."

The captain thought this was the first important step in winning the war. You can't attack an enemy three thousand miles away without having your armies safely sent across the sea and then consistently supplied and reinforced. Thinking about the last reports he had seen on losses in the Atlantic, especially tankers, it was apparent the war at sea was still in doubt.

James continued, knowing the captain was already doing the mathematics of new build tonnage, enemy sinkings, and convoy operations. "If we can reduce our losses by thirty percent from the high in November of one hundred forty-two ships, and increase sinking U-boats by twenty percent, then our new construction will win the war. This will take more escorts, more long-range bombers, and improved technology. Training new crews, for both ships and aircraft, takes time, but by the summer, we could see the Germans being pushed back from the convoy routes. This would allow us a full year to prepare for an invasion of Europe."

"James, do you think the president is going to push for an invasion during this conference?"

"Captain, I don't know for sure, but I think he is leaning that way. As you know, General Marshall wants to do it this year, but our analysis shows this to be improbable at best, and without the concentration of forces in Britain, I think it would be impossible. And until we secure the Atlantic sea lanes, there can be only a limited buildup of forces this year."

The captain looked at his protégée and waited as Brand worked through his next comment in his usual deliberate method.

"The meeting will be a challenge to General Marshall and Admiral King. General Arnold will be impacted, but as you know, he is way too focused on his area of operations and thinks his bombers will win the war. I told the president, the British were probably going to provide us with several options for planning the next phase of the war. Hidden in these options will be their real objective, which is to slowly wear down the Germans without an all-out ground attack across the channel.

"Seeing what they have put forward in previous meetings and from my conversations with Field Marshal Dill in Washington, the British are reluctant to hit the Germans directly. I believe they will push for closing out the war in Africa and then moving directly to Sicily, which I agree is the best option. This would push the Italians to the brink and probably get them out of the war. This has significance because the Italians currently man positions throughout the Balkans and Greece, plus they have units in Russia. Germany would have to send their units to replace the Italians and further stretch their manpower. Also, the capture of Sicily would open up the Mediterranean to our convoys and cut the time to get supplies to India and onto China by about six weeks."

"Do you think the president would go along with a campaign to capture Sicily?"

"I believe he would be easily convinced by Churchill for two reasons. First, we have a lot of men now in North Africa. Are we going to move them out of this front and back to England, which takes a lot of shipping? It would make sense to use them here in some sort of attack on the enemy. The second reason is experience. Our divisions have seen very little combat so far and have not operated as an American force. The men in Tunisia are fighting alongside the British and French and are brand new to war. If the next major offensive is in Sicily, we can involve several divisions in an amphibious operation and serve independently from the British. The same thing goes for our air force units. I think our air units are more numerous than the British in the Tunisian sector, but again, they haven't had as much experience fighting against the Luftwaffe."

Sensing the professor was probably exhausted by his flight from Gambia to Casablanca, Jameson decided to call it a night. "James, let's get some sleep. I know we're to be available to Admiral King at 0700 hours for anything he needs before the first meeting with the British."

James was sleepy, but his mind was full of facts and figures, plus some fears about what would be decided in the coming days. Much would depend on the conference plans, and many lives were now in jeopardy, waiting for the next set of decisions.

The place was dreary, damp, and cold. January in Lisbon could be temperate, but this year was proving anything but nice weather. Rains had tormented the area for the past week, and the skies showed little promise of sunshine. Albert von Karsthof's office was located on the second floor of the building. His window looked out on the gardens, which were well maintained and slowly inclined toward a massive brick wall. On top of the wall, ornamental spikes were placed and covered in rusting barbed wire. The German Embassy was not very large but still contained enough space for the accredited diplomats and associated staff.

Outside the walls were many more Germans not officially tied to the diplomatic post but in service to the Reich. Karsthof was listed as an assistant to the ambassador, Baron Oswald von Hoyniger-Huene, but he was actually the head of German Intelligence, the Abwehr, in Portugal. The man standing in front of him was listed as the new assistant naval attaché. The man was dressed in civilian clothes. Only when there were official duties, usually involving the host country's armed forces or other military liaisons, did the officers wear their uniforms. So far, the intelligence officer was pleased with the work of his most recent subordinate. Gebhardt Wagener proved to be a valuable addition to the staff, primarily because of his chemical engineering education.

"So tell me, Herr Wagener, what do you think of our Portuguese friends so far?"

"Sir, the Portuguese are working very hard to steal from the Allies and us, but at least they do it consistently."

The more senior intelligence officer and veteran of many clandestine operations in Portugal and Spain laughed. The Portuguese government tried to play both combatants against each other and make lots of money doing it. Salazar, the president of Portugal, was becoming suspicious of the unregulated trade in wolfram by both Britain and Germany. Shell companies had been established early in the war to own the mines and ship the ore to their home countries. Portugal and, to a smaller extent Spain, were the only locations in Europe to mine the ore from which tungsten was refined. This hardest of metals was key to significant improvements in steel. It was used for armor, armor-piercing shells, bearings, and the manufacture of high-speed cutting tools. Other uses were being found for the metal each day which drove the effort to secure more sources.

"Do you think our Portuguese friends are treating us fairly, or are they selling more to the British?"

Wagener was slow to reply. His mind was that of an engineer, and he didn't possess all the facts to form an answer, but he went forward with his assumptions.

"I think the Portuguese leadership is being as fair as possible. We have men watching the ports for all shipments, and I believe this information is accurate. Knowing the shipments we are moving, I believe the system is fair, but it's easy to abuse."

"What makes you say that, Gebhardt?"

"Sir, I believe the British could easily coerce Salazar to slow our deliveries or to make the cost very high, which would put an extra burden on us. Also, I think the British are still using their old treaty with Portugal against them. The English want to operate airfields in the Azores and Madeira, which could be troublesome for our naval forces."

The treaty in question was the Anglo-Portuguese treaty of 1373, the oldest alliance in the world, which Britain had not invoked. This treaty had not been used by either party for reasons which, at first, seemed obscure but later shown to be quite well thought out. By keeping Portugal neutral, the Spanish or the Germans had less reason to invade Portugal and the entire Iberian peninsula. The British didn't want to give the Germans any pretense for invading Portugal, which would necessitate a strike across Spain. From there, they would be able to attack Gibraltar and close down the Mediterranean. The sale of wolfram to both sides became a way to maintain Portuguese neutrality, which was in the best interest of both warring countries.

"My people in Salazar's government inform me the president wants to put more controls on the wolfram mines and possible shipments. I need you to slowly work your way into the navy ministry and other information channels to find out if this is going to happen. Also, we need to set up alternative plans in case there are more controls on exports. Find out about other means to get wolfram across the border to Spain. Our people in Madrid have told me the Spanish mines are not capable of more production, but once across the border, the border authorities will look the other way."

"Do you want me to begin working through official channels, or shall I be more discreet in my inquiries?"

Showing a big sinister smile, the senior intelligence officer replied, "Herr Wagener, you have a way with words. I think you should have some conversations at the Portuguese navy headquarters and start with someone of equal rank. Put on your best uniform and ask about support for any wounded sailors who might wash up on their shore. Perhaps you can inquire about using some of our ships to sail from Lisbon and then around Cape Finisterre into the Bay of Biscay and how they would react to this. Once you have established some willing contacts in the Navio da Republica Portuguesa, do some travels up north to Castello Branco and check out the mines in the region. I will give you some names of our associates in this area. Make inquiries on how more wolfram could be shipped out using alternative methods."

Wagener thought the order was open to interpretation. Knowing enough not to ask additional questions, the officer came to attention and left the office. On the way to his small office in the back of the building, he wondered about the war's direction. In Lisbon, he was now reading neutral newspapers from both Portugal and Spain as well as papers from Britain, Brazil, and the United States. The reports were often in total disagreement, but the more he read, the more he realized the German position was weakening. The American papers painted a surprising amount of information on war production, ship launchings, new army divisions, and thousands of airplanes. In particular, he saw a photograph of American B-24 bombers being assembled in a factory in Michigan. The engineer in him was quite impressed, but he also thought a lot of this was propaganda like he saw in Germany, but now he could see both sides of the story, and it made him wonder about the future.

16

16 January 1943
Casablanca, Morocco

- Guadalcanal--Commanding General XIV Corps orders a second coordinated westward offensive in order to extend positions through Kokumbona to Poha river; forms Composite Army-Marine Division (CAM) to drive west on 3,000-yard front in coastal sector.
- New Guinea--After preparatory bombardment, assault against enemy in Sanananda area opens.
- Libya--British 8th Army, having passed through enemy's main positions at Buerat, pushes energetically toward Tripoli.
- USSR--Soviet forces of Voronezh front are west of the Don at Rossosh, where Italian forces are routed. On Stalingrad front, progress is being made in the reduction of trapped German 6th Army.
- Germany--RAF bombers attack Berlin, using target-indicator bombs for the first time. This is the first raid on Berlin since 7 November 1941.

The general didn't look good. His face was red, and he lit one cigarette after another. The meeting had ended early in the afternoon and his performance, he acknowledged, was poor. General Brooke attacked his ideas for Tunisia and found the plan a total disaster. The issue of supporting forces was not evidenced in the presentation. If the Germans attacked Fredendall's American corps in the center, they could be checked and defeated before any assistance could be offered by General Anderson's army to the north. Even General Marshall failed to support the plan, and the commanding general of the Allied Expeditionary Force was told to rethink this operation. Eisenhower was now perplexed and looking for ideas. Luckily, he could get some solace from his old friend Patton and a young acquaintance discussing the campaign's progress.

As Ike walked into Patton's quarters, he immediately smiled at his old friend, and then upon seeing Professor Brand, his face lit up even more.

"Good to see you, Professor. What are you doing in Casablanca?"

George Patton answered for the navy lieutenant saying, "Brand flew in with Roosevelt and is working on future operations and logistics." Eisenhower's slumped shoulders and almost vacant eyes provoked Patton to ask, "What the hell have you been doing, Ike? Looks like you're in the dog house again."

Looking at the commander in Morocco, Ike slowly answered, "George, things didn't go well today. Brooke chewed up my ideas for II Corps and then attacked the overall strategy. Marshall didn't back me up either, which concerns me. I just finished a meeting with Roosevelt, who worked me over for a while and then asked when this campaign will be over."

James spoke up and asked, "General, what did you tell the president?"

With a gravely serious appearance instead of the normal confident Eisenhower seen in photographs, Ike replied, "Professor, I told him we should be completing this mission by late April or early May. The rains are causing us nothing but problems, and the Germans have moved in at least two full divisions since November. Rommel is falling back into defensive lines on the Libyan border, and our supply issues grow with each day." Sensing the lieutenant knew more than most people about grand strategy, the general asked, "So, what does Roosevelt think about what's going on?"

Recalling the deliberate method in which Brand thought, both generals waited for the young officer to respond. Eisenhower was far better at the waiting game than the short-tempered Patton.

"General, I think the president is patient and wants the best information available. If you think your forces can compel the Germans to surrender by May, he will agree and turn over anything you need to accomplish this goal. I believe he will also remove any officer who fails to deliver. General Marshall has made the same commitment to the president, and I expect people will be removed for failing to produce results."

As James let the words sink in, he added more details. "The situation in North Africa will take a few months to end, but you will be successful. That does not mean there will not be setbacks. I do have a concern about our Allies. The British officers I met with expressed doubts about the ability of our forces to close with the Germans and fight."

Patton was poised to make a crude comment but James continued. "General Patton has had some good experiences in Morocco, as did our forces in Algeria. Granted, we were fighting the French, who were not as stubborn as the Germans. But we still suffered many losses, and some of the units became disoriented, failed to meet objectives, and often were slow in responding to new situations. The Germans we are facing are battle tested and experienced in dealing with the desert terrain. They excel in a defensive war and, when attacked, immediately counterattack. Our men in Africa have not faced this type of pressure before."

Ike mulled over the information, which he knew to be true. Patton moved closer to the navy officer and responded. "Lieutenant, I don't think you know what the hell you're talking about. We met serious resistance and suffered a lot of casualties. Some French units fought hard. This was no cakewalk."

Eisenhower interrupted his friend, knowing how Patton could get up a full head of steam and charge into the unknown. "George, the professor is right. We suffered casualties we shouldn't have because of bad intelligence, poor leadership, and sometimes, strong resistance, but the Germans are not going to give ground. We will have to take the fight to them and be ready for a counterpunch."

The commanding general turned to the navy officer. "Professor, what do you think the Germans are going to do next? Are they going to sit back and wait for us to attack them, or are they going on the offensive?"

Patton wondered why Ike would ask such a question of a teenager from the navy who lacked professional military training.

"General Eisenhower, I believe the Germans will consolidate their positions in the south and improve the Mareth Line. Montgomery will have to attack head on with a possible flanking attack to the west of the German defenses. Arnim and his new divisions are holding the high ground in the northern reaches of the Atlas mountains. The central portion between these forces is where II Corps is located. If we had sufficient strength, perhaps two or three more divisions, we could push straight to the sea and cut the two forces in half. But, realistically, this will not happen for several months. I think the Germans will attack our positions first as a stalling tactic, perhaps dividing our forces in two. This way, Rommel could use his interior lines to good advantage and attack north toward Anderson. Any Allied setbacks or defeat would allow the Germans to consolidate for a long defensive battle."

Patton considered what the navy officer said and found everything was correct. The young lieutenant continued, "This analysis is preliminary and dependent on our ability to supply forces on the front line. Montgomery is plagued with the same logistics hurdles we have in Tunisia. Our ability to move supplies forward is dismal. The rail line is in poor shape and new tracks need to be laid. Additional locomotives are being sent, but it will be late February or early March before they can be employed. Aviation assets are under attack by the Luftwaffe, making our ability to move larger forces forward difficult. The lack of airfields close to Tunisia is a greater problem than the lack of planes. Fuel is also needed, which again takes trucks all fighting for space on the few roads heading from Algeria."

James was able to provide Eisenhower some good news for a change. "Sir, the situation will improve in the next thirty to sixty days. First, as the weather improves, road construction will be possible. The same goes for the railroad lines. Next, as we build more airfields, we can attack the Germans in Tunisia and slowly deplete the Luftwaffe. Third, the Germans are in much worse shape than we are. Everything they need to fight has to come on ships or in planes. You can carry seventeen men in their Ju-52s but very little cargo. If you want to bring in fuel, you need ships. The same goes for heavy equipment. They have a monstrous cargo plane called the Messerschmitt 323, which can carry trucks and smaller vehicles but not tanks. As we increase our air forces in North Africa and on Malta, these aerial reinforcements will be attacked. The Royal Navy is working diligently to close down the sea lanes from Sicily to Tunis."

Patton had not heard of the enormous Me-323s, but Eisenhower had been briefed by his air commander, Air Marshal Edward Tedder, about the huge plane. The RAF commander also stated the plane's inherent slowness and fragility and how it could be easily destroyed if not escorted by a large number of German fighters. Ike realized the Germans were in a difficult position, and only by cutting the enemy's ability to reinforce its tenuous positions in Tunisia would the Germans be forced into surrender. Yet, he knew his forces—land, sea, and air—were not quite ready to meet the challenge. He needed time and after today's verbal assaults, continued to wonder about his future.

Sensing his friend's situation, Patton offered some of his own ideas. "Ike, you need to get me the hell out of here and put me up on the firing line. I can whip those guys into shape and take on Rommel and the rest of his buddies. I don't think Lloyd is the man to do this. I know Marshall thinks highly of him, but the man is a planner not a fighter. We need to get our nose bloody and take the first step. Otherwise, Monty will wait until hell freezes over to move, and we might be sitting around here chasing camels through 1944."

"Now, George, don't worry about getting into action. Your corps will be needed soon. Just like the professor says, we can't supply the few divisions we have up in those damn mountains as it is. We can't put new units in until we get our supply problem solved." Turning to face James, Eisenhower looked more like his calm and confident self. "Professor, I think you just laid out our situation better than I have heard all day long. If you have a few minutes, could you share some of your ideas on our supply problems and how we might solve them?"

James acknowledged the request. As Patton pulled out several large maps showing various parts of North Africa, Brand laid out the situation and what convoys were coming in within the next sixty days, supporting the build-up in Tunisia.

The doctor poured a large amount of poor quality Scotch in what appeared to be a clean glass. The liquid was clear, which was the first indication the liquor was safe to drink. Upon smelling the golden-colored fluid, it seemed similar to the famous nectar made in Scotland. Tasting it slowly, the man's face turned into a grimace.

"Damn, is this supposed to be Scotch or some sort of liniment for an old horse?"

Jameson smiled at his friend saying, "Doc, I'm sorry, but that is all I could scrounge up from Admiral King's aide. All of the good booze is under lock and key, and strictly reserved for those wearing stars."

Feldman sipped the poor-quality booze once again. With a slight grin on his face, he said, "Beggars can't be choosers, but damn, this stuff is horrible. I guess we don't have any ice around here or perhaps kerosene to cut it?"

Laughing at his friend, Flannigan came to his assistance. He pulled out a bottle brought from America for such an emergency. Feeling this might be the proper situation and not to avoid listening to Hiram's belly-aching for the rest of the night, he poured a new glass for his friend. Handing it to the doctor, he stated, "Now don't get used to this stuff, Doc. I only brought one bottle from the States, and once this is gone, we're out."

"Bless you, my son. For a slow-witted Marine, you show promise. Thanks for sharing, but let me first drink some more of this rot gut, and then I can wash it down with your fine whiskey."

The men chuckled at the doctor as his expression reminded them of someone sucking on a lemon each time he took a sip. Again, Feldman asked, "Where was this made? Egypt or maybe the slums of Timbuktu?"

"According to the label," Jameson reported, "it was made in India from a Scottish formula, but then again, this might just be the label and not what's inside."

Duncan picked up the bottle and poured some in his glass, and slowly swirled it around. Sniffing the contents, he exclaimed, "This stuff would kill a cow! Bloody hell, I'm ashamed it has the name Scotland on it. I don't think this alcohol ever saw the inside of a barrel, nor was it made with anything resembling mash. I think it is some sort of Nazi secret weapon. You will go blind drinking this." Grinning, the Scotsman took a large swig of the counterfeit booze. "But you drink what you have."

Jameson laughed at the antics of the Scottish flyer. He was enjoying the man's company, and his knowledge of the British bureaucracy was terrific. Besides being a brave pilot, the man's engineering background had been extremely useful in the past few days. One of the British doctors had engaged Feldman in a conversation the day before Churchill and Roosevelt's arrival about bad food and possible poisoning. There were no known threats, but everyone was jumpy about having the two world leaders plus their top military staff located in a hotel near an active war zone.

Feldman thought the possibility was negligible, yet still plausible. He shared the discussion with Jameson, explaining how some of the British doctors and their American associates planned to test the foodstuffs, liquor, and other liquids which might be consumed in Casablanca. After telling the captain about the effort, Jameson asked Duncan to get involved in the process. Being an experienced chemist, the happy Scot was more than interested in helping the physicians. Military Police units were brought in to help Clark, who was put in charge of testing samples of everything perishable, liquid, or not containerized from Britain or America. Knowing that only three months ago, Nazi agents were located throughout the French territories, nothing could be taken for chance.

The teams assigned to perform tests, many personally supervised by Duncan Clark, worked for two days to clear every item brought into the compound. During this time, he "liberated" several bottles of spirits, which were added to the team's supply. The captain appreciated the gin. The rum was Gunny's favorite, while three Scotch bottles were pounced upon by Flannigan and the doctor. The Scot also found a couple of bottles of fine port, which helped wash down the local selections of goat and camel meat. As he told the team, "Even an old camel tastes good when you have a fine ten-year-old port."

Around midnight, James arrived from his meeting with Patton and Eisenhower. Lieutenant Waverly provided security during the meeting along with Sergeants Dean and Williams. Jameson's orders were explicit involving the professor; he was never to be without at least two guards anywhere in the compound. Additionally, Brand was never to go outside the compound unless ordered by the captain, and if this occurred, a four-man team must accompany him. Enough soldiers guarded the outside of the compound to thwart anyone wanting to attack it, but any possible threat to Roosevelt or Churchill could not be ruled out. The Secret Service had also brought a large advance team to Casablanca plus two teams that flew with the president from the States. This added security made Jameson feel better, but he was always concerned James would do something to place himself and others in danger. Admiral King had made it clear after James shot down two Japanese planes at Guadalcanal that the professor would not be doing anything heroic ever again.

Jameson was the first person to inquire about Brand's latest meeting. "James, how was Patton? Still full of fire and brimstone?"

"Yes sir, the general is still itching to fight. I think he would fly to Berlin and shoot Hitler himself if he could find a plane. I think he's bored to death sitting around Casablanca."

Looking at Waverly, the captain asked, "So, Lieutenant Waverly, are you ready for a drink?"

"Yes sir. If it's possible, I'd like to get something for Dean and Williams, too?"

"No problem. Here's a bottle of whiskey. I can't vouch for the quality of the booze, but it will help you sleep."

"Thank you, sir. Let me get the guys a drink, and I'll be right back."

As Waverly returned, Flannigan asked, "Anything unusual to report about the meeting with General Patton."

"No sir. A three-star showed up about thirty minutes after the professor went into the room with the general."

Overhearing Waverly's response, Jameson quickly asked, "Did you recognize the general meeting with Brand?"

"No, Captain. The professor told me his name was Eisen or something like that."

"Was the name Eisenhower?"

"Yes sir. I heard Mr. Brand call him Eisenhower. Seemed like a nice guy. When he entered the room, he was hunched over and looked like a whipped puppy. When he left the room, the man had a great big smile. Must have been a good meeting."

Flannigan looked at Jameson and saw the captain smile. As Brand walked back into the room carrying a glass of water, Jameson asked, "So how is General Eisenhower these days?"

Brand was nonchalant about the question, replying matter-of-factly. "The general is all right. Seemed he was concerned about the meeting he had with the Combined Chiefs of Staff. General Brooke thought the Tunisian campaign plans were not well thought out and would fail if initiated. Patton and I gave him some ideas on how to support the operation by improving the supply situation and moving up supporting units near Anderson's position. I told him about the probability of a German attack at his center position, and he's going to work with the II Corps commander to bolster this sector."

Turning back to look for something to eat, Flannigan shook his head in wonderment, and Jameson nodded in agreement. Waverly, still somewhat confused about the goings on involving the Science Team, would be told later about Eisenhower and his relationship with James Brand.

17

18 January 1943
Casablanca, Morocco

- Guadalcanal--Americans gain continuous line from Hill 53 northward to coast at point some 1,500 yards west of Point Cruz.
- New Guinea--Japanese, although facing certain defeat, continue to offer last-ditch resistance on the Sanananda front.
- Burma--Indian 47th Brigade opens attack on Japanese positions at Donbaik but can make little headway.
- Libya--British 8th Army continues to pursue enemy toward Tripoli but loses contact because of terrain and obstacles.
- Tunisia--Col.-Gen. Jurgen von Arnim, new Axis commander in Tunisia, opens offensive to restore Tunis bridgehead line by recovering ground lost to French on 12-13 January and then seizing control of passes west of Kairouan.
- USSR--Soviet forces of Leningrad and Volkhov Fronts have reopened land communications with Leningrad, isolated since fall of 1941, and hold corridor 10 miles wide in region south of Lake Ladoga.

The president enjoyed his day outside the heavily secured compound, touring the camp of the Thirtieth Infantry Division, which supplied the guards for the area. Roosevelt was in his element observing the Third Battalion perform a pass in review along with a band from the Thirty-Sixth Engineers. The commander in chief inspected equipment, including howitzers, machine guns, and half-tracks equipped with all sorts of weaponry. General Patton accompanied the president along with the battalion commander. The big FDR smile, cigarette holder, and hat were used to their expected advantage as he met groups of soldiers who had been kept in the dark about the presidential visit.

Upon returning to his villa, shortly before 1700 hours, the president met with the British prime minister and the Combined Chiefs of Staff. The meeting was a review of the progress so far in the military conference and the recommendations on how to wage war on multiple fronts. There were many roadblocks to overcome. Still, a significant number of agreements had been reached, with the top priority being the need to focus on securing the lines of communications, which required winning the Battle of the Atlantic. Without control of the sea lanes and reducing the U-boat threat, there could be little accomplished in establishing a western front or building up the bomber offensive. General Arnold and Air Chief Marshal Sir Charles Portal required larger deliveries of munitions, support personnel, and fuel to bomb German war industries and cities. Without shipping, the bombers were useless.

Admiral King won his battle on the American control of the Pacific campaign with the acknowledgment that the British would control the China-Burma-India theater of operations. With a free hand in the Pacific, the American navy would expand its strategic efforts in a two-pronged series of attacks, one in the Southwest Pacific under General MacArthur and a thrust up the central Pacific under Admiral Nimitz. The main issue yet to be resolved was what to do in Europe. Marshall still wanted to rapidly move on an invasion of France in 1943, while the British were united in their opposition. General Alan Brooke expressed their views on waiting until later in 1944 and, in the meantime attacking Sicily and Italy with the expressed desire to drive Italy out of the war. Brooke explained how Italy's surrender would cause Germany to further dilute their resources by forcing them to replace Italian units in places such as Greece and the Aegean and, more importantly, the many Italian divisions now fighting on the Russian front. The arguments continued, but the conference was fulfilling its primary goal of formalizing a unified battle plan to destroy the Axis powers.

After the meeting, Churchill, Roosevelt, and the senior officers from the two nations and their principal civilian advisors enjoyed cocktail hour. Later in the evening, the president planned to have a quiet dinner with Admiral McIntire, his naval aide, Captain McCrea, the president's sons Lieutenant Colonel Elliott Roosevelt and Lieutenant Franklin Roosevelt Jr., plus the son of an old family friend, Lieutenant Richard Ryan. Early in the cocktail hour, Roosevelt asked his naval aide to have Lieutenant Brand brought to the meeting to chat. Within fifteen minutes, a smartly dressed naval officer walked into the room and found himself the center of attention.

Seeing James enter the room, Roosevelt spoke loudly, so everyone would know what was happening. "Gentlemen, it appears that Professor Brand is now in our midst. Come over here as I have many questions."

James approached the president and stood at attention. Churchill sat next to the wheelchair-bound Roosevelt and spoke first. "Professor Brand, it is good to see you again. I believe you have been hard at work doing your magic on the reports supporting this conference."

"Mr. Prime Minister, it is good to see you again, sir. As to my efforts supporting the meeting, it has been an honor to help when asked."

Roosevelt picked up on the comment, inquiring, "So Professor, what do you think of the plans so far?"

Everyone in the room turned their attention to the young naval officer. All of the Americans knew him, as did General Brooke. Portal had not met the young man, nor had Fleet Admiral Pound. James saw the familiar face of Lord Mountbatten standing next to Field Marshal Dill—both smiled at the new arrival. General Ismay, the military assistant to Churchill, had briefly met the American naval officer once before but had no interaction with him. Sensing the need to provide an answer to the president, James took a deep breath.

"Mr. President, our plans are taking shape. Priorities are being established for winning the wars in both Europe and in the Pacific."

Chomping on his cigar, Churchill replied, "Diplomatic answer, young man, but I think you are not as reticent as I recall. Perhaps the presence of so many senior officers has slowed your answers."

Knowing he had to provide more detail and looking directly at the British Prime Minister, James said, "Sir, the plans are taking shape, but many conversations need to occur before the strategies can be finalized. Agreements have been made in the anti-submarine war in the Atlantic and the bombing campaign in Europe. The continuing need to supply the Russians is also of concern, and the northern route to Murmansk is still under direct threat of interdiction by the Nazi U-boats, surface fleets, and aircraft. The plans for the war in the Pacific continue, plus agreements are being reached on Burma's reconquest to open the road to China. The issue of what to do next in Europe is still under consideration."

Roosevelt, who liked the young man and his absence of fear in speaking his mind, decided to press further. "Professor, the prime minister and I have been briefed on the daily discussions of the military leaders, and I appreciate your candid assessment of what you have seen or heard concerning these discussions. What are the main sticking points going forward in coming up with a unified battle plan?"

Now facing a direct command from the president and hearing silence from the Allied military's senior officers in the room, James answered. "Mr. President, the Combined Chiefs are working on an agreement on what to do next once the Germans and their Italian allies are defeated in Tunisia. Should we immediately attack Sicily, Sardinia, the Dodecanese Islands of Greece, or attempt a cross-channel attack on northern France? All of these plans require greater analysis for the required logistic support, allocation of shipping, the need for greater numbers of landing craft, and the ability to control the skies by eliminating the enemy's aviation assets. I have been working on the shipping requirements for the rest of 1943 and into early 1944, and the build-up of personnel in the European theater will require we meet the construction estimates, as well as the elimination of the U-boat threat. If we prioritize the convoy escort plans, including constructing a greater number of escort carriers, we should defeat the German submarine force. However, the emphasis on building escorts, including destroyers, destroyer escorts, and corvettes, will diminish our ability to build enough landing craft to enable a large movement of troops to land on the coast of France until the spring of 1944."

Churchill pounced on the comments. "So, Professor, if we build up our ability to destroy the U-boats, we will not be able to commit enough landing craft until sometime in 1944?"

"That is correct, sir. The escort plan calls for the construction of eighty fleet destroyers and over three hundred destroyer escorts and corvettes. This also takes into consideration losses of approximately ten ships per month. By the end of the year, Britain and America should have 343 fleet-type destroyers and 829 destroyer escorts and frigates available for service. By the end of this summer, we should have forty-two escort carriers ready for operations as well. Also, the availability of long-range antisubmarine bombers should expand exponentially by the end of the year."

Thinking for a moment about the other part of the construction equation, James added, "The construction of landing craft is slowed by the need to focus on the escort program. Currently, a request for one hundred fifty LSTs for delivery to the European theater is in jeopardy. I estimate only eighty-four will be available by August. Every category of landing craft is in similar jeopardy. Both British and American industry is faced with supply, manpower, and space limitations. This necessitates scaling back operations requiring large numbers of these vessels."

As usual, Brand's comments were precise, unemotional, and without prejudice regarding the decision involved in making wartime allocations and production. Roosevelt knew most of the numbers and the implications for strategy. General Marshall wanted to drive straight into France. Admiral King knew nothing could happen until the U-boat danger in the Atlantic was eliminated or reduced to a minimum. General Arnold wanted to move quickly on his daylight bombing campaign in association with Air Chief Marshal Portal's nighttime RAF efforts. But these bombing attacks required vast amounts of supplies—bombs, spare parts, and most importantly, fuel—and until the shipping was available, the bombing of Germany would be limited.

Looking at his wartime partner, FDR commented, "Seems the professor has thrown some sand into the gears of our planning. I believe we need to get our people working on the best use of our forces for the remainder of the year and finalize plans to invade France early next year."

Knowing his staff had worked hard on winning his battle of delaying an invasion of France in 1943, Churchill replied, "I would agree with you, Mr. President. I will advise my staff to focus on what is doable after running the Hun out of Tunisia. I believe we should put maximum pressure on the Italians by quickly taking Sicily or Sardinia. They do not have the stomach for more war, and this would greatly help our Russian friends."

Marshall knew he was losing the battle for jumping across the channel and attacking the German homeland. Admiral King had advised him about the lack of sea transportation necessary to build up forces in Britain, and without air superiority, an invasion would be tenuous at best. Arnold just wanted to get moving on his bombing program and didn't care about adventures in the Mediterranean but would follow orders from the president. Brooke didn't smile but would have to thank the professor for his candor. Perhaps Sir John Dill's access to the young navy lieutenant was paying off. He felt the brash Americans were out of their league in the planning of war, and now the British General Staff showed its control of the battle plan.

The president thanked James for coming to the meeting and asked Admiral King to introduce him to the others in the room. The admiral, dutiful as ever and sensing the good impression Brand was making on the president, gladly walked him around the room to speak to the other attendees. James knew most of the officers but had never met Fleet Admiral Pound or Air Chief Marshal Portal. The Fleet Admiral was gracious but quick in his greeting and quickly pulled King to one side to continue their discussion on convoy protection. Leaving James in General Arnold's care, he quickly became engaged in an unusual conversation with the head of the Royal Air Force.

"Air Marshal, meet Professor James Brand. He's done a lot of work for the air force, especially in many of our development projects."

Portal was well thought of by the American Chiefs of Staff, and General Arnold agreed to most of the RAF's ideas on a joint bombing campaign of Germany. The two men and their senior teams worked tirelessly to build the airfields, supply depots, and maintenance facilities needed to make the bombing of Germany a success. The air chief marshal smiled as he shook the hand of the tall naval officer. "Lieutenant, I see you wear the wings of a naval aviator. Have you seen any combat?"

Before James could reply, Arnold answered the question. "Air Marshal, Lieutenant Brand shot down two Japanese planes over Guadalcanal in November. I'm quite sure he would be a very successful pilot, but he has been grounded. Isn't that correct, Lieutenant?"

Trying to avoid frowning, James replied, "Yes sir. I am not allowed to fly in combat anymore."

Arnold smiled and turned to Portal, saying, "Seems the professor went against orders and volunteered to fly a fighter supporting a bombing mission on some Japanese ships, which proved consequential in forestalling the reinforcement of the island by the enemy. He now knows as does every senior commander in the American armed forces that the professor's flying career is over."

Portal smiled, knowing the young man was both brave and probably a bit foolish. The Royal Air Force had many pilots but very few top scientists, which could not be easily replaced. "Lieutenant, I understand your dilemma, but I realize that some serve the greater purpose, and evidently from what I have heard you are too important to risk sending you off chasing the enemy."

Not expecting an answer to his comment, Portal continued with a different line of questioning. "I have a question for you, if you don't mind?"

"No sir, what assistance do you require?"

Seeing the change of expression on the professor's face, which awaited the inquiry, Portal provided James with a set of hypothetical questions. "Let's say you wanted to bomb a target but needed to be extremely precise. And this target is highly protected by enemy antiaircraft weapons. Plus, the target is large, requiring tons of explosives, perhaps several bombs. Now, if a pilot approached this target, let's say from the sea and needed to be at a shallow height to successfully hit the target, how would you approach this challenge?"

James quickly thought about the problem and the possible target. Submarine pens in Norway and France were a possibility. Knowing about the successful raid from the sea on the dry docks of Saint-Nazaire last March, this might be a possible target. There were other high-value targets in Bremerhaven, Hamburg, and perhaps the Kiel Canal. Whatever the target, a low-level attack would be suicide, if for no other reason, a bomb dropped from a low altitude would produce a large shockwave that could also destroy the plane. Quickly thinking through the problem, James responded.

"Air Marshal, the question requires a great amount of detailed analysis, but a brief examination of the facts provides a quick answer. Depending on the amount of the charge-weight ratio, an explosion would probably destroy the aircraft and the target. Approaching a strongly defended position at low altitude, even at speeds exceeding three hundred miles per hour, would result in extremely high plane and crew losses. If I may ask, can you provide more information as to the nature of the target and the amount of explosive charge?"

Looking at Arnold, Portal let out a small laugh, "Arnold, you were right. This man is just like so many of our boffins that we would need weeks explaining our ideas and then understanding their answers." Facing the perplexed American navy officer, Portal decided to add information.

"Lieutenant, let's say you were going to hit a large stationary target but needed to get below the surface of this target to amplify the effect of the explosion. I think Tedder told me about your work with him last year on skip bombing Italian ships in the Med. If you were to skip a bomb at a target, letting it sink to a depth which would maximize the effect of the explosion, would this work?"

James now had the information needed. Since it sounded more like an attempt to get a German battleship or perhaps blow up one of the hardened submarine pens on the coast, it would be essential to get close to a target, have the bomb sink to a depth, and then blow up. This would create a pressure wave, much like that found in a depth charge, which effectively destroyed submarines. A depth charge didn't have to physically hit a submerged submarine, just get close enough to explode near or underneath it. The pressure wave creates a force that could rupture the pressure hull if it exploded near a submarine and the submarine would either be destroyed or forced to rise to the surface, allowing the crew to escape.

Looking at Arnold first and seeing no reaction, James addressed Portal. "Sir, depending on the amount of charge in the weapon, a shock wave could be produced to destroy any target on or next to the water. It does require being extremely close to the target to not reduce the shock-wave's effect. The other problem is the depth setting and actual location of the weapon to maximize its effect. Locating the center of mass or some other critical physical feature would also magnify the blast. As to the skip bombing aspect, I think it would work, but if a large weapon was employed, the blast effect could still damage any aircraft engaged in such an attack."

Moving very close to the professor, Portal asked one more question. "My boffin on this project has said the same thing but devised a way to have the weapon bounce in such a way as to counteract the forward force of the bomb."

Brand reacted quickly and knew the answer. "Sir, would your expert be using backspin to help in the skipping as well as to give the bomber time to escape?"

"Yes, you hit on the idea, Professor. Do you think it will work?"

Not taking too long to think about the question but visualizing how the weapon would work, he replied, "Sir, I think if the casing of the weapon were strengthened and then with a significant backspin, a spherical type of weapon would bounce for quite a distance. I would need to come up with some speed, altitude, distance calculations, but I believe it will work."

Portal smiled and then looked at Arnold, said, "General, your professor just helped me decide about a project. If he thinks the bloody thing will work, I will move forward on the mission."

Seeing the expression on General Arnold's face, James knew something unique was being planned. The two senior air force officers shook Brand's hand, and Arnold admonished him not to say anything about the conversation to anyone else outside the men in this room. After agreeing to the command, General Arnold steered James across the room to where Admiral Mountbatten was speaking with Field Marshal Dill. As the two British officers inquired how things were progressing on the logistics issues for the buildup of men and supplies in Britain, it dawned on James that this unique weapon's target was not a ship or submarine pens but a dam. Later he would think about how this weapon would work and where the Allies might employ it to damage the German war effort. He tried not to think about the civilian lives which might be lost, knowing the war was taking on an even more terrible phase.

18

24 January 1943
Casablanca, Morocco

- Aleutian Islands--Enemy begins series of minor air raids on Amchitka.
- Guadalcanal--Continuing west in coastal sector, CAM Division reaches Hills 98 and 99 and gains contact with 25th Division. Bombardment group of cruisers and destroyers and carrier group bombard and bomb Vila-Stanmore area, Kolombangara, Solomon Islands.
- Tunisia--Implementing order of 21 January for Gen. K. A. N. Anderson to coordinate efforts of the three Allied nations, U.S. II Corps is attached to British 1st Army. Gen. Juin agrees to place French 19th Corps under British 1st Army upon approval of Gen. Giraud. Full-scale assault northward in Ousseltia Valley canceled. Germans order attack on Faid Pass as soon as possible.

Jameson, Flannigan, Brand, and Meyers, searched through the final report on the conference, looking for significant changes from the previous drafts. Having found nothing major, the men agreed the framework for

137

the war was complete. A strategic plan had been set, and the British and Americans agreed on what would happen in the war. James found the information on the manufacturing and shipment of war materials was exciting and more critical to the successful conclusion to the war, but the Allies had finally agreed on a broad worldview. As Brand studied the need for more synthetic rubber and the challenges in building factories to manufacture the new product, Jameson started to summarize the information, while Warrant Jones, Dr. Feldman, and Lieutenant Waverly sat and listened to his analysis.

"The conference lays out some big objectives in continuing the assault on Germany. Once the enemy is cleared from Tunisia, we will move forward with Sicily's invasion, possibly in July. The key to this is eliminating the U-boat threat, which will get a major boost in equipment and manpower during the year."

Seeing the men listening with great interest, the captain continued. "With the submarines pushed out of the way, the bomber campaign will be strengthened, and a night and day system of attacks will bomb German war industry, transportation, and major cities. The Allied governments have agreed to Admiral King's strategy of a two-prong thrust toward Japan through the Central Pacific and the Southwest Pacific. Next, the Allies will build up the CBI air forces and mount a major offensive into southern Burma later this year. The last item is the most important, the Allies will only accept an unconditional surrender of the enemy. There will be no deals or armistice. I think the president and prime minister are going to hold a news conference today and announce this as a major policy."

Gunny was the first to speak up. "Captain, what does unconditional mean? We had an armistice and then a treaty ending the Great War. What's different about this?"

"Good question, Gunny. As I understand it, the idea is to tell the enemy and our biggest ally, Russia, that we will not make some sort of last-minute deal to end the war. The Germans and the Japanese will have to stop fighting and let our forces into their country. The Allies will set the terms after this occurs. We will make all the policies and enforce international laws, meaning we will prosecute those guilty for the war."

Waverly, usually not one to ask questions, made an observation. "Captain, shouldn't we just shoot the bastards who started this and then go after the little guys who followed orders?"

Stifling a smile for the impassioned Marine, Jameson responded. "Lieutenant, I would agree with what you said, but when this war is over, we need to do the world a big favor and conduct real trials, submit evidence, hear arguments and then pass judgment. This way, the people of the world will see the difference between our justice system and that of the enemy. Does this make sense to you?"

Thinking for a moment, Waverly responded, "Sir, I guess it makes sense, but from what I've seen of the war so far, these are evil men who deserve to be hung. Shooting them would be a waste of ammunition."

Flannigan decided to change the subject for a moment. "Sir, what are the plans for the unit? Are we going to head back to the States?"

Not wanting to go into great detail but knowing these men were a tight group and highly involved in the war planning, Jameson decided to give them a quick overview of what would happen next.

"The president and prime minister are heading off to Marrakech this afternoon. I was informed they will spend one night, then the president will start his journey home. Brand, you will accompany the president on the return trip home. Waverly and Gunny will fly with you along with four of the sergeants."

Knowing the others were waiting for their orders, Jameson smiled and gave them the news. "I have been ordered to Algiers to work on the supply issues for the Tunisia operation and begin working on HUSKY, the code name of the invasion of Sicily. Meyers will stay with me. Lieutenant Clark will also come along since I may need help with the Royal Navy and to have an experienced aviator in case I need one. Flannigan and Doc, you two have been requested to help the army for a few weeks. General Eisenhower was pigeonholed by General Patton, requesting more training by experienced personnel. You two have been in the thick of the action in the Pacific, so the general wants you to tour the units here in Morocco and then move up to Tunisia and observe the situation. You will make recommendations on what you see and hear."

Flannigan was smiling at last as he thought, *Finally, a real mission, away from shuffling papers.* Feldman was intrigued to find out what the army's medical people were doing and how they handled the horrid desert conditions. Meyers didn't think of anything special about moving to Algiers, except he would get to see another part of the French colonial empire.

"Major, make decisions on the men you want to stay with you and those you are sending back with Mr. Brand."

Turning to Dr. Feldman, Jameson said, "I take it you want Hamlin to stay with you."

"That would be an affirmative, Captain. Jonathan has more experience in mass casualty work than anyone in North Africa and would be a good man to check out the situation."

"Good, I have no problem keeping Hamlin over here. I think Mr. Brand would agree that as long as he is with the president, his needing medical treatment would be well covered." Turning to look at James, Jameson asked, "What about Sparks? Do you think you will need him with you, or can he stay with me?"

James knew if he was back in Washington, his need for his experienced radio man would be negligible, he quickly agreed. "Sir, no reason to have Schmidt come with me. You will get better use out of him than I." Thinking about the changes going on with his friends, James suddenly thought about why he wasn't going to be staying in North Africa with the rest of the team.

"Sir, is there something special I'm supposed to work on when I get back to Washington? You know I'd rather stay here and investigate the field situation."

"James, I'm sorry, I don't know the answer to this. All I was told by Admiral King is he wanted you back in Washington to work on some new projects. I also think the president wanted your company on the trip back to the States."

James nodded his head in agreement, stating in a calm voice, "That makes sense, sir. The president asked me a lot of questions on the trip over, and perhaps he will share some of his ideas on future plans."

Waverly remained quiet but surmised the kid professor had a special bond with the president. As he watched the two on the long journey from Trinidad and then across the Atlantic, he saw two men, one old and one very young, engaged in long conversations. Often large maps were stretched across the table in front of Roosevelt, and sometimes the two scribbled notes or looked at large books labeled TOP SECRET. Bill Waverly didn't understand the relationship, but he understood the orders from the chief of Naval Operations to protect the professor with his life, which he intended to do.

Later in the day, Flannigan provided a list of assignments for the Marine security team. Staff Sergeant McBride would stay with Captain Jameson, Lieutenant Clark and Lieutenant Meyers. The three made a good team, and Jimmy McBride was devoted to the captain's safety. Chief Petty Officer Schmidt would also join Captain Jameson in Algiers to provide radio and cryptological support. Pharmacist Mate Jonathan Hamlin would accompany Dr. Feldman touring the American medical facilities in North Africa. Staff Sergeant Dean would stay with the major on his observation assignment with the American and British forces. Master Sergeant Laird and Sergeants Dillard, Williams, and Pride would be returning with the professor to Washington. None of them took the news well. All four men wanted to stay in Africa and shoot Nazis, but Flannigan was adamant with his decision, and the Marines followed orders.

Jameson pulled the professor aside before he left to join the president and prime minister on their journey to the fabled city of Marrakesh. The city was about one hundred fifty miles from Casablanca, and the trip would take several hours over what passed for good roads in Morocco. The captain warned James to avoid getting too involved in side projects for the president. Admiral King wanted James back under his control in Washington as soon as possible, but Roosevelt had requested the professor for the journey home. Knowing the president would ask or want all sorts of unusual items or discuss his ideas on strategy, King was concerned, but an order was an order. Brand would once again be on a twenty-four-hour call to do whatever the president wanted. James didn't mind his time with the president and found the conversations with the commander in chief stimulating and sometimes humorous.

The trip to the city in the Atlas Mountains was scenic and made James think of his home in Arizona. The mountains were extremely rugged, and as the long convoy of vehicles drove toward the city, the landscape changed from scrub desert to green valleys and lush vegetation on the hillsides. The temperature got cooler, topping out at fifty-four degrees Fahrenheit. The city was situated at an altitude of fifteen hundred feet, with the nearby Atlas Mountains ranging over nine thousand feet. The mountains were covered in snow, and the deep blue sky framed the mountain peaks like a painting. Staying at the home of the American Vice Counsel, the location was unique and at the same time the sandstone buildings with the dark red roof tiles created an image that was both breathtaking and romantic.

Churchill had President Roosevelt taken up to the top tower of the building to witness the sunset. James went to another location to take in the view, but nothing as spectacular as seen by the two war leaders. Looking out at the olive trees and gardens of the enormous villa, James thought of his fiancée. For the past few weeks, he had written only four letters to Lady Margret, and now he was feeling melancholy and longed for her company.

Seeing the expression on the young man's face, Gunny eased his way over and asked, "James, are you thinking of a particular young lady?"

James was slow to respond. He rarely showed his emotions, but he knew Gunny understood his dilemma. "Gunny, I haven't been thinking enough of Lady Margret. I've been all wrapped up with the plans and the meetings. I'm not sure if I'm cut out for marriage. What should I do?"

Never being a father, but knowing how it felt to be young and in love, the old Marine quietly pointed his finger at the last rays of sunlight glowing over the mountains. James followed the finger and studied the light and the few clouds working their way over the mountain peaks. Finally, the last vestiges of sunlight were gone. Stars quickly came out, a few at first, but suddenly the skies filled with thousands of lights, some flashing, some steady. Gunny finally replied, "James, the world is filled with mystery. I'm sure you could tell me all about the light we just saw. You could tell me all about the stars in the sky and probably about the composition of the mountains and every physical thing in sight."

James said nothing but waited as the old man continued gazing at the sky above him. Finally, sensing what the Marine was seeing, Brand looked up as well. Nothing was said for at least a minute. Finally, Gunny said, "James, Margret is like those stars out there. Mysterious, distant, luminous, and hard to understand. Love is the same. You'll find your way, just like you know how to navigate using those stars. Lady Margret is your north star, and that is all you need to remember. You will be back together, but knowing your mission, you will have to leave again soon. Take the time you have together and enjoy the mysteries of love and of the stars above us."

At first, Brand didn't quite understand the philosophy of what Gunny was saying but later that night, he began writing a letter to Lady Margret, at last he found his voice. He expressed his true feelings for her and made her a promise, which he knew might be hard to keep.

19

30 January 1943
Algiers, French North Africa

- Guadalcanal--147th Infantry takes up pursuit of enemy westward.
- New Guinea--Australian Kanga Force, which is being reinforced by air, decisively defeats Japanese at Wau and forces them to begin retreating.
- Tunisia--In British 1st Army area, Germans attack Faid Pass and overrun it, forcing French back to Sidi Bou Zid.
  - U.S. II Corps sends Combat Command A, 1st Armored Division from Sbeitla area to help defend Faid, but the combat command arrives too late.
- USSR--Rail junction of Tikhoretsk, south of Rostov, falls to Red Army, cutting main line of retreat of German Army Group A from Novorossisk area.
- Germany--RAF Mosquitoes make daylight attack on Berlin during the celebration of the 10th anniversary of Hitler's assumption of power. Grand Adm. Karl Doenitz succeeds Grand Adm. Erich Raeder as commander in chief of the German Navy.
- Rennell Island--Land and carrier-based naval aircraft engage Japanese aircraft attacking Rear

> Adm. Giffen's cruiser and destroyer forces. (Battle of Rennell Island, 29-30 January).
> • United States naval vessel sunk: Heavy cruiser **Chicago** (CA-29), by aircraft torpedo.

The papers were piled high on the desk. Every few minutes, another soldier or sailor entered the small office and added to the growing mountain. Staff Sergeant McBride tried to make room for another set of files but gave up and started placing everything on the floor with a large piece of paper on top listing the general nature of the reports underneath. Some sheets noted "Inbound Convoys," with the one next to it titled "Oil Storage." So far, Meyers had created two dozen categories to classify the incoming reports into some semblance of order. The army, army air force, and navy had different definitions, vocabularies, and symbols, making the situation difficult to understand. Meyers was not much of a drinking man, but the war in North Africa might turn him into a drunk.

The captain spent much of his time dealing with the British port authorities and American supply officers. The amount of infighting between the services was only exceeded by the indifference of the British. The Royal Navy didn't think it was their responsibility to help a Yank captain determine when or where ships docked, nor were they particularly concerned about the speed of unloading those vessels. But cargo intended for British forces received the highest priority. The Americans usually had to barter to get anything accomplished, especially with the French-controlled dockworkers. If the Yanks paid more money to get their supplies unloaded, the British would howl all the way to Eisenhower about the need to maintain standard labor practices and lower pay scales.

Attempting but not succeeding at sorting through the many dead ends of the logistics information war, Jameson refused to admit defeat. He had a few arms left to twist to secure the information he needed. The key man was the naval aide for General Eisenhower, Lieutenant Commander Harry Butcher. A reserve officer who joined the navy in 1939, the former vice president of CBS radio station WJSV in Washington, D.C., got to know the general early in the war. Their friendship was a stabilizing factor in Eisenhower's life as the commanding general in North Africa. Jameson had become acquainted with the radio man in

1940 when he returned to active duty in Washington. Both men shared many of the same interests, and as Butcher developed his association with the general, Butcher and Jameson stayed in close communications.

Tonight, Jameson was going to meet Butcher at Eisenhower's private residence, Villa dar el Ouard, a large villa near the beach. Here, the general's closest staff would meet with the commanding general late into the evening, primarily working but sometimes playing cards. Hopefully, the captain could nudge his friend Harry to open a line of communication to the beleaguered general. McBride would drive Jameson to the residence and wait outside with the general's large guard unit.

As Jameson went through the final security check to enter the building, he saw Butcher waving a bottle of beer in his direction. Greeting the smiling radio executive turned naval officer, the captain said, "Harry, you look natural in the uniform, especially with a beer in your hand."

Butcher saluted the superior officer with the beer bottle. As the two men shook hands, Harry escorted his friend into the foyer of the large house. Seeing the luxurious marble floors and ornate furniture, Jameson said, "Harry, it must be nice to live in a grand house. Beats the hell-hole-of-a-place I'm staying."

In grandiose style, Butcher extended his arms, showing off the salon with its concert grand piano, lavish adornments, and of all things a ping pong table. "Captain, or can I call you Fred, this place has no heat, the running water is a mystery, and the kitchen requires wood to make the ovens work. Otherwise, it's not bad," the commander responded with a smirk before pulling a cold beer from an ice-filled tub sitting on a small table next to the piano.

Jameson replied, "Harry, you can always call me Fred. Except in the presence of a senior officer. Until then, we'll keep it casual."

Noting the serious tone of the captain's speech, Butcher quickly agreed. "Understood, Fred. Still getting used to the situation around here. Ike, I mean General Eisenhower is besieged by every British, French, and American general, diplomat, or flunky on the whole damn African continent. Besides that, he's constantly replying to communications from Washington, London, and Cairo. The air forces are always mad for some reason, and the navy, really the British navy, is asking for more of everything to support their convoys and expand port operations."

Looking at his friend from pre-war days, Butcher quietly asked, "I hope you haven't come here looking for some sort of help with whatever the hell you're doing? I don't think Ike has the tolerance for more political games."

"Actually, Harry, that's the reason I'm here. Admiral King told me to get a hold on the supply situation in North Africa and then assist in the preliminary planning for the Sicily operation."

Not pausing long, Jameson looked around the room and then quietly said, "Based upon what I've seen so far, I doubt we could arrange to invade anything in the Mediterranean until at least 1944. Every command is proceeding like it's some sort of damn stateside maneuver. Each service is concerned with only their units and not the bigger picture. And when you throw the Brits into the mix, everything really goes to hell."

Harry took note of the lines in his friend's face and how they had deepened since their last meeting. He then thought about the man's mysterious role in the North African campaign. While Eisenhower waited out the invasions in Gibraltar's tunnels, Jameson was landing on the beaches of Casablanca within six hours of the initial attack. He had seen several memos with Fred's name on them, acting at the direction of Admiral Hewitt or Admiral King. Unsure of what the man's mission was, he decided to ask.

"Fred, you're still a mystery to me. I'm not sure what your role is, except being a science aide to Admiral King. Are you still doing the same thing?"

Jameson knew the relationship between Butcher and Eisenhower. The naval aide was more of a political officer and personal assistant, handling the press and being a sounding board for the many issues facing the general. Thinking about the best way to approach his mission, the captain decided to show Harry his orders. Pulling an envelope out of his inside coat pocket, he handed it to him, saying, "Harry, this will explain my mission."

Butcher opened the envelope, and upon seeing the opening lines, he looked up at the now even more mysterious officer and then quickly read the orders. The signatures at the bottom of the page were Marshall, King, and Arnold. Handing the letter back to Jameson, the commander said, "Seems you have significant friends that outrank Ike. I think you wouldn't show that to me unless you thought it very important."

"Harry, I don't like to use my orders unless it's essential. I think the time has come to get everyone in this command focused on the logistic issues, or otherwise we'll be sitting here a year from now."

"Is it that bad? I thought things were moving well in the ports, and the supply situation was only getting better?"

"Appearances are deceiving. Each service is trying to do its best, but the overall coordination suffers from too many chiefs. The British add to this problem as well, and the lack of unity of command makes decision-making difficult, slow, and sometimes, damn impossible."

Eisenhower's aide mulled the situation over in his head. The commanding general was being attacked from every angle, including the Germans. The British commanders thought he was a good politician but had zero strategic sense. Ike had never commanded combat units, leading most of his subordinate commanders to think him naive on how to fight the Nazis. Now, an obscure navy captain, who was an influential scientist, held orders that could counter anything Eisenhower said or did. But knowing Jameson as a gentleman and a man of great ability and integrity, he knew whatever the captain had to say was worth any short-term pain.

"All right, Fred. Ike will be back at the villa in about an hour. As soon as he comes in, I will set him up to meet with you. Since your orders are pretty clear cut, I'm sure the general will listen with great interest." With nothing else to do for the next hour, Butcher gave Jameson a tour of the villa, and then both men sat in the dining room waiting for the general to come home.

Two hours later the weary, somewhat agitated general walked into the villa accompanied by his chief of staff, Major General Walter "Beetle" Smith, who was holding a giant rolled-up map of some part of North Africa. As the two generals entered the dining room, Butcher and Jameson stood at attention, with the naval aide stating the obvious. "General, you look better than you did yesterday, but that's not saying much."

Both generals smiled at the good-natured officer. Seeing a navy captain standing next to his aide, Eisenhower said, "Captain Jameson, I heard you were up here helping out our supply situation, but I didn't know you knew Harry."

With a slight grin, Jameson said, "General, good to see you again, sir. I have known the commander since he found his way to the holy cause of the United States Navy back in 1940. I believe he is still trying to win you over to the true light."

Laughing at the observation and recalling the last time he briefly met with Jameson at the Casablanca Conference, the commanding general asked, "So you know Harry, and that's why you're here, or is there something I need to know?"

General Smith sensed something was up. He, too, had met Jameson back in the early days of the war when Jameson and his young protégée provided information on the war plans being formulated by Eisenhower and his planning team. He sensed that something was going on, and Ike would not be pleased.

"General, I need to speak with you considering the overall logistics effort in your theater of operations and the challenges facing not only the present situation in Tunisia but also HUSKY."

Ike's face went from a grin to a frown in a matter of seconds. Before Eisenhower could reply, his faithful chief of staff jumped into the conversation. "Captain, what the hell is your job anyway? Admiral Hall and our supply command are working on the problems."

Eisenhower recalled how the captain and the young man people called the professor were tightly linked to the American military's senior command. He quietly took over the conversation before anyone would become more upset.

"Captain, as I recall, you work for Admiral King. Is that still the case?"

"Yes sir. I report to Admiral Edwards, the CNO's chief of staff. Perhaps my orders will help you understand my mission."

Handing the letter over to the commander in chief, Ike quickly read the orders and then handed them to Smith. The chief of staff looked at Eisenhower and then handed the orders back to the navy captain.

"Seems you have me at a disadvantage, Captain Jameson. Knowing you and the young professor, I think you would not bother me unless something was going on which hindered my mission. Let's go into the study and tell me what's on your mind."

Turning to Butcher, Ike said, "Harry, you and Beetle should come along. I think the good captain is going to give us something to think about, which may not be to our liking."

As the four men walked into the study, Butcher closed the door behind him. Over the next thirty minutes, Captain Jameson outlined the current situation, the challenges caused by the lack of organization. The navy's Science Team leader offered up a set of recommendations to unify the command, set priorities, establish specific goals, and change the timing for significant projects and troop buildups. All of these ideas were backed up with examples and a few recommendations for leadership changes. Eisenhower saw the wisdom in the plan and the need to remove some deadwood, which was causing many of the delays in getting men, machines, and supplies to where the fighting was taking place.

Later, Harry Butcher escorted his friend out of the villa with a promise to check in on him in a few days to see if the new orders coming down from the commanding general were making a difference. The commander shook Jameson's hand and whispered, "Fred, you sure know how to shake up an organization. But what you have recommended is just what Ike needs. I think he's afraid that once the Germans get past this muddy season, they will come at us with full force, and he doesn't think we're ready for them."

Jameson didn't smile but replied, "Harry, I've seen some bad things in this war, and I can tell you, we're never ready for what may happen. You just have to do your damn best and do whatever it takes to prepare. Lives depend on it."

The Second Armored Division's headquarters was situated near Rabat, the home of the Sultan of Morocco. The two Marines didn't have time to tour the old city but focused on their mission. After spending the past few days with the Third Infantry Division, they moved on to see how the army trained their armored forces. Neither Flannigan nor Sergeant Dean had much experience with tanks, primarily because the Marine Corps had so few of them. There were several light Stuart tanks on Guadalcanal, but moving large, armored vehicles around in a jungle was arduous if not impossible. The desert conditions had proven the perfect terrain for fast armored assaults. Field Marshal Erwin Rommel had shown this many times, much to British chagrin, who were finally using their tanks to good advantage.

The two men were waiting in the outer office of the division's commanding officer, Major General Ernest Harmon, when they were ushered inside. Seated behind a large desk, probably taken from the previous French commander of the building, the general watched as the two Marines marched within five feet of the desk and came to attention.

"At ease, men. Welcome to the Second Armored Division."

"Sir, my name is Flannigan, and this is Sergeant Dean. We are pleased to be here."

Harmon looked at the two men in field uniforms with rows of ribbons across their chest. He noticed both men were highly decorated, seeing the major had been awarded the Navy Cross, Silver Star, and Purple Heart and saw similar awards on the sergeant's uniform. He knew he was dealing with professionals.

"Major, Sergeant, good to have you here. General Patton told me to expect your visit and to let you see how we operate. I understand you have done an outstanding job with General Anderson's Third Infantry and hope you will have some ideas which could help our command."

"General, we look forward to learning how your division operates, and if there are any things we could do to assist with their training."

Harmon directed the two men to take a seat and then asked a series of pointed questions.

"Major, I see you and the sergeant have both been in combat. Can you tell me where and to what extent?"

"General, we were at Midway Island and then the invasion of Tulagi and Guadalcanal."

"Were you wounded at Guadalcanal?"

"No sir, I failed to move quickly enough in the Philippines, but since then, I have learned to be much faster." Flannigan kept a straight face, not knowing if the humor would be out of line.

The general laughed and said, "Major, it looks like you have learned a lot since then. How did you get out of the Philippines?"

"General, I was serving as the Marine aide to Admiral Hart, and after I was wounded during the bombing at Cavite, I was sent out with the last ships leaving Manila."

Looking at the Marine again, he noticed the burns on his right hand. Figuring they went up to his arm and perhaps on the rest of his torso, Harmon changed the subject. He knew now these two men could be of help to his command. The invasion of French Morocco had been, in his own words, a "cakewalk," so anyone who had been in combat with a determined enemy was worth his time.

"Major, General Patton told me about your mission and how you work for Admiral King. He also told me General Eisenhower has used your team's services to his advantage on more than one occasion. If Ike likes you, that's all I need to know. I will arrange a tour of the command this afternoon and then tell me what else you would like to do. I will have my aide, Captain Thomas, be your official guide. I would also like your candid opinion on anything you see which could be improved or changed. Any questions?"

"No sir. We look forward to observing your men and learning how they expect to fight the Germans. We have been briefed by General Patton on the situation in North Africa, and one of our team has spent time with General Eisenhower to examine the strategic situation in Tunisia."

Harmon was immediately interested in the last comment about the supreme commander. Anyone who had access to Ike must be in the know as to what was happening in Tunisia. The tank general was itching to get into the fight but knew his division would probably not participate in the battles against Rommel. Patton had already told him his unit would probably be the spearhead for the recently approved invasion of Sicily. His assistant division commander was already working on the preliminary plans for this next phase of the war.

After the two Marines left his office, Harmon placed a phone call to his friend George Patton, making additional inquiries into how influential Major Flannigan was within the military hierarchy. The II Corps commander made it clear to the armored division commander to listen closely to whatever the Marine told him. Patton then shared how the major's youngest associate, a youthful navy lieutenant, who was also a physics professor, tutored Eisenhower and himself on German tactics and the current logistics problems facing Ike's army in Tunisia. After hearing this report, the general placed calls to each of his senior commanders to ensure they all took advantage of Flannigan's time in their units. Harmon knew the battle for Tunisia was in a confused state, and an experienced combat officer, even a Marine, could help his division improve.

If this was the dry season, the sweating officer wondered what the hell the wet season was like. As the man sipped on his cool, but definitely not cold drink, he waited for the bureaucrat to show up. Cavendish was a strange bird, or so thought Lieutenant Beck. The man was incorrigible, yet his many indiscretions meshed with the American's more extensive plans. As long as Rolle and his British associates were appropriately rewarded for their efforts, all would go well for his newest project. Today's meeting was to get the dates and times for the movement of trucks carrying foodstuffs north toward the air bases in Assam, six hundred miles north of Calcutta. Most of the transport ships had been sent to Karachi because of the presence of enemy submarines operating from India down to the straits of Madagascar. The Japanese started bombing Calcutta in early December, and nearly a dozen raids had occurred since then. The dock area had been hit but without much physical effect. However, the morale of the thousands of dockworkers was affected and many had vacated the area. The British were trying to cajole them back with more pay, which tended to sway the workers' opinions.

But a few convoys had made it, and the last one came from South Africa carrying flour, sugar, and other non-perishable food items. These supplies were meant for the workers building the airfields in Assam province and air shipment to Kunming in China, the terminus for the Air Transport Command. *Flying the Hump,* as it was called, was dangerous, and some of the pilots Beck had met when they were on leave in Calcutta were stressed and in poor health. Flying over the Himalayas at altitudes of twelve thousand to sixteen thousand feet in unpressurized planes, with only rudimentary navigation equipment was a dangerous occupation. If a pilot could not find the passes at these lower altitudes, he was forced to fly over the mountains, which ranged upwards of twenty-six thousand feet, far above the capabilities of a heavily laden aircraft. One of the exhausted pilots told Beck that it was easy to get to Kunming; all you had to do was look down and follow the silver aluminum pieces of crashed American planes.

Finally, Cavendish arrived and sat down next to the navy officer. No one would consider the meeting out of the ordinary. Both men were involved with port operations, so it was natural that some of their work would be carried out in a bar, part of a good old English tradition. Beck determined no one was watching them, and after Rolle received his gin and tonic, the two men got down to business.

"Beck, how goes the American war effort? Any news from the missing convoy?"

"Nothing new from the ships. Seems they ran into a submarine south of the Gulf of Mannar, which caused the convoy to scatter. A few ships turned around and headed back to Cochin. One was hit but did not sink and was escorted to the base at Colombo in Ceylon. I think the others will show up in another two or three days."

"Too bad the Japs are so busy punching holes in our ships. Bad for business, you know."

"I think the submarines doing the damage are German. One of the reports I read this morning said a German U-boat was sighted and attacked by one of the escorts, but it got away."

Rolle swished his finger in his drink. "Damn! Seems that Jerry wants to slow our supply ships as well as the Japanese. Anything being done about it?"

Contemplating whether to order another drink before they got down to business, Beck said, "I have heard something about the Germans getting some sort of intelligence about our convoy routing. Not sure, but one of the British commanders I met mentioned the Germans using a merchant ship holed up in Goa as the source of information. But I may be wrong about it. I'm sure the Portuguese wouldn't want to cause you Brits any anguish over enemy merchants interred in their harbor."

The British port official knew Beck was using Colonel Granger as an intermediary for the movement of money to Goa and eventually moving it to Lisbon for safekeeping. "Yes, I think our friends in Goa wouldn't want to be implicated in nefarious spy games by their guests. But perhaps this may be to our advantage. Any attention placed on a neutral country keeps eyes from looking into the diversion of supplies."

Nodding, Beck asked about the next large shipment. "When will the trucks start moving north to Assam?"

"I believe there will be some forty-five trucks, escorted by a platoon of Indian troops leaving on February 3. If all goes well, they will arrive at the Assam and Bengal Railroad terminus within a week, perhaps ten days. Then the train will move ever so slowly north to your aviation people in north India."

"Are we prepared to move some of this inventory to other locations? Do we have the timetables and overnight camps located?"

Rolle smiled and said, "Yes, all is set. Our man has arranged for a change of itinerary on day five of the journey. He has been instructed to relocate two trucks to Bhagalpur, where interested parties are waiting. Since this city is on the Ganges, it will be simple to move items of interest along the river. The entire province of Bihar has many buyers, and my old friend and associate will supervise the transaction."

"What about the payment?"

"Again, my friend will move the funds into more stable currency, and within ten days payment will be made here in Calcutta. The normal fee of five percent of the total proceeds assures his commitment and silence. He knows the punishment for any deviations."

Beck had thought about this problem early on. The underworld in India was more extensive than most believed. Small-time crooks, robbers, and burglars were everywhere in the major cities. Still, a few enterprising groups of men had agreed to areas of control based upon a geographical analysis of the many provinces within the giant country. Making inroads into these organizations was relatively easy, and once an agreement was made with the local Calcutta group, a nationwide formula was established. These men would take the majority of the risks and money, but as Beck told his British associates, the remaining amount dwarfed anything they thought possible. The criminal organizations were very pleased with the arrangement. They knew the Englishmen and lone American would keep their end of the bargain as well, and once the war was over, they would depart India, leaving the majority of the winnings in the pockets of local gang leaders.

The U.S. Navy officer gazed out the window, noticing the daily torrent of rain had slowed to a manageable downpour. Refocusing on the subject at hand, he asked, "What are the plans for the fuel shipments? I understand barges are being purchased to move drums of aviation fuel to the airfields. Any progress on having a few of these items disappear during the voyage?"

The civilian port manager sipped his drink and scanned the room. Seeing no threats to the conversation, he whispered, "This is still a problem. I know when the barges will start moving north, but there is still no regular schedule established. I think within the next month or so, I should be able to tell you exactly the number of barges headed up the Brahmaputra River each week. My sources tell me each barge will carry mainly aviation fuel, but twenty-five percent will be gasoline or diesel. Much of the fuel will then be transported on planes across to China. I think that if we could see a two or three percent waste factor for drums going overboard, no one would notice."

"Good idea not to get too greedy on the fuel. It has quick resale value, and no one would ever know what became of it. I'm sure the empty drums also have value in the secondary market?"

"Of course they do. I think each one will be quickly purchased for a nice profit. I need to inform our friends about this and set a price for both the fuel and the barrels so we know our share of the proceeds."

Beck wanted to smile but didn't. Here he was with a British civil servant plotting to "lose" war supplies and working out ways to cover these activities on the books by planning in advance a certain amount of what Rolle called "spoilage." The civilian government in India had centuries of experience on how things really worked in the sprawling country. It was expected that specific amounts of every item shipped into the country would go missing. This meant you planned for the losses and did not bother to explain what happened and instead simply placed another order for the same items. The American sipped his drink and thought to himself, *India is an exceptional place, and spending time on the subcontinent should be an extremely lucrative venture.*

20

2 February 1943
Logistics Research Department
Washington, D.C.

- Guadalcanal--1st Battalion, 147th Infantry, succeeds in crossing Bonegi River and makes contact with 3rd Battalion south of Tassafaronga Point.
- Tunisia--In British First Army's U.S. II Corps area, 1st Armored Division headquarters opens at Sbeitla: Combat Command D drives to ridge east of Sened, where it digs in and repels counterattack.
- USSR--Final resistance of German 6th Army at Stalingrad ends, concluding epic struggle that has turned the tide against the Axis. Action in other sectors is unabated as Red Army endeavors to drive enemy as far west as possible before spring thaw.

The presidential train arrived on Sunday night, January 31, to the ice and snow of Washington. The trip from Casablanca was memorable for each member of the Science Team accompanying President Roosevelt. When the plane arrived back in Trinidad, Admiral Leahy had fully recovered and rejoined the president for the final two legs of the journey home.

The Boeing Clipper flew to Miami, and upon arrival, Roosevelt and his entourage went directly to his train, left the warmth of the south, and headed back to the nation's capital. Along the way, Leahy spent most of his time with the president but had two meetings with James to discuss some of the personalities attending the Morocco conference.

The admiral was interested in the dynamics of the American and British military leaders, specifically, how General Marshall got along with General Brooke. Both men disagreed with one another, and James explained how the two were civil but often cold in their relationship. The professor said that Portal and Arnold were close and agreed on most of the air war decisions, as long as they got their way. Admiral King and Admiral Pound were cordial and only disagreed when discussing ship construction and Pacific strategy. James reserved his analysis on the overall outcome of the meeting. However, he told the president's military advisor that the Americans were still weak in planning and developing strategies. The British were well prepared and had backup plans for almost any question, whether supply, manpower, tactics, or intelligence. The Americans needed to improve their staff work before the next major meeting.

The president told James to take Monday, the first of February, off and told Leahy to communicate this information to Admiral King. Roosevelt knew the young man was desperate to see his fiancée, and the professor deserved at least one day off before returning to the problems the war effort was facing. James and Margret had a wonderful day together and spent much of the time at the British Embassy taking walks in the cold while James told her stories of his latest adventures. But the day ended quickly with a series of dispatches from Captain Jameson, who needed help on convoys heading to North Africa.

The second of February was cold and dreary. The snowfall from the weekend had turned into a gray slush, which messed up the shine on everyone's shoes. As James entered the Logistics Research Department, he was greeted by a different-looking office. When he left, four enlisted men worked diligently on typewriters or developing reports for senior officers. Now, there were eight desks, and four of them were occupied by women. The WAVES (Women Accepted for Voluntary Emergency Service) were seated doing the same job as the four men. As he came into the office, the four WAVES jumped to attention, while the four men

157

slowly got up from their desk, with one of them calling out, "Good to have you back, Lieutenant. Did you bring us a flying carpet?"

James laughed at the comment and quickly told everyone to take their seats. The four new members of the Naval Reserve had been told very little about the organization or the unit's leadership. They knew the group was top secret and employed a unique staff of highly educated officers researching various aspects of the war effort. As the Marines came into the room, smiles from the young women were quickly returned. Before Brand could speak further, Lieutenant Stevens walked out of his office with Ensigns Rollins and Billingsley, plus a young woman officer.

"James, good to have you back home. How was the trip?"

Looking around the office, James replied, "The trip was good but very long. It looks like there have been some additions since I left. Please introduce me."

"Sure, James. This is Ensign Nancy Pollard, who joined us two weeks ago. She was teaching at George Washington until she joined up in August."

"Good to meet you, Ensign. Please call me James from now on. What did you teach?"

"Good to meet you, sir. I taught mathematics and was studying for my doctorate degree when I volunteered to join the service."

Ensign Pollard was an attractive lady in her mid-twenties. Her hair was auburn, and she was tall for the day, standing five-feet ten inches. She wore glasses and had the look of a good researcher. James would soon rely on her ability to do statistical analysis of his many projects.

"Glad to have you aboard, Ensign. Please let me introduce Warrant Officer "Gunny" Jones and Lieutenant Bill Waverly, who leads our security detail."

Waverly moved forward and, being a bit awkward at first, mumbled, "Good to meet you, Ensign Pollard."

Nancy smiled at the officer, who she guessed was in his early thirties. She saw the rows of ribbons on the man's chest and knew he was not a staff officer but a warrior. Pollard had heard only a few stories about the men in this group. Lieutenant Stevens said little, but occasionally, she overheard whispers about where the professor was or how the captain was meeting with the chief of staff. When she was chosen to join this department, she had been told by Commander Allen the group was not only top-secret, but their leaders were associated with the senior command of the Allies.

As she met the young man called the professor by Rollins and Billingsley, she realized the unit was engaged in critical operations. The armed Marines' presence further reinforced her assumption, and she wanted to get to know more about the duties and responsibilities of the men in the command. She didn't have to wait long to find out.

James invited Stevens and his officers into his office, as well as Lieutenant Waverly. Gunny stayed outside the room, sitting at his desk. Nancy had not been in the locked office before, and when she entered it, and the lights came on, she saw a blackboard full of equations beyond her comprehension. Several large sheets of paper were pasted on the walls, each having either lists of projects or large maps with pins stuck in places all around the world. Before she could examine anything in-depth, James told Waverly to shut the door. Then he told everyone to grab a chair and prepare to take notes.

Stevens, Rollins, and Billingsley came into the room with note pads, but the newest member did not know to bring anything with her. She started to say something, but James seeing her plight, went to his desk and pulled out a pad of paper and a pencil. As he gave her these items, he smiled and said quietly, "Don't worry. You'll get the hang of things soon."

Moving closer to a large map of the Atlantic, the lecture began. "As you all know, my recent mission to Africa allowed me to get close to some of the senior British officers I had not met before. The meetings of the Combined Chiefs of Staff were difficult, and just like the last one, the British did a much better job in their staff work. The ideas they presented were well thought out and backed up with lots of supporting information. I think General Marshall had a lot of egg on his face, but that's all water under the bridge. The plans were set for the war effort for the remainder of 1943 and into 1944. The most urgent item was the Battle of the Atlantic and ending the U-boat scourge. Without control of the sea lanes, we cannot build up the forces required to invade the continent. There were many other agreements, but the president has tasked us with providing an assessment of the nation's ability to meet the construction timetable for the escort ships. This includes timetables for the delivery of materials, launchings, commissioning, and crewing of several hundred destroyers, destroyer escorts, and escort carriers by the end of the year. Also, we need to investigate delays in building more long-range patrol bombers, which will help neutralize the German submarines."

Looking around the room at the logistics officer and then at his Marine security officer, who had listened to many conversations on the long flight back to the States, James concluded his remarks. "This is only the first phase of the information we need to pull together for Admiral Leahy. I will work with Admiral Edwards on whatever delays we discover. We need to find every hinderance in obtaining these ships and planes. Any schedule not met will mean the death of an Allied sailor or soldier. We must destroy the German submarine fleet. Any questions?"

Looking around the room, Nancy saw only the look of grim determination on each person's face. These men knew their mission, and after hearing Lieutenant Brand's speech, she now understood the importance of her work. Nothing was more important than stopping the U-boats, and at last, she felt that she could make a real contribution to the war effort.

Only later did the new ensign find out how this problem was only one of hundreds affecting the war. She also would find out more about the navy officer who looked like he was still in high school and how he spent time with the war's leaders. Now, she would fight her way through reams of papers, searching for anything which might delay the building of the ships the Allies needed to win the war in the depths of the Atlantic.

It was late in the afternoon when James was ordered to Admiral Edward's office. Gunny remained at his post, with Waverly accompanying the professor to the admiral's office. Upon arrival, James was told to wait until called. Taking their seats, the two men were quickly engaged in a conversation with Commander Allen.

"Good to have you back stateside. How was Morocco?"

"Great seeing you again, Commander. I thought by now you would be out chasing U-boats on a destroyer."

Smiling at the professor, Allen replied, "I wish I was just about anywhere but here. Yet, as they say, it is my duty to follow the orders of my superior officer." Looking at Waverly, he added, "How do you like working for the Science Team? Anything interesting to report?"

"Commander, I'm not sure what to say about the job. I have met many important people, including the president. So far, things are going well."

Allen thought it was a diplomatic answer, knowing the Marine would instead prefer to be back with his old unit storming some beach in the Pacific. Not saying anything more, the commander told James what was going on in the admiral's office.

"James, the admiral has two visitors who want to speak with you. I know Admiral Train, the Director of Naval Intelligence, but I don't know who the general is. Not sure what's going on, but they want to talk to you." Turning to Waverly, Allen said, "Lieutenant, you are to wait here."

Not needing to reply to the order, Waverly nodded his head in understanding. Not that he liked it, the Marine was becoming accustomed to waiting outside meeting rooms until instructed to do something else. Allen was soon interrupted by Edward's secretary telling him to escort Brand into the room.

As the two men entered, both came to attention, waiting for instructions about what to do next. Edwards quickly said, "At ease, gentlemen. Commander, I will not need you in this meeting. Please make sure we are not interrupted."

The commander came back to attention and then walked out of the room. Edwards rose to shake Brand's hand and introduce the two men seated at the table.

"Lieutenant, good to have you back from Morocco. Admiral King has said many a good thing about you since he returned. I think he wants to meet with you tomorrow to discuss some of the agreements made with the British."

Turning toward the two men still seated at the table, Edwards introduced the senior officers. "Brand, meet Admiral Train, Director of Naval Intelligence, and General Donovan, Director of the Office of Strategic Services."

"It's an honor to meet you, Admiral Train, General Donovan."

Both men peered at the tall young officer. Train knew of Brand from his sources in the CNO's office but had never met the man. Brand's reputation was stellar within the navy. Yet, his exploits in developing intelligence outside normal channels had caused some concerns within his hierarchy. The old navy didn't like mavericks, especially ones who got results or questioned the official analysis of the Office of Naval Intelligence (ONI).

General Donovan was different. He was a personal friend of President Roosevelt and had been chosen to build and then lead the American foreign intelligence service. This caused the ire of both the army and navy intelligence services. This also included the FBI, whose director, J. Edgar Hoover, believed everything related to spying, including foreign and domestic intelligence, was his domain. Roosevelt thought differently. Over the years before the war, Donovan had been a one-man intelligence service for the president. "Wild Bill," as his friend called him, was a successful lawyer with international business interests, which allowed him to build an informal network of influential people throughout the world. These individuals fed the former Wall Street lawyer a steady stream of information concerning the leadership of nations and each country's economic situation. As head of the intelligence service, Donovan was leading the effort to garner information about the enemy and build an effective spy network.

Train remained seated, demonstrating the man's traditional navy behavior. Donovan stood and approached the lieutenant. "Lieutenant Brand, it's wonderful to meet you at last. The president has told me about you and the many great things you have accomplished for the war effort. He even told me about you jumping in a plane at Guadalcanal to shoot down two enemy aircraft." Laughing, he continued, "Splendid job, but he also told me you will never do this again."

James looked closely at the general's jacket. His ribbons signified the man had won every medal for valor the American army awarded, including the Medal of Honor. This was a warrior who knew firsthand the danger and cost of war. James was now captivated by whatever the general had to say.

Edwards sat down and pointed Brand to the chair next to him, stating the purpose of the meeting. "Brand, these two officers are working on our situation regarding the government of Portugal."

James quickly concluded it must be about the Azores and what was known as the Azores air-gap. The expanding series of bases and long-range aircraft such as the B-24 Liberator slowly filled the North Atlantic with air reconnaissance, which could hurt the German submarine campaign. These aviation assets were capable of searching great distances from bases in Newfoundland, Bermuda, Greenland, Iceland, and Britain's south coast. However, even with new long-range models coming off the production line, there was still a hole in the surveillance system in the middle of the Atlantic, which could only be filled by bases in the Azores.

Donovan could see the lieutenant mulling over the information and quickly added, "Lieutenant, based upon your anti-submarine work for Admiral King, you realize the situation with the hole we have around the middle of the Atlantic can only be filled by an airbase in the Azores. You also know of Portugal's neutrality in this war, and the Allies respect this decision. Great Britain has a treaty with the Portuguese dating to 1373, making it the oldest treaty still existing in the world. Our British friends have not invoked the provisions of this treaty and for a good reason. The dictator of Portugal, Salazar, fears an immediate retaliation from Hitler, including a full-scale invasion of his country. Also, there are other reasons which make Portugal's nonalignment important to our cause."

Admiral Train now entered the conversation. "Mr. Brand, we have other considerations besides building an airbase in the Azores. The Portuguese provide us with a good location to listen to what is going on in Europe. We have diplomatic posts in Spain, Switzerland, Sweden, Turkey and Ireland, but the Portuguese are the easiest to deal with. Our government doesn't want to jeopardize our ability to get into and out of Portugal. I think you might know what we're talking about."

The professor had taken in all of the information, knowing the two senior officers were speaking at a high level and not offering more details. This didn't bother James because he immediately connected the dots on what else was in jeopardy besides building an airfield. There must be significant intelligence operations underway in the small country, and being fearful of Hitler attacking this enclave of neutrality could jeopardize something more critical.

Donovan supplemented the information. "Another thing to consider about our relationship with Portugal is the export of wolfram. Salazar took over all the mines late last year and controls the mineral's export to both Britain and Germany. Interestingly, the Portuguese demand immediate payment for these exports, which are equally distributed to both warring parties. But the British pay in Pounds while the Germans must pay in gold. We aren't sure, but there must be millions of dollars' worth of gold sitting in Portuguese banks, probably stolen from countries the Nazis invaded in the war."

Edwards then offered up the reason for the briefing. "Brand, we have our *chargé d'affaires* in Lisbon, George Kennan, who is working with our intelligence services to watch what is happening with the wolfram exports. He is also working with the British ambassador and their sources to help influence the Portuguese decision-making on the Azores. He has requested help in understanding what is happening with the export of the wolfram and hampering the Nazi's efforts to acquire more wolfram than they are officially entitled."

James quickly thought they wanted him to go to Portugal, but that idea was quickly washed away by Edwards. "Professor, you are not being asked to go to Lisbon, but I had a recommendation on who we could send to help our people in Lisbon. We need someone with a legal background, someone who also understands logistics and is fluent in French. Not many people speak Portuguese, but Salazar's official communications are in French, plus many of his staff are French speakers. I thought we could send Lieutenant Meyers. What's your opinion?"

Lights went on in Brand's brain as he considered the options of sending Meyers off to Lisbon for what might be a long time. Captain Jameson depended on the man for his intelligence and ability to work through supply bottlenecks. However, this mission sounded too crucial to the war effort. "Admiral, I think Lieutenant Meyers would be an excellent resource. He is quite good at looking at all aspects of logistics management, and his legal training would be an asset. The lieutenant's experiences in North Africa demonstrate his diplomatic and intelligence gathering abilities. If I may ask, how long would this assignment last?"

Donovan answered the question. "Based upon what Kennan reports, I think a month or more would be needed at first and then a few more trips over the next year to inspect what we are putting into place to support our staff."

The professor analyzed the statement, knowing Kennan was a state department official and probably a member of the fledgling OSS operation. Additional sources were probably being put into the country, including clandestine operatives. Lieutenant Meyers would help set up a surveillance network of the wolfram mines and work with the local British officials on the Azores problem. All of this would take time, but it would not be necessary for the lieutenant to be in the country for the duration.

As Brand framed his reply, Edwards asked, "General Donovan, what do we know of the British efforts in securing Portuguese approval to put an airbase in the Azores?"

The general replied quickly and with the precise wording of a lawyer. "Admiral, our British friends are conflicted on how far they can push Salazar. Their ambassador has urged caution, but the Portuguese ambassador in London is pro-British and helping steer the conversation. I think we could get approval sometime this summer. The other concern is how this will affect our ability to maintain aircraft at a British base. Legally, we are not part of the treaty, and this may be a sticking point. I think your man would help us gauge Portuguese opinion and develop plans for our inclusion."

James considered his answer for a moment. "General Donovan, I think Lieutenant Meyers would be just the man for the job. Captain Jameson will need some assurance this will not be a full-time assignment, but based on your description of his activities, I think it would be a good use of the lieutenant's skills."

Donovan thought about the precision of James Brand's comment. Roosevelt informed him of the professor's strategic thinking and how the young man carefully thought through each problem. The OSS director wondered if he could borrow Brand for some of his future planning as the general ramped up his organization.

Watching the two warriors smile at each other worried Admiral Edwards that the man known as "Wild Bill" would soon try to "borrow" Brand for additional projects. For now, he would remain alert to requests coming from the White House, knowing Donovan might be the source. Sensing agreement on the Meyers issue, the admiral asked, "What do we need to do to get this project moving? I need to contact Captain Jameson to let him know he's going to lose his man. Also, I need to tell him how long the lieutenant will be away."

Donavan explained the next steps. "Once you notify Captain Jameson of the lieutenant's temporary assignment, I will have him meet our Minister to French North Africa, Robert Murphy, who will provide background on the situation he is about to encounter. The State Department is set to get Portuguese clearance for Meyers to be named an assistant naval attaché in Lisbon. This will be his cover, and upon arriving in the country, Kennan will guide him on the other aspects of his mission. Getting him into Portugal will be comparatively easy. We will look at him entering through Spanish Morocco, and from there, he could fly to Madrid and then take the train into Lisbon. One of our people in Lisbon would be waiting to guide him in his other duties."

Edwards pondered all of this with an eye to risk. Having diplomatic credentials would protect his man if he was accused of spying by the Portuguese government. The most significant danger would be from Nazi spies working to keep wolfram supplies flowing north to Germany. Meyers was not a trained spy, nor was he a warrior like Flannigan or the Marine lieutenant guarding the professor. But knowing Meyers as a resourceful officer, the admiral thought the situation would not be overly dangerous. Edward's biggest concern was the impact of Meyers' absence on Jameson's growing number of projects.

21

7 February 1943
Algiers, French North Africa

- Guadalcanal--161st Infantry, 25th Division, crosses Umasani River and advanced northwest to Bunina Point; patrols reach Tambalego River. Japanese force of 18 destroyers in route to Guadalcanal to evacuate troops is attacked by aircraft from Henderson Field; 2 enemy destroyers are damaged.
- China--Generalissimo Chiang Kai-shek, in letter to President Roosevelt, presents enlarged version of his three demands and agrees to take part in Burma offensive.
- Tunisia--In British 1st Army area, 1st Ranger Battalion arrives at Gafsa by air and is attached to U.S. II Corps. RCT 168, 34th Division, is attached to 1st Armored Division.
- USSR--Continuing toward Rostov, Soviet troops take Azov, on the Sea of Azov. In the Ukraine, Kramatorsk, southeast of Kharkov, falls to Red Army.

The men in the small office had worked like dogs for days, trying to get a handle on the supply problems in North Africa. The ports were jammed with cargo and more ships were waiting to unload, but there was insufficient dock space. Warehouses were at capacity and materials were being stored out in the open, ensuring damage by weather or pilferage by the locals. When available, trucks started their slow journey to the east. Road conditions were still terrible. The winter rains had caused flash floods wiping out bridges and roadways. The narrow tracks heading into the central part of Tunisia were in even worse shape. Engineers feverishly toiled night and day to keep the few roads passable, but they were short of equipment such as bulldozers, heavy trucks, cranes, and building materials.

Jameson looked at the last day's report and shook his head. Duncan Clark had just returned from the British port office and added to the captain's misery. "Sir, my countrymen are all cocked-up as usual. Getting any sort of summary of what the hell is coming in on the ships is impossible."

The captain found himself relying more and more on the Scotsman each day. Since the cable arrived outlining Lieutenant Meyers' temporary assignment, Jameson became buried in supply and transportation problems. The lieutenant was scheduled to leave this afternoon for his assignment in Portugal. Jameson had met with Robert Murphy, who briefed Meyers about the situation in Lisbon and how he should act in the neutral nation. An army intelligence officer gave Meyers more detailed information on his duties plus a few pointers on spy craft.

The man gave the lieutenant a list of key contacts, which he was to memorize and then destroy. Nothing could be taken into Spain or onward to Portugal, which could identify him as a covert asset of the American government. The other item discussed was how to deal with enemy agents and officials. Germany and Italy both had large embassies and staffs in the neutral country, and it was probable Meyers would meet them during formal events put on by the Portuguese. The logistics officer and now fledgling spy was also given instructions about meeting various Americans and refugees from European countries living in Lisbon who served as covert watchdogs of the wolfram trade. The best place to meet these individuals was at the seaside casinos at Estoril, some ten miles from Lisbon. Here, expats from all over Europe, including members of royal families, adventurers, and spies, wasted away the war while making financial deals or selling secrets.

Jameson was not happy about the assignment, particularly the amount of risk Meyers might be facing. But the order came from Admiral Edwards, and the lieutenant thought it would be an excellent opportunity. Now the captain was asking for more help, and his friend Commander Butcher promised to find two or three men who could help him clean up the supply situation in North Africa. So far, only one had shown up, a technical sergeant who had years of experience in warehousing for General Motors. Another man was supposed to report tomorrow who had similar qualifications from a trucking company in Ohio. Hopefully, these two new men could work their way through the piles of paper slowly filling the cramped office.

As he pondered the newest convoy report, Jameson heard Sergeant McBride loudly proclaim, "Damn, Major, you look like you've been digging ditches!"

Hearing these words, the captain quickly exited his office and saw Clark and McBride speaking to Flannigan and Dean. Both men were in army utilities, holding on to their helmets, weapons, and dirty beyond belief. Seeing Jameson walk out of his office, both men came to attention. "At ease, you two. Where the hell have you been? I expected you yesterday?"

Flannigan replied, "Sorry, Captain, we had to hitch two rides from Oran, and then the jeep we had broke down outside of town, so we had to get with some trucks heading to Algiers carrying supplies. It took forever, and every hour or so, a truck in the convoy broke down. What a mess."

"Glad to have you aboard. Did you get a good feel for the army units you visited?"

Dusting off his shirt sleeves and wiping his face with what passed for a handkerchief, the major responded, "Sir, the units all looked good. Most of them had some experience with the French, but a few of their battalion commanders told me their men were still way too green to fight the Germans. The equipment looked in good shape, and they maneuvered well in some exercises we witnessed, but I have to agree with one colonel who said his men weren't ready to fight in a bar, let alone in a battle."

The captain walked the exhausted major into his office and shut the door. Looking at the tired-looking Marine, Jameson asked, "What do you think of their officers? Are they ready to lead in battle, or are they better suited for garrison duty?"

Responding to his commanding officer, whom he trusted explicitly and knowing the man only wanted the truth, Flannigan gave his assessment. "Captain, the commanding general of the Second Armored Division knows what to do and has been working his men day and night to get them ready for a battle with the Germans. The infantry units we saw, especially at the battalion and company level, are a mixed bag. The men have no combat experience. Several officers blew off our suggestions, even though only a few of them fought the French. Sergeant Dean told me most of the army sergeants were well trained but led by officers they didn't trust. It all comes down to training and experience. One of the battalion commanders was more than candid, telling me that some of the officers who landed against French opposition were incompetent. Still, nobody wanted to relieve them from their commands. I think if we get into a major battle, we're going to be badly mauled."

"Okay, Robert, let's keep this between ourselves for right now. I know General Eisenhower would like to hear your comments, but he told me he wanted you to head up to General Fredendall's command and meet some of the soldiers who have been fighting the Germans. I think we're in for a big fight soon, and the general could use you and Dean checking on the men of the First Armored Division and the Thirty-Fourth Infantry. Each unit has had some combat against the enemy, but nothing major. Eisenhower wanted to punch a hole in the German center, but he was dissuaded at the Casablanca Conference. We know Rommel is ready to defend against Montgomery at the Mareth Line, but we aren't sure what the Germans north of his position are planning."

Flannigan decided to tell the captain something else. "Sir, I had a conversation when we got to Oran with a British captain, who had been wounded in the first push into Tunisia back in December. He led his company into the mountains near Bizerte when they ran into a determined defense by the Germans. They were able to hold onto their gains, but had to pull back after two days of enemy counterattacks. The Brit told me they had captured a couple of wounded Germans who he interrogated after he was hit. Evidently, these soldiers had been airlifted into Tunis a week before and rushed to the front. Both men had fought in Russia, and before that, one man was a veteran of the battle for France. The Brit told me these men were not only tough but confident."

"I take it that you think we're going to have a tough time fighting these people?"

"Captain, I think we're going to get our butts kicked if we don't toughen up and think smart. From what the Brit told me, and he had been at Dunkirk and then in Greece, the Nazis are not only fierce fighters but also intelligent when it comes to war. I saw a lot of our army officers who thought the Germans would call it quits once they see our troops."

"Don't think that will happen either, but we need to get Eisenhower our best assessment of what our people are capable of doing." Thinking a bit more, Jameson said, "Why don't you and Dean stay in Algiers for the next couple of days and rest up. Get some clean clothes and a shower, too. I'll get you set up to head to II Corps and arrange transportation."

"Thank you, sir. I would like to get the Sahara off me as soon as possible. I think some of the sand is actually camel crap. Sure smells like it, anyway."

Laughing, Jameson replied, "I'll have McBride take you to our billet so you two can clean up. The sergeant can scrounge up some uniforms as well. Plan on dinner with Clark and me tonight, say 1900 hours."

Walking over to the major, Jameson sniffed the air and smiled. "I believe it's more camel than sand, plus some old donkey thrown in. Glad you and Dean are here. Go get a shower and some rest, and we'll talk later."

Shaking the dirty officer's hand in gratitude and friendship, Jameson returned to his desk. The major's report added to his apprehension about the situation in Tunisia and how the novice citizen army of the United States would do against the experienced forces of the Third Reich. After a few moments of reflection, the captain picked up the office phone and asked to be connected to Commander Butcher's office at Eisenhower's headquarters.

The man had been sequestered in his office for four hours. The Marine sitting at the desk outside the door finally decided the man inside needed a breath of fresh air. Rising from his desk and then adjusting his uniform as prescribed by naval regulation, he approached the door and knocked. Hearing no reply, he knocked louder. Still hearing no response, Gunny opened the door. Knowing what he would see, nothing shocked the old Marine.

James Brand was standing by the blackboard with a piece of chalk in his right hand and his trusty slide rule in his left hand. The officer's tie was still on but loosened around his neck. The top button of his shirt was undone, and the man's shoes were off. Typical for the professor, or so the Marine warrant officer thought.

"Lieutenant, sorry for the intrusion, but I thought I'd check on you to see if you needed anything."

The improperly attired lieutenant turned to face his friend, a smile slowly formed on his face. "Gunny, I think I'm okay. Perhaps another glass of water would do me good."

"Sir, you need to get out of here once in a while. Go outside and get some lunch or at least take a walk around the building."

Seeing the old Marine's concern, James replied, "All right, Gunny. That may be a good idea. See if Stevens is free for lunch. I need to get some information from him anyway. Can you join us?"

"Sure, I don't seem to have anything keeping me at the desk, so let's get out of here for a while."

Grinning at the man's attempt at humor, James buttoned his shirt and slid his tie into its correct position. Gunny waited, but while James was putting on his shoes, another visitor walked into the office. Seeing the officer, Warrant Officer Jones came to attention.

"Commander, good to see you, sir," Gunny said in his usual command voice, which over his many years had made many a private fearful.

"Gunny, at ease. Just needed a word with the professor."

James stood with one shoe on and the other somewhere beneath his desk. "Commander, how can I be of service?"

The senior officer carried a folder, and couldn't help but notice James was wearing only one shoe and his tie was askew. It was obvious James was about to leave the office. "James, it looks like you were heading off. Going to get some lunch?"

"Yes sir. The Gunny just made me aware that I needed to move more and thought some lunch would be good for me."

"Good idea, indeed." Turning to Warrant Jones, Allen said, "Gunny, you might need to do this more often because the lieutenant is turning pale. Perhaps we need to get him some time in the sun."

James smiled and asked, "Do you mean they need me in Hawaii?"

Shaking his head no, Allen replied, "Sorry, James, but you and I are stuck in this cold climate for a bit longer." Holding the file up, the commander said, "I needed an update on your analysis of Project 61. The admiral wants to move forward with a large contract to buy these contraptions."

Moving towards the commander, limping with one shoe on and one off, the professor, took the file, saying, "Sir, I've been working on the final calculations from the test."

Pointing to one of the blackboards, James said, "I would be happy to take you through the numbers right now."

Smiling, Allen replied, "James, why don't we get some lunch, and then you can take me through your report. Both of us need food, and from the looks of it, Gunny needs to eat too."

James grinned at the comment and bent down to quickly put on the missing shoe. Then, donning his jacket, he asked, "Sir, what's your pleasure, the big cafeteria with Spam or the small lunch shack with Spam?"

Allen pointed at the door and the three men walked out. Picking up Stevens as they exited the office, they walked down the corridors to find the large cafeteria and the ever-present Spam.

Lunch was a good break for the hard-pressed professor. Every admiral in the office now wanted some of his time. Thankfully, Admiral Edwards carefully managed these requests, and any officer going outside the chain of command discovered to their chagrin the lieutenant was under the tight control of the chief of Naval Operations. Commander Allen was one of the primary guardians of the professor's time, which meant the request on Project 61 came directly from Admiral King.

After sitting down in Brand's office, Allen waited for the inevitable lecture to begin. The commander actually enjoyed the time he spent with James, primarily the intellectual stimulation from gaining new knowledge, or sometimes finding out that a once cherished idea wasn't worth his time or talent. Today's topic sounded straight out of a science fiction magazine, so the commander was hoping the secret project would work. It didn't take long for the facts and figures to come flowing out of the professor.

"Commander, the Office of Scientific Research and Development Project 61 is an excellent example of splendid cooperation between the scientific community and industry. I have been involved in only a few aspects of the Mark 24 mine design, as it is officially known, but it's really an acoustically controlled homing torpedo. Some development team members have started calling this thing Fido since it acts like a good hunting dog, but I guess there may be something else about the name."

Allen was familiar with the concept and saw the drawings and preliminary funding for the project, but thought it was a great idea that would not work. The scientists and engineers had proven him wrong. Such an invention could prove to be a significant advance in anti-submarine warfare.

Drawing on one of his blackboards, James delved into his explanation. "Essentially, we took the body of the old model Mark 13 torpedo and shortened the hull to reduce the length and weight of the unit. The scientists at the Harvard Underwater Sound Laboratories and the people at the Bell Telephone Labs came up with a couple of ideas, which were incorporated into a single design, which promised to work. The guidance system uses four hydrophones arranged around the middle hull of the torpedo and tied to a sound processing array built around a vacuum tube module directing the motions of the unit to follow the sound of a submarine."

Seeing the commander was following his commentary, James continued. "Now, once we had the design of how to hear and could point the torpedo to a precise set of sounds, we had to come up with a way to provide power and control. This was solved by General Electric's engineers developing an electric propulsion and steering system which would follow the command from the processing array. The last part of the puzzle was power. Western Electric came up with a compact, lightweight, shock-resistant forty-eight-volt power supply. Now, all we had to do was put the components together and see if a plane could drop one of these things from an altitude of a few hundred feet without breaking it. The report you have is the confirmation of a series of ten tests made from different aircraft, including Avengers, PBYs, and Liberators. The tests confirmed that most units survived their descent and activated, looking for their target."

Allen looked at the diagram James had created on the blackboard and scratched his head. "Okay, I see the components and how the thing basically works, but how does it find a submerged submarine?"

Anticipating the question, James had already sketched out an attack on a submarine by the M-24. "Once the torpedo hits the water, it begins a circular search at a specific depth. Initially, the first tests were done with a fifty-foot search depth, but the engineers determined it was best to go lower, down to one-hundred-fifty feet. As the M-24 circles, it's searching with its hydrophones to pick up the telltale 24kHz acoustic signal of a submerged vessel. At this point, control of the weapon goes from the circular search system to the passive acoustic homing system. Once the weapon establishes this contact, it heads for the sound, and as one of the engineers told me, locks on to the target until it hits it."

Writing more numbers on the board and then showing what the search pattern looks like, Brand scribbled depth readings on the side of the blackboard and explained more on how the system worked. "If the torpedo fails to find the target, it goes back to the circular pattern, which is the unit's default system. It will rise to fifty feet and stay there. If it goes to forty feet, it descends again, just in case any surface vessels are nearby. This is the safety feature for the system."

The commander studied the graphics on the board and the numbers that meant little to him but must have something to do with depth, speed, and explosive power. "James, this thing is a game-changer. What are the drawbacks, if any?"

"Good question, sir. The system has only a limited power supply, so a plane can't just sight a periscope on the horizon and then drop one of these things. The pilot has to get close, preferably within a few hundred yards. The torpedo is small compared to the standard load of the torpedoes on one of your destroyers. The power supply will only operate for ten minutes with a speed of twelve knots. This speed sounds slow, but underwater, a German Type Seven has a top speed of seven knots, so the operations procedure on this thing stresses the need to get in close before dropping it. The maximum range will be about four thousand yards, so if a pilot drops it near a submerging U-boat, the torpedo has to obtain depth, start its circular pattern, listen for the enemy, and steer itself in finding the target. Yet, I think it will be a great weapon because the enemy submarine will think it's safe once it gets underwater, but the M-24 will find it and kill it."

"How much explosive does it carry?" Allen wondered if the thing packed enough of a punch to sink a submarine.

"The unit is smaller than a standard ship or plane torpedo, so the warhead had to be made smaller to accommodate the planes dropping them. The explosive charge doesn't have to be huge to be effective underwater. Especially if the torpedo makes direct contact with the sub. The M-24 has a ninety-two pound warhead filled with HBX high explosive. This seems small compared to a Mark 14 torpedo's six hundred pound warhead. But underwater, all you have to do is crack the pressure hull. This compares favorably to the Hedgehog, which has only a thirty-five pound warhead. Either weapon will kill a sub underwater."

As the commander listened further, James went into a mind-numbing set of facts and figures on the drop height, speed, testing parameters, and the maintenance aspects of the weapon. Fido, as he began calling it, was a spectacular breakthrough in anti-submarine warfare. Understanding the unit's capabilities, he knew it was essential to get the "mine" into production quickly. James was still writing things on the blackboard, but Allen had to ask his question.

"James, where are we on the contracts for this thing? Are they being produced, yet?"

"Commander, things are already moving forward to ramp up production. An order is about to be processed for four thousand of these things, and I expect we will have some of our ASW planes equipped by the end of April at the latest. The British requested hundreds of these as well, and the operations plans will be finalized by the end of March."

As usual, the professor answered the question but added nothing more. Allen thought the lieutenant would make a good lawyer someday. As he closed the Project 61 file, he felt the Americans were beginning to get on top of the situation in the Atlantic, thanks in part to men like James Brand, who worked in research laboratories at universities and corporations throughout the country. But quickly, he came back down to earth and asked another question.

"James, have you heard anything new on the Mark 14 problems? Since the death of Admiral English, I wondered who was going to shepherd this project."

James knew about the untimely death of Commander, Submarine Force Pacific, Rear Admiral Robert English, in a plane crash on January 21. Along with some eighteen others in the Martin M-130 flying boat *Philippine Clipper*, the plane had crashed into a mountainside near San Francisco after the experienced pilot became lost in fog north of the city. It had taken a week for the plane wreckage to be found. Now, the well-liked submarine commander would have to be replaced, hopefully by someone aware of the issues and challenges the Pacific submariners were facing. English was fighting with the Bureau of Ordnance about the Mark 14 torpedoes his subs were using. The rate of premature explosions, inaccurate depth settings, bad contact exploders, and even circling torpedoes had worn down the members of the "silent service."

"Commander, I haven't seen anything new since before I left for Casablanca. The last set of reports came in from Admiral Lockwood, who did a damn good job documenting failures. I have a few hunches on this, but the torpedo people at BuOrd don't want to hear anything bad about their weapons system. There have been a series of reports on the Mark 6 magnetic exploder and how they either don't go off or explode too early as they near an enemy ship. Neither situation is good, but the reports I've seen coming out of the Brisbane-based submarines have enough merit to push people in the right direction."

Allen added a new bit of information. "The Southwest Pacific subs are under the command of Admiral Lockwood, who I believe will become the next COMSUBPAC. If he gets the job, I think you will receive whatever information you need to fix the torpedoes."

James thought for a moment. A man had tragically died, like other men he had met since the beginning of the war. Without delay or even a short pause to reflect, he was replaced and the business of war continued. The professor didn't think long about the philosophical issues of life and death in the war but silently said a prayer for Admiral English, whom he met many months ago at Pearl Harbor. Now another admiral would be put in charge of American submarines while he sat safely in his office and figured out more and better ways to kill German submarines and the crews they carry.

22

13 February 1943
II Corps Headquarters, Tunisia

- Tunisia--Commander in Chief, Allied Force visits U.S. II Corps area to review disposition of forces since an enemy attack is imminent. Axis commanders meet to review attack plans.
- USSR--Germans are containing Soviet attacks toward Novorossisk, last enemy stronghold remaining in northwest Caucasus. Red Army gains complete control of the Rostov-Voronezh rail line with the capture of Novocherkassk and Likhaya.

The trip got underway the previous evening as an eleven-vehicle convoy departed Algiers in the middle of the night. Temperatures dropped throughout the darkness as the trucks, armored cars, and staff cars slogged their way through the hills and mountains leading into Tunisia. The destination was the headquarters of II Corps near a village named Tebessa. General Fredendall had established his HQ far from the front lines, and as they drove into the area around noon, Major Flannigan knew things would not go well. Engineers were blasting their way into a ridge line and apparently were building a bomb-proof fortress to house the staff of the American forces.

Dean shook his head and whispered, "Sir, this looks like the army is going to stay put for a long time."

The Marine officer nodded his agreement but said nothing. The two men had been added to the convoy after Captain Jameson asked Commander Butcher to include them on the inspection tour by the newly promoted General Eisenhower. The general now had four stars on his shoulder, which gave him a rank equal to most British commanders he was nominally leading. General Anderson of the British First Army was a lieutenant general, but the new Allied ground commander for the North African campaign was General Harold Alexander. He was commanding what was known as the Eighteenth Army Group, which included all Allied units, including Montgomery's Eighth Army now fighting Rommel along the Mareth Line in southern Tunisia.

Pulling themselves out of the half-track equipped with dual-mounted .50 caliber machine guns, Flannigan told Dean to tour the area and talk to as many senior non-coms as he could. These conversations would reveal more about the current situation than all of the briefings being held by the II Corps commander. General Eisenhower and Major General Lucian Truscott hailed the Marine major to join them on a quick command center tour. Truscott, who had been the commanding general of the northern forces landing in Morocco in November, now served as Eisenhower's deputy on the front. Both men appeared upset by what they saw at the command center.

As Flannigan joined the two senior officers, he heard Truscott commenting to Eisenhower about why Fredendall was building a bunker in the middle of the desert, fifty miles away from the front lines. Ike didn't respond but frowned as he looked around. The general saw an engineer officer and pulled him into a conversation. Evidently, this unit had worked for weeks on the command post and was proud of the work his men were doing. When asked about supporting front line units, the officer said they had their own engineers. Angered by the words, Flannigan said nothing. The Marine's experience with rear echelon support units had been negative, and this situation just increased his dislike for people who stayed far behind the lines.

As the officers toured the area, there was no sign of the corps commander. After another half hour of waiting, General Fredendall arrived, followed by the British First Army commander, General Anderson. The meeting began shortly after with a briefing by the II Corps intelligence officer, Colonel Benjamin Dickson, who painted a disturbing analysis of the enemy's plans, explaining that Rommel was holding off Montgomery in the south behind the fortifications of the Mareth Line, which would allow the Afrika Corps to move its armored forces north to attack the Allies. The Americans were strung out along a line that included Gafsa and Faid Pass. The II Corps forces were thin and exposed to a violent attack at these locations, with little hope of reserve support.

General Anderson disagreed with the assessment and thought the American officer was a pessimist. He reviewed his army's deployment showing the British V Corps in the north, the Free French units in the center, supported by both British and American units, and the American II Corps holding the south. Further south were scattered French units, which acted as early warning defenses if the Germans tried a sweeping attack far out into the desert. The weather continued to be horrible, which stymied aerial reconnaissance, but simultaneously allowed the Luftwaffe time to build up its forces for a future offensive. The British general believed any German offensive would be focused in the north, where his reserves were held—both British and American. The general ended his briefing by stating any Nazi attack in the south at Gafsa or Faid would be a diversion for a major operation against his forces in the north.

Flannigan sat in the back of the room, surrounded by II Corps staff officers and members of Anderson's entourage. No one, including Eisenhower, seemed to question the analysis of the British general. Colonel Dickson's report had been sidelined for the time being and soon relegated to the pile of unheeded reports so often found during wartime. The Marine major wondered why General Eisenhower seemed to accept Anderson's version of expectations along the front lines. As the major sat back in his chair trying to see the maps of Tunisia, he thought back to his conversation two nights ago with Captain Jameson.

The captain told Flannigan about a conversation with Commander Butcher. Apparently, during a meeting at Ike's headquarters, Butcher overheard the British staff supporting the Supreme Allied Commander saying they had no confidence in Eisenhower's ability to lead the Allied forces. The Brits also had little faith in the capability of the American troops to fight the Germans. Most agreed Ike was a good organizer and worked well to improve inter-Allied relationships, especially with the mercurial French generals. Still, they felt the American general was out of his depth when commanding an army in the field.

This was evidenced by naming three British deputies, one each for the navy, air force, and army units in the theater. Alexander was selected as ground commander based upon his experience in France, Burma and commanding the British troops in Egypt, including Montgomery's Eighth Army. Eisenhower had never commanded a unit in battle and was forced to sit out the First World War training troops. The British had suggested they were following decisions made at Casablanca pushed by General Brooke, who also had no confidence in the American leader. As the story was told, Ike was "kicked upstairs" to remove him from significant decision-making for field forces.

Now, as Flannigan listened to the British general, followed by the II Corps commander, Major General Fredendall, he was concerned the British might be correct. Eisenhower asked excellent questions but made no tactical suggestions. The American commander was appropriately worried about how the thirty-seven thousand II Corps troops were being dispersed across the valleys and hillsides of their assigned territory, yet he made no attempts to change Anderson's decisions. Later, General Truscott told the Marine he wanted to yell at somebody, but Ike wouldn't let him. Flannigan thought the same thing.

Later in the day, after looking over the construction of an airfield south of the II Corps command bunker, the convoy moved north to meet the commander of the First Armored Division, Major General Orlando Ward. The general and Eisenhower were old pre-war friends, and they were happy to see each other. Ward provided an overview of the way his division had been scattered into three separate combat commands. The commanding general of Combat Command B, Brigadier General Robinett, gave Eisenhower a summary of the situation. Evidently, Anderson, the British commanding general, ordered the First Armored Division to be split up into separate combat commands covering the passes and valley of the central region of Tunisia. They were spread thinly which would stop their ability to assist one another in a powerful enemy attack. Each command unit consisted of tank units, artillery, armored infantry, and combat engineers. It looked like a sound idea on paper, but these units had not trained together and didn't understand each other's capabilities.

Like the meeting at II Corps headquarters, General Ward didn't criticize the plans or leadership. Flannigan saw pre-war politics showing its ugly face. Even though the situation called for someone to stand up and argue the worst-case position, no one pointed out the errors being committed. Robinett was not a West Point graduate but had met Eisenhower earlier in his career. He knew his command was scattered about, with some units being placed on hilltops which could easily be cut off and surrounded by an enemy attack. Reserve units were far away and might take days to come to the aid of a beleaguered unit. Ward didn't comment on his orders from Fredendall but complained about the dispositions ordered by General Anderson.

Questions were asked, and men looked at maps. Discussions on increasing air support and getting more supplies sent to the forward units occurred. Still, the Marine thought the senior generals were dancing around the room, each reluctant to address the situation. Eisenhower was not taking charge, nor was he challenging the field commanders, whether they were in command of an army or a battalion. Flannigan became more concerned with each meeting. The next few days would see more of the same, and the major feared the inevitable battle and its outcome.

Was it really February? The officer's uniform looked like it had just been immersed in muddy water. Sweat stains grew from his arm pits around to his back, where they merged, and then one could almost see drips cascading down into his khaki pants. Wiping his brow with a dirty khaki-colored handkerchief, the man peered out of the open window hoping for a breeze. Luckily, the bar had the marvel of a sizeable electric ceiling fan, but the simple air movement was not enough to end the humid unpleasantness. Lieutenant Beck had been waiting for thirty minutes, and after consuming two tepid beers, he was getting angry. The heat made him more upset but knowing the man he was going to meet, Beck expected a late arrival.

Major Peter Smythe-Jones was not punctual. Even when he was sober, lateness was his operating mode. Yet, the American also knew security was imperative, and both men took pains to make sure they were not under surveillance. Beck thought the risk was small, but his enterprise was growing more prosperous with each day, and he didn't want to end up in some Indian prison. Yesterday, their banker, Colonel Granger, provided an update on recent deposits made in the banks of the Portuguese colony. The old man knew most of the financial people in the major Indian cities and was on excellent terms with the Portuguese bankers in Goa.

Moving money in small amounts was the key to secrecy, so said the colonel when he was lucid. The man would do what he was told as long as his bar and hotel bills were paid. If nothing else, the banker was detailed and knew his way around banking laws. The last ledger of accounts showed deposits in seven banks located in the four largest cities of India. Each account was in the name of a newly created company, all legally chartered by the British authorities. Beck marveled at the man's ability to establish credible organizations, get them incorporated, pay the tax stamps which were required by the Crown and then move monies about without any fear of discovery.

These activities had some degree of risk, but Beck felt the odds of being discovered were slim. His British accomplices knew full well the price of indiscretion. The Indian criminal gangs were well equipped to keep out of jail and would use large bribes when needed to get the local authorities to look the other way. If this failed, more extreme measures would be used, including murder. Life was cheap in the subcontinent, and accidents could be easily arranged, or people simply disappeared. The American's biggest problem was not to get overly greedy. Each day ships brought new loads of American supplies for the war effort. Knowing that one ship might carry ten thousand tons of cargo, it would make sense that some would get lost or mislaid. Figuring that one of the convoys would be attacked somewhere between ports in the United States and India made the loss of one truck, a bulldozer, bales of wire, cases of food or ammunition meaningless in the larger scheme of things.

As he waved at the bartender for another beer, Beck noticed Smythe-Jones walk into the bar. As the man slowly made his way to the American's table, the British supply officer stopped to speak to officers seated together. Laughing and pointing to his business partner seated across the room. Peter finally sat down, turning to wave at the table full of his countrymen, the major softly said, "Just wave at the fools and smile."

Beck did as he was told and held up his beer, and the British officers all waved back, most of them holding up bottles of the local brew. The major then turned and said in a regular voice, "Good of you to meet me here, Lieutenant. I hope this bar was not an inconvenient location for you?"

Playing the game, Beck replied, "Yes, Major, this seems to be as good a place as any other in Calcutta. I hope you have time today to discuss our warehousing issues."

Noticing the British officers were now engaged in their own conversations, Smythe-Jones whispered, "Keep up the conversation. I don't think they can hear us, but let's use the time wisely."

Agreeing to the terms of the meeting, the American picked up his beer, looked at it, and pointed to the bottom of the bottle. "Appears things are moving quickly. The warehouse is going to be moved in two days. Can we arrange to have somebody help with the transportation issue?"

Understanding the need to find more people to move supplies from a temporary holding location to where the buyers would meet to bid on the stolen items, the British officer said, "Yes, I think we can hire some locals to help out on the warehouse. Transportation may be an issue, but if the price is right, people can be found."

Beck agreed additional people would cut into their profits but they needed to move the inventory to the point of sale. "So long as it doesn't get too expensive, I will agree. Now, make sure this is a one-off deal. I would hate to add to our costs."

Holding his beer up and looking at it intensely, Peter whispered, "Shouldn't add more than five percent to the total. I think we will clear a sufficient profit on this transaction."

Smythe-Jones was quick to see the look in Beck's eyes following his utterance of the word "profit." The partners had an unwritten rule of saying nothing in their conversation that could be construed as illegal activity. "Sorry for the slip, Lieutenant. I will make sure it doesn't happen again."

Beck changed the subject. "I understand a large convoy has reached Karachi. Orders are being made for some of the trucks, perhaps as many as sixty, to be shipped to Assam. It might be worth our effort to make sure these arrive in good shape. Sometimes there are accidents, especially during the last one hundred miles after being offloaded from the trains. The information will be available within two days."

Smythe-Jones grinned and looked at his hand, using his fingers to count the days from unloading until the trains would move from Karachi through Dehli and delivered to a siding south of Assam. "I would think it would be twelve or more days before the trains could make it to the depot. Perhaps we should be planning for some losses along the way. I think four or five might suffer breakdowns. I will see what kind of maintenance support I can arrange for this contingency."

The conversation sounded quite ordinary, but now the British major would send information to his Indian partners to steal trucks somewhere south of Assam. If they were filled with other items, so much the better.

"Tell me, Major, I understand the Portuguese have some sort of Carnival in March. Is it something like the Carnival in Rio or the Mardi Gras in our state of Louisiana?"

Holding his beer and taking a sip, Smythe-Jones smiled, knowing the final connection in their movement of money was taking shape. "Yes, Lieutenant. The people of Goa, being good Catholics, have a big festival each year similar to the one in Rio de Janeiro. Quite a good show with feasting and lots of pretty girls. Are you planning on attending?"

"I have some leave coming, and my commanding officer told me I could go anywhere as long as I don't leave Asia. I don't think I want to visit the Japanese, and I had thought about going on a tour up to Kashmir, but someone told me about Goa, which sounded like fun."

"If you have permission to travel, all you need to do is get an entry visa for the Portuguese colony. I think I know someone who could arrange it for you. The British government would want to know the purpose of your trip, but I doubt it would be an issue. When do you want to go?"

Looking again at the table of British officers nearby, Beck said, "Sometime in early March. Do you see any problem in making this happen?"

The British supply officer held the requisite stiff upper lip for the query. "I will have to contact a friend in Dehli and get the paperwork going. If you can get me a copy of your authorization, it shouldn't be a problem."

Knowing the trip completed the chain to funnel money from India to Goa and onto neutral Portugal, Beck's contented smile grew with each sip of beer.

The files were marked Top-Secret with name and signature pages attached to the inside, indicating the contents, date, and when the file was returned to the secure storage area. A large number of folders disclosed the person who was reviewing the contents and why it was essential to the war effort. Lieutenant Waverly had watched an army lieutenant walk into the professor's office carrying a briefcase handcuffed to his left wrist two or more times each day for the past week. Warrant Officer Jones staffed the desk outside Brand's office and signed in every file on his own report log, ensuring that none of the important documents were lost. The Marine lieutenant didn't understand any of the information in the files, which Gunny told him made no sense to anyone but the lieutenant.

James had examined the last four files sent over by Vannevar Bush of the OSRD, and with each new report asked for additional information. The latest piece was about the site of the first key installation for the Manhattan Project, known as Y-12. This was the project name for the electromagnetic isotope separation plant, producing the enriched uranium for the atomic bomb. The location had been selected by General Leslie Groves near Oak Ridge, Tennessee, to take advantage of the electrical power generated by the TVA's dams. Y-12 was the first part of the Clinton Engineer Works, including the X-10 graphite reactor, the second reactor in the world after the pilot program at the University of Chicago. Three additional facilities were to be built on the site, including the K-25 gaseous diffusion plant, and the S-50 liquid thermal diffusion plant. Lastly, a large power plant would be built containing eight coal-fired twenty-five thousand kilowatt generators, which would augment any power needs not covered by the TVA hydroelectric facilities. The more James read about the size and scope of the operation, the more concerned he became. The forecast for the number of employees alone dwarfed any of his preliminary estimates. If things progressed on schedule, over eighty-two thousand people would be employed at Oak Ridge by 1945. The existing small farming community had no infrastructure, roads, schools, or housing. All would have to be built, and this would take time.

As he worked through each of the plans, knowing construction was about to begin on the first facilities—Y-12 and X-10—he thought about the need for raw materials. Concrete and steel would be needed by the thousands of tons. Wood, steel, piping, lead, copper all would be required in massive amounts, which had to come from the nation's factories, with most already allocated to various war projects. The other concern was manpower, not just for the construction phase but also for the systems' operation. Electricians, scientists, engineers, and maintenance personnel would have to be hired, moved, and trained in new technologies. Other parts of American infrastructure, including schools, hospitals, stores, roads, and railroads, would have to be built where there was currently nothing.

James knew the project's priority and had been asked by General Groves to look into the critical need for copper, which was required in enormous amounts for the Y-12 electromagnetic coils. Wartime production was high, but the demand by the armed services was higher than could be mined and refined by American sources. Canada and new mines in Latin America were ramping up, but the need far outweighed the supply. The professor was asked about alternatives, and the one he recommended made sense but caused some internal squabbles in the government. Copper was the go-to metal for conducting electricity. However, the best metal for electrical and thermal conductivity is silver, but its rarity and high value caused James to recommend the use of the American silver supply used in coinage. He estimated a total requirement of 14,700 tons of silver would be needed to make the coils. Knowing the recommendation would be challenged, the professor told the Manhattan Project engineers that once the war was over, it would be necessary to return the silver to the treasury. He waited for a reply from the Treasury Secretary to this unusual request by his friend Vannevar Bush. James knew Bush would get the silver.

As he examined other strategic materials, he needed more help. Knowing Stevens was working night and day on aluminum requirements for the aviation industry, James had Billingsley and Rollins focused on the destroyer escort program. He had one more asset, so James decided to put the team's newest member on one of the high-priority projects.

Ensign Nancy Pollard had been working on convoys since being assigned to the Logistics Research Department. She enjoyed the work and found the job rewarding. She was able to use her math skills to examine the loading of ships in convoys to maximize the total amount of what was called sea-lift across the Atlantic and Pacific. If a ship could be configured to add just five percent more cargo per voyage, the results would be enormous to the war effort. Requiring several different skills, she quickly learned about ship design, displacement, cruising speeds, loading and unloading capabilities at various ports, and the utilization of manpower both on the ships and in the ports. Lieutenant Stevens had praised her on both ingenuity and mastery of new information. The only thing she had not accomplished so far was to work directly with the famous professor. Now, as she entered his office accompanied by Lieutenant Stevens, both excitement and doubt filled her.

As usual, James was in his stocking feet, without his tie and his sleeves rolled up. Stacks of files covered his desk, plus another metal table that sat next to a line of three full-size blackboards. As Nancy looked at the formulas and calculations on the board, she worried about her mathematical skills. Seeing the woman staring at the boards with uncertainty, James grinned. "Don't worry, Ensign Pollard, I won't ask you to add to the equations on the board. They are my way of asking complex questions in different ways."

The smiling young man could have been her younger brother. "Sir, I think I would need a few hours of your time to even come to understand the questions you're asking, let alone comprehend some of these equations."

Having felt the same way many times, Stevens couldn't help but grin as he said, "The ensign is ready for her next assignment. I think she has done a great job on the convoy problem and is ready to tackle something difficult."

Much to Pollard's chagrin the convoy problem was not that simple, taking her over two weeks to come to grips with the knowledge on how ships were loaded and how displacement mattered in terms of ship stability. James came to her rescue, asking her to sit down. Stevens pulled up a chair as well.

Leaning against the front of his desk to face the ensign, Lieutenant Brand tried to settle the newcomer's nerves. "Please call me James while we're working in this office. As you have gathered, I want to keep everything on a casual first-name basis. We're involved in way too many serious things without adding rank protocol to the complexity and stress of our mission."

Pointing to one of the blackboards he continued, "What you're looking at is part of the most secret and probably most costly program in our country. I will need help working through some of the logistics issues this project faces, and I want you to be my partner in this project."

The ensign wondered about the equation, which might be a unique form of calculus, but she could not make out the relationships expressed. As she listened to the explanation, she appreciated the words coming from Brand. He wanted a partner, not an assistant—a revelation to any woman in academic life who was often treated as a second-class assistant to a male colleague.

"Nancy, if that is all right with you, I need you to be my eyes and ears for this program. It will entail you traveling a lot across the country to various sites in the early stages of construction. You will be provided the highest security clearance in the nation. Before you were assigned to this office, you were vetted by the FBI and the Office of Naval Intelligence. Your prior experiences in secret programs were verified, and many of your former colleagues, teachers, and even neighbors were interviewed. Nothing was learned which would make you a security risk, but I must warn you that anything you divulge to anyone not approved for this project will result in a charge of treason."

The professor allowed the warning to sink in for a moment before asking, "Nancy, do you understand what I just told you? I need a yes or no answer."

"Sir, I understand the seriousness of the situation and will abide by all rules and regulations."

"Good. Lieutenant Stevens will provide you a few more forms, which have to be signed and witnessed. Please read each one carefully. If you do not understand anything stated in these documents, please ask. Once you sign them, you are locked in for the duration of the war, and perhaps beyond."

Noting the seriousness of Brand's comments, she quickly acknowledged his words.

"Lieutenant Brand, I look forward to doing whatever I can to help the war effort. When do I get started?"

Smiling again, James said, "As soon as you review the documents and sign them, I want to give you an overview of your new duties. Of course, sometimes I will need to pull you from one project to work on something else, but for right now, you will be focusing your efforts on one thing only."

Stevens and Pollard left the room and went into Captain Jameson's vacant office to read and review each of the national security documents. Later in the day, James gave Ensign Nancy Pollard an overview of the Manhattan Project. James had provided the other officers of the team only a high-level overview of the project weeks before. Pollard was now going deep into the super-secret program with all of its complexity, unknowns, and stress. The WAVE ensign would find her future in atomic energy.

PART 3

23

15 February 1943
Lisbon, Portugal

- Northwest Africa--Gen. Alexander, selected at Casablanca Conference to head all Allied Forces in Tunisia, arrives at Algiers for conference at AFHQ.
- Tunisia--In British 1st Army area, Gen. Anderson orders forces holding high ground west of Faid withdrawn and Kasserine Pass organized for defense. Anderson directs Gen. Fredendall to withdraw all forces after isolated troops have been extricated to positions defending Sbeitla, Kasserine, and Feriana. Axis forces, moving cautiously against Gafsa, discover it has been evacuated. French 19th Corps is quietly and gradually moving right flank forces back to Sbiba.
- Guadalcanal--Joint air command designated Aircraft, Solomon Islands (Rear Adm. C. P. Mason) is established with headquarters at Guadalcanal.

The trip had been easier than Meyers thought possible. The British had helped by flying the American officer directly to Gibraltar without going first to Spanish Morocco. This eliminated diplomatic discussions with

Spanish authorities. A British Lockheed Lodestar operating as a civilian transport for BOAC was flying to Lisbon to deliver three new members of the British embassy and then returning with two people who were going to new postings. The flight to Gibraltar was on a Short Sunderland flying boat, which shuttled key personnel between the Allied command center on the Rock and Eisenhower's headquarters. The American had to wait for two days in Gibraltar while the British and Portuguese agreed to the postings of new diplomatic personnel, including Meyers.

The lieutenant enjoyed his two days on the British possession, even though the accommodations deep inside the mountain were not comfortable. His British host, a Royal Navy lieutenant commander, informed him that things were quite nice now, since so many Allied command groups had moved to Algeria. The British had built miles of tunnels throughout the mountain, and as these were dimly lit, dripping with moisture and often cold, John Meyers thought fondly of his cramped quarters in sunny Algiers. The food was worse, and he wondered how the garrison on the island fortress could deal with the isolation, dark and damp tunnels, and horrible food.

He was happy to leave the British post and fly off on the Lodestar for Lisbon. The plane was reasonably fast and flew way out to sea, skirting the Spanish coast of the Iberian peninsula to avoid patrolling aircraft. Within a few hours, the pilot made the approach to Lisbon's airport and landed with barely a sound chirping from its tires. Once the plane came to a stop at a place indicated by a small man waiving a red flag, the on-board steward opened the door, and the five passengers deplaned into what was a lovely day. The sun was shining, the north winds brought a chill, resulting in much cooler air than he had experienced on Gibraltar. As the men entered the terminal, they were greeted by officials from the Portuguese government. Each passenger was dressed in civilian clothes, which for Meyers had been hastily acquired in Algiers. The border guards watched each man fill out several pages of forms, and then what appeared to be senior officials, wearing immaculate grey uniforms with peaked hats, began asking questions, all in English.

"Lieutenant Meyers, United States Navy, is that correct?"

"Yes sir. My name is John Meyers, and I am an officer in the United States Navy."

"And you are going to be an assistant naval attaché to our country?"

194

"Yes sir. That is my position."

The man looked at the forms then pulled a list from his briefcase. He put his finger on the second page of the list and then looked up at the American.

"All seems to be in order. My information from your *chargé d'affairs* states you are on temporary assignment and may be required to leave from time to time." Looking up from his list, the man asked, "What is the nature of this temporary duty?"

John Meyers had been briefed by the OSS officer in Algiers on the questions he might be asked. Smiling at the official, John replied, "Sir, my government has requested assistance from your government on issues relating to the security of both our countries. I believe your officials understand these and would advise you accordingly."

The official didn't smile but knew he would not get any more information. The American basically told the border official to take his questions back to his senior officers, who had agreed to let Meyers into the country.

Knowing the conversation was over and the American had diplomatic immunity granted by the Portuguese government, the only thing the officer could say was, "Welcome to Portugal, Lieutenant Meyers. I hope you enjoy your assignment."

Once through the small terminal, Meyers was approached by a tall man, who introduced himself as Thomas Murdoch of the American legation. The two men grabbed Meyers' luggage and got in their car, a 1938 Ford, driven by a Portuguese employee of the American legation. As the car drove away, Murdoch looked around, and then while keeping his hand low, so the driver couldn't see it, he pointed toward the driver, indicating to John not to say anything meaningful.

"Good flight, Mr. Meyers?"

"Why yes, it was just fine. I was fortunate to get on the BOAC flight from Gibraltar."

Seeing the hand move again to signify all was well, Murdoch replied. "Glad to hear that. Most of our people fly in on the Clipper through the Azores, which runs infrequently these days. Otherwise, you have to take the British flight from London at night, flying way out to sea to avoid German patrols from France. With the Allies now in control of North Africa, things will be much easier."

Moving into small talk about the city, just like any tourist would do, the men discussed the local economy, restaurants, transportation issues, and Lisbon's lovely ladies. The driver listened to every word, but nothing of consequence was said. Murdoch later told Meyers the embassy driver was an agent with the Portuguese Secret Police known as the PVDE. Any person who was not American was in the employment of Captain Agostinho Lourenco, the PVDE's director. Murdoch was listed as an assistant to George Kennan, but in reality, he was the intelligence officer for the OSS. The two men would become very close in the coming months.

That night, Meyers was given a briefing on the situation by Kennan and the American Financial Attaché, James Wood. The Americans in Algiers, including Ambassador Murphy, provided an overview of the current diplomatic situation, but now the two leaders of the American effort to win over the Portuguese provided a realistic assessment of the problem.

"Lieutenant Meyers, the situation in Lisbon changes daily. Our British cousins have been active in the country for hundreds of years, and we, by necessity, follow their lead. Yet, the president wants to move more rapidly than Mr. Churchill on building bases in the Azores. Their ambassador, Sir Ronald Campbell, is an old-school diplomat. However, he doesn't push very hard. We depend on David Eccles with the Ministry of Economic Warfare on the wolfram issue. He's also up to speed on the Azores problem."

James Wood continued the briefing with additional information on the situation and what the United States wanted. "The wolfram issue was put in play by Eccles last year when Salazar nationalized the mines. This threw thousands of miners out of jobs. Now, we are faced with many clandestine mining operations throughout the northern part of the country. The official Portuguese government's position is to be neutral in its approach to the Allies and the Germans. Each country gets an equal amount of the mineral, but the British get to pay in cash, while the Germans must pay in gold. We figure millions of dollars in gold has been shipped to Lisbon since 1940, much of it stolen from other countries."

The lieutenant let this sink in for a moment. The plight of the Jews was becoming well known in Allied countries, and since Meyers had access to much of the secret information about the war, he realized much of Germany's payments were made with gold stolen from conquered countries but much more came from private citizens. As he listened, he became unsettled over the ongoing dilemma facing all of Europe. Not only the war but also the morality of the conflict. Stolen property, missing people, refugees, death, and destruction were now a part of his war.

"There are growing constraints on the Portuguese economy, which the British are using to push them toward our way of thinking. Everything Portugal imports—food, machinery, or oil—must come by ship. Spain is a financial disaster zone. Since their civil war, they can barely feed themselves. Portugal has colonies in Africa, plus their commercial enclaves in Goa, Macau, and Timor. The Japanese occupied Timor in early 1942, but the Portuguese are still there. Macau survives only because the Japanese allow them to remain neutral. On the coast of India, Goa is a bright spot for the Portuguese because of their ability to trade raw materials with the British. The same goes for the African colonies of Angola, Mozambique, Guinea, and the Cape Verde Islands."

Picking up a map of the African continent, Wood pointed to each of these places, all part of a colonial empire dating to the 1500s. "From these colonies, Portugal gets coffee, rubber, rice, cocoa, sugar cane, oils, and spices. All of these raw materials are highly sought after by the nations of the world." Pointing at another map that showed the Atlantic Ocean, the economic aide pointed out the nation's location and its principal islands off their west coast. "Here is Madeira to the south, and right here in the middle are the Azores. This is the thing we want more than anything else. The president wants to exert more pressure on Salazar to allow the British to put a base on one or more of these islands. Once this occurs, we would put our planes on British bases without any formal approval by the Portuguese. Once the British get in, we are their allies, and so we just join them."

Meyers studied the map and then looked at the African map as well. Pointing at the large colony of Angola, he asked, "How does Portugal move its raw materials around without running into problems with the enemy or us?"

"Good question, John. Our British cousins set this up early on in the war. Not wanting to have Portugal or Spain become black markets for the Nazis, our Allies set up a system called NAVICERT, which requires neutral governments to get approval or certification to import or export materials in approved quantities. The British Ministry of Economic Warfare developed a plan based upon historical amounts of trade that the neutral nations can buy or sell. There are certain levels, for instance, of oil which can be brought into Portugal or Spain. The same goes for other strategic materials like iron or copper. Finished goods such as radio equipment, aircraft parts, engines, vehicles, etc., are also covered by a NAVICERT certificate. If a Portuguese ship wants to travel between New York and Lisbon, it must have this certificate detailing what is on board. The situation is the same for people traveling to and from neutral countries. You are going to find out that this country is full of refugees trying to escape the Germans, and they will do anything to get to America."

Smiling at the new arrival, Keenan added, "John, what James just told you includes anything, including marriage proposals or just sex. You need to be very careful in your dealings within the refugee community. In the next few days, you will be propositioned by women who were once members of royal families or daughters of financiers. You will be an outstanding catch, but don't put yourself into a compromising situation. Remember, wherever you go in this city, someone is watching you. It may be the Portuguese police, or it could be the Gestapo. Even the British are watching us, so don't confide too much in them as well."

The comments about the surveillance aspect of the job unnerved Meyers. He had been instructed by Captain Jameson not to get too close to anyone while on this assignment. Now, he understood what the captain was telling him. As he listened to the wolfram discussion, including an attempt to preemptively purchase all of Portugal's output to keep it away from the Nazis, John thought again about the morality of the war. He hoped he was strong enough to avoid entanglements in this new job.

The shelling grew more intense. Dean glanced at Major Flannigan, who lay a few feet away, peering through his binoculars at the dust clouds marking the enemy's movements. The major's face showed no emotion, only resolution to do his job. This helped the sergeant feel better about the situation. As Dean looked down the line to his left, he saw Captain Marvin Stonebridge, prone and visibly trembling; the man's face contorted in fear. Dean had witnessed fear many times on Guadalcanal, but never expected to see it on an officer's face. Further down the line, men were trying to dig into the hard rocky soil while lying on their sides. The grizzled Marine thought these men were not trying to get into a deeper hole but actually crawl into the earth itself.

Looking again at the major, he saw Flannigan motion to him to move back down the hillside. Seeing the command, Dean quickly responded by crawling backwards, all the time watching Flannigan do the same. The army officer didn't move an inch. As the two Marines got close to one another, Flannigan spoke over the roaring sound of cannon fire. "Dean, get the men on the left off the crest of the hill. Leave one OP only with three men. Don't let those guys go further than twenty-five feet down this hill and keep them at least ten feet apart."

"Yes sir. What about the captain?"

"Tell that SOB to move! I'm not going to risk any more men on his stupid ideas."

"Aye, aye, sir. Do you want me to get the company commander over here to talk to you?"

Flannigan looked to his right, where the hill dropped to a gully. He knew the Germans would try to envelop this small command whenever they got around to it. The enemy's tank forces were rapidly moving forward and not bothering with isolated American units sitting on top of hills, at least for the moment. Whosoever's idea it was to spread out these units in the mountains near this pass was beyond stupid. The company he was assigned to was dispersed along a hill at the extreme flank of the pass the Germans poured through. Nothing was going to stop them until they decided to rest for the evening. If, that is, they stopped at all.

"Good idea, go find Captain Rigsby and tell him to work his way around the bottom of the hill to where we are."

"Sir, what's the plan?"

Flannigan stated resolutely, "Hell if I know, but if the Germans do what I think, tonight we should be able to work our way through the gully and make for the northern boundary of Combat Command A."

Dean knew it would be risky for the company's remnants to creep through darkness down a hill and near enemy positions. "What about the guys over on Lessouda, Colonel Water's men from the One-Sixty-Eighth?"

Speaking as softly as he could, Flannigan said, "Willie, the Germans are crawling all over that hill. I don't think anyone made it off. This company is far enough away to not be worth the effort. The enemy will probably wait to capture anyone left in their own good time." Looking around at the men of the two platoons assigned to the hills north of where Waters unit was surrounded, the major added. "I don't want to spend the rest of this war in a POW camp, so I'll take my chances."

Dean nodded. He knew how badly the Japanese treated their prisoners, so he didn't want to find out if the Germans were any better.

The company's captain crawled to Flannigan's position before Dean had a chance to find him. "Major, are we going to hold out here or scatter tonight?"

Looking at the young officer, who until three weeks ago was a first lieutenant at a replacement depot near Algiers, and now commanded a rifle company, the Marine told him the plan. "Captain Rigsby, an hour after sundown, we're going to get these men off this rock and head northwest toward Sbeitla. From looking at what the Germans have been doing to our tanks, I doubt we can hold the pass. If we can move as quietly as possible, I think we can pull out without being discovered."

The young officer, an ROTC product from the University of Iowa, looked at the major's map and thought this was a good idea. The last known position of Combat Command C was a mystery. A large unit had been posted at Hadjeb El Aioun, twenty miles due north. Across the valley floor and the now enemy-occupied village of Sidi Bou Zid, Lieutenant Colonel Robert Moore was still fighting for his life with the Third Battalion of the 168th Regimental Combat Team. The Germans had first enveloped Lieutenant Colonel John Waters' battalion and now were doing the same to Moore's men. The small company Rigsby commanded had been attached to Waters command but dispatched two days ago to take up positions on the small hills situated west of the road heading north to Sbeitla.

Flannigan was amazed at the haphazard locations of American units along what was called the Eastern Dorsal. The collection of small but rugged mountains created a natural boundary and a good defensive position if enough troops were available to defend them. The Americans had placed units along the valley floors and on some of the more prominent hills, causing problems since the distances between each unit prevented mutual support. Any enemy attack could be made separately against each stronghold and then destroyed in detail. As he had witnessed through the day, American units were being eliminated in appalling numbers with the remnants trying to flee. The ninety-three survivors of Rigby's understrength company could not be counted on to stem the German advance. Their mission now was to live to fight again.

As the two officers studied the map, and Dean checked the sky for the Luftwaffe, which had devastated many American tanks and artillery units, Captain Stonebridge slid down to their position. The man's eyes betrayed his condition as he asked, "Major, what's the plan? Are we re-treating now? Which direction should we go?"

The Marine major and the young company commander were trying to save the men in the unit, but Stonebridge wanted to save only himself. Flannigan didn't need to nursemaid the staff officer assigned to be his guide. Only four days ago, the army captain was introduced to him by General Fredendall as his junior aide. The general told the Marine that the young captain was a top graduate at West Point, class of 1941, and had been instrumental in building II Corps into a strong unit. The man was full of swagger but had never been in combat, yet he claimed he was ready to lead men into battle. The arrogant officer had Dean drive the jeep around to different units within the First Armored Division and the Thirty-Fourth Infantry Division. At each location, the pompous officer introduced the Marine major as an advisor to Admiral King, who need-ed to see how the United States Army was winning the war.

Most of the combat commanders, mostly lieutenant colonels, weren't happy to see the staff officer and by association, neither were they pleased to meet the Marine. Only after a few minutes of conversation did the army officers come to appreciate the major's experience. Flannigan's questions on enemy movements, defensive positions, and lack of mutual support quickly made him a valuable commodity. Most of the battalion commanders were well aware of their situation and were fearful of engagement. A majority of units had experienced the Germans and found the enemy skillful and deadly accurate, especially their use of artillery and dive bombers which effectively nullified many of the American's advantages. The army officers were quickly losing their bravado about besting the Wehrmacht.

The company commander, Rigsby, answered the question. "We are planning to move out an hour after sundown to give us the best chance of escaping."

Before he could continue, Captain Stonebridge exclaimed, "Good plan. Why don't we go now? The Germans seem to be occupied on the other side of the valley. If we leave now, we can escape."

The look on the man's face showed stark fear. Ever since the first artillery rounds exploded near the little town and the American units came under attack by Stuka dive bombers, the staff officer evidenced fear—or was it cowardice. Dean thought the man wasn't just scared, he was a coward. All of the braggadocios was gone, and now the highly placed junior officer just wanted to save his own ass. The Marine sergeant wanted to put the man in his place, but Dean knew it was not his role.

Flannigan replied quietly, "Captain, we are going to wait until it gets dark. Then we will move quietly down the hill and use the gully to hide our retreat. Within a mile from here, there are a few more low hills which we can use to mask our movements."

Stonebridge looked at each man and then started speaking rapidly. "Good plan. Good idea. I think it will work. We should get someone to notify HQ about this plan. Get some more support for our evacuation."

The man's short staccato sentences could not mask the captain's collapse into a fearful frenzy. Flannigan had seen the same thing happen at Guadalcanal, but usually, it was after days or weeks of continuous engagement with the enemy. Now, he witnessed a professional officer who had been highly educated in the arts of war fall apart.

The man said nothing for a moment but pulled back down the hill. The major and the company commander ignored his movements as they searched the map for ways to get their men off the hill and safely away from the Germans. At the same time, Dean noticed the staff officer swiftly walk down the hill. The sergeant thought the man was going down the hill to relieve himself in privacy, so Dean looked away. As he continued scanning the sky for German intruders, he heard the sound of an engine.

Flannigan and Rigsby heard it too, and both men fell to the ground thinking the Germans were moving around the hill to attack. Dean looked at the gully and saw a jeep driving away at breakneck speed. "That dumb son of a bitch!" was all the sergeant could say as the highly respected army captain drove the jeep to the end of the gully and then sped away to the north across the dry but rocky floor of the valley.

The company commander stared in disbelief at the jeep as it drove away, wondering what kind of idiot would pull this kind of stunt. Flannigan thought the same thing, asking Dean, "How far do you think he'll get?"

Dean turned to his commanding officer and good friend, shrugging his shoulders before recognizing another noise, this time above his head. "Hit the ground. Stuka at one o'clock."

The two officers sat next to a prominent outcropping and quickly laid flat on the ground, hugging the biggest rock they could find. The men in the dirty khaki uniforms were hard to spot from the air unless they were moving or at the top of a hill. The soldiers were all in their foxholes, so no one could be easily spotted. The two officers and the Marine sergeant buried their faces in the ground and waited for what felt like an eternity.

Dean was the first man to pick up his head. His hearing was excellent, something he improved as he stood watch in the darkness of Tulagi. His brain told him the plane was moving further away, and he didn't think there would be anymore, at least in the next few minutes. The major and the army captain looked up, and Dean gave the all-clear. Dean crawled to the top of the hill and carefully looked at the situation. Far off toward the north, he could see the jeep making a cloud of dust heading north to safety. The Stuka saw the cloud of dust and quickly determined the dust meant a target. Quickly descending, the German let loose with his machine guns, not wanting to waste a bomb on a lowly jeep. The vehicle was shredded by the two M-17s, firing 7.92mm ammunition. The jeep flipped over and blew up in a ball of fire. The German gained altitude and headed back to his base near Tunis.

Flannigan focused on the ground, shaking his head in disgust at the waste of life as Captain Rigsby stared at the smoke rising in the valley floor. Dean scanned the area and saw the Germans still moving to attack Colonel Moore's position and consolidate their hold on the small village. The major looked up and told Captain Rigsby, "We'll keep an eye out for any movement by the Germans to the north. I don't think they saw the attack on the jeep, but if they did, it would be just another American fleeing the battle. Get your men briefed on the plan and have your sergeants check each man for anything that might make noise. Don't take everything, just ammo, water, and food. We have to travel light and fast. Any questions?"

Captain Rigsby said no and went to round up his two platoon lieutenants and senior sergeants. The Marine had a good plan and the experience to save his men. The army captain was happy to have the major leading him.

An hour after sundown, with Dean and a corporal named Hudson out front, the bedraggled company made their way slowly down the hill into the gully. Per the major's orders, the company's heavy equipment was left behind. The three trucks camouflaged in the dry river bed known as a wadi were stripped of their sparkplug wires, distributor cap, and the fuel lines were cut to incapacitate them. Five wounded men were carried on stretchers, and the dead left behind in makeshift graves. Dean had walked up and down the line of men to ensure nobody's gear would create noise. Silence was the watchword, but fear would be the force pushing the soldiers to follow orders.

It took two hours for the group to slowly work their way through several wadis, climb up and around a group of small hills, and march their way to the dirt track that passed for a major thoroughfare in Tunisia. Flannigan had instructed Dean and the army corporal to keep as close to cover as possible and avoid contact with anyone they met. In the dark, friend and foe become hard to detect. As the battered soldiers of the company skirted the roadway, Dean stopped the march. Flannigan, who had stayed with the lead platoon, quickly moved forward.

Slipping next to Dean, he looked in every direction and then whispered, "What do you see?"

The sergeant pointed across the floor of the small valley and whispered, "Looks like vehicles moving slowly up the track. I think they're ours, but I can't be sure from this location. Hudson and I will move to the right for a closer look."

With the only illumination coming from the stars, peering into the darkness, Flannigan could now see some trucks and possibly a tank moving north on the road. "Go ahead. Keep low and keep the corporal behind you. Seems to be a good man, but you know how to stay quiet."

Not saying a word, Dean crawled over to the corporal, and then the two men moved forward in a crouch position, quickly darting to the left and then to the right and then stopping to watch and listen. In five minutes, Flannigan lost sight of them and waited. The platoon sergeant came up to his position, and the major told him to spread the word to stay down and not move until ordered. The army sergeant followed orders and passed the word to the men spread out for two hundred yards. The five stretcher cases were cared for by the one surviving medic. His dead compatriot remained atop the hill.

Ten minutes passed, and no sign of Dean and Hudson. The Marine knew not to get too anxious. At least this was not Guadalcanal, where at night you couldn't see your hand in front of your face, and the jungle was filled with strange noises. Seeing a few more vehicles moving north and the absence of gunshots gave him comfort, thinking the column in the dark were Americans fleeing the debacle at Sidi Bou Zid. Five more minutes passed. Anxiety among the men behind him grew by the moment.

They had endured a day and a half of fear and loss. The Germans had pounded the town and quickly overrun the Allied armored forces. Then they enveloped the battalions on the hills above the village. A few scattered outposts, such as the one Flannigan was attached to, survived. The enemy knew where they were from aerial observation, but the Panzers searched for much bigger game. The Luftwaffe did the most damage, strafing and dropping a few bombs on the Americans. Captain Rigsby urged his men to dig deeper, but many managed only a foot or so into the rock when the first Stukas came over. An exposed machine gun location was obliterated in seconds. Several nearby men were wounded, with some dying from those wounds the first day. The company was tired, scared, and praying for safety.

Dean came over the small pile of rocks hiding the major. Out of breath but smiling, he reported. "Sir, they're our people. Some individual units from the Combat Command C. Most of their tanks were destroyed when they charged into the village."

Taking a second to catch his breath, Dean was joined by Corporal Hudson, who added to the report. "Sir, there is space on the trucks for our wounded if we move fast. The rearguard units are coming up quickly and have been ordered back to Sbeitla."

"Corporal, good work, get to the back of the column and find the captain. Tell him to move the wounded forward first."

The corporal moved quickly down the line of men. Seeing the platoon sergeant approaching, Flannigan repeated his order. "Sergeant, the priority is getting our wounded secured on one of those trucks. Take a squad and head to that column and tell them to wait for our stretcher cases. Don't take no for an answer."

The sergeant smiled and responded, "Yes sir. Nothing will move without them."

The army sergeant returned to the column, pulled six men from the line, and quickly moved toward the trucks. Looking past the sergeant, Flannigan watched the first of the stretcher cases moving forward. Each was being carried by four men, with the medic walking next to the wounded men. As the men passed the Marine major, each one acknowledged the officer leading them to safety. After another five minutes, the last man in the unit stopped in front of the major and his sergeant. Rigsby quickly affirmed no one was left behind. "Sir, everyone is out in front of us. Any orders?"

"Captain, I told your sergeant to find space on those trucks for our wounded. If there is more space, have your men mount up. If not, get them marching north."

Flannigan and Dean stood and began walking to the distant column of vehicles. Rigsby followed and watched as the two Marines kept looking in every direction with their Thompsons at the ready. The young army captain quickly learned how to be a warrior from watching these two men react to the situation and their surroundings—an experience not taught in officer training schools. As they neared the line of vehicles, he was enormously relieved to see the Americans waving him toward the lead truck. As he got close, he saw Major Flannigan approach a jeep containing a senior officer. Rigsby decided to stay with the Marine and learn more about being an officer.

The jeep contained a Lieutenant Colonel and two junior officers. A sergeant was driving the jeep. Flannigan approached the jeep and saluted.

"Sir, my name is Flannigan, and this is Captain Rigsby of the One-Sixty-Eighth."

The colonel was a staff officer from the First Armored Division. He looked at the filthy men and asked, "What's your unit, Major?"

"Sir, I'm an observer for General Eisenhower. I report to Admiral Edwards in Washington."

The colonel stared intently at the officer and finally recognized the eagle, globe, and anchor on the man's collar. He recalled hearing General Ward talking about a Marine visiting the front lines but had not met the man. "Glad to see you made it out. How many men did you bring out?"

Pointing to Captain Rigsby, who responded, "Sir, I have ninety-two men with a few stretcher cases and seven less severely wounded."

Not knowing Rigsby or his mission, the colonel asked, "Captain, where were you and the major during the battle?"

"Sir, we were set up as an observation post on the small hill west of the river bottom and just off the track heading north to Hadjeb. Colonel Waters put us on the other side in case the Germans came in from the north."

The colonel thought this over. He was unaware of small unit positions. He knew about the two battalions on the large hills overlooking the valley leading to Sidi Bou Zid but realized some units would be scattered about to serve as observation posts. "What do you know of Waters and Moore?"

Flannigan decided to jump in to keep the captain out of the argument. "Colonel, since the Germans attacked, we were without communications to either major unit. The captain had two platoons from his company assigned as the OP on the hill a day before the enemy attacked. None of the units, including the captain's, could provide mutual support. We had two .30-caliber machine guns, three 60mm mortars, and rifles. Our orders were to be ready to advance or withdraw based upon commands from battalion."

The colonel looked at the Marine major and recalled what General Robinett had said about the observer. Evidently, the officer was a veteran of several major battles and knowledgeable of the strategic situation. Before the colonel said anymore, the Marine spoke again.

"Colonel, the captain's unit should never have been stuck out on this hill, far away from any support. I think this happened on the other side of the valley, and the outcome was easy to see. From what we saw today, Waters' battalion had been enveloped by the Germans, and I doubt they will last the day. Not too sure about what happened to Colonel Moore, but I think he was being blanketed the same way. Perhaps he was able to move out, but I didn't see anything to report."

The colonel looked at the experienced Marine and knew the man standing in front of him probably had more combat experience than he did. Being a staff officer in charge of supply for the division, he told them what had happened.

"Major, Captain Rigsby, we were ordered to blunt the attack by the Germans today, and so units of Combat Command C, reinforced, moved forward. The enemy picked off our tanks and vehicles from a great distance. As we surged forward, our tanks exploded and became separated. Then the biggest tanks anyone has ever seen appeared, and from a distance greater than our tanks 75mm guns can reach, they methodically destroyed our remaining units. I think we came in with forty-six tanks, one hundred thirty trucks, nine self-propelled guns, and god knows how many men we have left. We are pulling back to form a line at Sbeitla. I understand that Combat Command B is heading there now, and we have been promised air support in the morning."

Flannigan mulled over the situation report and knew the Americans had been bloodied badly but could make up its losses. Yet, he was unsure of the leadership going into the next few days. Any more "cavalry charges" into the muzzles of German tanks would be suicidal. The generals in charge needed to improve their decision-making soon, or they would be back in Algiers.

The colonel commandeered a jeep for the Marine and Captain Rigsby and told them to move quickly up the road to find the command post for General Robinett and report on the situation. Dean drove, and Corporal Hudson kept an eye out for the enemy. It would be a dry and dusty nighttime drive in the desert, allowing Flannigan to mull over what he had seen and experienced in the past few days. The longer he thought about it, the angrier he became.

The wounded had come in slowly, but now as more trucks pulled into the receiving station near Sbeitla, the reality of the carnage of battle came into focus. Men were burned from being in tanks, hit by the deadly German 88mm antitank gun. The armor on the Sherman tanks was easily pierced by the high-velocity weapons. The tankers had gone into the battle against the Germans, thinking their tanks were the best in the world. As reality set in, the tankers wished they had joined the navy instead of the army. The enemy's antitank guns sliced through the Sherman and Grant tanks like they were butter. Most of the time, the tanks caught fire or exploded. Many crewmen were critically burned if they were lucky to escape a direct hit. The doctors now faced the reality of dealing with deadly burns, which often took the life of the seriously injured.

"Doctor, can you help me with this patient?" The calls kept coming from the army doctors. Few of them had dealt with severe burn victims, and now the field hospital was quickly filling with blackened bodies.

"Let me see what you have, Dr. Samuels." Hiram Feldman held forceps and pulled on the burnt tissue, which fell off in sheets. The critically burned man had been given morphine and was thankfully unconscious, but earlier, his screams were deafening.

"Looks bad." Feldman examined the man whose clothing had burned into his flesh to the point the doctor didn't know where one started and the other ended. His hands looked more like the webbed feet of a goose, rather than a human being. The vile odor of burned flesh filled the air causing some of the less experienced doctors to turn away in an effort to contain the contents of their stomachs. As the doctor continued his evaluation, he observed the man's lower torso and what remained of his scrotal area. Dr. Feldman knew if the man lived, he would never function and pulled the sheet over the blackness that was once a young man in his early twenties.

"I doubt he will survive, no matter what we do for him. It looks like seventy-five percent coverage with third-degree burns. He must have covered his face with his hands when the fire erupted in the tank. I am amazed he's lived this long. Give him morphine, cover the burns with ointment, and wait."

Samuels, who was a year out of a residency program for internal medicine, was appalled by the comment. "Doctor, shouldn't we try to save him? I think there must be some hope."

Hiram touched the man's shoulder and then pointed to the tent's entrance as the wounded arrived in droves, and an orderly was overheard explaining to a medic that two more trucks were waiting outside to be unloaded. "Samuels, I want to help him as well, but you know with burns this severe, we can't help him, but we can ease his pain. There are more wounded coming in, and we need to help those we can save."

The young doctor searched the face of the physician who had been introduced to the field hospital's staff three days ago. The man was here to observe and provide suggestions for the care of the wounded. Many of the doctors wondered about the navy doctor in their midst but said nothing. The hospital had seen a few casualties, but nothing they couldn't handle. This ended yesterday when the Germans attacked. Now, casualties mounted, and decisions had to be made—many involving life and death situations never encountered by most of the physicians. Word was passed the navy doctor had been involved in South Pacific battles and worked with severe burn cases. Hiram Feldman was again asked to make decisions on the life or death of young men.

Feldman heard the familiar voice of Jonathan Hamlin, his pharmacist mate, standing near the tent's flap entrance to the surgery area. As Hiram came near, Jonathan ushered him outside to see another two trucks driving up to disgorge their contents of human misery. Pointing to the newest arrival, Hamlin calmly stated, "Doc, we need someone out here to triage. Lots of them need immediate care." Looking back to the truck, he added, "Burn cases need special attention. Reminds me of the *San Francisco*, when the plane hit the antiaircraft mounts and dumped fuel on the gun crews."

Recalling the grizzly scene of dozens of burned bodies, Hiram quickly agreed to Hamlin's idea. Grabbing the pharmacist mate by the arm, they walked to one of the ward tents searching for the hospital commander. The staff of medics, orderlies, and doctors were surrounded by blood, burned flesh, and human suffering to an extent unknown to inexperienced medical personnel.

Spotting the lieutenant colonel in charge, Feldman came up beside the man going over a chart held by an orderly. "Colonel, we need to go to full triage outside. Trucks are piling up, and if we don't act fast, men who should live will die."

Colonel Couch, who was perhaps ten years older than Feldman and a career army doctor, had the face of a man in pain as he was torn between his duty as a physician and that of an army colonel. The doctor had never been placed in a situation this critical, and it was overwhelming. Noticing the stoic demeanor of a colleague who had been through this trauma and survived, the colonel pulled himself together. "What do you recommend, Doctor?"

"Colonel, we need one doctor outside working with a couple of your best medics to triage the incoming patients. Those whose treatment can be delayed due to less serious wounds should be placed in a holding area. The ones with severe wounds who could survive with emergency surgery can be funneled into the operating area. We will have to make hard decisions in some of the worst cases. You know what I'm talking about, sir."

The colonel didn't like to think about letting men die but realized the current situation changed the rules. The forward hospital had seven medical doctors, three being qualified general surgeons. The doctors were supported by three surgical assistants and twelve medical technicians. Assisting the doctors were a dozen trained medics, as well as fifteen orderlies trained in medical hygiene and record-keeping. Stretcher-bearers, ambulance drivers, and a full field kitchen made the field hospital self-contained. But now, the unit was being inundated by incoming casualties.

Colonel Couch viewed the crowded room, stacked with cots full of men covered in bandages and in agony. "Feldman, do what you can to make the right decisions. Set up an area and get at least three medics working with the worst cases. I've contacted Division. They are sending help, but it will be sometime tomorrow morning before we get relief. I asked for ambulances to take cases to the rear, but the roads are packed, and the damn Germans are bombing our relief columns."

The man mumbled a few more words and walked away, leaving Hiram with the challenge of playing God. Turning to his trusted assistant and friend, he said, "Jonathan, find one or two men who you think can handle this job. It will not be easy, but we have to do our best. Grab as much morphine as you can so we can ease as much of their pain as possible. I'll work the incoming trucks. If you need me, come find me."

Hamlin didn't need to acknowledge the command. The pharmacist mate had seen the worst of mankind's inhumanity in the Pacific. This was just a different version of the insanity of war, and now, the price for man's stupidity had to be paid. As Jonathan walked away to find capable men to assist in triage, he was glad Dr. Feldman was here to do the job. Few were prepared to make the decisions required this night, but he knew Hiram was the man to do it. As he watched another wounded soldier pulled out of a newly arrived truck, Hamlin hoped help arrived soon.

24

19 February 1943
Office of Admiral Edwards
Washington, D.C.

- SWPA--Naval elements of SWPA force are redesignated U.S. 7th Fleet.
- Tunisia--Gen. Alexander, upon visiting front, finds situation so serious he takes command of 18th Army Group at once, a day ahead of schedule. Upon taking command, the general orders British, U.S., and French forces organized under separate commands and their respective commanders at once; the front is held by static troops while armored and mobile forces are withdrawn as reserve striking force; plans made to regain the initiative.
  - In U.S. II Corps area, enemy opens attack on Kasserine Pass with tanks and infantry, supported by artillery and succeeds in gaining positions within it but cannot drive defenders out. Some reinforcements are sent forward to bolster Allied positions. CCB, 1st Armored Division, is alerted for possible commitment.
- USSR--Red Army reports progress southwest of Kharkov and announces that Kharkov-Kursk railroad and highway are cleared of enemy.

Reading another report which included the CNO's action items written in the margins, Admiral Edwards wondered if this battle of paper would ever end. The Chiefs of Staff had met earlier in the day to prepare for a meeting with the British representatives based in Washington. Sir John Dill was the senior member for the British and spoke with the prime minister's authority, who rarely overruled his own Chief of Staff, specifically General Brooke. This did not mean that he didn't have violent disagreements, policy shifts, strange strategic ideas, and other wisps of fancy, which all drove Brooke to despair. Eventually, the British got to a decision and stuck to it.

The Americans were different in terms of involvement by the president. He set a general strategic direction and then let his three service chiefs—Marshall, Arnold, and King—do their jobs. The fourth man in this organization was the chairman of the Joint Chiefs, Admiral Leahy, who rarely intervened in the final decisions made by these three men. Leahy preferred to work in the shadows and individually exert influence on critical strategic decisions. He was astute enough to let each service chief run their own organization unless there was a conflicting view or sometimes a lack of consensus on future plans. Then, the admiral would intervene, speaking on behalf of the president to move the agenda forward.

Admiral King had pushed for more support in the central Pacific, pulling more ships out of the Atlantic. Troop transport was the most significant issue, and with the decision to invade Sicily in July or August, King wanted to use his amphibious forces to support Halsey in the Solomons. The CNO was working to finalize plans to retake the Aleutian Islands, which had been agreed to at Casablanca. The cantankerous Admiral was still chafing at getting approval from the Combined Chiefs to move forward with kicking the Japanese out of American territory. The planning phase was underway for the islands of Kiska and Attu to be attacked by sea and air in preparation for a land invasion sometime in late spring or summer. The only thing holding the operation back was horrible weather, lack of ships, shortages of trained men, additional aviation assets, good intelligence, and some good luck. Edwards was given the task of finding the resources to get this operation underway.

Admiral Edwards had received the preliminary plans, which dated back to November. More of a planning exercise, but indicated the many problems in attacking well-defended islands twenty-eight hundred miles from Seattle in the north Pacific. There were no nearby major facilities for support, and these islands had the worst weather found on the planet. The document contained a preliminary plan on how to neutralize the enemy far away in the Aleutians. The war plans staff had pulled together information from the Alaskan commander, Rear Admiral Thomas Kinkaid, who had replaced Rear Admiral Theobald in January. The new commander had built a solid fighting reputation in the Solomons, and now Admiral Nimitz expected the same fighting spirit in the north.

The previous day, Kinkaid's sea force commander, Rear Admiral Charles McMorris, attacked Attu with his four destroyers and the cruisers *Richmond* and *Indianapolis*. The weather was terrible, and visibility awful due to low clouds and swirling fog. No ships were found in Chichagof Harbor, so the vessel bombarded anything visible. The damage was slight, but the enemy now knew the Americans were coming. Aerial attacks were just as problematic due to the horrible conditions. The Americans had occupied the island of Adak some two hundred forty-four miles away from Kiska and four hundred forty miles from Attu in August and built an airbase on the island. The next nearest base was Dutch Harbor on the island of Unalaska, some four hundred miles further up the Aleutian chain. Adak gave the Americans a jumping-off point for the invasion of both islands.

As Edwards penned notes to his staff on what Admiral King wanted to do, a knock on the door derailed his thought process. "Come!" he yelled.

Commander Allen knew he was not to interrupt the chief of staff without a good reason. "Sir, I have an eyes-only message from Admiral Leahy for you."

Edwards had only received one previous message like this from the president's advisor, so he immediately took the message and read it. Allen stood in front of the admiral's desk, waiting to reply to the message or support his commanding officer as required. The face of the admiral betrayed his emotions. First, there was a grimace, followed by a muttered expletive and then a frown. Not looking at the commander, Edwards reread the message and then picked up a message tablet, which he rarely used. Normally, he told others to send messages, but this request required his immediate personal attention. The admiral quickly wrote his note, which was short and to the point. Handing the message to the waiting commander, he finally spoke.

"Allen, get that sent out immediately with top priority under Admiral King's name. Send a copy to General Marshall, General Eisenhower, and Admiral Leahy. Then go find Brand and bring him here."

The commander took the message and was about to do a perfectly executed about-face that would make a Marine drill instructor proud when he was stopped.

"Aren't you interested in what's so damn important?"

Allen saw the grin on the man's face, so he answered, "Sir, it's none of my business, but if you think it would be helpful to me in my duties, then yes sir, I would like to know."

The admiral, who was exhausted from twelve to fifteen-hour work days dealing with the navy's many problems, actually smiled. "Commander, you will be an admiral one day, so I'll let you in on a little secret. Politicians have no shame, and sometimes they don't see the big picture of what's important. It appears the president of the United States wants to know where the members of the Science Team are, and furthermore, he wants them back in the country to work on other projects. I think our commander in chief believes the world of supply management, convoy organization, and anti-submarine warfare can be handled by just about anybody. I'm unsure of what the man wants, but if the president wants something, we follow orders."

"Admiral, once I get information on the whereabouts of Captain Jameson and his men in Africa, shall I arrange priority transportation?"

His smile erased, Edwards said, "Good thinking. I'm not sure what we have coming back this way, but let's see how fast we can make this happen. I just hope Jameson has all of his men under one roof, but I have a feeling Major Flannigan is sniffing gunpowder somewhere dangerous."

"Sir, I'll send the signal and then get Brand to report. Do you want Stevens too?"

"Yes, it's probably good to have both of them present to find out what is happening. Do you have any idea what Brand is working on right now?"

"Admiral, the last thing I heard was some special requests on torpedo problems which are upsetting the BuOrd boys. I also understand he has something brewing with Professor Bush."

The admiral thought the Bush projects were taking more of Brand's time than Admiral King desired, but the requests came directly from

Admiral Leahy and would overrule anything the CNO wanted. The torpedo issue gained more attention from CINCPAC, and as a submariner, Edwards was also interested in anything that affected the "silent service." Knowing James Brand, the admiral knew the professor was probably making waves, which would eventually end up on his desk.

✵

The list was long and impressive. As the admiral looked at each numbered item, which contained a short sentence of explanation followed by the page number in the appendix with greater detail, he let out a long sigh. Only the professor could be this detailed and thorough with recommendations for either improvement or often killing a program in its entirety. Many people would be unhappy to see their pet program or idea listed like this, but few could rebut the facts listed in the paper. Edwards wanted to smile but knew it would just encourage James more, so he finally looked up and asked a few questions.

"Lieutenant, you commented on Commander Parsons' recent trip to the Pacific and the successful use of the VT fuze on board the *Helena*. Any further recommendations on the expansion of the program?"

"Admiral, Commander Parsons was enthusiastic about the success of the fuze and how it shot down a Val dive bomber on its first attempt. I think that we should move into full-scale production, but keep the restrictions on using the weapon only at sea, to minimize any chance of the enemy getting a chance to look at an unexploded warhead."

"Agreed, I will put this item to Admiral Purnell and make sure it gets priority at the next meeting of the Joint Committee on New Weapons and Equipment. Do you think Parsons is ready for more challenges?"

"Sir, the commander is the navy's top ordnance expert and is very inventive. I think he would do well on any project." James gave the admiral a long stare which told Edwards that Parsons would do well with another secret project needing engineering talent.

"I'll take that under advisement, Mr. Brand. If you see the commander, tell him, 'well done' from me."

The man's finger slid past report items needed for speeding up the building of destroyer escorts and the expansion of the synthetic rubber factories. Edwards wanted to ask about Brand's push in hiring additional mathematicians for the Harvard Computation Laboratory. The facility was working on analog systems for fire control of naval cannons and other methodologies for improving gun ranging, bombing accuracy, and faster design and development for radar and radio equipment. He lingered for a moment, but decided to move on to other hot topics.

Stopping at the B-29 program, he read the description. The super bomber had nothing to do with the navy, but Brand had discovered implications for naval strategy. "Brand, what are you doing with the B-29, and why is it important to the navy?"

Deciding not to grin, as was his custom when James found a project which he found especially interesting, he said, "Sir, the Superfortress, as Boeing calls the plane, will be a game-changer for the war against Japan. I doubt it will be of great use in Europe because of delays in getting it finished. By mid-1944, when the plane should be operational in small numbers, the American and British air forces will have thousands of large bombers attacking Germany. This big bomber has a much longer range and bomb load, which can be brought to bear against the Japanese from bases in China and some of the islands we plan to attack in the coming year. This will require the navy to support these planes by taking island bases and supplying these airfields with bombs, fuel, food, and support materials for thousands of crewmen. I think the navy should start planning joint operations with General Arnold for the middle of 1944."

Returning his focus to the report, but quietly telling himself Brand's comment made total sense and would require another immense support and supply operation, he would add this to his list of items for Admiral King. After discussing a few more mundane topics, such as the construction of small landing craft, training thousands of engine mechanics for the expanding naval air arm, and building more support bases for all theaters of the war, Edwards found the item which most interested him.

"Tell me about the torpedo problems. I understand the Mark 24 Mine issues, but my interest is the complaints about the Mark 14 torpedo. What have you found out so far?"

Glancing at Stevens sitting next to him, James began his discussion. "Admiral, since the start of the war, submarine captains have been complaining about their torpedoes. This includes failure to explode on contact, running deep, circling, 'porpoising,' premature detonation, and I think the item which concerns me the most is the serious loss of trust in the weapon by the submarine crews. I have read forty-five combat patrol reports from our boats operating out of Freemantle, Brisbane, Alaska, and Honolulu, and they all read-alike. This would mean that submarines working in different areas all have reported the same issue."

Edwards thumbed through the pages passed to him by Stevens, itemizing the submarine, dates, targets, results, and other circumstances, which would concern even a skeptic.

Brand continued. "Admiral, when I was in Brisbane last year, I talked to a few sub commanders, and they all said the same thing. They would set up an attack, make their approach within range of the weapon and then launch a spread toward the target. Nothing happened. Or they would hear an explosion, but when they looked at the target, it was sailing away. No damage, no fires, but the escort vessels were headed straight at them."

The professor added another point about the situation. "Admiral Lockwood ran tests back at Freemantle last June and determined the Mark 14 ran eleven feet deeper than the depth programmed. BuOrd fought the report until the fall when they said the torpedo ran six feet lower than planned. Changes were made, but many submariners report the depth is still not accurate, resulting in captains setting torpedoes to run shallow, which allows enemy escorts to spot and attack our submarines. The magnetic exploder is still not working properly, plus the contact exploder appears to be failing as well."

Edwards, the former commander of the Atlantic Fleet submarines, was deeply troubled at the loss of boats and now the failure of their primary weapon. The internal politics were a problem with reputations called into question and the veracity of combat skippers being second-guessed. Looking up from the statistics Brand presented in his report, he asked, "Lieutenant, are you willing to stake your reputation on these numbers?"

"Admiral, I am certain with the numbers in the report. The submarine crews that are attacking the enemy with faulty torpedoes deserve answers and weapons that work. My reputation means nothing compared to their sacrifices."

The admiral thought the response was spoken with a fervor the professor rarely used. Usually, his words were expressed in unemotional tones, using facts and figures to express his opinion. Now, the young officer was willing to stake his professional reputation on his analysis. This was good enough for Edwards to get involved.

"All right, Mr. Brand, I will message Admiral Lockwood to begin getting to the bottom of this. I want you to get his information and also contact BuOrd to get their latest story. Somebody has the answer, and I want this weapon fixed."

The admiral became emotional. He saw the reports on submarines that were reported lost. Weeks would go by with unanswered replies to signals sent to submarines. Finally, the boat would be declared lost, with no indication of where or how it sank. No one knew if any of the crew survived, but if a submarine was attacked underwater, crew survival was doubtful. Relatives received a telegram stating their husband, brother, or son was considered missing in action and further information would be forthcoming when available. The majority would be later declared dead, their boat on eternal patrol.

Pushing the image of lost submarines out of his mind, Edwards searched the final pages of the report and put it down. Looking to the window on his right, the admiral asked a final question. "Lieutenant, do you have any idea what Admiral Leahy wants? He has ordered Captain Jameson and his men back to Washington."

James replied quickly, stating, "Admiral, I haven't spoken to Admiral Leahy in two days, nor have I made any requests on bringing the captain back. Do you want me to ask him?"

The admiral was always amazed at the young officer's naïveté on the politics of the command situation and how power was exerted by the country's politicians. Trying not to grin, Edwards responded. "No, Lieutenant, that will not be necessary. I'm quite certain you will receive more information later from Admiral Leahy or this office about what is happening. Until then, continue the good work, and I will review your recommendations and activities tonight and send you my comments tomorrow. Any questions?"

"No sir. Thank you for taking the time to see Lieutenant Stevens and me. If there is anything you need, let me know."

Standing up and coming to attention, Brand and Stevens each carried a box of support materials not needed by the admiral. As the officers left the room, the admiral leaned back in his chair and asked his aide, "Allen, do you think the professor knows what's going on, or is he so wrapped up with his projects, he's clueless?"

The commander had wondered the same thing many times. The

reports and recommendations the professor offered encompassed so many of the war issues from production to global strategy that he was having difficulty keeping up with the deluge of information. "Admiral, I think the professor is trying to do everyone's job at the same time. And what's unsettling is he does it better than most men who have to focus on only one aspect of the war."

Edwards pushed forward in his chair and stood. Allen immediately followed suit but was told to sit back down. The admiral walked over to the window and peered out to the courtyard. Men and a few women passed through the area with most intent on getting from point A to point B using the most direct route. For the past hour, Edwards had witnessed James go to every letter in the alphabet and most of the points on the compass. Brand grasped the big picture, but also had the facts to put things into perspective and in the correct order to make things happen. Admiral King had the same ability, which often unnerved his subordinates and fellow military leaders. "I guess that's why the boss likes Brand—they are so much alike."

Allen watched the admiral as he stood next to the window and knew his commanding officer was contemplating something. The sudden words seemed out of place, but the commander was unsure. "Sir, were you asking me a question?"

"Sorry, Allen. I was just thinking about the admiral and the professor and how the two of them think along the same lines. They complement each other, and don't suffer fools. I hope the lieutenant doesn't do anything to turn Admiral King against him, but perhaps, he's too smart for that. Maybe that's why Leahy wants Jameson back. Someone needs to be the buffer between the two."

The commander thought this was a wise decision, and perhaps the president's chief of staff saw problems on the horizon which needed the intercession of a shrewd captain. Later, Allen would speak to Warrant Jones about what was going on and how well James was doing without Jameson's guidance.

"Can't this thing go any faster?" The man kept looking to the rear of the truck as the vehicle careened down what passed for a road.

"No sir, I can't go any faster than the truck in front of me, but

I wish I could." The corporal was tailgating the truck in front of him despite orders not to bunch up. The German planes were attacking anything moving on the roads heading north to Sbiba. The convoy full of wounded men was headed to a defensive position set up by the British south of the village, and once there, they could feel somewhat safe.

The rout had been going on since the night of the sixteenth. The Germans attacked in great strength toward Kasserine Pass, intending to drive west to Tebessa. Other enemy units headed north to Sbiba, but the American Combat Command B fought well and slowly withdrew on February 17. British and American formations raced toward the town, while American units were starting to blunt the Germans coming out of Kasserine to the west. The enemy failed to control the heights on either side of the pass. The Afrika Corps moved extra panzer units into the fight on the nineteenth, but the Americans slowed the enemy advance while reinforcements bolstered defensive positions.

Feldman sat next to the driver, a tough-looking sergeant holding his M-1 Garand who kept sticking his head out of the window to scan the skies for Stuka dive bombers. For most of the past hour, the sergeant had made astute observations as to the parentage of the pilots of these aircraft and found similar characteristics of the Allied air forces that had not made an appearance to defend the trucks. The doctor agreed birth certificates should be verified, and the pilots notified of their new status.

"Bastards, I think there're hiding in the clouds waiting to clobber us again." The sergeant spit out a wad of chewing tobacco through the open window only to have a portion of it fly back into the truck's cab. Wishing he was in the back of the truck with Hamlin, Feldman looked out the cracked windshield searching for enemy dive bombers. Seeing nothing, the doctor commented, "Seems the Nazis are working in other areas."

The driver, who switched his focus back and forth between the road ahead and the sky above, added, "If we can keep up this pace, we should be in Sbiba in another hour."

"That would be good for the men in the back. I think if the British set up a field hospital nearby, we can get some of these men the attention they need." Hoping Hamlin was holding his own with the wounded cases, he knew most of these men were not in immediate danger. The critical cases were moved a day earlier. These men, many considered "walking wounded," would be okay if they can get their wounds cleaned and stitched up by a proper surgeon. There were only four wounded men in the back with Pharmacist Mate Hamlin, but the truck also carried every kind of medical supply imaginable. The last thing the unit commander ordered was to burn the tents and anything slightly valuable for the Germans. Nothing was left behind for the enemy.

Twelve trucks led by a few jeeps and two armored cars carried the remnants of the field hospital and twenty-six wounded men. The hospital was ordered out the day before by a battalion commander shaken by the German attack's ferocity. The colonel had told the hospital people to get out within six hours or become prisoners of Rommel. No one wanted to stay and see the field marshal's version of Teutonic hospitality, so everyone went to work moving men and equipment. Feldman volunteered to remain with the last unit departing the village, which he knew sounded noble but told Hamlin this was the best way to earn their keep in the army. Jonathan didn't think the army would pay anything additional to their navy salary, but he agreed they could help out the wounded on the way north.

An hour and forty-five minutes passed before the convoy entered the British lines. The trucks were waved through with an escort to the British field hospital two miles north of the village. The hospital was on the back side of a set of hills, next to a wadi that allowed them camouflage from aerial observation. The American hospital commander was excited to see Feldman and the trucks show up at last. He had worried they would be attacked by the Luftwaffe or captured by Rommel. The British field hospital was commanded by Major Cyril Ramsey who was also glad to see the Americans arrive, although his interest was more in the supplies his Allies carried than their well-being.

As Feldman described the status of the wounded men in his care to the American hospital commander, the British major approached. Feldman didn't salute, a habit he had learned on Guadalcanal, but the British officer saluted like he was on a parade ground.

"Doctor, my name is Ramsey, and we are glad you made it out with your wounded and your supplies. Perhaps we could share some of your supplies? We moved here rapidly and arrived last night with nary a tongue depressor."

Seeing the look on Lieutenant Colonel Couch's face, Feldman answered for him.

"Major, we're happy to share with you and hope we don't have to use many of these supplies in the coming hours, but the Germans were pushing hard toward this location. The American units are slowing them down, but I think they are running short of supplies. It's good to see your soldiers ready to fight."

The major seemed to appreciate the Yank doctor's manner of speaking. "I would agree with your assessment. It is not unlike the bloody Germans to ruin a man's tea time. The tank regiment commander holding this line told me your lads were doing a good job of slowing down Rommel's advance. I believe part of your Thirty-Fourth Division is coming into the line now, which should be adequate to blunt their advance. If our position holds, we can push them back into the desert."

The man's calm demeanor and resolute outlook impressed Feldman. Having met several British officers, including Sir John Dill, the doctor was not surprised by the relaxed attitude.

"What supplies do you need?"

"We are short on bandages, whole blood, surgical equipment, blankets, pharmaceuticals of all kinds, and whiskey. Anything would be appreciated."

Smiling at his new colleague's needs, Feldman happily replied. "We have most of what you need. Our whiskey supply was devastated by increased consumption during several bombardments, but I do think we can share some of our last few drops with our distinguished Allies."

"Splendid! I do think we will do a good job for your men, and later, we can see if your selection of whiskey meets our needs."

The major and Feldman walked off to look into the trucks. After each unloaded their wounded, the officers would see what supplies they contained. Outmaneuvered by Feldman and the British major, Colonel Couch went in search of a senior American commander to tell him what to do next.

It was impossible to be alone. No time for thinking about tomorrow, let alone the next hour. The men were exhausted, thirsty, and running low on ammunition. Decisions needed to be made, and it seemed everyone looked to him for guidance. Since leaving Sidi Bu Zid, the men of Captain Rigsby's company moved to positions north of Kasserine Pass. They were attached to an ad hoc force of remnants from Combat Command A and a few survivors from the One-Sixty-Eighth Regimental Combat Team. The battalion commander, a lieutenant colonel, tried to get his men situated for the German onslaught but suffered from unclear commands and poor terrain. The night before, the man left his command post to find someone to tell him what to do and never came back. The second in command had been wounded in the opening engagement, and an artillery captain was in charge until Flannigan appeared with his rag tag company.

The army captain in charge quickly relinquished command to the senior officer, even though the man was a Marine. Sizing up the situation, Flannigan moved the four hundred men into new defensive positions further up the valley and into some high ground. Examining the terrain and now knowing how the enemy deployed his troops, the Marine officer went to work. The first thing he did was to get Rigsby set up as his assistant. He needed someone he could rely on, and the young officer had proven himself worthy in the past few days. Dean took an inventory of weapons, ammunition, and other supplies. Water was the most important item on the major's mind, and after two days without having much to drink, the sergeant realized the importance of something so simple.

The major was a whirlwind of activity starting on the evening of the eighteenth and drove the soldiers to dig their fox holes much deeper and made sure the men were not spaced too close together. The improvised battalion had three 37mm antitank guns, which he knew were useless against the large panzers, but could do well against troops and vehicles. Fourteen Browning .30-caliber machine guns were set up along with eight 60mm mortars. The artillery captain, who was delighted to have Flannigan take command, also found four 80mm mortars, and late last night, two stragglers entered the line, and both had half-tracks with 75mm howitzers. At least the unit had two artillery tubes that could slow down a tank, but he didn't count on it.

It was near dawn when a jeep drove up to the rear of the unit, and a colonel came looking for the unit commander. Finding Major Flannigan, the colonel, brought up a small number of light tanks and some large howitzers, then briefed the officer.

"Major, looks like you know what the hell you're doing, so I'll be brief. The Germans are moving up the valley, and I don't think our position will hold. You did the right thing by getting your men up in the heights, but I don't think the units on the valley floor will be able to hold out very long. This is my first rodeo, Major, so give me some idea of what we're facing."

Flannigan appreciated the man's honesty. Not having experience fighting the Germans, the colonel might repeat the same mistakes made over the past few days by charging head first into the German antitank guns and being overwhelmed by the panzers and their well-trained infantry units moving forward with them.

"Colonel, the Germans want you to move forward, which will let their long range antitank guns hit you before you can even shoot back. Let them come to you but remember, these new tanks are huge. I've seen our Shermans hit them with no effect. The only way to hurt these damn things is to strike on the side or back. Aim for their tracks is what I was told by a few of the survivors from Sidi Bou Zid."

Thinking a bit more and seeing the colonel was listening well, Flannigan continued his briefing. "You need to get your men to dig deep. I saw lots of men get killed by not being in a deep hole. The rock is hard, but it sure beats getting hit by German shells. The enemy likes to use their artillery to keep our heads down and then envelop any opposition they encounter. This is what happened to Colonel Waters. They were isolated, and the enemy moved around them and slowly pinched them into a small pocket. Not many men escaped. Also, make sure you have a good line of retreat open. If we can keep the heights, we can slow them down for a day or so. I think the high command is working fast to bring up units probably north of us at Thala and west of us toward our supply center at Tebessa."

Everything the major said made great sense to the colonel. Knowing the British were moving south to support the American forces, he knew the dirty-looking major was either well informed or had the strategic sense to understand the situation. As the senior officer looked around the small command post, Sergeant Dean ran into the tent.

"Major, I've got a count on the ammunition."

Ignoring the colonel for a minute, he asked, "Any good news, Willie?"

"Not much, Major. The artillery boys have less than fifty rounds for each of the 75s, and the 37s have only forty rounds left. Most of it is antipersonnel, but it's all we have. The mortars have maybe enough to fire thirty times, and then they can throw rocks. The machine guns have lots of ammo and so do the rifle units. The medics are nearly out of morphine and bandages. Food is nearly gone, and there may be enough water to get through tomorrow, if we're lucky."

"Thanks, Willie. What's the morale like?"

"Sir, the guys we came in with are going to be fine. A lot of those who escaped from the hills aren't ready to fight much. The artillery guys are nervous, and the mortar men are looking scared. Sounds like a dark night on Guadalcanal to me."

Smiling at his sergeant and friend, the Flannigan replied, "Go around again and keep these guys focused. Rigsby's men are good, but try to move some of them around with the stragglers we picked up yesterday. Give them a pep talk—tell them the Germans aren't that tough."

"Aye, aye, Major. You want me back here when things get hot?"

"Good idea, Willie. Keep your head down."

The sergeant exited the tent, and the colonel watched the man leave, holding onto his Thompson submachine gun like a small child. Turning to speak to the major, he asked, "Major, it sounds like you've been in some tough fights. What's this about Guadalcanal?"

Not wanting to get into great detail but knowing he had to respond to what effectively was now his commanding officer, Flannigan replied. "Sir, the sergeant and I spent time at Guadalcanal in August and again in November."

"I thought the Marines did all of the original fighting."

"Yes sir. I'm a Marine assigned to the staff of the chief of Naval Operations."

The colonel was astonished and asked, "What the hell are you doing in Africa?"

"Colonel, my unit was tasked to assist General Eisenhower, and I have toured General Patton's command in Morocco and now General Fredendall's II Corps."

Looking at the officer, the colonel grinned. "Damn long way from the Pacific, but I'm glad to have you here to help out. From looking at what you've done to deploy these men, you know the score. Any advice for me and the units I brought down to help?"

Flannigan didn't like giving advice to anyone in the army, let alone a colonel, but the man asked. "Sir, move your men to higher ground. Get them to dig in and keep your tanks back. The light ones are not worth the effort and will only get chewed up by the Germans. Move your artillery back but have a way for them to move quickly up the road to Thala. Establish a reserve that can plug any holes because once the Germans open up a line of attack, they pour through it. Rommel is opportunistic, and his men will move quickly without considering a counterattack."

Flannigan thought some more then added his last comment. "Sir, keep your units in contact with each flank. Establish some sort of communications so that if the Germans push through, you will know it before you are rolled up by their tanks."

The colonel thought the advice was sound. Just like the units he was given to move south to defend the pass, they were all new to combat, making for many mistakes. The colonel couldn't afford to make any errors. General Ward told him to plug the hole and pullback only if there was no alternative. Perhaps the general wanted him to sacrifice himself, if needed, to complete his mission. Looking at the quiet but confident Marine, the colonel asked one more question. "Major, when do you expect the enemy to attack?"

Looking at his watch and then looking at the sky, which was just beginning to lighten, Flannigan replied. "Sir, I think Rommel will be coming in the next two or three hours. Expect him to make a move at the center of the valley, hoping we'll expose ourselves by shooting early. Keep your men under cover and let them get close. It's our only chance to slow them down."

The colonel shook Flannigan's hand and wished him well. The man got back in his jeep and drove away. The Marine major looked around the small tent, grabbed his Thompson and walked toward the forward observation post and the reality of war.

The order to pullback came late in the day. The provisional battalion commanded by the Marine major had held its position despite three attacks. The men had acquitted themselves well, but the casualties mounted with each new German push up the hill. Ammunition had been brought in at midday and quickly expended to help close the gaping hole in the American line in what was now known as Task Force Stark.

Elements of Combat Command C, survivors of the One-Sixty-Eighth Regiment and most of Colonel Stark's Twenty-Sixth Regiment of First Armored Division were scattered in the floor of the valley. Other units were on the heights on both sides of the pass which connected what was known as Highway 17 leading north to Thala and the road to Tebessa. As Flannigan looked down into the valley, all he could see was smoke and devastation. American tanks, trucks, and field artillery pieces were strewn about the valley floor. Some of the tanks were still on fire, or as the soldiers called it, "cooking off." The Germans and Italians suffered significant losses as well. The howitzers had hit many enemy tanks and destroyed them, but not enough to stop the advance.

Sergeant Dean laid next to the major. He looked up and down the line of men who would serve as the rearguard as the men retreated. Dean hated the word and wanted to stay and fight it out with the Nazis but knew it would not make any difference. A good Marine filled with all of the skills and bravery known in the Corps couldn't stop a German tank. Flannigan looked behind him and saw the last group of men heading north to catch up with the other units making their way to what would be a new defensive line. At least the Germans had stopped coming up the hill. But the knowledge was only a slight reprieve. The enemy would move to flank his position soon, and now with his remaining rearguard of less than thirty men, there was no way to stop a concerted attack.

Waiting five more minutes to ensure the enemy was not massing for another attack, the major gave his signal to withdraw. Slowly, men crawled backward, and upon arriving at the reverse slope, they ran down the hill in a crouch position, fearing another barrage from the enemy artillery. After seeing the men pullback, Flannigan said, "Okay, Willie, it's time we got the hell off this hill. Stay low, and let's see if we can catch the bastards asleep at the wheel."

The two men crawled on their bellies until they were further down the hill. Finally reaching a point where they could stand but still crouching forward, they headed down to where one of the army sergeants was waiting for them. Signaling for the rearguard to move out, the men sprinted down a small wadi heading toward the road, but far enough to the east of it as not to be seen. The majority of his battalion had moved to waiting trucks, which Flannigan had hidden two days earlier for their escape. His rearguard would be walking for most of the way north, but were far enough off the road to avoid detection. Darkness fell quickly now, and Corporal Hudson was again on point. Flannigan told Captain Rigsby if they made it out of this mess alive, he would get the corporal promoted and given a medal for doing a great job.

As the men moved north, paralleling what was called a highway, Flannigan stopped every few minutes and listened for any sound from the south. Every so often, he heard the clank of a tank far off in the distance. The engine noises were distant, so Rommel's panzers were not trying to chase the survivors at close range. The wily German commander wondered what the Allies were planning ahead of him and didn't want to run into a heavy defensive position at night. The Afrika Corps would bide its time and move forward after consolidating its power into a central striking unit. Other German formations were moving toward Tebessa while another strong unit moved directly toward Sbiba. The enemy wanted to push the Allies back to consolidate their defensive positions around the Eastern Dorsal and destroy as many American, French, and British units as possible.

Around midnight, the small rearguard ran into some of the escaping units from the Stark Force, and the men were able to catch a ride north toward the relative safety of the new Allied defensive line now being formed south of Thala. As soon as he knew his men were safe, Flannigan fell fast asleep in the back of a half-track, filled with other dirty and exhausted men. Sergeant Dean kept a watchful eye over the major and wondered what had kept the man going the past five days. Hoping the small convoy reached the new defensive line before dawn and the appearance of the Luftwaffe, Dean gazed up at the night sky and kept his vigil.

25

23 February 1943
Algiers, Algeria

- Tunisia--Rommel assumes command of German Army Group, Africa, as Axis forces continue reorganization.
  - 18th Army Group: Gen. Alexander informs Gen. Montgomery that situation at Kasserine has improved and orders him not to take undue risks.
  - In British 1st Army's U.S. II Corps area, final enemy forces withdraw into Kasserine Pass during morning, followed unaggressively by Allied forces. Enemy and Allied planes are active during the day.
- USSR--Sumy in the Ukraine, northwest of Kharkov, falls to Red Army.

The Royal Navy lieutenant was still trying to match up the inventory of an American ship with what was supposed to be the shipping orders. Nothing matched. Sherman tanks were being rushed to the front, but spare parts, extra treads, and lubricants were unavailable. The last week of fighting had seen the loss of one hundred eighty-three tanks, one hundred four half-tracks, more than two hundred guns, and five hundred jeeps and trucks. More importantly, some six thousand men had been wounded, killed, or captured. Replacement units had been rushed to the front within the first days of the enemy offensive, and now additional units were being pushed forward to bolster the front lines. British units had held the front at Thala aided by the timely arrival of the Ninth Infantry Division's artillery, which helped stop the German tanks. Small groups of Americans were moving forward to the front from as far back as Oran and cobbled together into some semblance of a fighting organization. Commanders were unsure of where they were going or what they would do when they reached their positions. The Americans had been pushed back eighty-five miles from their lines along the Eastern Dorsal, but finally held at Thala and Sbiba, ably aided by British units rushed to their aid.

Duncan Clark sat behind a makeshift desk, searching diligently to find the correct report. Sergeant McBride held another report which might help the Scottish officer. The two men had developed a close friendship, and with Meyers away in Portugal, they tried their best to help Captain Jameson, but the task was far from easy. The captain received orders to pull his men out of Algeria and return to Washington as soon as possible. Jameson had signaled Admiral Edwards his reluctance to leave until he could locate his other men somewhere in Tunisia. Finding them was difficult because of the raging battle and tenuous communications. Harry Butcher had provided the last sighting of Major Flannigan when he joined Eisenhower on a tour of Fredendall's command center. The last information on Flannigan's whereabouts had him checking out the front line troops.

Dr. Feldman's situation was similar. His last known sighting was three days ago at a field hospital near the town of Thala. The battle near the village raged for two days, and so far, all attempts to get a message through had been fruitless. The captain sought out Butcher for his help, but the battle up and down the Tunisian hills and valleys proved the old adage about the "fog of war." Little was known about the actual situation because of incomplete or non-existent communication.

At Eisenhower's headquarters, the air force liaison had offered his help, but the forward air bases had been overrun by Rommel's forces. Aerial observation was spotty at best and no one was sure what units were in which areas. General Fredendall had little idea of what his unit commanders were doing, but he issued orders to hold positions and drive the enemy back at all costs. The only problem being the commanding

231

general never left his headquarters, and his original distribution of forces caused many holes in both communications and command.

Clark's work was interrupted by a messenger from the Supreme Commander's headquarters. The American sergeant appeared to have taken a camel to find their office—what used to be the French Navy's command center. The French were still here but begrudgingly gave space to the American naval staff at the port. Captain Jameson was lucky to find two offices in the complex, which the team shared with the American liaison's staff working to turn around American convoys. The sergeant handed the Royal Navy officer a form to sign and then gave him an envelope for Captain Jameson. The sergeant knew the protocol and asked if he should wait for a reply, which the Scot thought was a good idea. The phones rarely worked in the building, and getting through to Eisenhower's headquarters was a hit or miss proposition. Men like the sergeant spent their days tooling around on motorcycles delivering messages to various command centers and nearby air bases.

Taking the message into the captain's office, Clark came to attention and handed Jameson the envelope. "Sit down, Clark. I think this should be an update on the location of our lost sheep. At least that's what I hope it is."

Duncan hoped it was good news and not the kind often transmitted on message forms. As the battle raged in Tunisia, Clark received reports from a few RAF pilots trying to help the beleaguered ground troops but often tangled with Luftwaffe fighters instead. The situation, as they reported it, was confused and evolving. Knowing this meant no one knew what the hell was happening on the ground, the lieutenant grew more concerned for his new friends.

Jameson opened the envelope and read the message. It didn't say much, but at least there was some good news on Dr. Feldman and Pharmacist Mate Hamlin.

Smiling for the first time in a few days, the captain reported, "Looks like Doc and Hamlin are working their butts off at a British field hospital north of Sbiba. Eisenhower sent a request to General Anderson to see if he could find our boys, and it appears they are doing good. They will be sent back to us tomorrow, with a convoy of wounded men being evacuated from the front."

"Good news, sir. Anything concerning Major Flannigan?"

"Unfortunately, nothing new. My friend Harry has heard that

Flannigan and Dean worked their way to the front lines and got tied up in the attacks around Sidi Bou Zid. He told me the men escaped to new positions at Kasserine, where Robert was commanding a makeshift battalion holding the hills above the valley floor. Sounds like something he would do. There's been nothing else reported since the nineteenth."

"Do you think he withdrew with the people heading toward Thala or more toward the Tebessa area?"

"I wish I knew, but all Harry had was that the order came to retire during the evening, and most units pulled back in good order with Rommel not following too closely. I heard that we lost many men, and some units were captured, including General Patton's son-in-law."

Both men said nothing for a few moments, but finally, the plucky Scot added his thoughts. "Captain, I'm quite certain the major would not surrender, and he has enough sense to know when to beat a quick retreat. I would think he is somewhere close to the enemy complaining about the army, the lack of food, and the commanders who messed this thing up in the first place."

Jameson did not take offense at the remark about senior officers. He knew from Harry Butcher that Eisenhower was mad at himself for letting this battle get out of control. The commanding general was furious about how poorly some American units had been led and how they had fought. Some of the reports showed how the commands had been decentralized and often too far away for mutual support. The Germans were amazed at the sloppiness of their newest enemy and how poorly they were organized. Deciding to stay on the positive side of the equation, Jameson said, "There will be enough time to figure out who did what later. For right now, it appears we have contained the enemy's penetration into our lines. General Eisenhower has sent General Harmon to find out what's happening and make recommendations. From what I've heard about the general, many people will not be happy."

Clark, knowing how the British Expeditionary Force had been manhandled by the Germans in France, realized there would be many changes in the American army's command. He hoped Flannigan and Dean were safe but knew from his own combat experience that luck is meted out strangely and without consideration to friend and foe alike.

The previous day had been a fight to the finish. The British Twen-ty-Sixth Armored Brigade commanded by Brigadier A. L. Dunphie had blunted the German attack and, with the help of artillery from the hast-ily deployed Ninth Infantry Division, stopped the panzers from reaching Thala. Additional American units were thrown into the line, including engineering companies, cooks, and clerks who had not held a rifle since basic training. So many men had pushed through the British lines in their flight to safety that the British were seeing their new Allies as in-competent at best and at worst, cowards. Not a good way to start a war, or at least that is what Flannigan had said when his unit arrived three days ago. As haphazard as it was, his command still had fight in it, and they took up positions to the right of a company of British antitank guns.

For two days, the fighting ebbed and flowed with Germans trying to push men forward during the night but running into stiff Allied re-sistance. Three times, Flannigan's men had repulsed attacks and quickly developed a good working relationship with the British units on both sides of them. Soon, the more experienced Brits expressed confidence in these fighters, especially in the officers. The last attack had been stopped by the timely interdiction of Ninth Division's 105mm howitzers and a few 155mm guns being fired from their positions near the town. The German tanks were targeted effectively, and after several of their Tigers had been rendered useless, the panzers pulled back and slowly retreated back to Kasserine Pass.

Early in the morning of the third day, hours before sunrise, Major Flannigan received a message to head to the command post of the Brit-ish brigade. Leaving the now experienced Captain Rigsby in command, the major and Sergeant Dean made their way back to find the British general. On three occasions, Flannigan had met the Brigadier when the man came to visit each of his units on the front line. The commanding officer was quite a sight walking around without a helmet and carrying a riding crop like he was out to inspect his brigade on a parade ground, not a battlefield. Both men took a liking to each other quickly, with Dun-phie assigning the American command over two British companies and a battery of antitank guns. The sun was just beginning to come up in the cold desert. Men huddled around in small clumps drinking tepid tea and trying to chew on British biscuits. Dean thought the best thing about the hard crackers, as he called them, was to remove bad teeth. Staying outside, he went in search of coffee, hoping the Brits had something to drink besides tea and canned milk.

Flannigan entered the tent and stood at attention in front of the Brigadier as he finished speaking with another officer engulfed in a long heavy coat with an army green winter cap pulled over his ears before turning to the American Marine. "Major, good to see you made it through the night. Well done! Did you take any casualties?"

"Sir, we lost three men in my unit and four men from one of your antitank guns hit by enemy fire. Two died, but the other two will make it."

Not saying anything about the losses, which would be added to the number of men his brigade had lost in the past few days, Dunphie introduced the man standing next to him, studying the map on the table.

"General, I'd like you to meet one of your officers. Splendid job he and his men have done. He held his position despite repeated attacks by the Germans. I gave him command of some of my units as well, and he seems to be well-liked by our men."

The general turned and looked at the officer and suddenly said, "Damn it, Flannigan. Where the hell have you been? People have been looking all over for you."

Major General Ernest Harmon had been pulled out of Morocco by Eisenhower five days ago to find out what was wrong with the American units fighting in Tunisia. Officially, he had been made second in command of II Corps and authorized to replace any man he thought was not doing his job, including the Corps commander. So far, the hard-charging general was traveling the front to find out what was going on, something General Fredendall had failed to do.

"Sir, I've been too busy being chased over the hills by Rommel to worry about anything else."

Smiling at the Marine major, who was a known commodity, Harmon asked, "What's happening at the front?"

"General, I think the Germans have had enough for the time being and have pulled back. I would think they are going to hold up at the pass and consolidate their situation. They will probably fall back to their original line of departure in a few days because their lines are too extended to defend against a major Allied attack. Rommel did most of what he wanted to do, but he didn't get as far as he probably planned. If I was in his shoes, I would push to our major supply points, capture or destroy them and then withdraw. This would put us in a bind for at least another month and allow the enemy time to beef up his defensive positions."

Dunphie listened to what the major said and added his own commentary. "General Harmon, the major speaks accurately as to the enemy's intent. I think if we had not stopped them here and over toward Tebessa, the bloody Germans would have easily destroyed our ability to maintain our push into Tunisia. People like the major and his men did an outstanding job in delaying Rommel's movement until we could move south to stop them."

The American general was impressed with the Brigadier, and what he had seen so far in this sector, his appreciation for the British defense was growing. Now the Marine major had added his view of the situation, and he needed to get more information on what had happened from someone who was an active participant.

Looking at the British Brigadier, he asked, "Sir, if I could borrow the major for a few minutes, I would like his assessment before joining up with your unit."

Sensing the American wanted to talk in private with the major, Dunphie replied, "General, I need to go check on my men. Perhaps we can continue our conversation in an hour."

Acknowledging the diplomatic way the man spoke, Harmon said, "Thank you, Brigadier. I look forward to hearing your thoughts."

The British officer picked up his riding crop, and as he walked out the tent, he added, "Hope to see you soon, Major Flannigan. Don't leave without saying goodbye."

Before the Marine could reply, the senior British officer left the tent. Harmon pulled Flannigan toward maps of the battlefield. Keeping his voice down, but with the same commanding presence, Harmon asked, "What the hell happened out there? It seems our army failed to fight."

Flannigan, who had become more diplomatic in the last year working with Captain Jameson, took a deep breath. "General, I am unaware of the orders other units received, so I cannot comment on what I do not know. However, the original set up for the battle was ill-conceived, poorly executed, broke all the laws of war, and led by incompetent fools."

Harmon's lack of facial expression did not lessen his appreciation for the officer's candor, so he pushed for more information. "Major, I know your reputation and your experiences in the war. Saying that, what did you witness from your perspective in the last ten days of fighting?"

Thinking back to what seemed like another lifetime, Robert Flannigan threw caution to the wind. "General, whoever broke up the units into these small commands shouldn't be in charge of a kitchen, let alone a field combat organization. Every battalion commander I encountered was working on the premise that mobile reinforcements were ready to come to their aid. The command I was attached to was positioned on a hill without receiving or capable of providing aid to nearby units. Without concentration of forces, the enemy took on each unit in order and destroyed them. I witnessed the destruction of two battalions because their supporting units were too far away to provide assistance."

Taking a moment to collect his thoughts, Flannigan added, "The situation called for good communications, which were non-existent. The commanders of the armored units charged through the valley like they were Custer's cavalry and were cut to pieces by the German's antitank guns before they could get in a single shot at the enemy. Our tanks performed heroically but haphazardly. Time after time, I saw two or three tanks move forward, and the enemy targeted the rear tank first, so the front tanks didn't know what was happening until it was too late. Evidently, no one but me had taken the time to read about the British experiences fighting Rommel and how they allowed Allied tanks to be lured into their firing range and then destroyed."

Harmon looked on as the man seemed to be back on the front lines watching fellow Americans being killed then routed by the professionals of the Afrika Corps. The general had heard other stories on his tour and from some of General Fredendall's staff who had been near the front lines. Trying to keep his poise, Harmon asked, "Tell me about your pull-back to the Kasserine Pass. I understand from the Brigadier that is where you took over a battalion."

Taking a deep breath, the Marine tapped two fingers against the map to indicate troop positions. "General, when I got the company I was attached to off the hillside, we moved over to the Kasserine Pass area looking for friendly units. Luckily, the Germans reacted slowly to the collapse of our lines. Otherwise, they would be approaching Algiers by now."

Harmon weighed the comment and decided the German commanders were unprepared to take advantage of the American failures to defend the Eastern Dorsal at Sidi Bou Zid. If he were in charge of an experienced group of tanks like the Germans, he would have pushed on until his men ran out of fuel or hit the Mediterranean Sea.

"Sir, I was given command of a bunch of platoons, squads, and rear echelon troops who luckily wanted to keep on fighting. The company commander, Captain Rigsby, did an excellent job helping pull these men together as a fighting unit. I just provided guidance on dispositions. I received orders to hold the hills on the right side of the pass with my force, which I think may have numbered four hundred, maybe more. We were lucky the Germans spent most of their effort in the valley, destroying the units that were trying to hold out there. The other hillside units did a good job and held until nightfall when, like my command, retired to the British lines south of Thala. This is where I put the unit under the command of the British."

"Why didn't you continue heading north? I think you had done your job so no one would say you were bugging out." General Harmon needed to ask the question because he knew so many American units passed through the new Allied defense positions and kept moving away from the battle.

"General, the British needed all the help they could get, and there was no way I could keep heading north. I told the officers they could continue moving because, officially, I was not their commanding officer. Still, every one of those men stayed and rallied their men to fight like demons against several enemy attacks. I'm proud of them all."

Sensing an opportunity to get more of the man's unvarnished views on the battle, Harmon asked, "What kept you going? Why did these men fight while others ran away?"

Taking his time and not wanting to air more dirty laundry, Flannigan slowly responded. "Sir, I think it's a matter of pride. These men needed someone to tell them why they were fighting and why it was important to put themselves in harm's way to stop the Germans. If an officer can do this, his men usually, though not always, will follow him. I think, sir, if the average soldier sees a senior officer willing to die for the cause, they will stay and fight. My biggest concern was to convince them to keep fighting when they saw so many men run from the battle. If I could do anything different, it would be to try to convince those heading for safety to join up with my men, not for me, but to help themselves. I believe it's going to take some time for some of these men and units to regain their courage."

"Major, what about the officers who ran this show? Should we get a new team in here to lead these men?"

Sensing the general was asking for his opinion, the major responded. "General, the men will fight if they have trust in their senior officers. The same goes for their battalion, company, and platoon leaders. If we try to cover this up and move people around, things will not change. It's not my job to make recommendations on senior leaders, sir."

Harmon decided to push. He already had the commitment from Eisenhower to make recommendations on removing anyone from command he thought was not measuring up to his standards. This included the II Corps commander and the commanding general of the First Armored Division. "Do you think we need new blood, Major, or can we just move a few pieces around the chess board and see if anyone notices?"

Knowing the pressure Eisenhower was under and being tutored in power politics by Captain Jameson and Admiral Edwards, Flannigan responded with his version of the truth.

"Sir, whoever was leading this mess, should be replaced. Several senior officers are not fit to command this type of new warfare. They aren't cowards; they just don't see the big picture of how this war is being fought. The same goes for colonels and majors who have been given field commands but failed to lead their units in combat or, worse yet, pulled back, leaving other units without support. General, I saw men die over the last ten days, and it makes me mad as hell to see good men killed or wounded without a good explanation of why we are asking them to make this sacrifice. We owe it to the dead and the living to get this army moving in the right direction."

The general had sensed the same thing when he came to Fredendall's headquarters and found out the commanding general had not been to the front. As he examined the situation and found how General Anderson had broken up both British and American units to set up defensive positions, he was livid. What bothered the man most was that the American II Corps commander didn't object to these orders. Now, he was confronted by an honest officer who knew war more than most men he had ever known. The man's reputation was exemplary. He didn't have to fight but instinctively took command of several units, including British units, and successfully fought the enemy to a standstill.

"All right, Major, let me get in touch with II Corps HQ and arrange transportation for you and your sergeant back to Algiers. Do you have a recommendation for who will take over your unit, which I guess is about the size of a small battalion?"

"Sir, Captain Rigsby is the perfect man for this job and I would recommend that he be promoted to major as well. The man is the type of leader the army needs now. I would also like to add a corporal named Hudson to your list of promotions. He should be a platoon sergeant."

"Very well, I'll get with the brigadier and tell him Rigsby will be taking over, and I will make a recommendation that he should be promoted to major as soon as I get back to HQ. Same for Corporal Hudson."

"Thank you, General. Let me get back to the unit to make sure everything is in good order, and then I'll get my gear and Sergeant Dean and head back to Algiers. Do you have any idea as to what I'm to do in Algiers?"

"All I heard from General Smith was if I found you, to get you back to Algiers. The order came from Admiral Edwards, but Beetle told me it actually came from Admiral Leahy. You must work in rarefied air, Major, to get this kind of interest."

Not saying anything in response, but immediately wondering what was going on in Washington. "Sir, it was good seeing you again, and I know you will make the recommendations necessary to move the army forward."

"Major, I'll tell General Eisenhower how much you have done for this command, and I know he will pass that on to Washington. I hope to see more of you in the future, and if you have any ideas on how to improve our situation, please keep in touch. I would like you for my staff one day, but I doubt Admiral King would be willing to let you go to work for the army."

Shaking the outstretched hand of the hard-charging army general, Flannigan replied, "Sir, it would be an honor to serve with you in the future."

As the man left the tent, General Harmon took out his notebook and scribbled a few notes on what the Marine officer had told him. Returning the notebook to his coat, the general knew precisely what he would recommend.

26

25 February 1943
Hotel Palacio
Estoril, Portugal

- SWPA Command--Rough draft of the long-range plan for advance to the Philippines (RENO) is drawn up.
- Russell Islands--Torpedo boat base at Wernham Cove becomes operational.
- Tunisia--18th Army Group: In British 1st Army area, U.S. II Corps, hampered only by land mines and booby traps, recovers Kasserine Pass. 9th Division is concentrating in Tebessa area under corps command.
- United Kingdom--RAF begins round-the-clock air offensive against enemy.

New to the casino, the man was better dressed than many of the customers, at least in terms of the newness of his clothes. Many of the regulars were doing their utmost to conserve their wardrobe. Frayed collars and cuffs showed under the jackets of the well-dressed men. Some of the pants and suit coats showed signs of becoming threadbare or shining where there should be the dull luster of a heavy woolen fabric. The ladies were in the same situation. Only the richest could afford to buy new clothes, and even then, the selection was limited to whatever could be brought in from South America. Clothing from the United States and Britain was difficult to purchase, not only because of the import restrictions but also the un-availability of materials. European clothing manufacturing had ceased to exist unless you were wearing a uniform. Yet, the jewels sparkled, the men smiled, and the cigars seemed as plentiful as the local wine.

John Meyers had worked every day since arriving in Lisbon, and finally, his boss told him to enjoy a night out. Not being allowed to be by himself, at least on his first night, Thomas Murdoch would serve as his guide to the high-end nightlife of Portugal. A car from the legation drove them to the coastal town of Estoril, about eleven miles southwest from Lisbon. Facing the Atlantic Ocean, the Palacio Estoril Hotel had the grandest casino still operating in Europe. Warned to be careful with his contacts, the naval officer in his civilian clothes felt good at being in a place that appeared to be free of the worldwide conflict. As the two men walked into the bar, John could feel all eyes were on him. The dark wood paneling and subdued lighting made everyone seated around the bar even more mysterious. Murdoch pointed to two empty seats, and once settled, the bartender approached, asking in Portuguese what they wanted to drink. Thomas replied in his rudimentary Portuguese that the two men wanted Scotch. The bartender immediately switched to English, saying, "We have only a poor quality of whiskey. Perhaps a fine aged rum would be of interest?"

The American quickly agreed. Pouring each man a large amount of dark rum into a short glass and placing a single ice cube in it, the bartender followed with an artfully carved piece of lemon. The two men graciously accepted the drink and slowly sipped the rum as the bartender watched their expression.

"Excellent!" John stated and took another sip. He had never had an aged dark rum before and found the elixir better than most bourbons. It was smooth and slightly sweet, with the small amount of lemon peel adding just a hint of flavor to the liquid. The bartender smiled and asked, "You are new to Estoril, and you must be an American, yes?"

"Yes, on both counts," Meyers replied. "You speak excellent English. How did you learn the language?"

The bartender, who later told the Americans his name was Bento, meaning "blessed one," said he learned it in school first and then served on a Portuguese passenger ship before the war, where he met many English people. He also added that he spoke Spanish, German, French, and Italian and was learning some of the Slavic languages spoken by members of royal families from the now occupied Balkan countries.

As the man took another order from a nearby customer, the two men slowly sipped their drinks and surveyed the situation. Murdoch looked at his drink and whispered, "Two o'clock, that's the local Portuguese secret police officer who hangs out in the bar. Don't get into any conversations with him."

Knowing from his many lectures since arriving in Lisbon about spy craft, Meyers looked in a different direction and raised an eyebrow to show his understanding. The two men continued to check out the local patrons, and in another moment, Thomas pointed at the bottle of rum sitting on the back bar and said, "Check your six. That guy is Gestapo. Don't know the man he's sitting with."

Again, not moving or saying anything, John grabbed the piece of lemon and swirled it around the rim, and placed it at the six o'clock position, again signifying his understanding. He would take a casual look later. There was little fear of being targeted by the enemy, but he had been told to remain cautious around any person unknown to him. As the bartender refilled their drinks, several other men were pointed out. Two were British diplomats. Another was the Free French liaison in the city. Looking to his right was a member of the Zionist movement working on relocating Jewish refugees. Several Italian businessmen who were probably with their nation's intelligence agency huddled near a corner table. And finally, two members of the former Romanian royal family who showed little interest in the board game they were playing.

The two Americans talked about life after the war and how each man wanted to do something meaningful with their lives. The war had shown how their lives could make a difference to others, not just making money or, in John's case, building trust funds for the wealthy and finding ways to hide corporate cash in tax havens around the globe. Murdoch had worked at a Wall Street investment company and wanted to serve in the military but was recruited ostensibly for the State Department. Actually, the OSS found him based on his university connections at Yale.

Within six months, he found his way to North Africa to work for Murphy, and right after the invasion of North Africa, he was sent to Lisbon to work on the Azores' problem. The man spoke French and Spanish and was now mastering Portuguese, allowing him to work in both the diplomatic world and the intelligence communities.

As the men continued their discussion of post-war lives, a beautiful young woman approached and smiled at Thomas saying, "Mr. Murdoch, do you have a light?"

The American quickly grabbed his lighter and lit the lady's cigarette. She exhaled as the OSS officer closed the top on the lighter, and she asked, "Please introduce me to your new friend."

"Duchess, this is Mr. John Meyers. John, this is Countess Christina. Her father was the brother of the late Count of Covadonga of Spain."

"It is good to meet you, Countess."

"Mr. Murdoch, your friend can say more than that, can't he, or is he on official business tonight?"

John was entranced by the woman. She was tall, reddish-blonde hair, dark brooding eyes, and poured into a tight-fitting dress which left little to the imagination. Sensing he needed to answer the lady, Meyers responded, "Countess, Thomas and I are not on official business tonight. Perhaps you would like to join us?"

Standing up to allow the lady to take his seat, John asked the bartender to bring the Countess a drink. Asking for Cava, the Spanish equivalent of champagne, the three people were soon engaged in a conversation, at once straight forward and then turning provocative. Murdoch caught John's eye to tell him not to get involved too deeply, which Meyers understood as a security warning. But for now, the threesome enjoyed the time together. After her one glass of bubbly, the Countess politely excused herself because she needed to see other people who had just entered the bar.

Murdoch later explained she was checking out John to see if he was possibly helpful to the royal families currently exiled in Portugal. The Spanish monarchy was deposed in 1931, with its last king, Alphonso XIII, exiled to Rome where he died in 1941. Many former royal family members left their homeland for other European nations, especially Italy and Switzerland, but the Countess' father stayed close to his native land and lived north of Porto. His youngest daughter, Christina, elected to be in the more vibrant Estoril close to other members of the aristocracy. Whispering, Robert said, "A good thirty percent of the people in this bar are members of some royal family. Most are penniless and live off the good fortune of friends or have found jobs in banking, commerce, or crime."

Not entirely understanding the last comment, Meyers leaned in to pick up his drink and asked, "What crimes are you talking about?"

Picking up his glass and smiling as he appeared to toast John, he quietly said, "Import and export of contraband. Think wolfram, oil, food, cloth, drugs, and of course, prostitution."

Now understanding the warning he had received on his first day in Lisbon, John understood the business of war in a neutral country. Survival, by the nation and the individual, was the preferred end-state of being. This was accomplished by dealing with both sides and not caring too much about the winner. In the early days of the war, Portugal wanted to keep Germany from invading. But as the war progressed, everyone could see the Axis powers losing ground, especially in North Africa. Now the government of Salazar was bending to more requests from the British and Americans. Each day brought news of more German set-backs and Allied victories. It might not be soon, but the Germans were slowly losing the war.

Murdoch saw someone he knew and told John to stay at the bar and defend his chair. Smiling at the thought of fending off boarders like in some pirate movie, Meyers ordered another drink. He was starting to develop a great liking for the rum and wondered how much a bottle cost. Waiting for his drink, John sensed a man standing behind him. Turning to see who it was, he heard the man speak in English but with a heavy German accent, "Herr Meyers, it is good to see you are having some fun at last. Everyone told me you worked very hard, but now I feel much better at seeing you enjoying the scenery."

The man was dressed in civilian clothes and held a cane in one hand. His left eye seemed distant, and John figured that the eye was seriously damaged. Composing himself, Meyers said, "I seem to be at a disadvantage, sir. May I know your name?"

The man with the cane almost came to attention, saying, "Kapi-tanleutanant Gebhardt Wagener, assistant naval attaché in the embassy of Germany. Lieutenant Meyers, I believe you are also a naval attaché?"

245

The German did not extend his hand, nor did Meyers. This scene was awkward enough already, but George Kennan told him it would probably happen. The two countries were at war and mortal enemies, but they were guests of the Portuguese government and behaved accordingly, at least in Lisbon.

John decided to act like the nonchalant American, asking, "So, Herr Wagener, how long have you been in Lisbon?"

Smiling at the American, the German officer replied, "I arrived in January and hope to head back to the Fatherland soon. I find this place strange. Too many lazy people waiting out the war and not caring who wins or loses. Is this the same reaction you have?"

John Meyers decided to play along. "Not the same thing. Most of the Portuguese I have met are industrious and worthy of our help. As to the clientele of this establishment, well, let's say things are not what they seem."

The German naval officer was informed of his new American counterpart within a few days of his arrival. There were no secrets in the city's diplomatic circles, and any officially accredited member of an embassy or legation staff was open knowledge. The man's rank, title, and official job were posted by the host government, but if a person was a member of a nation's military, it was understood they were probably working in intelligence. Yet, the officer of the navy of his country's enemy was worth talking to, if for no other reason but to talk about the sea.

Before Wagener could reply to the American's comment, Meyers opened up the conversation. "Since you know about me, what should I know about you? Since we're both not in uniform, I cannot see your insignia of rank, awards, or qualifications. I'm a reservist who left legal training before the war and worked on contracts. I am not a warrior, but it appears you have seen the worst aspects of the war. Am I wrong to say this?"

Gebhardt was quickly taken back by the man's candor. Americans were quite different from their English cousins and had a tendency to get down to business quickly, as they would say. Finding the openness refreshing and knowing the man seated at the bar was an enemy as well, Gebhardt responded. "I served on destroyers and then had the honor of serving on the *Scharnhorst* during one of its cruises in the Atlantic. I cannot tell you more than that, but I did have an unfortunate encounter with British bombs, which ended my seagoing career. I now serve the Reich in another capacity."

John waited for more information, but the enemy naval officer didn't add anything else. Deciding to keep the discussion going, John commented, "It is always difficult to deal with the tragedy of war. It's a nation's leaders who make war, but it is the people who suffer the consequences. I hope your condition improves with time and that you will be able to return to your country after the war."

Sensing the diplomatic nature of the response and the personal aspects concerning his health, Wagener decided to push his luck. "Yes, Lieutenant Meyers, I hope I will be able to return to Germany soon, preferably after you stop bombing our cities. But I know we did this first to England. I think you Americans call it payback?"

The American sensed something else about this man. Perhaps it was his wounds, or maybe there was a sense of honor and humanity in this enemy. Not smiling but being as sincere as possible, he jumped into the unknown. "My grandfather came from Bavaria in 1898 to escape being conscripted and sent off to war. Several of his brothers died in the First World War fighting for Germany. My father fought for America, and now three generations have passed, and again I am fighting Germany." Switching to German, John added, "There are many Americans from Germany, but now all of us are Americans, and we fight for our ideals, not just honor. Perhaps after the war, you can immigrate to my country."

Leaving the thought hanging for a moment, John studied the German officer. The man was stoic and proud. Yet, he appeared to have many doubts about his country and his present situation. Gebhardt slowly responded, in German but speaking very slowly to ensure the American understood him. "Lieutenant, I too have relatives in America. Many Germans have family who immigrated to your country over the last one hundred years. Perhaps I will join them after the war."

Raising his glass, John offered a toast to the German. "To the end of war, and may peace be restored and the rights of man guaranteed."

Wagener grabbed his glass and said in English, "To peace and cooperation." Both men sipped their drinks, and then the German began to walk away but suddenly stopped and moved closer to the American. He slowly placed his glass next to John's and whispered, "Tell Allen that his friend Wilhelm will be in Madrid in late April."

Standing back from the bar, the German made a point of saying in a loud voice, "Good meeting you, Lieutenant. Good luck in your new post." Then the man walked away, limping slightly and leaning on his cane. Several people watched the men, with more than the usual interest. Some were part of the Portuguese secret police. Others represented British, Italian, German, Swiss, Soviet, and even the Vatican, all looking for information. Reports would be issued to their respective bosses, but most would be ignored. But the one American who watched the conversation, Murdoch, was pleased by the interactions and the message. The Abwehr was not as pro-Nazi as many suspected, and the new German naval attaché had made the first move. Now, people in Washington and London would become very interested in two naval officers, one American and one German, working toward a common goal.

The new orders were hand-delivered two days ago. Commander Allen was told to pack his bags for temporary duty at Pearl Harbor. His elation on hearing the news and the chance to go to sea was quickly quashed. Admiral Edwards was sending him to CINCPAC to help Lieutenant Brand work on the new Central Pacific strategy, which was approved at the Casablanca Conference. The Combined Chiefs of Staff approved the American plan to strike deeper into Japanese territory, and Admiral Nimitz would control these operations. General MacArthur would move further into New Guinea, with the eventual task of destroying the Japanese forces at Rabaul. The SWPA campaign would have many parts characterized by breaking Japanese offensive capabilities in New Guinea, New Britain, and the other islands controlled by the Japanese in MacArthur's area.

The Bismarck Archipelago spanned thousands of miles of ocean starting in New Guinea and ranging through New Britain, New Ireland, the Trobriand Islands, and further east through the Solomon Islands. Only Guadalcanal was in the hands of the Americans. New Guinea was going to be a long, arduous campaign. The goal was to isolate the island of New Britain and the sprawling Japanese base at Rabaul. The town and its excellent harbor had been captured in late January 1942 from its Australian defenders. There were now over a hundred thousand enemy troops, four major air bases, and an excellent deep-water port with naval support capabilities for the Imperial Navy. From these island airfields, the Japanese had nearly destroyed the Americans on Guadalcanal. The Tokyo Express started in the harbor and supported all Japanese offensive and defensive capabilities for thousands of miles. MacArthur knew Rabaul had to be eliminated for his command to move north to the Philippines and then onto Japan itself.

Admiral Nimitz was ordered to move forward with his Central Pacific strategy while supporting MacArthur and Admiral Halsey in their battles with the Japanese in the air, islands, and waters east of Rabaul. The admiral's planning team suggested a set of long-range strikes starting in the Gilbert Islands and moving north to control key islands in the Marshalls. In addition, the Combined Chiefs authorized Nimitz to consolidate the American position in the Aleutians by eliminating the Japanese units on Kiska and Attu. All of this had to be accomplished with limited men and ships. The Mediterranean campaign would continue after the conquest of North Africa with a mid-summer invasion of Sicily, quickly followed by amphibious landings in Italy. American landing craft for these European operations would take precedence over any craft being made available to Nimitz. The American Pacific commander would have to wait for new construction, more men, and supplies, but he decided to move forward with advanced operational planning.

These new objectives were supported by the war plans group under Admiral Cooke. Still, Admiral King decided to send the professor to Pearl to help CINCPAC develop its strategy and the hundreds of support requirements for several unique operations. James provided Admiral Edwards with a twenty-five-page briefing paper that itemized each operation's logistical support needs. The requirement for advanced operating bases alone would take thousands of sailors and Marines plus thousands of tons of supplies before any invasion could take place.

Admiral King's chief of staff understood the situation, but Brand had crystallized his thinking on the enormity of the task. Everyone on the staff appreciated the professor's capability to synthesize information and reduce it to coherent and interconnected requirements. James told the admiral to think of Newton's third law, "When two objects interact, they apply forces to each other of equal magnitude and opposite direction."

If the navy wants to move a thousand men from point A to point B, what is required and what else will not be accomplished by this movement? Edwards realized the man's quiet reasoning made more sense than most of the staff work presented so far. The war could only be won by the calm and resolute work of millions of people doing their utmost to deliver the implements of war and everything associated with making these things work. Commander Allen had said it another way, "Only good planning can make things happen in a war."

Now, Allen would get a chance to work with CINCPAC's staff and, at the same time, keep James Brand under control. Admiral King met with the commander to make sure he comprehended his assignment in Hawaii. The CNO called Allen, Waverly, and Warrant Jones to his office to give them last-minute instructions. The meeting began as most sessions did with Admiral King, formal and dead serious. The men entered the office and stood at attention in front of the admiral's desk. King did not waste his words.

"I'm sending Brand to Hawaii to help Nimitz and his staff on war plans. The professor will not, I repeat not, leave Hawaii without my express orders. He is not to go flying around in planes. He cannot hitch a ride in a submarine, a PT boat, or an aircraft carrier. Do you understand my orders, gentlemen?"

All three men, still at attention, responded in unison, "Yes sir."

"Good. Stand at ease. I have a few more things to tell you about this particular mission."

Standing and circling his desk, King proudly looked at the men before him. He admired both Gunny and Lieutenant Waverly. These men were proven warriors and knew how to protect the professor. He was also appreciative of the work Allen had accomplished in his year working on the staff and knew the man wanted to go back to sea, but for right now, he was needed more in Washington.

"I received orders from the president to get Brand involved in the plans for the Pacific theater. Roosevelt likes the way the professor thinks and how he gets things done. I agree with the president. But hear me out on this, the lieutenant has a lot of energy and needs to keep both feet on the ground and do his work. Commander, you are going to supervise the lieutenant and the security detachment. Captain Jameson and his men are not due back for another week to ten days, which requires someone to keep the professor under control. You know him well, and you also know

Gunny and Waverly. They can fill you in on things you need to know on how Brand operates. Don't let him bamboozle you into anything other than the staff work on the island. Admiral Nimitz has been given the same orders, and his staff has been informed as well. Any questions?"

No one on staff ever asked Admiral King questions, except for a young lieutenant who was not only brave but ready to spar with the CNO. Luckily, for the three men standing in front him, the professor was in his office working on something to do with rockets. Moving directly in front of Commander Allen, King added, "Commander, I know you want another sea command. I will not commit to one right now, but I am sure Admiral Edwards will release you soon. You have made great contributions to this command, and you will be rewarded in time." The admiral gave the man a very slight grin, something Allen had never seen before. Perhaps, something was about to change in Washington.

Admiral Edwards stood by the large wall map of the Pacific, listening to the CNO's orders. He smiled at Allen, informing him that things were in the works to get him out of his staff position. But for right now, the commander's work was too important to give him command of a new destroyer. King turned to face his chief of staff, who knew what to do.

Edwards moved forward and gave a folder to Allen. "Commander, here are your orders for your travel to Hawaii and what you will be doing at CINCPAC. You will also find a special set of orders signed by Admiral King, General Marshall, General Arnold, and Admiral Leahey, which grants you emergency authority, if required. If you have any questions on these orders, Warrant Jones knows what to do. Brand has a set of codes which only he is authorized to use, to contact this office or the White House."

Moving his eyes to Lieutenant Waverly, the admiral continued. "Lieutenant Waverly, you will ensure your men don't let their guard down in Hawaii. I know you understand the situation and will do your duty. Warrant Jones will provide any assistance or guidance you need. Any questions?"

None were offered. The men were dismissed, with Allen accompanying Waverly and Jones to the Logistics Office to review the orders. Admiral King arranged for a new R5D, the navy version of the C-54, to transport the men to Hawaii. The plane would leave early in the morning and make only one stop for refueling before reaching San Francisco.

The team's favorite pilot, Lieutenant Commander Shoemaker, and his co-pilot, Lieutenant Miller, would fly the team all the way to Hawaii. The plane seated twenty-nine, so other passengers would fill the spaces not occupied by Brand and his team. This flight would be a much more comfortable trip than flying a cold bomber across the Pacific.

Allen knew about most of the Science Team's deployments, but since this was the first to include him, he asked lots of questions to Warrant Jones.

"Gunny, fill me in on the procedures for the trip."

"Not much to tell, Commander. The security team is always armed and ready to move at a moment's notice. We will keep all confidential and secret information in weighted bags in case we have to ditch. Since Dr. Feldman isn't with us on the trip, we don't have to carry his extra supplies. There will be the four Marine sergeants, the professor, and the three of us. The plane will be met at every stop by additional security personnel. Once we're at Pearl, we will be given accommodations near CINCPAC on Makalapa Hill."

As Allen filed this information away, Gunny added another comment, more political than anything the old Marine had ever said before. "Sir, you should take your best uniforms with you, plus your dress whites. There is an unusual social scene on the island, and you may be invited to some of these shindigs. The place we are billeted is full of senior brass, so the orders you're carrying may be needed. Admiral Nimitz and Admiral Spruance are down-to-earth officers, but since the build-up in Hawaii, there are more brass hats there than I've seen in my entire career."

Thanking Jones, Allen said, "I appreciate your candor, Gunny. I have heard similar things from some of the men who have come back from duty in the Pacific. The navy has been building more housing units than warships, so if you see something I need to do, call me on it."

The three men double-checked the information, and then in concert with Lieutenant Stevens, pulled together the information the professor wanted to take along on the trip. The files, reports, and books would fill four suitcases, but as Warrant Jones told the men, "Mr. Brand likes to have lots of back-up information to make his recommendations."

Later that evening, Allen came by the house to speak with James about last-minute requirements. James was in a sullen mood because he had spent the afternoon with his fiancée, Lady Margret, and knew it might be weeks or longer before he returned. Margret was pushing for a wedding date, but James was holding out on the decision because of his assignments. She wanted a June wedding at the latest, but Brand could not commit to anything that far away. The commander knew the young lovers wanted to get married but realized the war made these plans nearly impossible. Allen knew he would have to keep a close eye on the love-struck professor over the next few weeks. Hopefully, Captain Jameson would join them in the Pacific within the month to relieve him of his duties so the destroyer officer could push for a new command. That was his hope, but he understood better than most that plans were made to be changed.

27

27 February 1943
Allied Headquarters
Algiers, Algeria

- New Guinea--162nd Infantry, U.S. 41st Division, reaches Milne Bay.
- Tunisia--18th Army Group: In British 1st Army's 5 Corps area, hard fighting continues around Bedja, but enemy is unable to advance.
  - In U.S. II Corps area, 9th Division relieves 1st Division at El Ma el Abiod and Dernaia Pass, northwest of Feriana, and 1st Division assembles east of Tebessa.

The men were still packing their belongings, plus boxes of files and reports. Some of these papers were to be used planning the invasion of Sicily, while others provided context for what had happened in North Africa. Several files detailed the problems of supplying the land offensive while others provided information on the special logistical needs of the air forces fighting in the campaign. Two files were to be hand-delivered to the Chiefs of Staff on what was learned from the fighting in Tunisia.

The past twenty-four hours had seen Captain Jameson, Major Flannigan, and Dr. Feldman in meetings at Eisenhower's headquarters. The general had received a preliminary report from General Harmon on what had gone wrong at Kasserine Pass and was told about the heroic efforts of the Marine major and the splendid work by the navy doctor. Their first-hand accounts helped the supreme commander get a better picture of the situation. Harmon was furious by what he saw and recommended removing several senior officers and several regimental and battalion commanders. Eisenhower slowed the hard-charging tanker's desire to make changes, because the commanding general needed to collect more information on what happened. One source would come from the two highly respected officers in Captain Jameson's command.

Ike was blunt in what he wanted to know, and Major Flannigan was willing to comply with the command. The Marine detailed his experiences and how the original placement of troops provided the enemy an easy victory. The major declined to incriminate any senior officer by name but commented on the lack of common sense and tactical knowledge. Flannigan did provide several glimpses of hope for the future by discussing individual heroism. The Marine provided examples of line officers who did their duty and acted professionally. Flannigan also stated he was most grateful to the efforts of the British units to stem the enemy's advance.

Feldman added to the analysis by sharing his thoughts on how the medical units worked in aiding the wounded, even when their efforts could not save lives. He pressed for more forward aid stations, greater mobility of field hospitals, better communications to senior commanders, and access to emergency transport for the wounded. The doctor saved his most critical observation for last. "General, the army needs more support for the medical corps. Men were horribly burned in their tanks. Men succumbed to infection when they could have been saved. The field medics were beyond brave, but if a man cannot be quickly evacuated in combat, his chance of survival drops with every passing minute. He must be taken to an emergency station that can do more than dress wounds."

Eisenhower listened to the comments knowing he was the man responsible for each and every decision. Others might decide at the division or battalion level, but it was his army, and he owned this defeat. Ike thanked the men for their openness and told Jameson he looked forward to working with him again and to contact Harry Butcher if there was anything that could help his command. As the three men left the commander in chief's headquarters, Commander Butcher grabbed his old friend and pulled him aside for a private chat. Harry had sat in on the briefing and watched as Eisenhower listened to the report.

"Fred, the general appreciated your men's willingness to open up and tell him what they saw. Not everyone is willing to do this."

The captain realized what his old friend was saying. "Harry, nobody wants to damage his career or hurt someone else's reputation. Protecting the other guy, the old friend from academy days or days spent at the command school, is ingrained in most officers. But this war requires every officer to tell their commanding officer exactly what they saw and provide a solution. I think the general will learn a great deal from this battle. I hope it doesn't ruin his career."

Butcher looked toward where the major and the doctor were waiting for the captain and then said, "Fred, I think he understands, and Ike has learned. You will see some big changes shortly. General Marshall has told him to make whatever adjustments he needs to make, and the old man will back him up all the way to hell, if needed."

Smiling at the comment, Jameson replied, "Hope it's not all the way to hell. I've been very close to it, and it is not a nice place. I think the general will do fine, and as I hear things that might be important for him, I will contact you through a secure channel."

"Thanks for the vote of confidence. I think General Eisenhower is the only man we have who can hold this coalition together and keep Churchill from running the entire show. Marshall likes him, but if my man screws up, he'll be replaced, too. Keep in touch and have a safe trip home."

The two men shook hands, and then Jameson caught up with his two officers. No one spoke until they were inside the staff car to take them back to their temporary office. Feldman was the first to speak. "So, what does the commander think of our performance?"

"Doc, you and Robert did just fine. Eisenhower appreciated your candor and your suggestions. There will be changes coming. That's all I can tell you for now. Keep this to yourselves, and later we can talk. We need to be at the airport in four hours to catch our ride south to Casablanca, and then hopefully, make the jump to Brazil the next day. Are the men ready to go home?"

Flannigan replied to the question saying, "Sir, everybody is ready, and the documents are secure for the flight home. Both Dean and Hamlin are in clean uniforms, and both smell much better than when they arrived from the front."

Laughing, the captain said, "I know you and the doctor smell much better, but Dean must have slept with a camel or a dead goat for the last week you were out there with the army. Is he feeling all right now? He seemed to be very sleepy yesterday when I talked to him."

"Sir, I think the sergeant, like Pharmacist Mate Hamlin, had only a few minutes of sleep over the last ten or so days. Whenever possible, he would put his head down on a rock or propped up to some stone wall and close his eyes. With any noise, he was awake and moving. The man is amazing, and I don't know how he does it."

Feldman added to the conversation. "Jonathan was the same way. I found him sleeping next to the cot of a wounded man, but before I got close to him, he would wake up to check the man's vital signs or change a blood-soaked bandage. Then he would find another wounded man who needed surgery or sometimes just hold the hand of the dying. I am very proud of him, and when this war is over, I will make it my mission to get him into medical school."

The captain knew both of the officers did similar things for the days they spent in the field. Each man took enormous risks to save others. One man saved the lives of men horribly damaged in the war, while the other man saved men by leading them to fight the enemy and, when necessary, withdrawing to new positions. The captain thought he was a lucky officer to have men who would sacrifice everything to save others. He wished that he didn't have to ask anyone to do more in the war but feared with his new orders, he and his team would see more of the war than most and experience more loss. Wondering where James Brand was, he commented, "I'm not sure of what we'll find once we're back in Washington. I didn't get any specifics on the orders except to return immediately. I hope James hasn't caused any problems, but knowing him, he's probably volunteered us to march into Tokyo."

Feldman looked at his friend Robert Flannigan and said, "Nothing that simple, sir. I think the professor wants us to parachute into Tokyo and capture Hirohito."

The Marine rolled his eyes. He thought the comment was probably correct and hoped Waverly and Gunny kept Brand in check. Perhaps chains were a better way to keep him down, but that required a direct order from the president.

Arrangements had been made to fly to Delhi and then take the train to Bombay. A meeting of Allied supply officers was scheduled for March 4, which offered Lieutenant Beck the perfect chance to see the sights and conduct some personal business. His commanding officer, Commander Appleton, hated meetings, especially with the British high command. A visit with the British could come in handy for Beck whenever special favors were needed from the Allied supply chieftains. The commander thought highly of the lieutenant and could still not understand the cloud the man was under back in Washington. The officer had done everything asked and had come up with some excellent ideas on the use of local transportation companies, warehousing facilities, and speeding up the transfer of supplies to the railheads for delivery to Assam.

Telling the lieutenant to take a few days of leave, Beck asked if he could first continue on to Bombay to meet the Americans at the port. The lieutenant explained that meeting his counterparts in the city would facilitate the constant reconciliation of what was arriving at the various ports. Often a ship would be diverted to another port, causing nothing but headaches as men tried to find missing cargoes, personnel, and records. Commander Appleton thought this was a good idea and tacked on another week to Beck's travel orders.

Beck asked one more favor of his commanding officer. Since he would be visiting the port of Bombay, would the commander approve a visit to the nearby Portuguese territory of Goa? Carnival would be in full swing, and the local British officers highly recommended attending the days of partying and dancing. It was quite different from the festivals of India, and Beck thought it would be an excellent chance to see this special place. The commander agreed and said he would make sure Beck had the correct paperwork to get into the colony and, more importantly, get out again. The lieutenant feigned ignorance of what the commander was saying. Beck already had his business associates provide him with the details for obtaining the necessary permissions to cross into the neutral territory and how to deal with any issues concerning what he was bringing into the country. Nothing could be left to chance, and Beck didn't like to take chances with what he would be carrying.

Before the travel north to the British headquarters in Delhi, the lieutenant met individually with his partners. Each man provided an update on their part of the business, including recent additions to the support team. Each team operated in different parts of the country, providing either the intelligence or the muscle for the operation. The partners in Calcutta built the master plan for diverting supplies or skimming deliveries and then delivering these resources to third-party buyers. The local teams provided detailed knowledge for hiding the supplies, cannibalizing machinery, delivering foodstuffs, and selling fuel on the black market. Each team was at least three steps away from the men in Calcutta. Proving a connection between Beck and his partners would be very difficult, thus making a legal indictment nearly impossible.

At last, the American would collect the proceeds from these operations and make the initial set of deposits in a neutral country for postwar distribution. Secrecy was now more critical than ever. A fortune was at hand, requiring the movement of money, gold, and precious gems to be made soon.

Beck had made reservations at one of the best hotels in Goa for March 8 through March 11. The colonel would already be there in a different hotel and make discreet inquiries about banks willing to act on his behalf. Most of the institutions were only too glad to take new deposits, and for a fee, they would not ask too many questions on their origins. The only thing they desired was where the funds would be transferred once they were in the bankers' hands. Each Portuguese ship leaving for one of the African colonies or back to the home country contained many illicit items, which again for a fee, would safely make their way to a new home in a Portuguese vault. Here, these items would sit with similar items of wealth acquired in similar ways, but that was not in the bankers' interest to know or care about. The fee was the critical thing, as it was in every capital in the world. Security would be provided by his bodyguard, Habir, who was being handsomely rewarded for his many duties and discretion.

On February 25, Torpedo Boat Squadron Two began moving some of its boats to the new forward base at Wernham Cove on the island of Barkia in the Russell Islands. The island was thirty miles up the Slot from Guadalcanal. The Russells had been occupied on February 21 by the Americans in an unopposed landing by the U.S. Forty-Third Infantry Division and the Third Marine Raider Battalion. Admiral Halsey wanted to control the southern side of the channel heading toward the growing base at Guadalcanal. The Americans feared the Japanese would quickly contest the move, but nothing happened. Construction units immediately began building the infrastructure of war, including an airfield, docks, housing, and a station for the PT boats. Having a base further up New Georgia Sound, the official name for the "Slot," would provide early detection of Japanese movements, especially in the nearby enemy-controlled islands.

Conditions on the island were worse than on Tulagi, but the Seabees promised to make the site as hospitable as possible. The days of begging in the Solomons were coming to a close. Each day saw the arrival of more men and equipment, providing a few comforts of home—if your home was in an equatorial swamp filled with mosquitoes, leaches, black flies, and snakes. The new ensign didn't care about the location or lack of proper facilities. All he wanted was to see some action.

The young ensign was the executive officer of an old Elco boat, which had arrived at Tulagi with the first torpedo boats in October. Now the boat was worn out, barely capable of thirty-two knots, and crewed by a combination of old hands and new transfers. The condition of the boat mattered little to the ensign. It was his first boat, and he was proud of it. The five old-timers on board called her the *Tulagi Maru* because the boat spent more time beached on the island getting repaired than fighting. The chief of the boat told the new officer the vessel had been damaged on four separate occasions, and the man he replaced had been seriously wounded in a battle with a Jap destroyer, along with three other men, one succumbing to his wounds.

Ensign Marcus Jameson, USNR, arrived in the war zone after postings at the training base of Taboga in the Panama Canal Zone and then to the staging base at Noumea. Having finished his training at Melville, Rhode Island, in late September, he had hoped for a quick trip to the south Pacific. His superiors had other ideas, and he spent three months in the Panama Canal learning how to operate an eighty-foot Elco boat in the tropics. The heat inside the boat was unbearable. Each torpedo boat could accommodate three officers and fourteen enlisted men, but usually, a crew of twelve to fourteen was typical for an operational boat. As a new officer, he expected to be made the second in command of the boat, which is precisely what happened. He learned a lot in Panama from a prematurely graying lieutenant aged twenty-five named Pruitt. Like everyone else in the "Zone," he wanted to get into the war and not chase phantom submarines or run the mail to forward outposts along the coast.

Luckily, the new ensign was ordered to the South Pacific. At Noumea, he was assigned to the USS *Niagara* (AG-P1), the first PT boat tender in the navy. Originally a civilian yacht named *Hi-Esmaro* built in 1929, the thousand-ton ship was narrow at the beam and 267 feet in length. The twin-screw diesel-powered vessel had a top speed of sixteen knots and a complement of 139 officers and men. The accommodations had once been lavish, but since the navy bought it in 1940, the ship had been stripped down for wartime service. The men on board had sailed the ship across the Pacific, arriving in New Caledonia on January 17, and began supporting the growing fleet of PT boats, known in the navy as "mosquito boats." The vessel had spare parts, mechanics, and shipwrights who could overhaul the small warships and allow them to fulfill their ever-evolving assignments.

Just before the departure of the *Niagara* to the forward base at Tulagi, accompanying four new boats assigned to Torpedo Boat Division 23, Ensign Jameson was ordered ashore to meet Admiral Halsey. No one on board knew why a brand new ensign would be sent to see the South Pacific Area commanding officer. The ensign waited outside the admiral's office for an hour before he was marched into the commanding officer's presence. Halsey was looking at a set of charts and speaking to his chief of staff, Captain Miles Browning, when an aide said, "Admiral, Ensign Jameson."

Quickly standing, Halsey smiled. "Thank you, Lieutenant. That will be all." The admiral walked toward the now terrified ensign and stared at the young man's face. "Damn, you look like your father."

Turning to his chief of staff, he continued, "Miles, doesn't he look exactly like Captain Jameson?"

Browning, not known for smiling, replied in kind. "Yes sir, he looks like his Dad. I hope he has some of his father's horse sense. He'll need it up in the Slot.

"Stand at ease, Ensign. I'm happy to meet you and welcome you to my command."

Ensign Jameson stared into the admiral's battle weary eyes buried deep under shaggy brows, and shook hands with the much respected admiral who appeared even older than his age.

"Have you heard from your father lately?" asked Admiral Halsey.

"No sir. I last received a letter from him in late December. I know he's busy, and I've moved twice since then, so the mail may be hung up somewhere."

"Well, I know where your father was, and I don't think that's a state secret. He's been in North Africa with the president at the Casablanca Conference. I heard he was still in Algiers helping straighten out the convoys and supply mess-ups that are the plague of everything we do."

Marcus didn't know what his father did, except he worked on Admiral King's staff. Otherwise, he was told very little about the elder Jameson's assignments. The last time they saw each other was at Bethesda, as the captain recovered from wounds received at the Battle of Savo Island. Any news was important to hear but learning his father was attending strategic conferences with the president was huge. Before he could say anything more, Halsey pulled him over to his desk.

"Ensign, let me show you the situation we're facing in the South Pacific." The admiral pointed out several islands and then moved his finger to the island of New Britain at the end of the Slot that ran down to Guadalcanal.

"We have secured Guadalcanal. The Japs left in early February and moved to some of these islands." Halsey pointed to New Georgia, Bougainville, New Ireland, and finally to New Britain. "At Rabaul, the enemy has his biggest base. This is where they have ships, tens of thousands of troops, and at least four big airfields. They may be licking their wounds, but the bastards are still in the fight. You and your PT boats will be instrumental in keeping them from sneaking down to attack us. Each night the PTs run up the sound and check out these islands to find out where they're hiding. Every night the enemy runs barges to supply their outposts, and the PTs are the best solution to ending their delivery service."

As the admiral continued his analysis, Marcus wondered about his future. He was not afraid, but as the admiral continued his briefing, the new ensign worried about the mission. The situation was much improved since the invasion of Guadalcanal, but the enemy was still strong and contested every island with a fearsome tenacity never seen by the Americans. The Imperial Navy continued to be a potent force and had exhibited strong tactical abilities, especially in night fighting. The American PT boat was one of the few weapons which could contest the Japanese at night. Stealth, speed, agility, and courage had been evidenced by the Tulagi-based boats, and the enemy was becoming more vigilant in their operations. Soon, Ensign Jameson would have to test himself against an enemy who neither gave nor sought any quarter.

Admiral Halsey finished his remarks telling the new officer, "Mr. Jameson, the Japanese are masters at fighting at night. You and the other PT boat officers must become even better at fighting in the dark than they are. A lot depends on small boats facing tremendous odds, but you and your men have the skills and courage to beat the bastards."

As the young officer was escorted out of the office, Halsey asked one of his junior aides to send a confidential message to Admiral King informing him of the young Jameson's new assignments and to pass this information to his father. After the aide left, Halsey looked closely at the nautical chart of the Solomon Islands. "Browning, these young men, like Jameson, will have their hands full if the Japs decide to push back down the Slot. If they don't come back in force, the mosquito boats will have to search these islands and make them come out and fight. Either way, these crews will be tested in the near future. The new carriers and battleships won't be arriving in the Pacific for at least six more months."

Browning didn't say anything. He knew how the admiral thought through strategic problems, and the one facing him and his command was daunting. He had to support the push against the Japanese on Rabaul by attacking islands in the New Georgia group and then attack Bougainville. At the same time, his forces would support MacArthur and his push deeper into New Guinea. These offensive actions required adding forces he did not possess or, worse in his mind, dividing his forces to accomplish the objectives coming out of Washington. He had only one aircraft carrier, a couple of battleships, some cruisers, and not enough destroyers to cover his larger units or escort convoys.

"Damn poor way to run a war, Browning." The man in command turned to his chief of staff and added, "Get me a report on our air assets and what we can loan to MacArthur. Check on the bombers coming our way in the next month, as well as our aviation fuel supplies. I'm worried that soon we'll get hit by the Japanese, and we must be prepared to meet any major attack."

The chief of staff dutifully noted the requests and walked out of the office. Halsey paced the room, gazing out the window at the few destroyers and one light cruiser anchored in the harbor. The other ships were scattered around the South Pacific, searching for the enemy or escorting convoys bringing reinforcements of men and equipment to the string of island bases that seemed to grow each day.

Ensign Jameson spent a sleepless night on board the tender. The next day, in a convoy of four merchant vessels, a sea-going tug, and two destroyers, the ships moved north to Guadalcanal and the war. Marcus thought about what he had heard and seen in the admiral's office. A few of the junior officers on the *Niagara* wanted to know about the mysterious meeting. Jameson said it was a courtesy call because his father had served with Halsey. This seemed to stop the inquiries and allowed Jameson to spend time on the bridge, seeking out information from the ship's navigator about the seas surrounding Guadalcanal. No one on the vessel had ever been there, but the charts provided information about future battles. Now in the Russell Islands, Marcus wished he had a copy of those charts he had seen in Halsey's office. The naval charts on his boat were old, tattered, and woefully out of date.

28

1 March 1943
CINCPAC Headquarters
Pearl Harbor, Territory of Hawaii

- Bismarck Sea--B-24 detects Japanese convoy, well-protected with fighters, en route from Rabaul to Huon Gulf, New Guinea.
- Burma--Sumprabum is evacuated by British civil authorities. Japanese move into the village and continue to skirmish with Kachin levies in the area but make no further progress toward Fort Hertz.
- North Africa--Gen. Spaatz takes command of 12th Air Force.
- USSR--Moscow announces that an offensive of Northwest Front, begun a few days earlier by Marshal Timoshenko, has regained Demyansk, Lichkova, and Zaluchie.
- Alaska--Naval Auxiliary Air Facility, Annette Island, Alaska, is established.

The place felt like home to everyone but Lieutenant Waverly. Every time he walked down a hallway, he encountered an admiral or a general. Colonels and captains moved about the offices like they were new recruits at Parris Island. The lieutenant had never seen so many officers in one place in his entire twelve years in the Corps. The Gunny told him to stick close to Brand, but that was proving difficult. Marine sergeants stood guard outside the offices of senior admirals and generals, and no one without authorization could enter. Lieutenant Brand had *carte blanche* approval to go anywhere he wanted to go, but his security detail would have to wait outside. After only one day at CINCPAC, Waverly was tired of the waiting.

Warrant Jones pulled James aside to see if there was something else Waverly could be doing while the professor was in his long meetings. The new member of the security team was bored. Gunny explained to James there would always be at least one of his Marine security specialists with him at all times, and he didn't think the Japanese would infiltrate the headquarters of the United States Navy in the Pacific.

Smiling at the old Marine's sarcasm, James said, "Gunny, let me see if we can find Lieutenant Waverly a more fulfilling task. I expect to spend the next few days locked in meetings with Commander Layton and Admiral Spruance, so there shouldn't be a need for babysitting duty."

Gunny acknowledged the remarks and waited for James to formulate an idea on what to do with the unhappy Marine lieutenant. It only took a few moments. "Do you think Lieutenant Waverly would enjoy training new troops?"

Knowing the combat-hardened Marine would enjoy getting dirty again, dealing with mud, flies, and raw recruits, Warrant Jones couldn't help but grin at the suggestion. "Sir, I think that would do the trick. The lieutenant needs to get out in the real world again. He's finding the number of brass unnerving and fears doing or saying something which will reflect badly on you."

The comment alarmed James as he awaited further explanation from his trusted friend.

"The lieutenant feels out of place as an officer. As a platoon lieutenant leading men in the field, sure, that's a natural progression for a Marine sergeant—the same duty but with more authority. Being around all these senior officers makes him uncomfortable because he knows he's not college-educated."

James was probably the one person on the team that understood the situation better than anyone. As a prodigy, he was always out of his element in social gatherings. Everyone wanted to show off their star student, professor, or researcher, making Brand feel like the trained monkey doing tricks in the circus. Now, Waverly's actions over the past few months made more sense. Being the odd man out always unnerved James, and his new security officer was feeling the same way.

"Thanks, Gunny, for the insights. I'll talk to the admiral and see if I can get him some time with a newly arrived unit. I believe new soldiers could learn a lot from Lieutenant Waverly."

Later in the day, James broached the subject with Admiral Spruance, who thought it was a good idea, especially after the professor explained Waverly's dilemma. The quiet admiral understood how the Marine officer felt and said he would take it up with Lieutenant General Emmons, the commander of the army units reporting to CINCPAC. The army was shipping new formations into the Hawaiian Islands every week. Units were scattered on Oahu, Maui, Kauai, and the Big Island, either in defense positions or training for future operations. Every unit waited for orders to move closer to the action, and Hawaii was the staging area for the Pacific.

After he met with Spruance, James was asked to meet with Commander Layton. Evidently, something urgent had come into the "dungeon," and the intelligence officer wanted Brand's input. The conversation was confidential, meaning that Commander Allen would have to step out of the room. The commander knew the situation and had handled many of the high-level intelligence reports reaching Admiral King's office. But Allen wasn't cleared to see the source material, which was the most exclusive information in America. After the commander exited the room, Layton gave the intercepted message to Brand.

"MacArthur flew a B-24 reconnaissance plane up toward Rabaul every day since we got the preliminary intercept. Today we received a confirmation of the movement of the Japanese convoy. Any thoughts?"

Other measures were introduced to protect the source information, knowing that protecting all MAGIC intercepts was vital. This included flying a plane in the area or having a submarine surface near a fleet movement, thereby being visible to the enemy to remove any doubt the Allies could read their radio traffic. All this was critical to maintaining the secrecy of the American code-breaking activities.

"Commander, this fits the Japanese pattern perfectly. They have now realized that they have been throwing small units into New Guinea and haven't built up a significant force to deal with MacArthur. Their forces are scattered along the coast, which makes the general's jumping along the coastline easier. He gets behind their main forces, which causes them to pull back into the jungle or fight against hopeless odds. Seems like someone in Tokyo has figured out they need to expand their army quickly. If General Kenney can intercept them with his bombers, I think he can destroy them or at least force them to return to Rabaul."

Looking at the professor and grinning, Layton handed another message to James. As he read the communique, James started to smile as well. "Looks like Kenney's people are making it difficult on the Japanese. With enough fighters to keep the Zeros occupied, the B-25s will destroy the transports and their destroyers." As he read more of the report, James added, "The Aussies are flying their Beaufighters in as well, and these planes are perfect for attacking ships. I saw a few of these planes in Britain last year. With four 20mm cannons mounted in the nose and four more machine guns in their wings, these planes can make a mess of a transport."

Seeing the look on the face of the professor, the intelligence officer commented, "James, I know you'd love to be up there flying against the enemy, but everyone at CINCPAC knows the score. You aren't allowed to even touch a plane, let alone fly one."

With a sheepish grin on his face, James replied, "Yes, I know the score, but damn it, I would love to get in a plane and fly again. But, for now, I'll do my job and dream."

Layton remained silent on the subject but moved on to another set of intercepts. As the two men looked through the enemy communications, James began to see a pattern of some concern. It took a while for the commander to see what Brand was reviewing, but finally, it hit him. The Japanese were moving forces south to Rabaul to support the New Guinea campaign and slow the American advance north from Guadalcanal. James couldn't quite comprehend the enemy's plan, but the two officers were now aware something was up. Nothing immediate, but perhaps in another month, the Japanese would be going on the offensive. Layton alerted the team in the dungeon to be even more diligent with every intercepted radio message. The Americans needed to look under every rock to understand the Japanese plan, starting with the movement of the all-important merchant ships carrying the supplies of war to Rabaul.

The city was still physically undamaged by the war, but emotionally things were different. Spring was a special time in the city, and except for the large number of men in uniform, nothing seemed different. Food was rationed, but it had been that way for many years. Influential people did not worry about rationing, but most everyone else did. It was good to be back home, but his mission was one of great complexity and fraught with peril. Prince Kaya Akihito, a lieutenant in the Imperial Navy, served as an intelligence officer to Admiral Yamamoto, the commanding officer of the Imperial Fleet. He was accompanying Vice Admiral Gunichi Mikawa and General Hitoshi Imamura, Southeast Area Army Commander, to brief and hopefully sway the opinions of the Naval General Staff on future plans.

Admiral Yamamoto moved to Rabaul along with Vice Admiral Ozawa, who had moved his command to get closer to the battle zone. The defense of New Guinea was becoming more of a problem, as well as the expanding American presence in the lower Solomon Islands. Ozawa now commanded the Third Fleet and was directly responsible for naval operations supporting the Japanese strategy in the area. Kaya knew the situation was deteriorating, and based upon the lack of army-navy coordination so far in the war, he realized the war was moving in a way not intended. The prince had informed his cousin of this two days before at a private luncheon at the Imperial Palace.

Being the cousin of the emperor was both a good and a bad thing. Access to the leader of the country was often an exercise in futility. Yes, the emperor was the head of state, a revered near-deity whose orders were followed by the one hundred million citizens of the Japanese Empire without question. At least that's what everyone believed. Actually, the emperor ruled through his government, which was now under the control of General Hideki Tojo. Acting as the prime minister of Japan and dominating his few opponents in government, Tojo and the military ran all aspects of the government. Emperor Hirohito was the one hundred twenty-fourth direct descendant of the first Japanese emperor, Jimmu, but he controlled very little. Only by directly intervening during meetings of the privy council could his will be expressed, and then only at great peril. Throughout the

1930s, those who spoke out against the military were often assassinated. The killers often faced little or no repercussions, as well as those in charge of the attacks. Prince Kaya knew this well and made sure conversations with his cousin were always private and short.

Kaya had gone to the palace ostensibly to see his aunt, who served as an attendant to Empress Kojun. Upon arrival, his presence was made known to the emperor, who quickly arranged for an informal meeting in his study. Knowing the palace had many eyes and ears reporting whatever Hirohito did or said, it was essential to keep the conversation quick and obtuse. Upon entering the emperor's study, Kaya immediately came to attention and then performed a deep ritual bow of fealty. Hirohito appreciated the ritual and the devotion of other members of his extended family. Signaling him to come close and enjoy some tea, the two men sat down at a small western-style table, covered with maps and papers.

"Kaya, it is good to see you. How have you been?"

"Your Majesty, I have been well. You appear to be in good health. How are the children?"

"Good of you to ask, Kaya. My three daughters grow taller each day, and my sons are full of energy, which only a child could possess."

"Children are a blessing, sir, and perhaps one day, I will have a family as well."

"Prince Kaya, should I have my wife find you a suitable young lady, or do you want to select your own?"

"Sir, I have little time for a wife or a family. The admiral has me moving around quite a lot, and the war requires everyone to make a sacrifice to the nation."

"Tell me, how is the admiral? Are things going well in the south seas?"

"Sir, you know the situation in the lower Solomons. You authorized a repositioning a few months ago, and now things are calmer. We have much to do in New Guinea, but I fear the enemy is gaining strength with each new day."

Hirohito knew the conversation was now touching political matters, which had to be very carefully entered. "So tell me, Kaya, are there new plans to counter the American threat?"

"Sir, I am here to meet with the Naval General Staff to brief them on a future operation which might help check the American advance."

The emperor picked up on the wording and asked, "If the operation goes badly, does the great admiral have another plan to put forward?"

Kaya knew the words were carefully chosen by his cousin. He needed to be clear in his answer to alert the emperor to the risks of failure. "Sir, we estimate the operation will succeed, but we are unsure of the American strength in the waters of New Guinea and in the Solomon Islands. If our estimates are correct, and we maintain the element of surprise, the operation will succeed, but only for a short time. Our ability to replace planes and pilots is not advantageous at this time."

Hirohito had been trying to dig deeper into the economic realities of the war. Plane and ship production was up, but the emperor knew the Allies were building more. In March, five hundred naval aircraft of all types were made, but the pilots did not exist. Losses, especially in the air, were bleeding the naval air arm white. The emperor asked another question to clarify the prince's response.

"Kaya, if we can consolidate our gains in the south, do you think the enemy will push harder in this area or move to another front?"

The intelligence officer and cousin of the emperor realized what the man wanted. The answer was not obvious but based upon the available intelligence and his own gut feeling, he knew the answer.

"Sir, if we hold the enemy in the south, they will move in a different direction. More ships arrive every week. Some of the new American planes are making many of our aircraft obsolete. The American submarines sink our merchant ships at an alarming rate. I fear the enemy will move against us soon, and not just in the southern ocean."

The emperor put up his hand to touch his glasses, signaling Kaya not to say anything else. Either Hirohito sensed someone was eavesdropping, or he feared what was being said. Turning the subject to something more personal, the emperor asked, "How is your mother? Have you seen her since you returned to Tokyo?"

The conversation was over in another five minutes. As the prince departed, he noticed the frown on the face of the emperor. He realized the ruler of Japan knew things were getting worse, but he could do nothing about it.

The captain was angry. Not at anyone in particular—perhaps at one man, but more so at himself. As soon as he and his team returned from Algiers, he learned about the deployment of James Brand and his security team to Pearl Harbor. Admiral Edwards assured him Brand was being supervised by Commander Allen, but that didn't stop his concern about his protégée. After spending weeks in North Africa, working with the Allied command under Eisenhower, the captain had a better feel for the political nuances of high command. The professor was not so skilled, and he feared the young physicist would fall into the world of infighting in the headquarters of the Pacific Ocean Area.

Jameson didn't worry about the top commanders, Nimitz, and his chief of staff, Admiral Spruance, taking advantage. It was the other sparring partners with stars on their collars occupying the major commands in Hawaii. Each admiral and general protected their turf to the last lieutenant, and only under the direct orders of CINCPAC would an individual give way. Knowing how Brand operated, often too trusting in the actions of others, the captain feared the worst. Thankfully, Commander Allen understood the politics, and hopefully, James would spend most of his time with Commander Layton working on high-level intelligence. Few people had clearance for MAGIC, which would hopefully keep James away from individuals who would like to avail themselves of the professor's talents. Warrant Jones would advise James on who to trust and when to back away, but the worldly Gunny could only do so much. Lieutenant Waverly and his Marines would protect Brand from any physical danger, but these men knew little of the politics flowing about at the Pacific headquarters.

As soon as he had been debriefed by Admiral Edwards, Jameson asked about getting the rest of the team shipped off to Pearl to help Lieutenant Brand. The admiral had standing orders to do this, but several people wanted to be briefed by Jameson and his officers before heading to Hawaii. Flannigan and Dr. Feldman had been ordered to brief General Marshall and members of his staff on what they had experienced in Tunisia.

The battles had ended, with only skirmishes and patrols continuing. The Germans had pulled back to a new defensive line, and the Americans licked their wounds, trying to regain their pride after being humiliated at Kasserine. The British gave Eisenhower advice on deployments but talked behind his back about the lack of training, leadership, and overall capability of the American forces. Ike was having to listen to his British commanders while working on making changes. General Harmon had issued a scathing report on the ineptness of the American leadership and offered many suggestions, including the replacement of the senior officers. Thus far, General Marshall backed Eisenhower on any decision he made, but the chief of staff wanted the American army to start an offensive soon.

Admiral Leahy requested a similar meeting with Jameson and Flannigan to discuss the situation and recommendations to improve the situation in North Africa. Leahy also wanted a detailed report on the logistics situation and how it had hopefully improved since the Casablanca Conference in January. The captain had Lieutenant Stevens create a detailed account of the supply situation starting back in November with the TORCH invasion and the convoy program since then. Stevens and his team developed several charts showing ship sailings, warehouse issues, manpower allocation, Allied cooperation (or lack of), transportation difficulties moving goods from the ports to the front, and ongoing communication challenges. These were all boring details. Yet, nothing happened in a war without the transportation and delivery of supplies and manpower to fight the enemy. America was learning faster than many thought possible, but not fast enough to meet the evolving threats from the enemy.

Late in the afternoon, Admiral Edwards pulled Jameson into a meeting with Admiral King to discuss the next phase of the war. The admiral welcomed Jameson back to Washington and commented on his brutally honest reports, but as King stated, "Jameson, the facts are just that, facts. We can't win this war on wishing. Your reports are making a difference, and I want you to continue doing them. Whenever you see something that Edwards or I need to know, tell us in the same blunt fashion. I am tired of people making excuses or trying to sugar coat the truth."

King sat behind his desk, with Edwards and Jameson seated across from him. The man was in a dark mood, but a common emotion for a man facing global challenges. After glancing at a report on the war in the Pacific, he began speaking, "Jameson, you and your men did a good job in North Africa. But I don't like Major Flannigan traipsing all over hell and back trying to get killed. His reports, though, are making a difference. General Marshall told me that he needed men like Flannigan on the front lines giving him this kind of hard information. Same for Dr. Feldman. Both of these men are credits to you and the navy."

The only sound in the room was the rhythmic tapping of the admiral's fingers on the edge of his desk as he considered his next action. "Once you and your men brief Admiral Leahy, I want you to head out to Pearl to check out what is happening in Nimitz's command. We have an overall plan for the remainder of 1943, and at Casablanca I received approval for a push up the central Pacific. MacArthur wants everything to go to his command so he can crawl up the coast of New Guinea and then move on to the Philippines. This will take too much time and slow down the war. The only way to stop the Japanese is to go right at his throat, which means taking the war directly to Japan."

Gathering his thoughts, the admiral continued. "To do that, we need to leapfrog to the Gilberts, then the Marshalls, and finally onto the Marianas. Brand gave us ideas on why this will win the support of General Arnold. It will place air force bases close enough to Japan for the new B-29s. I don't think bombing will stop the enemy, but it will surely hurt them enough to slow their ability to wage war. These bases will also bring our submarines closer to the Japanese sea lanes, which will strangle their industry. I want you and your men to look at the plans Nimitz is working on and poke holes in anything that looks weak."

Seeing an opening, Jameson asked, "Sir, what strategies are being developed in Admiral Cooke's planning group?"

"Right now, there is an outline based upon pre-war ideas. I think we need to revisit everything we have and come up with a plausible way to move north from the Solomons and then right up to the Marshalls. I would like to make a major move by the end of this year and then have an aggressive set of offensive actions set for 1944."

As Jameson and Edwards looked on, King again went silent. The CNO was thinking about many alternatives and how in war, plans are required, but reality often makes them useless. Finally, he regained his focus. "We also need to be looking at any opportunity to destroy the enemy's fleet, whether in a single battle or in a series of smaller actions."

Staring directly at Jameson, King said, "Look at ways to use our submarine assets to destroy key units of the Japanese navy along with the destruction of their merchant fleet. If we can erode Yamamoto's ability to fight, by whatever means, having a large empire means little. Isolating enemy units and bypassing most of their bases will win the war in the long run. I'll have Cooke work up some ideas as well, and upon your return, we'll finalize our plan."

With the meeting over, Jameson and Edwards went to the chief of staff's office and conferred on what King wanted. "Sir, how long do you think we should be in Hawaii?"

"Jameson, you know as well as I do that you might stay at Pearl for a month or a year. I doubt the latter but plan to be there through April. We have several operations planned, and I would like some of your team to participate." With a steely stare, he added, "That does not mean the professor. He is to stay at Pearl. Also, keep Commander Allen at Pearl for a few more weeks. He would love to get back to sea, but Admiral King wants him to remain on the staff for a few more months. Don't tell him this, but if there is any operation going on in the next thirty days which he could observe, by all means, set it up. Nothing extensive, but a journey aboard a cruiser or carrier would do him some good."

Jameson agreed it would benefit Allen to get his sea legs back by spending time aboard a warship. He didn't believe Admiral Nimitz would object, so he committed the idea to memory and would address it as soon as he got to Pearl Harbor. Edwards arranged for the team to fly out in two days. Hopefully, things would be calm until then, but the war was raging everywhere. A few days in transit could be a lifetime for many.

29

3 March 1943
CINCPAC Headquarters
Pearl Harbor, Territory of Hawaii

- Aleutian Islands--Adm. Kinkaid recommends limited offensive with available forces be conducted against Attu, bypassing Kiska, the objective for which planning has been in progress for some time.
- Bismarck Sea--During heavy coordinated attacks, Allied planes severely cripple Japanese convoy, which arrived off Huon Gulf. After nightfall, PT boats of 7th Fleet destroy one of the vessels previously damaged by aircraft.
- Tunisia--German Afrika Corps issues plan for attack from Mareth Line.
  - In British 1st Army's 5 Corps area, fighting around Bedja subsides. U.S. II Corps continues to patrol actively without making contact with enemy. Sidi Bou Zid is free of enemy.
- USSR--On Kharkov-Bryansk rail line, Soviet forces capture Lgov and Dmitriev Lgovsky.

The map was a study in contrasts—vast amounts of blue waters interspersed with tiny specs of land. Each island's name was exotic and conjured up images of happy natives, swaying to the sound of distant drums. Smiling at the picture in his mind, the professor knew full well most of the islands were uninhabited, had no fresh water, contained few natural harbors, and many were occupied by the enemy. Looking to the far north of the Pacific was another string of islands creating an arc of some thousand miles from Kodiak Island to the Japanese-held islands of Attu and Kiska. James was working with Admiral Nimitz's staff to develop plans for each of the islands in the Aleutian chain, but the eventual goal was to push the war to another set of islands, known as Japan.

The challenges were immense, not only because of the hundreds of thousands of square miles of empty ocean but also the logistics of war. Where do you find the troops, planes, ships, and stores, especially oil? The oil problem had long plagued navy commanders, but it became the most important logistical question in the Pacific. Before the war began, the navy decided it needed to protect its oil supplies. A large tank farm near Pearl Harbor was the central "gas station" for the navy in the Pacific. One errant shot or small bomb could destroy millions of gallons of fuel oil, diesel, and aviation fuel. Luckily on December 7, the Japanese were more intent on sinking ships in a decisive sea battle than destroying America's ability to fight back.

Starting in 1941 and onward, the navy created a monstrous underground storage facility at Red Hill near Pearl Harbor. Each of its twenty vertical underground chambers was the equivalent of a twenty-story building. Each tank was one hundred feet in diameter and two-hundred-fifty feet in height, all lined in quarter-inch steel plate and reinforced concrete. Over thirty-nine hundred workers toiled day and night to build the complex. A total capacity of two hundred fifty million gallons of petroleum products could be stored in this facility. The first tank was finished in September 1942, and the last tank should be ready by the end of September 1943.

The other petroleum challenge facing the navy was obtaining the necessary number of tankers to transport fuel from the West Coast to Hawaii to fill the tanks. Then, specially constructed navy fleet oilers would take the oil further into the Pacific and refuel the American warships while they were at sea. America had developed *underway replen-*

ishment or UNREP, before the war, which allowed the fleets to stay at sea and not have to return to refuel at a port. Each of the *Cimarron* class of fleet oilers could hold up to eighty thousand barrels of fuel oil, eighteen thousand barrels of aviation fuel, and sixty-eight hundred tons of diesel fuel. The ships had a maximum speed of eighteen knots and were designed to fuel two ships simultaneously, even in challenging sea conditions. This moving fuel depot and resupply capability would be another key factor leading to Japan's downfall.

Every new strategy had to be checked against the limitations of American supply. If the Central Pacific strategy was going to work, all of the logistical issues needed to come into alignment. Moving thousands of troops from California to staging bases in Hawaii and then on to some tiny island required extensive research, planning, and leadership. James knew the army used the "tooth to tail" ratio to describe the challenge of putting one infantry soldier to fight the enemy. In an army division, it meant that only thirty percent of the people actually engage in combat. When you add the naval support to move the troops, supply them once they face the enemy, and then support them with fire support, aviation units, and the need for medical evacuation, the figure moves to one man fighting and sixteen men supporting. The tail in the Pacific was very long and required enormous numbers of people to take the war to the enemy. Admiral Nimitz understood this better than many of his staff, and James was tasked with developing the plan to support the men fighting the battle.

As he worked on the first set of plans for the Central Pacific thrust starting in the Gilbert Islands, he was called to Admiral Spruance's office to discuss movements in the far north Pacific. Commander Layton and Commander Allen were also in attendance as Spruance briefed the group in his usual precise way.

"The Combined Chiefs have authorized our movement against the Japanese in the Aleutians. However, we will not be given additional support to do this. Admiral Kinkaid has recommended against an invasion of Kiska for several reasons, but especially the number of troops required to successfully capture the island. Layton's latest intelligence assessment shows around fifteen hundred soldiers on Attu and perhaps as many as ten thousand on Kiska."

Pointing to a map of the Aleutians, Spruance stated, "Attu is at the end of the chain, and since we have positions on Adak and further back to Dutch Harbor, Kinkaid recommends bypassing Kiska for now and taking Attu. We have a division of Army troops already assigned to our command, now training in California. We can control the air above both islands and use superior sea forces to control the sea approaches. This way, Kinkaid believes we can shut off resupply efforts to the Japanese troops on Kiska and wait for more combat units later in the summer."

Layton added, "If we can take Attu, we can use it as a base of operations against Japanese resupply efforts and cut off enemy shipping before it gets close to Kiska. James, what do you think?"

The professor looked at the chart of the islands and did a quick set of calculations. Knowing the distances and how Attu was at the extreme end of the island chain, he agreed. "Sir, this makes good sense for two reasons. First, like you said, it would further isolate the Japanese garrison on Kiska and allow us to successfully patrol farther out toward the Kuriles. Second, since we don't have the troops necessary to maintain a three-to-one margin against the enemy, it would be best to attack the smaller garrison first."

Looking at the admiral, James continued, "Sir, by attacking the smallest garrison, we will learn a lot about the enemy's ability to defend in these cold conditions. The same goes for our soldiers and sailors. We need to understand the conditions on the ground and how we'll support these units once we are in control. I have read reports on the situation at Adak, and the ability to conduct flying operations in what one pilot said, was the worst possible conditions. We should proceed, but with caution."

The admiral liked James because he got to the point without a lot of extraneous information. Spruance had read many of the same reports on the navy's problems with operating in the frozen conditions of Alaska. The number of operational casualties was causing senior commanders to rethink their plans. Men stationed on these islands were going mad at an alarming rate. Ships were lost or damaged because of the high seas, constant fog, and poor charts. Like his boss, Spruance knew the Aleutians were a side show, but it was American territory, so they had to be recaptured.

"All right, Layton put together an intelligence briefing on Attu. What does the enemy have on the island, what are his defensive positions, what kind of supply issues does he have, and what is the Imperial Navy doing to support it."

"Yes sir. I'll have my team pull everything we're getting out of Japan and focus on their northern fleet support from Paramushiro to see if we can get any feel for their force levels."

"Thank you, Layton. I'll advise Admiral Kinkaid to begin his planning. Lieutenant Brand, if you and Commander Allen could help in these activities, I would appreciate it."

"Yes sir. More than happy to help." James replied and then quickly added, "Sir, would it be possible to check out the situation in Alaska to help in our understanding of the challenges of fighting in the Arctic?"

Knowing the professor well, the admiral smiled and replied, "Lieutenant, you will do your planning here, not in Alaska. For right now, you are not to leave the Hawaiian Islands. Any more questions?"

"No sir. I understand the orders."

After the three officers left Admiral Spruance's office, they returned to a conference room James had set up as his temporary planning room. Layton closed the door and, with a big smile on his face, said, "James, that was a good try, but you know Admiral Spruance isn't going to let you out of CINCPAC until you are recalled by Admiral King. But I admire your spunk!"

Allen added his thoughts, saying, "James, keep on trying, and maybe one day soon, you'll get out of this office. Remember, we all serve a purpose, and we are doing our best to win the war. I would love to get on a destroyer and battle the enemy, but here I am. At least I'm closer to the action here than in Washington."

The intelligence officer agreed but wanted to get back to the business at hand. He needed James to help on the recent intercepts from the Imperial Navy to see what they were doing in the Central Pacific. Later, he would begin his search for information on Japanese intentions in the North Pacific.

The men crawled in red mud under several belts of barbed wire. The activity had started before dawn when the platoon sergeants called out their men to form up with full packs and weapons. After a hurry-up breakfast of powdered eggs, Spam and toast, the platoons formed up into companies and marched toward the jungle training center along the Wailua River. The camp for the first battalion of the One Sixty-Fifth

Infantry Regiment was located near the town of Wailua on the island of Kauai. The training center was in the foothills of Mount Kawaikini, with an elevation of over five thousand feet. Other units of the regiment were scattered around the island at Barking Sands, Koloha and Port Allen. The other regiments of the Twenty-Seventh Infantry Division were in Maui and the island of Hawaii. Major General Ralph Smith commanded this former New York National Guard unit, which traced itself back to pre-Civil War days. The One Sixty-Fifth was formerly known as the Fighting Sixty-Ninth Infantry, which had gained great distinction in World War One.

But all of the history and citations didn't mean a thing to a determined officer watching the former weekend warriors push themselves through the jungle mud of Kauai. Another officer observed the men and stood next to the lieutenant. Samuel T. Brown was the assistant commander of the battalion, a major who had worked on Wall Street and graduated from Yale. A good officer and product of the ROTC program at the university was not only green but unsure. Looking at his struggling men, the major asked the lieutenant a question.

"Lieutenant, do you think the men are getting the hang of it?"

Bill Waverly had been on the island for only two days but quickly recognized the need to get these men into good physical shape, focused, and trained to kill. Nothing about the battalion appeared organized or ready to fight a war. Knowing his place in the command structure, the Marine lieutenant chose his words carefully. "Major, your men need a lot more practice at working in bad conditions." He pointed to men attempting to move through the mud and barbed wire, snagging their clothes or equipment in the rusting strands of wire, adding, "Sir, if this was an infiltration on Japanese units, half of these men would be dead or wounded already. Every time someone picks up his butt or head to move forward, he becomes a target. The men are bunched up, making it easy to drop a mortar round right in the middle of them. You can't afford to have your men running around in groups of more than two."

The major looked at men who had their heads up or were trying to unsnag their equipment. Several were no longer crawling but up on their knees to see where they were. The major was dejected by the performance and knew the Marine was speaking from experience.

Pulling a whistle out of his pocket and blowing it hard enough to be heard for several hundred yards, he motioned for an officer's call. Platoon and company officers closed in, overlooking the men in the mud. The battalion commander drove up in his jeep to find the officers huddled around his assistant. What he heard did not make him happy.

"Men, I have been watching this training session, and I am annoyed by your performance. Your men are sloppy handling the barbed wire entanglements. They don't crawl on their bellies but like to get up on their knees and scamper about like toddlers." Getting up a head of steam, the major acknowledged the presence of his commanding officer but continued speaking. "Men are lollygagging about, bunching up in large groups, slowly advancing, and from the looks of it, half of their weapons are full of mud and couldn't fire if their lives depended on them."

The battalion commander had never heard his deputy speak this forcefully and wondered what had gotten into the man. Seeing the Marine standing next to the major immediately answered the question. The day before, he received a call from the regimental commander about General Smith sending a decorated Marine officer to observe his battalion's training. The colonel told his battalion commander that the man was connected to Admiral Nimitz and knew what the hell he was doing, so he was to listen and learn. Evidently, the listening was happening, and hopefully, his soldiers would learn from this process.

About to continue, Major Brown stopped before his anger rose further. Turning to the Marine, he asked, "Lieutenant Waverly, do you have any words of wisdom to impart to these officers?"

Waverly had met only a few of the battalion's officers since arriving on a plane from Honolulu and had spent an hour with General Smith at his HQ near Schofield Barracks on Oahu before flying out to Kauai. The general was impressed by the Marine and had heard directly from Lieutenant General Emmons on the man's background and, more importantly, his connections to Admiral King. The army general gave Waverly the green light to observe any training underway and make recommendations for improvement. Waverly now wished he had learned to be a better writer because he could fill a book on changes needed by the unit.

"Major, the men need to do several things to improve their likelihood of accomplishing their objective and staying alive. Let me give you a quick idea of what you should be working on to improve your units. First, above all else, don't bunch up. This is what the Japs like about

Americans. We like to be in groups. Stay fifteen feet apart, moving and looking at all times. Next, have your men stop talking. The more you talk, the easier it is for the enemy to find you. On a jungle trail, you can't see ten feet ahead of you, but you can hear men's voices from a long distance. The last point, for now, keep low. Don't stick your damn head up to see what's going on. If you're low, you have a better chance of surviving a mortar round. When you need to get on your belly and crawl, crawl like you're a worm. It's slow going, but you'll live longer."

Hearing the last comment, many of the army officers were unsure why they were talking about things as mundane as staying low, not bunching up, and not talking. Seeing some of the faces of his officers, the battalion commander spoke up.

"Men, most of you have not met the lieutenant, so let me do a proper introduction. Lieutenant Waverly is first and foremost a warrior. This officer has spent twelve years in the Marines and is a member of the First Marine Raider Battalion. He fought at Tulagi and was given a battlefield commission. Later at Guadalcanal, he was wounded three times. He was severely wounded at the Battle of Bloody Ridge. He was decorated with the Navy Cross for volunteering to man a forward observation post, carried three wounded men back to safety, and personally operated his machine gun until he ran out of ammunition. Then with only a Thompson, he held off another attack and crawled back some three hundred yards to the main defensive line…in the dark…on his belly…and under fire."

The battalion commander let this set of facts be absorbed by the captains and lieutenants of his battalion. The silence was as good a teacher as talking loudly. All of the officers were staring at the colonel and then glanced over to see the Marine officer. "So, if Lieutenant Waverly recommends you and your men doing something, do it. This is not a request; it's an order. The lieutenant is providing this training as a favor to the army. He is on another mission but volunteered to help out his fellow countryman. We shall all be seeing combat soon enough, and I want you and your men to be ready. Are there any questions?"

No one spoke, which is what the battalion commander expected. He turned to Waverly and asked a question. "What else do you think these officers should be doing to prepare their men for battle? And, lieutenant, that includes me. What should I be doing to help these men succeed?"

283

Waverly had never in his life been asked by a senior officer, especially a lieutenant colonel commanding an infantry battalion of some twelve hundred men, to recommend anything. But now, the Marine was in his natural element. He knew what to do to make men ready to fight and, if necessary, to die for their country.

"Sir, if it would be agreeable to you and your officers, I would like to take you out for a night patrol." With a slight grin on his face, Waverly added, "Sir, it's only for officers. No enlisted men. We need to learn from each other, and everyone needs to be able to lead a patrol in the dark, so if we could assemble at 1700 hours for a briefing, then we can head out for a little excursion in the woods."

The colonel loved the idea. The major was not so sure, and the rest of the officers, many of them being older, didn't like the idea at all. By midnight, everyone, including the colonel thought Waverly was mad, but they all agreed later, it was the most helpful training they had ever received.

Daytime temperatures remained cool, often with a chill in the air—skies were brighter and spring was near. Yet, the peasants of Portugal were not experiencing the glow from the new season. Most people were poor, and unless involved in the financial business or tied to the government, most of the population dealt with the same problems that existed before the war started. Food was scarce. The fishing industry sought their bounty close to shore out of fear of being attacked by either Axis or Allied forces. Imported goods were becoming more scarce or, if available, too expensive for the poor or the middle class to purchase. The nation was full of immigrants who had escaped war-torn Europe, but now wanted to leave for a new life elsewhere. The aristocrats held out in the casinos and resorts, with a few ultra-rich caring for some of the more impoverished princes and princesses from countries now under Nazi rule. All of this made Lisbon more mysterious and, at times, similar to a bazaar trading on hopes, lies, and subterfuge.

Meyers and the intelligence agent Murdoch had been trying to understand the pieces of the puzzle set in motion by the German navy officer. The reference to the American OSS station chief in Switzerland, Allen Dulles, was unmistakable. Wilhelm, the other name mentioned by Wagener, could be several prominent Germans, especially Admiral Wilhelm Canaris, head of the Abwehr. Coded messages were sent to Dulles and to Donovan in Washington for direction. It took a few days for Dulles and the OSS offices in Washington to agree on the next steps in what was a bizarre dance of espionage, intrigue, and treason. John Meyers had been the point of contact, and now he was being pulled into a position for which he was unprepared. His military experiences provided a good background in naval intelligence, but supply and contracts were his areas of expertise. He was more than a little bit concerned when he received his new orders.

Murdoch looked over the message. Evidently, it took Washington a few days to agree on what they would do with the newest Lisbon situation. Handing the note to John, the OSS man stated what was going to happen next.

"John, for whatever reason, this Wagener fellow has chosen you for contact. We don't know what's he looking for or if he's working in counterintelligence. We have our London sources checking, but nothing shows up so far. Sources in occupied countries are trying to locate information on the man, but it may take some time to build an assessment. What matters now is for you to take the next step. This is a delicate dance, and sometimes you lead, sometimes you follow. Don't think of yourself as Fred Astaire. Think Ginger Rogers, because as I heard it said, she makes the same dance moves as Fred, but backwards and in high heels." The man laughed at his own joke but then turned deadly serious.

The dance analogy is closer to reality than Meyers would have thought possible. "You will follow the moves this German makes. You need to be clear about what we want and don't ever give this guy a break. We are winning this war, and I think this officer is only one of the first who may want to jump ship."

Meyers took all of this in and re-read the message from Donovan. Admiral King had been advised about this new mission, and the admiral's orders were explicit. Do whatever Donovan wanted. The OSS provided suggestions on how to proceed but left the details to Murdoch, and eventually, the decision was made by John Meyers. It was his life, and he would not be asked to do something he didn't want to do. Looking at his new and now critical friend, he asked, "Bob, how do we set this thing up?"

Murdoch had already laid out several scenarios to set up a meeting of the two men. The challenge was to conduct a meeting in secrecy when the city was full of spies, not only American and Germans, but also British, Portuguese, Spanish, Italian, Polish, Russian, and even the Vatican had people looking out for their interests. Bob laid out a plan which would involve a drop of information to the German to see if the man wanted a meeting. Next, a series of maneuvers that would make Napoleon happy would be taken to isolate any spies trying to determine why two sworn enemies were meeting. The location had to be chosen carefully, with only highly trusted agents aware of what would occur. Although part of the spy game, people would be compromised if handled incorrectly, and a few, even John Meyers, might become casualties of war.

The first phase of the operation was the drop to secure an agreement to meet in some secret location. Murdoch had chosen a middle-class hotel in the outskirts of Lisbon, which had several entrances, making it difficult for any third party to consistently monitor. If the German was agreeable to the location, then a time and date would be offered. Finally, the meeting would occur between two enemies, but perhaps one would no longer be considered dangerous.

The next night, at the same bar in the casino, the two men met. A message was passed in such a professional manner that only the most seasoned agent could see the move. One such man was watching, but he already knew the game was on. In tonight's dispatches, the man from MI6 would report on the progress of the colonials in their attempt to compromise the new assistant naval attaché in Lisbon. They were unsure of the reason for the action, but that could be determined later. The Americans were amateurs at spy craft and had a penchant for talking too much about what they were doing. "Thank God," one of the top men in London said about their ally's unprofessional behavior, "only the bloody Germans are worse."

30

6 March 1943
CINCPAC Headquarters
Pearl Harbor, Territory of Hawaii

- Russell Islands-- Islands undergo enemy air attack. This is the first indication that Japanese have learned of American occupation of the islands.
- Tunisia--In British 1st Army's 5 Corps area, enemy maintains pressure against north flank of corps in Tamera area. In U.S. II Corps area, Gen. Patton takes command of corps, relieving Gen. Fredendall. Gen. Omar N. Bradley, who is to succeed Gen.Patton after operations in South Tunisia are completed, becomes deputy corps commander. In British 8th Army's 30th Corps area, Rommel makes his last attack in Tunisia and is decisively defeated.
- USSR--Gzhatsk, on rail line between Moscow and Smolensk, falls to Red Army.
- Solomon Islands--Three cruisers and seven destroyers (Rear Adm. A. S. Merrill) bombard Vila and Munda, Solomon Islands.
- Two Japanese destroyers sunk: **Mineguymo** and **Murasame** in Kula Gulf.

The final reports of air attacks on the Japanese convoy in the Bismarck Sea were spread about the conference table. James was updating Captain Jameson, Major Flannigan, Dr. Feldman, and Lieutenant Clark about the destruction of the eight transports carrying several thousand troops plus the sinking of four of the eight escorting destroyers. In addition, sixty Japanese aircraft were shot down by the American fighters. American PT boats attacked later that night and sank a damaged transport and tangled with one of the escort vessels. Allied losses were only six planes and twenty-five crewmen.

Major Flannigan had seen some of the press releases coming out of MacArthur's headquarters. "James, SWPA stated that they had sunk twenty-two ships, killing some fifteen thousand troops and crewmen. Any reason for the discrepancy?"

Quickly looking at his information, James replied, "Major, the public affairs office in Brisbane often inflates numbers. I think General Kenny's flyers reported what they saw, and then someone added more to the score. It's been a slow press week, so I think the Southwest command wants to make the headlines."

Thinking a bit more about what he had seen in the intelligence reports, Brand added, "We knew how many ships left Rabaul and how many came back. Only four destroyers made it back, and it appears only one of them is in good working order. No merchant ships came back, and we also know the Japanese fighters covering the convoys were decimated by our P-38s flying high cover for the bombers." Smiling at his friend, he added, "Just looks good to the people back home to show what the bomber boys are doing."

Duncan Clark smiled at the professor and asked, "James, did they use the skip bombing technique we have talked about?"

"Apparently, they used their B-25s with short-fused bombs at extremely low altitude. A flight of B-17s dropped their loads from less than eight thousand feet and reported some hits, but based upon everything I've seen in the past, I find these reports highly unlikely."

Jameson enjoyed the banter from his men. It was good to get everyone back together to work on new operations. The captain and his men arrived the day before from San Francisco on a new C-54, which was more comfortable than being stuck on another cold bomber. James brought him up to speed on his activities and how he had sent Waverly to observe troops in Kauai. The captain approved since he knew James was guarded by Gunny and the rest of the security detail. Having Lieutenant Waverly working with raw troops was a good thing, knowing these men would soon be put to the test of battle.

After the briefing on the Bismarck Sea victory, Jameson and Commander Allen left to meet Admiral Spruance to discuss the planning challenges for the Central Pacific campaign. James would not attend the meeting. He and Clark headed to the harbor to visit the newly arrived British aircraft carrier HMS *Victorious*. Flannigan and Dr. Feldman were slated to meet with members of the planning staff to review plans for expanding the Solomon operations, which aimed to launch an invasion of New Georgia in early summer.

Admiral Spruance was glad to see Captain Jameson again. The two had developed a good relationship during the Midway operation. Now, with the increasing power of the American military, the chief of staff knew the war would be won, but not when. There were many battles yet to be fought, and except for the Doolittle Raid and the presence of American submarines in the waters off the home islands, Japan had not been directly attacked, making the Central Pacific strategy so important.

As he laid out the scenario to Jameson and Commander Allen, the admiral described the strategy. "Gentlemen, if we can quickly take the primary islands in the Gilbert and Marshall groups, we can control the skies a thousand miles in every direction. We need only a few islands in each group to make this strategy work. This will stop enemy reinforcements from getting to countless numbers of Japanese controlled islands, making them spend huge amounts of energy to support their forces. It will also allow us to control the Caroline group without having to invade all of them."

As he pointed out the various specs of land strewn over the Pacific, Spruance continued his appraisal. "This strategy requires not only the advance forces to attack and seize these islands, but a huge logistical tail winding its way back to the West Coast. Without a thorough analysis of the manpower and supply capability needed, we cannot make this plan work."

The admiral found the latest intelligence reports for the targeted islands and continued. "Each of these islands becomes a stepping stone to Tokyo. We don't need to occupy every island in these groups, only the ones that allow us good airfields and anchorages for the fleet. Once an island is secured, our construction battalions will build the airfields, docks, oil tanks, barracks, and other infrastructure to make them useful to our strategy. Any island not occupied will be harassed by our air forces but not invaded. The enemy troops left behind will cease to be a threat and left to starve. Each step toward Japan will isolate thousands of Japanese who will not be able to defend their homeland."

Jameson was familiar with the overall plans for the Central Pacific strategy but was new to the tactical methods and timelines. The captain looked at the wall chart of the Pacific Ocean behind the admiral's desk and asked, "Sir, what is our first objective?"

Spruance took a few steps back to the large chart. "Captain, we have a strong foothold at Guadalcanal. Halsey is tasked with supporting the isolation and destruction of the enemy fortress at Rabaul. Under General MacArthur's direction, his forces will move up the Solomon chain and either neutralize Japanese forces by either invading specific islands or neutralizing them with air and sea forces. MacArthur will continue his push up the coast of New Guinea, then turn to cut off Rabaul by controlling islands in the Admiralty group and, if necessary, invading New Britain."

Moving his finger northeast of Guadalcanal, Spruance discussed the first phase of the Central Pacific campaign. "The first target in the Gilbert Islands is Tarawa, which was the British headquarters for the Gilberts. The island has a Japanese airfield on it now and controls the airspace for hundreds of miles in every direction. The island is about twelve hundred miles away from Guadalcanal, so we must have enough carrier aircraft to support any invasion. The other targets we are looking at are Nauru and Makin. By capturing at least Tarawa, we will have land-based air cover for the move north to Kwajalein, about another five hundred miles northwest as well several other possible targets in the Marshall group."

Commander Allen had attended several planning meetings on the Central Pacific offensive, but this was the first time he really understood the distances involved and the logistical hurdles that needed to be overcome. He asked, "Admiral, in looking at Admiral Cooke's original document, the major concern made was the lack of aircraft carriers and landing craft. With Admiral Halsey's need for ships and planes, do we have sufficient forces available to make this happen by year end?"

"Good question, Commander. Admiral Nimitz is very concerned about over-stretching the ships we currently have and the deployment dates for new ships. We don't feel the move into the Gilbert Islands could occur before October of this year. We estimate we will have six large carriers and at least four of the new light *Independence* Class ships available by September. The deployment of eight or more escort carriers will add to this mix for anti-submarine and ground support. This fleet will have a half dozen battleships, maybe more, depending on the number of older ships now undergoing modernization. Getting all of these new ships and their crews to work well with one another will be a colossal challenge."

Looking at Jameson, Spruance frowned and added, "We might have big ships, but the major problem in all of these plans will be landing ships. Big ones like the LSTs are more precious than gold, and the small landing craft and new LTVs or what the Marines call amtracs are even rarer. Captain, I think you know more about this problem than I do, so if you can share any insights, it would be most helpful."

Jameson knew more about the problem than he would like to admit. Part of his work in Algiers was the advance planning for the invasion of Sicily, tentatively planned for July or August. This invasion has precedence over all other operations, and every other theater of the war got what was left.

"Admiral, I'm afraid you're correct in your fears. The planning for additional offensive action in the European theater has the priority and approval of the Combined Chiefs of Staff. Allocations for LSTs are all spoken for through at least July. The same goes for the small landing craft. I'm unsure of the LTVs, but they are listed as a priority production item. MacArthur wants them as well as the British, so we'll have to fight to get our share."

"Thought so, but we go to war with what we have. Correct, Commander Allen?"

"Yes sir, but perhaps once we get back to Washington, we could see if we could push more of the production to the Pacific."

"I would appreciate anything you and Admiral Edwards can do to help us get more of these contraptions. The Marines have been using every one we can get, and they think it's the best piece of equipment for landing troops." Spruance stopped speaking for a moment and then asked another question. "Captain, how much do you know about the Aleutian plans?"

Jameson was new to the issue, but Allen was already working on some ideas with Commander Layton. Spruance quickly covered the latest plan coming from Admiral Kinkaid. "Seems that Kiska may be too hot to handle, so the North Pacific planners want to take out Attu first. They don't think it will be as tough, and a new army division has been authorized to our order of battle, so we might as well use them. Kinkaid needs some help on this, so I was wondering if you had any thoughts?"

"Admiral, if the commander can bring me up to speed on what he has seen, I'm sure we can build an assessment of the situation."

"Good, I look forward to any suggestions you have. Layton has the newest intelligence reports, and I can get you the current plan submitted by Admiral Kinkaid. If possible, I'd like to get back to you in two days. I hope that's enough time; if not, let me know."

"Sir, I'll get Lieutenant Brand to help us out and get back to you shortly on our progress."

As Jameson turned to leave, Spruance had one more thing to say. "Captain, I had one of my aides checking out an officer in my command that might be related to you." Seeing the slight fatherly grin on Jameson's face, the admiral continued. "Your son, Ensign Jameson, is on a PT boat in the Russell Islands. If I hear anything about him, I'll let you know. Perhaps, you can go see Admiral Halsey and arrange a visit with your son. If you need any assistance, let me know."

Taking the information Spruance handed him on Marcus, Jameson responded, "Thank you, sir. I have not heard from him for several months but knew he would be deployed somewhere. I'm familiar with the islands near Guadalcanal and suppose this is a new advance base. Hopefully, my letters will catch up to him soon." Later that evening, a father would write a long letter to his son, wishing him good luck and urging him to be careful.

The two officers left the admiral's office and headed to the conference room they were given for their use while in Hawaii. Once in the room and with the door shut, Allen spoke first. "Captain, I think this Attu thing is going to be very rushed, and I don't think anyone has any idea about fighting a war in the Arctic. From the reports I have read about the ships and planes operating in the Aleutians, the Japanese are not the biggest threat; the weather will kill you just as quick."

Knowing some of the issues the British faced in moving ships to Russia across the Arctic Ocean, the captain realized the Americans were in for a hell of a battle. As the two men looked at the nautical charts strewn across the conference table, Jameson suddenly remembered what Admiral Edwards told him about the commander. With a grin on his face, the captain asked Allen a question.

"Commander, may I call you by your first name while we're locked up in this room?"

"Certainly, sir. I haven't heard my first name used in a long time."

"Good, but you must call me Fred. Okay?"

"Captain, I mean Fred, it would be an honor."

"John, I know you want your own command, but you and I both know you have proven your value to Admiral Edwards many times over. He told me he wanted to let you go back to sea, but for right now, he needs you back in Washington."

The commander knew his desire to return to sea duty was not a priority in the war effort and realized he may be stuck in a staff role for the rest of his career. "Fred, you and I do what we are told to do just like they taught us when we were plebes at the academy. If the navy feels I can be of more use steering a desk than a ship, so be it, but I don't have to like it." John Allen grinned, knowing the captain felt the same way.

Both men were in agreement about their present situation. But Jameson decided to improve the commander's disposition. "John, before I left Washington to relieve you of preventing the professor from making some major political error, Admiral Edwards told me to allow you a little sea time. I think I have an idea which ties directly into what we're currently doing."

The commander's face lit up like a kid at Christmas, wanting to know what was in the shiny wrapped box which held out the hope of a sea posting.

"This Aleutian campaign is going to be run on a shoe string with whatever forces are available. Knowing Admiral Kinkaid, he's going to rush to attack Attu. I believe he will try to isolate it first from reinforcements before he invades. This means he will need more ships. Admiral

Spruance told me that *Salt Lake City* is heading north to add to the ships under Admiral McMorris's command. It's scheduled to depart for Dutch Harbor on the tenth or eleventh. I think you should go along as an observer, and once you get to Dutch Harbor, Admiral Spruance can get you posted as an observer with McMorris as he attempts to stop the Japanese ships heading to Kiska and Attu. Do you want to go on a very cold voyage?"

Allen was beaming and replied, "Sir, I mean Fred, if you can arrange only a few weeks at sea with the possibility of action, I will be forever in your debt. I know the ship's captain Bertram Rogers. He was on the planning staff for Admiral King. I think you know him as well?"

Jameson quickly replied, "Yes, I knew he was up for a ship, but I was gone when he received the posting. I guess he took over in January. I never had a chance to serve with him because he spent the late '20s on a submarine while I was out in California teaching ROTC."

John Allen was ready to leave now and join the ship but realized everything needed to be set in motion, and then in a few days, he could go join the heavy cruiser on its way north and possibly see some action. The captain was happy for the commander but recalled his enthusiasm for joining a ship to see some action back at Savo Island. That didn't turn out very well. He hoped Commander Allen fared better in the cold seas of the North Pacific.

The British aircraft carrier appeared quite different from their last visit in January. The HMS *Victorious* was similar in size to the American *Enterprise* but a hundred feet shorter than the new *Essex* class carriers. The ship had added several antiaircraft guns, new radars, and extended the flight deck to enable the landing of the larger American Avenger (TBF) torpedo bombers. The vessel retained the Royal Navy's disruptive camouflage pattern but would soon wear the U.S. Navy's sea blue to match the *Saratoga*.

An armored deck increased the British ship's displacement by a few thousand tons but would prove essential in the Pacific War, something the Americans soon wished had been done to their own ships. Aircraft on board *Victorious* was limited to sixty whereas the *Enterprise's* usual complement of war planes was eighty-five with space for one hundred. The new *Essex* class carriers now in production were a hundred feet longer with an increased displacement of thirty-three thousand tons, fourteen thousand greater than the *Enterprise*. The new carrier's usual aircraft complement was one hundred three, with a top speed of thirty-three knots and a crew of twenty-nine hundred men. The British warship had a crew of only sixteen hundred. Still, even with fewer men, the on-board ventilation systems were designed for duty in the North Atlantic. The men suffered terribly on their transit through the steamy Caribbean and Panama Canal and into the Pacific.

Lieutenant Clark led Brand and Warrant Jones up the gangplank of the warship and was greeted by the American liaison aboard, Commander Mitchell. The visitors were given a tour of the vessel to see the modifications made during its time in Norfolk. The additional antiaircraft guns and flaring on the ship's sides improved the *Victorious'* ability to fend off Japanese air attacks. Two extra arrestor wires were still needed to handle the sizeable American torpedo planes. The combat information center had been expanded to accommodate the new radar systems plus the additional American air controllers. Mitchell explained how the trip down to Panama and then onto Hawaii proved more changes were needed. All of them could be done at Pearl, but it would add another few weeks before the ship could be deployed to the South Pacific. Luckily, the Japanese fleet had made few moves toward the American positions.

Leaving the American and his British pilots, James, Gunny and Duncan made their way to Captain Mackintosh's cabin to invite the captain and his senior officers to a party in their honor on the ninth. The British pilots were getting ready to head ashore to sample the local culture, and Mitchell would join them, or as he put it, provide chaperone and interpreter services in case anyone got into trouble. Clark told Mitchell he would join them later, but first, James needed to visit the captain. The captain was happy to see Clark, Brand, and Warrant Jones, knowing how much of his mission was based upon the professor's ideas. The captain provided the three men with an overview of the voyage, including losing two pilots to accidents. The need to add the arrestor hooks became evident on the passage to Hawaii as the hook on the Avenger was too narrow for the British cables. The tension system was also too weak to handle the bigger American planes, so this was one of the changes that would have to be done before heading into the war zone.

"Overall," the captain stated, "The ship and crew are ready to meet the Japanese head-on. I look forward to telling Admiral Nimitz that the Royal Navy is ready."

James thought the ship looked good, even though it had been at war since 1939. Now, it would join its American counterpart and meet the Japanese threat. That evening, at a hotel bar in Honolulu, Lieutenant Duncan Clark and the other members of the Fleet Air Arm discovered American booze and hula girls. Except for some black eyes and tremendous headaches, the British officers were able to recall little of their late night adventures.

31

8 March 1942
USS *Salt Lake City* (CA-25)
Pearl Harbor, Territory of Hawaii

- Tunisia--18th Army Group: Takes command of U.S. II Corps but leaves French 19th Corps attached to British 1st Army. II Corps continues planning for offensive in mid-March. In British 1st Army area, 5 Corps continues to withstand pressure against north flank in Tamera area.
- USSR--Red Army troops capture Sychevka, forcing enemy back toward Smolensk.
- West Indies--German submarine, **U-156**, sunk by naval land-based aircraft.

The heavy cruiser was getting the last of a new paint job. The ship had been damaged at the Battle of Cape Esperance back in October and spent the next four months being repaired. The vessel had sustained four major hits from Japanese shellfire during the battle and required a significant overhaul of its engines. Since the attack on Pearl Harbor, the ship had been in continuous service, escorting carriers and participating in the Midway and the Guadalcanal campaigns. New radars were being

fitted as well as additional antiaircraft weapons. The ship, affectional-
ly nicknamed the *Swayback Maru*, had acquitted herself well in every
operation and luckily had not sustained many casualties. The new commanding officer, Captain Bertram Rogers, had inherited a well-trained
and experienced crew. The ship had lost many of its experienced junior
officers and ratings to new construction, but luckily, it had held onto
enough "old-timers" to keep the ship running smoothly.

Captain Jameson, Commander Allen, and Lieutenant Brand went
aboard the cruiser at 0800 hours to meet with Rogers and his executive
officer, Commander Bitler. Admiral Nimitz had sent the captain a signal
informing him of Allen's temporary assignment with Admiral Kinkaid
requiring his passage on the cruiser to Dutch Harbor. Rogers was glad
to see some familiar faces from Washington and had enjoyed working
with Allen on war plans. Bitler was also happy to see Jameson, who was
a year ahead of him at Annapolis. Lieutenant Brand stood back as he
witnessed the meeting of old friends and marveled at the recollections of
times gone by. His college and work experiences were limited by his age
and his chosen profession's reclusive nature. Finally, after a few minutes
of smiles and laughs, Captain Jameson introduced James to the two officers, and the five men sat down to talk about the ship's new assignment
in the cold seas of the Aleutians.

"Captain Rogers, your ship looks in fine condition and should be
ready to make the passage north in a few days. Admiral Spruance wanted to know if there were any last-minute problems or requirements."

The ship's captain asked his executive officer, Commander W. S.
"Worthy" Bitler, to answer the question. "Captain Jameson, I think we're
set to go. The ship needs its final bunkering to top off the tanks and load
the final ammunition stores. The provisioning should be completed by the
ninth, and the crew has been called back to the ship with no more liberty
calls for the men. We have seventeen new men yet to arrive, but we have
been told by fleet personnel they should be here in the next two days. None
of these men are deemed critical except for one engine room pump expert."

Rogers then added one other item. "Jameson, we're still waiting for
cold-weather clothing. We have received some, but we can only equip
half the crew. We are told the sea conditions will be rough and the two
destroyers escorting us are in the same position. Do you think you could
make some inquiries?"

"Certainly, Captain. If there are any heavy clothes in Hawaii, I think we can find them. Admiral Spruance has some excellent scroungers on his staff, and it's amazing what they can come up with when needed."

The small talk continued for another minute. The ship had finished its repairs and improvements and was ready for sea. Like so many ships in the fleet, crews aboard were constantly changing due to the need to transfer experienced men to new vessels. Officers who once would have waited five years for promotion were now being promoted after only six months of service. An ensign in 1940 would be a lieutenant now and, by the end of this year, possibly a lieutenant commander in command of a new destroyer escort. Brand was aware of new reserve officers being placed in command of landing ships with only a year of training. The enlisted ranks were in even worse condition. The old-time petty officers, the core of the navy, were trying to take amateurs and change them into old sea dogs in six months. The war was not slowing down and the number of ships being launched required crews, even barely trained ones.

Commander Allen asked about the passage north and how long Rogers anticipated the voyage would last. The answer was longer than he expected, but he knew the ship would not be charging full speed straight to Alaska. "Allen, based upon our sailing instructions, it will take us six days to get to Dutch Harbor. We will meet up with our destroyers south of Dutch Harbor and refuel once we enter the harbor. Admiral McMorris will command the cruiser force, and he plans to sortie within a few days of our arrival."

Jameson introduced James to the two officers but did not tell them why Brand was at the meeting. When posted to King's staff, Rogers was aware of the professor but had not met him. Few people were acquainted with him on a personal basis as if the scientist was some kind of monk the CNO kept in a cave. Captain Jameson provided the reason for James's appearance at the meeting.

"Gentlemen, I introduced Lieutenant Brand when we walked into the room, but now I want to provide you the reason he's here. Captain Rogers, I know you recognize the lieutenant from your time on Admiral King's staff. My official position is the commanding officer of what is known as the Science Team, reporting to the CNO. There are several other individuals on the team, but the primary member is Lieutenant Brand. James is a professor of physics at Colombia and provides technical support to the Chiefs of Staff and Admiral Leahy. He is also highly involved in the intelligence community, and Admiral Nimitz wanted James to provide you a briefing on the situation you will encounter in the Aleutians."

The two officers stared at the navy lieutenant, who appeared no older than a high school student, and were amazed at the young man's connections to the senior leadership of the war effort.

James, in his usual calm manner, began his talk. "Thank you, Captain, for the introduction. Captain Rogers, Commander Bitler, you and your ship's company are about to encounter the worst weather known to mankind. The situation in the Aleutians is about to get even more dangerous. Admiral Nimitz has been ordered to eliminate the Japanese forces on the islands of Attu and Kiska. The Japanese are constantly making efforts to reinforce their garrisons. But the horrible weather and our forces have stopped many of these attempts. They are trying to build an airfield on Attu but don't appear to have the machinery necessary to accomplish this as quickly as we do. They do have a large number of Rufes and large flying boats at Kiska but none at Attu. The garrison's size on Kiska is much larger, and for this reason, Admiral Kinkaid has recommended the Allies attack Attu first. This does two things to the enemy position. First, it allows us to destroy the smaller garrison, using only the forces currently available to our North Pacific command. Second, it sets up an additional barrier for the enemy to cross in their attempts to resupply Kiska. The islands are two hundred miles apart, and with Attu in our possession, we can use this island as an early warning post for any Japanese movements toward Kiska."

James waited for the first piece of news to sink in. He used a chart Allen had brought along to help make his point. "If the Japanese try to reinforce either island, it is imperative that naval forces stop them. Our ability to perform aerial reconnaissance is limited due to the foul weather and long distances from our nearest base on Adak. This requires Admiral Kinkaid to stretch out his naval forces to search out toward the Japanese bases on the Kuriles, about seven hundred miles away, and then patrol north to the Bering Sea."

The professor was now hitting his stride and continued with an as yet incomplete timeline. "The timeframe for operations against Attu is early May. This is dependent on weather, the addition of more bombers and escort fighters at Adak, and prepositioning troops to the marshaling sites in the Aleutians. The Seventh Division, now training in California, will be used for this operation. It's a brand new unit with no combat experience. It has moved to Fort Ord to begin amphibious training. Admiral Rockwell has been named Commander Amphibious Forces North Pacific and has assembled a staff to develop plans for the invasion. Currently, the sea forces for this operation are still being assembled. Admiral Nimitz has assigned three older battleships to provide gunfire support, and perhaps one escort carrier will also be added. The situation is fluid, and changes will be made up to the invasion date."

The men were staring at the young officer as he continued with a list of support units, air force, and navy land-based aircraft, submarines, and for the stockpiles of supplies, fuel, and medical supplies, now being assembled for the offensive. The commanding officer of the *Salt Lake City* knew he was going into battle but was unsure of the conditions he would be dealing with, both on the sea and with the enemy. As he and his executive officer began asking questions of the professor, he began to worry about his ship and its crew. *Would they be ready?* And would he meet the challenge of leading men into battle? Rogers would spend a lot of time with Commander Allen on the voyage north to help him prepare and calm his nerves.

The sun was low on the horizon, with an hour or so of daylight remaining. The meetings had gone exceedingly well, and since arriving in the coastal city, the American was enjoying the attitude of its people. The natives were a little less pushy than those of Calcutta. The colonial officers, businessmen, and soldiers were pleasant and straightforward in their dealings. Beck had been told by Colonel Granger not to expect the chaos found in India. The locals, citizens of Goa but of Indian descent, were cordial in their bearing and attitude toward foreigners. The small colony was surrounded by hundreds of millions of Indians, plus their British masters, who for centuries were unhappy about the Portuguese presence. But the tiny enclave of Portuguese civilization had survived since the early 1500s, with few problems and a strong sense of doing business with anyone, as long as they didn't cause trouble.

Beck and his bodyguard Habir arrived early in the morning from meeting his American naval counterpart in Bombay. This pompous port officer was another example of the wrong man doing the wrong job in the wrong place. The officer's name was Unger, and he was so incompetent Beck thought he could get the man to sign over the entire American base to the Japanese. All of this emboldened him more, so that by the time they arrived in the Portuguese colony Beck was ready to do business on a bigger scale than even the colonel imagined.

His business partners were happy with the arrangement negotiated with the navy officer. Each man received a ten percent cut of the profits from the various scams and outright thefts established by Beck. The Indian criminals who did the dangerous details of robbery, warehousing, and eventual sale of the goods, received a fat thirty percent of the monies, plus their expenses, which usually averaged another five percent. This left thirty-five percent of the proceeds to the American, who in turn paid members of his personal staff, including Habir, five percent. The remaining amount was free and clear profit for Beck. As he traveled around India in his official role of port officer and logistics manager, he saw how this percentage would be sufficient to yield a few million dollars over the next two to three years.

As Beck enjoyed the sunset and drank another gin and tonic with the colonel, Habir entered the room and handed his employer a note. It came from the banker he had met a few hours earlier. Senhor Diogo Souza had made several inquiries based upon the request Beck and Colonel Granger had provided. The note asked for a meeting that night at nine o'clock with two of the bank directors. Nothing else was stated but the name of a restaurant, Passaro Azul. The colonel commented, "Sounds like the bankers are interested in doing business. I think Senhor Souza will be offering us an opportunity to transfer our hard assets into some sort of cash instruments or gold credits. I told him we wanted a safe way to transfer our assets to Lisbon without significant risk. I think he understood what we needed."

The navy lieutenant understood this as an agreement for the bankers to receive the jewels, gold, and other forms of hard currency and change these items for an easily transported and hard-to-trace form of wealth—gold coins, gold bars, and American money. British currency was also a possibility, but the Indian government carefully controlled its paper money and limited its use in the country. The traditional Indian

Rupee fluctuated in value and was not easy to change outside of India. The currency of Goa, the Portuguese Indian Escudo, was pegged on Portugal's Escudo, but it was also challenging to exchange for other currencies. This left American dollars, which were the most stable form of currency. Still, their availability in India was minimal because neither the Americans nor the British wanted to create a black market in dollars. Beck looked forward to the meeting with the bankers, knowing they would like to do business with him but they also planned to charge a hefty fee for their efforts.

That night, Beck, Colonel Granger, and Habir went to the restaurant and had a delightful meal with the three bankers. Senhor Souza talked around the main reason for the dinner until after the meal had concluded. The conversations were about everything except business. Politics in India, America, the war against the Axis, the climate of Goa, and the lovely ladies of the colony were all discussed at great length. Finally, Souza pulled out a two-page contract, written in English, and presented it to the colonel. As Granger examined the agreement, the Portuguese banker explained what they planned to do with the deposits being made into their bank.

"Senhor Beck, my associates, and I are happy to accommodate your needs in dealing with the financial issues we discussed earlier. We will arrange to transfer these assets for a fee of six percent of the total value. For this fee, we will take charge of the items in question and arrange for the disposal of those objects with some form of value into hard currency. Upon your approval, which will be accomplished monthly, we will reconcile the account and transfer the agreed-upon amount to Lisbon for deposit in the home office of the Banco Nacional Ultramarino. Each deposit will be certified and held in a numbered account. If this meets your expectations, we are ready to fulfill our part of the contract."

Knowing the colonel had already negotiated with the Portuguese banker for two days before Beck arrived in the colony and understanding the probable terms, the American agreed to the contract. "Senhor Souza, these terms are acceptable as well as the suggestions on the transfer of these assets to Goa. We understand the fee structure and the timelines. The deposits we have made so far will increase significantly over the next few months, and I want to be assured that you will be able to process these on a timely basis."

Souza was told about the size of the deposits, much of which would have to be sold to other buyers. In the case of the jewels, perhaps they would be forwarded directly to third parties outside of the subcontinent. The middle east was the most likely location for the sale of diamonds, rubies, and emeralds, because of the increasing desire of various sheiks and lesser nobility to hold hard assets. The fee agreement would allow the bankers to pocket excess profits from the sale of jewels and other items, thus making the six percent sound low. But for now, the deal suited both parties and would make the Portuguese bankers a lot of money.

Later that night, after consuming some excellent Port provided to Beck by his new banking partners, the colonel returned to his room. Habir stayed close and drank only water. He rarely drank and was always at the ready to defend the American. The Sikh knew what the American and his English partners were doing, but it didn't bother him. The criminal gangs working in concert with Beck were only stealing from the Europeans, and many Indians benefited from these thefts. Habir was personally gaining wealth at an alarming rate. If the war continued for another two or three years, he could buy a vast estate and take care of his extended family for many generations. For this fact alone, the bodyguard was dedicated to the safety of the navy officer.

Beck stood up and walked out on the patio overlooking the street and beyond to the harbor. He noticed a large number of ships, all illuminated, with none darkened like in Calcutta. Several of the ships were moored close to one another and swung at anchor in the darkened sky. The colonel had pointed out four of them earlier. "Three of those ships are German and the other one Italian. They were caught in the Indian Ocean when the war began in 1939 and found their way to Goa. Being a neutral port, they have been interned with their crews staying aboard their vessels, bored out of their minds."

The navy officer wondered why the British had not come into the harbor and taken them away but knew they didn't want to upset the neutral Portuguese, with whom they had a long-standing alliance. But knowing the need for merchant shipping, it was strange these ships sat unused in a neutral harbor without anyone doing anything about it. As he returned to his room for the night, he heard the sounds of bands playing further up the street. Tomorrow, the colonel told him, Carnival festivals would be in full swing with lots of parties and food and drink available for his enjoyment. Others would be watching for the start of festivities, including two men now interested in what Beck and the colonel were doing in Goa, especially tonight.

The boats had received a warning of a possible attack, and luckily each was at sea when the enemy planes arrived. The island was still in a primitive state, but there were many juicy targets, especially around the small harbor. Two small landing craft were sunk, while several other boats were beached to avoid sinking. The Seabees were hit hard and lost much of the equipment being used to scratch out the airfield. No one died in the attack, but several men were seriously wounded. The most significant loss was to the generator plant, which had just started to operate, dashing hopes for electricity and perhaps even some ice.

Marcus Jameson and the six boats now stationed at Wernham cove transported the most seriously injured men to Tulagi. They then waited a day to load repair parts for the construction battalions. While at the headquarters for the Solomon Islands torpedo boats, the men swapped stories of their nightly forays up the Slot. Lately, the boats had been harassing enemy barge traffic, and a few short but spirited battles had broken out. Most of these were over quickly, with the Americans coming out on top. The Japanese rarely had anything heavier than a machine gun on the diesel-powered barges, which were about fifty feet in length with a top speed of nine knots, but usually traveled no faster than seven knots. These boats had a three-foot draught, and used extensively by the enemy for moving men about the islands or from ship to shore. They were no match for the Americans.

The PT boats mission was to constantly patrol up the channel to Vangunu, Rendova, or New Georgia. The Japanese were building an airfield at Munda but moved many men to the nearby islands to slow any American advance. Further up the channel, the American navy laid a minefield in Blackett Strait between Kolombangara Island, the Gizo Island reefs, and Makuti Island. Three old four-stack destroyers—converted to minelayers—escorted by the destroyer *Radford*, dropped two-hundred-fifty contact mines in the channel. Even before the American flotilla made it back to Tulagi for refueling, four Japanese destroyers ran into the new minefield of the early morning darkness. One destroyer sank, and two others were seriously damaged. Only one warship escaped the American trap.

Early in the morning, the PT boats on Russell were notified to prepare for a move north after dark to search for crippled enemy vessels but were warned off late in the afternoon. Planes from Guadalcanal finished off the two damaged destroyers and severely damaged the lone survivor. Operations were shelved for the evening, knowing the enemy was now taking extra precautions. Ensign Jameson and the other PT boat officers returned to their boats, instructing their crews to stand down. There would be no late-night tours of the Solomon Islands. Marcus thought this would be his chance to show what he could do. Running his boat on a high-speed torpedo attack is what every man in the PT boat service dreamed of, but tonight he would once again drink his warm beer, play poker, and wait along with three other ensigns who shared the same dream.

32

9 March 1943
Lisbon, Portugal

- New Guinea--Japanese planes attack Wau in force. The first in a series of heavy air attacks on strategic points in New Guinea.
- Burma--Columns of Indian 77th Brigade (Chindits) begin crossing Irrawaddy River in order to harass enemy farther east.
- North Africa--Axis reorganization of forces continues. Field Marshal Kesselring's authority over ground, air and sea units in the Mediterranean is extended. Gen. von Arnim takes command of Army Group Africa, succeeding Field Marshal Rommel, who leaves Africa.
- Tunisia--In U.S. II Corps area, 1st Division is joined in Bou Chebka area by RCT 18, which reverts to it from attachment to 34th Division.

The confirmation of the meeting was handled with great care, using the busy casino as the perfect cover for a discrete hand-off. The message was a time, date, and location, using a simple substitution code based upon a set of pages in the local newspaper published the same morning. Armed with this knowledge, the message gave Wagener today's date, a street address, and a room number. The time was the most challenging part to uncover. Using a compass heading from an article in the paper as the tool to discern the time, the German quickly figured out the message. Two hundred, ten degrees indicated a southwest course, but adding another zero became 2100 hours.

Being careful in his movements around town and giving a cover story to his superiors about meeting a new illicit mining partner, the tall man hobbled down narrow streets with his cane, ducking into passageways to ensure he was not being followed. Taking three taxis like he was taught at the Abwehr school in Berlin, he further dirtied his trail. Finding the building, a middle-class hotel frequented by businessmen and a few high-class prostitutes, Wagener climbed the stairs to the third floor and stopped at the last step. Slowly poking his head out to look each way into the hotel corridor, he saw a man with a lady of easy virtue entering a room. He saw no one else, but Gebhardt waited another thirty seconds to be sure. Again he scrutinized the empty corridor. Walking in a slow though not overly cautious manner, the German located room 314 and knocked. Being unarmed, he didn't know what to expect. Would it be the Gestapo or one of their criminal partners waiting to kill him? Perhaps it was someone besides the American navy officer, which would force him to quickly retreat down the stairs. Holding his breath, he waited.

John Meyers had waited alone for an hour—a snub nose .38 pistol at the ready and a bottle of good Portuguese wine from the Douro Valley on the table. He hoped to drink the wine instead of firing the gun. Two American agents were in the next room. Two other agents posed as drunks in the alley next to the building, boisterously holding court. The agents were first-generation Americans whose families had immigrated from the Azores before World War One. Even with excellent language skills the agents were identified as being from the islands and not Lisboans. When the knock at the door finally came, Allen caught his breath and slowly made his way across the room. Cracking the door just enough to recognize Wagener, he opened it fully allowing entrance. The German quickly entered, held a finger to his lips to keep Meyers quiet, and pulled back the curtains John had closed tightly and peaked out to see the street. No one was there, at least no one he could see in the dark roadway.

Speaking barely above a whisper, Wagener said, "I believe your commanders are interested in what I have to say. We need to be quick because I have to make another meeting to cover this one."

John walked to the small table and pulled out the chairs. Sitting down, he stated, "Herr Wagener, my high command is interested in any communication which could be beneficial to the peoples of our respective countries."

The German sat down and slowly looked around the room. Seeing the paper and pencil in front of John Meyers, Gebhardt pulled them toward him and began to write. Pushing the scrap of paper toward Meyers, he said, "This is a way to contact Wilhelm. He knows your Mr. Dulles and would like to renew his association. It appears many other members of the leadership express deep misgivings on the direction of our country. Perhaps, we can jointly address this problem in the future."

Meyers looked directly at the German navy officer who returned an expressionless stare. Both professionals, but their countries were at war. Yet, the man seated in front of him hinted there were perhaps senior officers and officials who wanted out of the war.

Wilhelm meant only one thing. Admiral Wilhelm Canaris was exploring options. Not to save himself, which would also have to be considered, but to save his homeland from utter destruction. The chief of German military intelligence knew things were going badly in Russia. The North Africa campaign was nearing its end, with the defeat of the German and Italian armies in Tunisia. Italy itself was seething in resentment, foretelling its collapse, leaving Germany alone to control an ever-shrinking empire. The U-boat war continued, but the losses in submarines and their experienced crews could not be replaced. And worst of all, the Allies were growing in bomber strength, threatening to obliterate the Fatherland from the air. It didn't take a genius to see the noose was slowly closing on the Nazis, and Canaris knew there was only one future—total destruction.

Wagener understood this early in his naval career. At Narvik, his destroyer flotilla was utterly destroyed by superior British naval forces. The Kriegsmarine was not ready for war in 1939, nor would it be prepared by 1944, which was the Fuhrer's promised timeline for starting the war. His duty on the battle cruiser *Scharnhorst* proved the total inadequacy of the navy to fight a war at sea. The foray into the North

Atlantic with its sister ship did sink many Allied merchant vessels, but they had been fortunate in not meeting British warships. Once the two ships arrived at Brest, they were under constant attack until charging up the English Channel to safety in German waters. The British were caught off guard and failed to stop them, yet the *Gneisenau* hit a mine as it neared the security of a German port and never again went to sea.

The *Scharnhorst*, now hidden in the northern fiords of Norway, waited to attack British convoys but rarely exposed itself. The battleship *Tirpitz* did the same thing, never leaving port, low on fuel oil for its bunkers, and harassed by British bombers. The few remaining cruisers of the German Navy were in the Baltic, and there were no plans for reinforcements. The Kreigsmarine was barely a "force in being," and except for the aggressive patrolling by the U-boats, inconsequential. Gebhardt understood things scientifically and understood the requirements of having the raw materials required to fight a modern war. Germany still used more horse-drawn artillery than trucks. Tank production was sluggish, as was the availability of fuel to power them. The Luftwaffe manufactured more airplanes but failed to understand the need for a long-range bomber, so as its enemies shrunk its borders, the Reich could not reach out and attack the industries and cities of its opponents. At a quickening pace, the tools of war were becoming more difficult to supply, and the loss of hundreds of thousands of men in Russia was bleeding the nation dry.

Meyers had been carefully briefed on what to say and what to ask. Looking at the note the German handed him, he said, "I know we are interested in any information which would prove these claims. Can you share something which would indicate the sincerity of this request?"

Wagener knew there would be a requirement to prove his credentials in opening this clandestine line of communications. He also knew his statements were an act of treason, punishable by his death and those of many others. His religious beliefs had always influenced his life, and now he needed to do the greater good for mankind. "Herr Meyers, on February 27, some British commandos stormed the industrial plant in Telemark, Norway. The plant was heavily damaged, but much of the "heavy water" is still in tanks. More work is being done to resume production. I know your command knows the results but not the complete story."

John wrote down the essential information, including the dates. He had no knowledge of the British operation or, for that matter, *heavy water*. As he finished, the German added one more piece of information. "There is a major push to resupply Tunisia. Additional air units are being sent to Sicily and Tunisia. A large ship convoy is planned for a run from Palermo to Tunisia. This will also be in coordination with a major airlift using several hundred transports. The target date is April 5, with an additional hundred seventy-eight fighters reassigned from the Eastern Front to fields on Sicily. The Luftwaffe will probably have three hundred fighters in Tunisia by April 1."

This was the kind of intelligence rarely given by an enemy agent. The message's source wanted the Allies to understand its significance and allow the Americans to react. Meyers dutifully wrote down the details. "Why does Wilhelm want to tell us these things? Germans will die, and the war might hinge on this information."

Gebhardt arose from his chair, peeked out the windows one last time, and headed to the door. Turning to face the American, he said calmly, "The war is already lost. If a few hundred men die today but ten thousand live tomorrow, is it not a good thing?"

As the door closed, Meyers exhaled and wondered about the next step. He probably would not be involved in any meetings with Wilhelm, but wondered about the chess game he was now playing. Later at the American legation, he would be debriefed several times and asked to write a report, recalling the exact words used by the German officer as well as his facial expressions, posture, and even the man's eyes. Each non-verbal clue might offer additional insight into the man and his mission. Finally getting to bed at 0300, sleep passed him by. He wondered about the commando mission and the future convoys to Tunisia. The German had told his enemies about war plans and secrets which came only from one source. Murdoch told John to be ready to meet the German again, but possibly not for many weeks. Instructions and approvals would be slow, but eventually, senior people would begin discussing future clandestine meetings.

The town of Vasco de Gama sat along the harbor of Mormugao in Goa. The merchant ships and the few Portuguese naval craft were moored in the harbor or tied up alongside the many wharves of the town. The beaches were nice, and the warm sand felt good to tourists visiting the colony. Today was the last day of Carnival, and the biggest party of the holiday season would begin after sunset. Already, party revelers strolled down the small quaint streets of the town, drinking the local liquor as well as savoring good quality Portuguese wines. Food stalls opened early, and the bars were packed. Traditional music from Portugal was heard throughout the town. Occasionally, a guitar and sitar were heard playing simultaneously in a strange rhythmic confluence of musical cultures.

Beck had abstained from booze most of the day. The same could not be said for Colonel Granger, who started early but still could rally enough to imbibe after dark. The two men were scheduled for dinner at one of the best restaurants near the waterfront—a setting out of central casting, with garish costumes, soft music, and breezes from open verandas facing the water. They were seated on the second floor in a special section, reserved for their exclusive use by the bankers of Goa, who seemed happy with their important client. Tonight, with their business complete, the two men would watch the festivities. The colonel, would fall into a deep drunken sleep by midnight and moved to a lovely room in the back of the hotel next door. The American, drinking more than usual, would stay more or less sober as he enjoyed a moment of triumph.

Joy came at a high cost. Over the last twelve months, the navy lieutenant had gone from a "survivor" of the Pearl Harbor attack to a drunken scoundrel, a disgrace to his uniform, summarily demoted and shipped out to waste away the war in the backwaters of India. Now, as he sat in a lovely restaurant overlooking the bay of a Portuguese colony on the Indian Ocean, he reveled in his success. His years in the navy were never part of his plan. His father decided every step in his life and pulled strings for the young man to attend Annapolis. He only had to spend four years in the navy, then with a military background, his father's business interests would ensure his future success.

The plans crumbled when the Japanese attacked Pearl Harbor. Beck was in the hospital with the flu when his ship, *West Virginia*, was damaged and slowly settled to the harbor's bottom. After recuperating and doing odd jobs at the navy base, he was sent to be a staff officer at Main Navy. Another promotion to Lieutenant Commander came with the new assignment, again arranged by his father, and he settled into spending the war in a safe office in Washington. Then a young officer

named Brand came into his life, taking things from bad to worse....
Snapping himself out his pathetic trip down memory lane, he had become master of his future, which had nothing to do with helping his country win the war, but everything to do with acquiring great wealth.

As the night progressed and the colonel fell deeper into a drunken state, Beck tried to pay the bill but was informed that everything was taken care of by his new banking friends. The manager agreed to get Colonel Granger to his room. The American naval officer, now wearing a tropical tan suit, white shirt, no tie, and a matching white straw Fedora hat, walked down the stairs and strolled down the street alongside the bay. It was nearing midnight, so the music was getting louder. Beck walked by an outdoor stage with a Portuguese band playing expressively, but not that well. Never mind, it was the last night of Carnival, and everyone was enjoying themselves. What sounded like fireworks were heard coming from the dark bay where several ships were moored. These were the same ships the bankers had pointed out the day before—the German ships *Braunfels*, *Drachenfels*, and *Ehrenfels*, plus the Italian cargo vessel the *Anfora*.

Beck continued gazing into the darkness of the harbor, watching the dim lights burning on the Axis vessels. Other ships were anchored in the harbor, mainly Portuguese and a few British flagged vessels used by Indian merchants transporting goods between the subcontinent's ports. Under the Hague Convention, ships of belligerent nations can use a neutral port, but a warship can only remain in harbor twenty-four hours. If it stays longer, it is interned for the duration of the war and made incapable of movement and crews can be held ashore or on the ship to maintain the vessel in working order.

The rules for merchant vessels were similar, but if they left the neutral port, they were fair game for their enemy. The four Axis merchant ships had entered the port of Goa in the early days of the war seeking refuge and were now under the control of the Portuguese government for the duration of the war. Under Article Four of the Hague Convention, belligerents cannot use neutral harbors or lands for communication or engage in hostile actions against their enemies or the neutral host government. Yet, sometimes, warring nations fail to follow the terms of international agreements. Thus was the situation in the harbor tonight.

Noises in the harbor grew louder, and now other people looked out into the darkness at what looked like a small war taking place on one of the ships. Suddenly, a series of large explosions occurred. Fires broke out in several areas of the ship and people crowded the dock to get a better view. For a good ten or fifteen minutes, fires raged on the vessel. Another explosion occurred. This time on a second ship, followed by two significant blasts on the other enemy ships. Each of the four vessels was on fire and sinking. The Portuguese navy reacted slowly, indicative of the sailors relinquishing their posts in favor of a party. Beck watched as rowboats came ashore and tied up at the dock. Crewmen pulled their friends from the boats—several men apparently hurt or burned. Many of the crews had been ashore attending a party and rushed to help their friends.

The American watched for another few minutes as the ships slowly burned and began to sink in the bay. No longer interested in the situation, he walked back to his hotel, needing a night cap to celebrate his business success. Beck was unaware of two men in civilian clothes who also watched the festivities. One of the men noticed the American heading back to his hotel, jotting down the time and location of his meeting with Colonel Granger. The other man smiled as he watched the fires on the ships slowly burn out as the vessels sank below the sea.

"We should report Colonel Granger to headquarters. I know he had no knowledge of the operation, but we should check it out since he was in the Light Horse. As to the American, we must make some inquiries." The two men quietly strolled back to their hotel and waited for sunrise.

Out in the Indian Ocean, a derelict-looking old hopper barge named *Phoebe* slowly navigated south along the coast. It left the harbor shortly after the sinking of the German cargo vessel. Its volunteer crew of eighteen men from reserve units—fourteen from the Calcutta Light Horse and four men from the Calcutta Scottish—had agreed to the mission in January and now headed back to the safety of Calcutta. Every member of the British crew was over forty, and had just ended the German naval presence in Goa.

33

11 March 1943
CINCPAC Headquarters
Pearl Harbor, Territory of Hawaii

- China--U.S. 14th Air Force is activated under Maj. Gen. Claire L. Chennault.
- Tunisia--In British 1st Army area, 5 Corps remains under enemy pressure in Tamera sector.
- USSR--Continuing counteroffensive toward Kharkov, enemy reaches the town, which Red Army staunchly defends.

The work was monotonous. Papers overflowed from the desk to the conference table, and into boxes stacked along the back wall. Files, briefing books, and reports filled the room. Folders filled with reports included information on the amount of fuel oil consumed in Admiral Halsey's command for each month since November. Every ship, boat, and barge utilizing any kind of petroleum product was noted somewhere in the hundreds of pages marked PETROLEUM UTILIZATION—SOUTH PACIFIC AREA.

Then there were similar fuel reports for vehicles, aircraft, lubricants, and miscellaneous light oils used for high tolerance weaponry and another report on the amount of hundred eighty proof ethanol used to power torpedoes. As he looked at the file in front of him, the recent-ly returned Lieutenant Waverly thought the paper failed to capture the amount of propellant siphoned away for use by American personnel as an intoxicant. He recalled several evenings on Guadalcanal when en-terprising Seabees mixed this highly volatile liquid with various types of canned fruit juice and raisins to create an elixir that could make the war-weary happy and then happily pass out. Gunny caught the smile on the man's face and asked what he had found in the incredibly dull papers, which made him grin.

"Gunny, you know how we make torpedo punch, right?"

"Sure thing. Did you find a report on it in that pile?"

"Not really, but I did see the amount of hundred eighty proof alco-hol used by Halsey's command since November. I don't think they used that many torpedoes."

Grasping the situation, Warrant Jones replied, "I doubt the senior enlisted men in charge of accounting for this product accurately reported the amount being used in the weapons and that which may have spilled in transit."

Laughing at Gunny's choice of words, Waverly commented, "I'm sure some CPO has a little black book of accounts which would satisfy the navy as to the missing amounts, but then again, a senior NCO knows how to make things work and how to make things disappear."

As both men laughed at what was probably a booming business on many South Pacific islands, Major Flannigan walked in with James, Dr. Feldman and Lieutenant Clark. Eyeing the papers strewn across the floor and the unopened boxes piled halfway to the ceiling, the major asked, "What's so funny? Couldn't have been what you've seen in these boxes?"

Gunny quickly filled in the major as to Waverly's observation and then explained it to the professor and the Scotsman. "Seems the navy uses high-grade alcohol to power torpedoes, and drinking it straight would kill or blind you."

Hearing Gunny's comment Dr. Feldman quickly added, "Anything over one hundred fifty proof will kill you if you consume more than a few ounces straight. You would pass out first, and if you didn't die, it would mess up lots of your internal organs, and yes, you could go blind. The problem with this stuff is that it is blended with methanol and other denaturants to decrease volatility during storage."

Seeing the look on Brand's face, Feldman continued the lecture. "Now, I'm sure that if some enterprising sailor or Marine cut the liquid with lots of juice, sugar, raisins, canned fruit, even Coca-Cola, the proof level of the actual product would drop to maybe one hundred, making the batch palatable but not lethal." Smiling as he said these words, the doctor added, "Now, I have only sampled this once while aboard the *San Francisco*, but it wasn't very tasty. It was a great way to sterilize operating room tables, however."

Everyone but James was laughing at the doctor, whose expression was that of a child caught in a cookie jar filled with a powerful intoxicant. Brand was trying to do the math on how much juice it would take to reduce the toxicity level of the torpedo fuel to make it compatible with the human body, but before he got far in these thoughts, Commander Layton walked into the room.

"Looks like you have been having a hell of a time opening Christmas presents in here. Find anything useful?"

Major Flannigan, being the senior officer present, replied for the team. "Sir, I'm not sure what we've found so far. The professor, Dr. Feldman, Lieutenant Clark, and I have said goodbye to Commander Allen and then watched the *Salt Lake City* leave the harbor." Turning to James, the Marine asked, "James, have you found anything useful so far?"

Immediately going into research mode, Brand stated, "Commander, we are getting a good feel for the supply situation in Admiral Halsey's command as well as the situation in MacArthur's area. It appears the fuel issue is still of paramount importance. The number of oilers remain far below the number required to supply the bases we have from here to New Guinea."

Moving over to the large wall map of the Pacific, James continued. "Hawaii serves as the origination point for everything currently moving to the other Pacific commands. The fuel situation here is improving daily, especially with the remaining new underground storage tanks becoming available in the next few months. The issue facing CINCPAC is in providing adequate convoy support to the islands beyond Hawaii. Another problem is the slower merchant oilers we're using to supply Australia by skirting the contested areas by steering far south to avoid the Solomons. This adds a week to ten days to any delivery schedule."

Pointing at Halsey's area and his headquarters on New Caledonia,

James provided more information. "The South Pacific Area has some storage capability in Noumea, but we're having to keep at least one oiler tied up in the harbor to service ships moving north to the Solomons. One of our recommendations is to put together a Seabee unit to build nothing but oil storage facilities."

Layton looked at the map and knew the situation well. More engineers were being sent to help the army massing in Australia as well as in the Solomons. New navy construction battalions were engaged in building airfields, docks, and naval support facilities across the Pacific. More units were desperately needed, but the professor had a good point. Without sufficient capability in the transportation and storage of oil, the war would be on hold.

"James, what do we need in terms of men and machines to do this type of work?"

"Commander, I'm no expert in construction, but from watching a few of the projects underway in Hawaii, we need more five-hundred-man Seabee battalions composed of welders, iron workers, and heavy equipment operators. I'm certain Admiral Moreell has established parameters for the various types of projects for these units. We just need to get more men shipped out to help us."

Thinking again about the gargantuan construction required to allow America to build new bases across the Pacific, Layton asked another question. "After the Seabees and engineers build these facilities, what else is required to continue the attack?"

Maintaining his usual calm expression, James gave the intelligence officer his assessment. "Sir, if we can fix the fuel oil problem for the navy, we still have a huge hole in our ability to support our air forces. Before I left Washington, it became widely known that the aviation gas problem was becoming critical."

Sensing that Brand was going into a detailed explanation, Duncan Clark jumped into the conversation. "Commander Layton, how much do you know about aviation gasoline, specifically one hundred octane fuel?"

The commander quickly admitted his ignorance. "Lieutenant, I don't have the foggiest idea about aviation gas or, for that matter, what makes it so special."

Seeing the Scotsman take over the explanation, James sat down and listened. Clark gave a brief history of fuel oils without making it sound like a chemistry class. "Sir, as you are aware, gasoline is a product derived from crude oil. Certain properties exist in this fuel that may or may not make it acceptable to different engines. Your normal automobile can handle sixty octane fuel. It will knock a lot, but it will run. Octane is part of a rating system that informs one of the qualities of the fuel. For example, a fifty octane fuel would have an n-heptane rating of zero, and an iso-octane rating of one hundred giving you the number fifty. The n-heptane is the cause of knocking in fuels, it burns in an explosive manner, so if you reduce this attribute, the engine runs smoother. Before the war, eighty-seven octane was deemed by the powers in Whitehall or in your Washington, as being sufficient to make an aircraft engine operate smoothly."

Looking over at James for confirmation and seeing the grin, the Scotsman continued. "Now, if you're flying a trainer or a transport, a little knocking is all right. You are not looking for high performance. But if you have a bloody German on your tail, you don't want your plane spitting and coughing. So, before the war, we experimented with some of your splendid one hundred octane fuel. By increasing the engine manifold pressure, we were able to correct the knocking problem and increase the power without expanding the size and weight of the engine. You can see the logic in this, can't you, sir?"

Layton knew he was in for a different kind of briefing from the affable British pilot, so he played along. "Lieutenant, so if you get more power from your engines, you fly faster and perhaps longer than your enemy?"

"Precisely! Well done, sir, if I may say so for an intelligence officer." Layton took no offense, but Flannigan gave Duncan a stern look.

"Sir, by using additives such as tetraethyl lead and using a process of hydrogenation, your American scientists were able to increase the octane rating of aviation fuel to one hundred and perhaps beyond. The difference in performance is breathtaking and will help win the war. The problem Professor Brand is concerned with is the ability to make millions of gallons of this fuel in America and then ship it worldwide. Your country, sir, is the only major supplier."

James added another piece to the puzzle. "Commander, what Clark is talking about is building more specialized refineries to make the fuel.

These facilities use the Houdry process of catalytic cracking. There is currently inadequate capacity for the production of enough aviation gas to support the war effort. Add this to the need to produce toluene for TNT, butadiene for synthetic rubber, and of course, the normal range of fuels for ships, trucks, and automobiles. The American oil industry is working hard on expanding these capabilities, but it's taking a long time. I have made some suggestions to the Petroleum Industry War Council, but so far, I haven't heard anything back from their technical committee."

Layton wondered how Brand kept all of these facts and figures in his brain and then pulled them together to make sound arguments. Looking at the other piles of paper in the room, the commander asked another question.

"I know I will get more information than I need, but what else have you discovered in our supply organization?"

James decided to handle this one gently and not go into great detail. "Commander, the situation is one of relationships. For every soldier or Marine fighting the enemy, we will need fourteen, perhaps as many as seventeen men working to keep him supplied with the munitions, food, fuel, and other support necessary to fight a war. Every man we add to this supply chain, starting on the West Coast, needs the same level of support. For example, our naval air station in Bora Bora has nearly five thousand men. The garrison supports the airfield, engineers build infrastructure, mechanics keep the planes flying, etc. As we continue to build more forward bases to support the Central Pacific plan as well as MacArthur's push through New Guinea, we may end up supporting some three hundred separate bases."

The professor let the number settle in the minds of Layton and his colleagues. In the past year, bases such as Midway, Johnston, Palmyra, Dutch Harbor, Noumea, Fiji had all been expanded to support the offensive against Japan. New bases in the New Hebrides, Solomons, New Zealand, Samoa, Australia, and New Guinea were all being built and then expanded to support thousands of soldiers, Marines, and airmen. Fleet support bases and smaller installations were being planned to maintain the expansion of the navy. There were thousands of new troops, ships, airfields everywhere in the Hawaiian Islands, and as these units moved forward, new units would be brought in to replace them. America was on the move, but it needed more of everything.

Layton pondered the information, knowing Brand was discussing the realities of a global war. The Pacific theater was receiving perhaps only thirty percent of the total Allied effort, which meant the situation in Europe was even more significant in scope. The commander turned to James. "What do you need in terms of help to finalize your review for Admiral Nimitz?"

"Sir, if you can loan us about a dozen men with accounting backgrounds, a few experts from each service on their supply situation, then we should be able to complete our report by next week."

Knowing the need to come to grips with the logistical needs of CINCPAC's command, Layton said he would find the needed support and have them report in the morning. As he was about to leave the room, the commander said, "James, let me know if you find any big roadblocks to the Central Pacific plan. The admiral wants to get this right."

After the commander left, Feldman was the first to speak. "Sounds like you've opened a huge can of worms, James. I hope you can find all of them soon. I don't think I want to spend the rest of the war looking at reports on the number of prophylactics consumed by the Marine Corps."

Everyone laughed and began looking into the unopened boxes. Flannigan took off his jacket and started going through reports and wondering how Commander Allen was doing on board the *Salt Lake City.*

The Marine major shouldn't have worried too much about his friend aboard the heavy cruiser. The ship had sailed mid-morning with a tug leading the way out of the bay. At the narrow harbor entrance, a small vessel opened the heavy anti-submarine net, which closed the gate to Pearl Harbor to all ships, especially to a submarine trying to sneak their way into attacking the American navy. Several Japanese midget submarines had attempted this on December 7, 1941. One of them was sunk by the old destroyer *Ward* before the devastating attack by the enemy's bombers and torpedo planes.

After clearing the harbor, the cruiser was escorted out to sea by a pair of subchasers. These one hundred ten foot vessels were sturdy and manned by a crew of twenty-five enlisted men and three officers. The wooden ships, often called the "splinter fleet," were reasonably fast—capable of twenty-one knots—fast enough to run down a surfaced submarine. The subchasers were used mainly near coastal waters but could stay at sea for a few days, making them a potent deterrent to any enemy submarine. Further out to sea, a destroyer pinged the depth with its SONAR system, searching for Japanese submarines lurking below. As Commander Allen peered through his binoculars at the destroyer, he wished he was in command of the distant ship, but for right now, he was just glad to be at sea.

Captain Rogers gave Allen unfettered access to the bridge, and even though he was not required to take an active role in the ship's operation, he volunteered to stand watches. The captain appreciated the gesture for many reasons. First, there were the many new officers who had joined the crew, including many rookie ensigns and lieutenants who had never been to sea in their brief careers. Some of these men were in college eighteen months ago or were recent graduates of the Naval ROTC programs. Others were Annapolis graduates who had been sent out early from the academy. The nation needed officers, and graduation was moved up for several hundred men in 1942.

The situation in the enlisted ranks was more of a problem. Twenty-five percent of the crew had joined the ship at Pearl Harbor, with most never being at sea or, for that matter, in the navy. Men had been inducted in the service, trained at the boot camps, and then advanced schools such as gunnery or electronics and shipped out as fast as possible. The loss of so many ships at Guadalcanal had forced the navy to put many untested men into combat situations before they were fully trained. Petty officers of the *Salt Lake City* would have to build their crew from the ground up.

Commander Bitler, the executive officer, enjoyed having Allen aboard for no other reason than to help him work with the new officers. The ship's navigator was an experienced man, but his assistants were new to the navy and needed significant tutoring. Allen was happy to help. The ship's first lieutenant, the officer charged with the vessel's deck department, had only two seasoned petty officers and perhaps a dozen experienced sailors. Everyone else was new to the navy. Allen relished the opportunity to work with these officers and enlisted men. It was like he was back on his destroyer, working with every man, no matter his position. On a destroyer, the captain knew every man and their duties. A heavy cruiser is different. The *Salt Lake City* had a crew of over seven hundred men, with every possible job from a dentist to a barber aboard.

As it became dark and the night security watches were set to ensure total blackout conditions, the ship increased speed and set a course north to the Aleutians. The next several days would be filled with drills, inspections, and more drills. Captain Rogers wanted to get the ship working on a wartime basis, which meant no downtime for the crew. Commander Allen appreciated the work ethic of Rogers and Bitler and took mental notes on how these two men operated. He hoped he would be able to take command of another warship soon, but at least he was now at sea and not shepherding a desk in Washington.

34

15 March 1943
Office of Admiral Edwards
Washington, D.C.

- New Guinea--1st Battalion of 162nd Infantry, U.S. 41st Division, occupies positions at Mambare River mouth without opposition.
- Tunisia--Gen. Eisenhower visits U.S. II Corps headquarters as preparations for offensive continues.
- U.S.--Commander in Chief, United States Fleet (Adm. E. J. King), establishes fleet numbering system; all fleets in the Pacific to have odd numbers and those in the Atlantic even numbers. Central Pacific Force is redesignated, 5th Fleet.

A lieutenant commander sorted through a batch of radio messages for the admiral. The officer, Jerry Tillman, had been assigned to cover Commander Allen's desk while he was out in the Pacific. Everyone on the admiral's staff was happy to see Allen have an opportunity to get out of the office, even if only for a few months. Until the commander returned, Tillman would have to fill in and hopefully not screw up. Tillman had joined the staff after his release from the hospital.

The newly-promoted officer had flown Wildcats from the *Enterprise*, but was shot down in the battles around Guadalcanal in November. Spending two nights in a tiny lifeboat a few miles from the Japanese-occupied island of Santa Isabel was only one of his worries. A broken leg, cracked ribs, a badly injured back, and facial lacerations kept him occupied as he paddled toward the middle of the Slot, hoping to be found by American forces or perhaps some of the friendly natives he had been told about. A PBY found him on day three of his ordeal and flew him back to Tulagi for medical treatment. From there, he was sent to New Caledonia and then onward to Pearl Harbor. His bones mended, but his back remained an issue. He was sent to medical experts stateside where he was poked and prodded by top-notch physicians. Yet, none of them could say with any certainty that he would regain his ability to fly or, for that matter, serve his country. Only with the efforts of several senior officers did he remain in the navy and receive a desk job in Washington. He was also awarded his second Distinguished Flying Cross. Tillman was credited with nine kills and three probables during his months aboard the *Big E*.

Jerry knew he was fortunate to still be in the navy and was thrilled to be assigned to the billet in the chief of staff's office. Edwards had explained that he needed to be his expert on naval aviation and would be given every opportunity to regain flight status, but he was flying a desk for now. Tillman gladly accepted the posting and worked hard to show the admiral he could do any job thrown at him, but after taking over for Commander Allen, he wasn't so sure anymore. Allen had a knack for making sense of all of the reports and messages flowing into the admiral's office and then prioritizing which ones were most important and putting these in context to the current situation. Tillman was plugging away but unsure of his capabilities.

The phone on his desk rang, and he quickly answered. "Lieutenant Commander Tillman speaking."

The voice on the other end of the phone barked a set of orders, not requests. Nearly jumping up and saluting, the commander replied, "Sir, Admiral Edwards is attending a meeting with Admiral Cooke. Shall I interrupt him or have him call you back when he's finished?"

The voice shouted to have Edwards come to his office before

abruptly disconnecting. Sensing the importance of the demand, Tillman jumped up in search of Admiral Cooke's office. Usually, the secretary to Edwards would handle the admiral's calls, but the chief petty officer was ill, so Jerry played a dual role.

Finding Admiral Cooke's office, he first asked permission from a member of the admiral's staff to barge into the meeting. The officer, another lieutenant commander, asked what was so important. When he heard the man's name wanting information from Admiral Edwards, the aide quickly stood and walked to the door and went inside. A minute passed, and then Jerry was ushered into the room. Admiral Edwards was sitting next to Cooke, and seated across from them was General Wedemeyer, the army's head war planner. Coming to attention, Tillman waited.

"Tillman, what's so important that you had to interrupt this meeting?"

"Sir, sorry for the interruption, but Admiral King wants to see you."

Slowly standing up and looking at his fellow senior officers, Edwards stated, "Sorry, gentlemen, but I must go find out what the boss wants. I will try to come back soon or send word if I cannot rejoin the meeting."

The admiral walked out of the room, followed closely by Tillman. Once they were in the hallway, Edwards turned to speak to the staff officer. "Commander, you did the right thing. If Admiral King wants something from me or any other officer, he wants it now. Come along, and maybe you'll get a chance to see the boss in action. Quite a show he puts on."

Jerry fell in lock step with the chief of staff, and both men quickly marched to the office of the chief of Naval Operations and the Commander in Chief of the United States Fleet. As the two men entered the outer office of the CNO, a captain stood and told Edwards the admiral was on the phone with General Marshall, but he was told to send Edwards in when he arrived. Signaling for Tillman to stay in the outer office, Edwards opened the door and entered the office. Jerry sat down and felt the pain in his back subside. Standing for more than a few minutes was difficult, but he rarely showed any signs of discomfort. Aspirin didn't help, and the other pain killers offered by the navy doctors were addictive. So, the former fighter pilot suffered in silence.

Ten minutes passed, and the CNO's secretary answered a call, quickly saying yes and then put the phone down. Looking at the lieu-tenant commander, the old chief petty officer barked, "Commander, the admiral wants you to join him and Admiral Edwards."

Quickly standing and making sure his uniform was in perfect or-der, Jerry walked into the room and quickly came to attention in front of King's desk. Edwards was seated in a chair beside the admiral's desk, and there were two other chairs positioned in front of the desk. "Lieu-tenant Commander Tillman, reporting as ordered."

King looked at the naval aviator and examined the officer from the top of his head to his shoes. All was in order, he thought. The man had the gold wings of a navy aviator, ribbons denoting several decorations, and war experience. Edwards told him about the young man a few days earlier and how he was filling in for Commander Allen. The chief of staff told King the man was quick on the uptake and was not only a warrior but a team player.

"At ease, Commander. Take a seat."

Tillman sat down but stayed ramrod straight. He was an Annap-olis graduate and was reverting to his plebe days at the academy. Jerry had fought the enemy on many occasions and won most of his battles, except for the last one. Now, he was more fearful than when he fought the Japanese. King's reputation was known throughout the navy. It didn't matter if you were an old academy graduate or a ninety-day wonder from Iowa; the CNO was not only the boss but the closest thing to Neptune, the mythical god of the sea, than anyone else in the world.

"Admiral Edwards tells me you're doing a good job filling in for Commander Allen. What do you like about the job?"

Jerry kept his composure and quickly replied, "Sir, the position re-quires a great amount of concentration and the ability to make quick adjustments to policies and even faster decisions. It's not like flying a Wildcat, but it keeps me on my toes."

Edwards thought the response was politically sound and directly answered the question. Not knowing what King was up to, he waited.

"Commander, I know you have an excellent record and were an ace aboard the *Enterprise*. You graduated at the top of your class and chose to become an aviator. Why did you do that when you could have gone to sea and taken a fast track to command a warship?"

"Admiral, the future of the navy is in combined arms. Flying is one aspect of what the future of fighting a war is becoming. My experiences in combat proved to me the navy must have a strong air capability along with surface and submarine forces. Without all three working together, we might not be able to win the war."

King thought the answer captured the essence of what the war in the Pacific was becoming. A strong surface fleet could not survive without a strong aviation capability. Submarines had already proven their ability to damage a nations' war capability, not only by the American submarines attacking Japanese ships but also by how the Germans used their U-boats to nearly strangle the British.

"Commander, once Allen returns from his present assignment, I want you to work with a small group planning the next phase of the war. I need an experienced pilot who knows the enemy to address both carrier and ground-based aviation issues. This includes logistics for the advance toward Japan and the manpower needs of the navy and Marine Corps."

Stopping after this comment, King saw the man seated across from him was void of emotion. His only reaction was to continue looking the admiral in the eye and wait for his next command. The CNO liked men who focused on the issue at hand and demonstrated self-control.

"You will continue working for Admiral Edwards as one of his principal aides, and as the planning moves forward for future operations, you will be called upon to quickly move to address these new challenges. Any questions?"

"No sir. I look forward to the opportunity."

Again, King liked the mettle of the man. No extraneous words or self-doubt, similar to another young man on his staff. Edwards, knowing the briefing was over, said, "Commander, I will provide you more details on this assignment later. You are dismissed."

Standing quickly, which caused him to grimace in pain, Tillman came to attention, executed a perfect parade ground about-face, and left the office. After the door closed, King commented, "I think this man will work well with Cooke's people. We need to have combat veterans involved in these planning sessions. Most of our senior people have not been tested in battle, and we can't afford mistakes."

"Sir, do you want me to introduce him to Brand and the Science Team?"

Thinking about the question, King slowly replied, "Yes, get him linked with the Stevens' logistics people first and when Brand comes back from Pearl, introduce him to the rest of Jameson's command."

Edwards had expected this would happen, especially with Allen being seconded to the Science Team already. "Admiral, I'll get him connected with Stevens today. When do you want to recall Brand from Hawaii?"

King had already fended off several requests from the army, Admiral Leahy and Vannevar Bush wanting to "borrow" the professor. Thinking about the question, King responded, "No, keep him at CINCPAC until Nimitz finalizes the plans for the Aleutians. Plan on bringing the boy back in April. His last communication indicated the Japanese were planning something, but no one knows yet what this may be. Layton and Brand have some ideas on an enemy offensive toward New Guinea or our bases in the Solomons. Still, no one has been able to read the tea leaves well enough to understand the enemy's intentions."

Edwards understood the political dynamics the CNO was operating within and knew sooner or later, Brand would be pulled back to work on other priority programs. But out in the Pacific, far away from Washington politics, the Science Team directed their attention to the navy's pressing needs. Wondering about the intelligence concerning a Japanese offensive, the chief of staff was concerned about the ability of the navy to react to any attack. The *Saratoga* and the newly arrived HMS *Victorious* were the only large aircraft carriers in the Pacific. The *Enterprise* was still being repaired, and the first of the new *Essex* class carriers were still undergoing operational tests and shakedown cruises. It would be early summer before these new ships could become a factor in fighting the enemy.

The ships were swinging at anchor in the tropical breeze. Even the large battleships were slowly dancing about in the shifting winds. The prince had returned from Tokyo the previous day aboard one of the Kawashini seaplanes, which regularly transported men and high-value cargoes to the far-off bases of the Japanese Empire. The flight had been routine, with a stop in Taiwan, Manila, and finally Truk. He was glad to be back aboard the *Yamato* and away from the politics of Imperial Headquarters.

Admiral Nagano had finally agreed to the new operation. The army had demanded more support from the navy in their battle to hold New Guinea. The recent losses in the Bismarck Sea had delayed their timetable for launching a counterattack against Allied forces, and their men were suffering from supply problems, including ammunition, but most importantly, food. The Americans were adding more aircraft to their offensive, and the Japanese air forces were increasingly at a disadvantage. Without air superiority, the army was under constant threat of attack. Admiral Yamamoto was given orders to bring in additional units to bolster the forces on Rabaul and the other airbases in the region.

Lieutenant Akihito had argued long and hard against the plan. The army positions spread along the northern coast of New Guinea were vulnerable to seaborne attacks. The Americans and Australians were proving the value of amphibious assaults against poorly defended positions. MacArthur was not hitting hardened enemy positions but leap-frogged around them, cutting off troops from supply. The Japanese army had to fight the Allies in front of them, and then all of a sudden, they were behind them, isolating them from support. The prince thought the tactic was well-conceived and foretold the strategy for the remainder of the war. He had told his key intelligence expert, Petty Officer Shibuya Haruki, "You cannot defend every beach and every island. If you do so, you will quickly run out of men, and the enemy will bypass those locations it deems unimportant."

But the decision had been made, and even the emperor could not change the plan. As he pulled out the briefing papers and began his report, he looked at the man who had to execute the orders. Admiral Isoroku Yamamoto seemed older than when he last saw him only a month ago. The war was wearing men down, and the man in overall command of the navy was tired and worried. The admiral told the prince to begin his briefing, which was short and to the point.

"Admiral, the Imperial Headquarters commands the navy to provide maximum support to the army's efforts to regain the advantage in New Guinea. In addition, it wants the navy to support the efforts on Rabaul to push the Americans back from this vital location."

Seeing the admiral looking at the briefing paper and the charts of the seas from New Guinea to the Solomons, Kaya continued. "Sir, Tokyo has stated it is imperative that we hold the entirety of our South Sea positions. The key to this strategy is the operation of the four airfields on Rabaul and the subordinate bases at Buka, Kahili, Ballale, Vila, Munda, and Rekata Bay. We know the Americans want to increase air assaults

330

on the major bases in Rabaul and have been attacking the bases in New Georgia and Bougainville with greater numbers of planes. Their cruisers have been bombarding the base at Munda but have so far not been successful in curtailing our operations."

The admiral listened to the report and examined charts showing the islands from Rabaul on New Britain, down toward Bougainville, New Georgia, and Guadalcanal. The outlying bases should have been built months earlier to support the Solomons campaign, but the men and materials were slow in coming. Now the Imperial Japanese Navy was paying the price for their slow response to the American advances.

"The operation, code-named *I,* calls for the reinforcement of land-based planes by the aircraft from the four carriers of the Third Fleet at Truk. With several hundred additional aircraft from the navy, mass attacks can be made on Guadalcanal. Then more attacks will be made on American bases in New Guinea at Oro Bay, Port Moresby, and Milne Bay. The plan calls for the destruction of American airpower at these bases. Additionally, these attacks will eliminate the shipping at each of these locations. Our intelligence shows several enemy cruisers and destroyers working out of the Guadalcanal area. If these can be destroyed or heavily damaged, the enemy will have few combat ships available to attack our bases."

Kaya paused his presentation as Yamamoto examined the plan. The great admiral looked at the charts and the targets outlined in the report, then making no sound, he closed the document and looked at the intelligence officer. Yamamoto respected the prince's ability to realistically assess the enemy's intentions, and so far, he had been right more often than not.

"Kaya-san, what do you think of this plan?"

Vice Admiral Ugaki, the chief of staff, scanned the report and watched as Lieutenant Akihito responded. "Admiral, the plan sounds simple. Too simple. I doubt the Americans will be fooled for long. We know they have added many planes to their base at Guadalcanal. We don't know where their carriers are, but we believe they are working out of Noumea and have two large carriers currently available. The American bases on New Guinea are strengthening and have gained much-needed operational experience over the past few months. Bombing attacks on Rabaul and the army garrisons in New Guinea are increasing. Our army planes seemed to have made little headway against the American Fifth

Air Force in New Guinea. The few American pilots we have captured tell us about their increasing numbers, which I believe is true."

Taking a deep breath, Kaya expressed his opinion, which earned him the wrath of the Imperial Army planners in Japan. "Sir, by stripping the planes and pilots from the Third Fleet carriers and using them in this attack, we are wasting our best offensive asset. Without experienced pilots, our few remaining carriers are worthless. I fear that we will lose many of our best people fighting a holding action which should be done with army pilots, not navy men."

Ugaki quietly agreed with the assessment. It took many months of training to create a competent carrier pilot. The army had so far invested only a small portion of their aviation assets in the South Pacific. The navy had lost many of its best men. Losses were high at Midway and the battles of attrition around Guadalcanal further reduced the number of experienced pilots. Now the army needed the navy to save them. The chief of staff saw Prime Minister Tojo's hand in this effort, and it angered him.

Nonetheless, the plan had been ordered by Imperial Headquarters, and orders must be followed, even if you disagreed with them. Looking first at Kaya and then at his chief of staff, Yamamoto calmly stated, "Admiral proceed with the movement of the Third Fleet's planes and pilots to Rabaul and the outlying bases. We should start this operation after the first of April. Ensure that each carrier retains at least one-third of its aircraft and crews. I want to be able to follow up any success with a carrier operation."

Admiral Ugaki stood and bowed to the commander in chief of the Combined Fleet and then walked out of the conference room. The intelligence officer stood erect and bowed as well, preparing to leave the room, but Yamamoto stopped him. "Sit down, Kaya-san. I need to speak to you about this operation and how you think it will affect the war. I am unsure of its ability to change the course of the war, but it may end the lives of many of our best people."

As the young man sat down, he saw the war-weary admiral slump in his chair. Yamamoto began a monologue of what he saw happening in the war and where the situation was heading. It was not defeatist, but it was realistic. The war was not going in Japan's favor, and he knew many men would die soon.

PART 4

35

24 March 1943
USS *Richmond* (CL-9)
North Pacific

- U.S.--JCS approve plan to occupy Attu in the Aleutians.
- Tunisia--In U.S. II Corps area, 1st Armored Division attacks Djebel Naemia in greater strength but cannot dislodge enemy. Gen. Patton orders the position taken during the next morning's attack. Maj. Gen. Ward, CG 1st Armored Division, personally commands attack which begins midnight 24-25 without artillery preparation.
- Pacific Ocean Area--Naval and army aircraft bomb Nauru Island, South Pacific.

The seas were high, the wind blew from the north; the temperature was near freezing. Visibility was limited to only a few thousand yards. The light cruiser bobbed up and down in the rough ocean like a cork. The heavy cruiser *Salt Lake City* had it even worse. The *Swayback Maru* was always a "wet" ship, and even though it had a displacement of three thousand tons more than the *Richmond*, the vessel was rolling heavily. The four destroyers, *Dale, Coghlan, Bailey,* and *Monaghan,* were doing their best to stay upright, but with each colossal wave, the little ships rolled from side to side, with their crew holding on for dear life. Commander Allen held on as well but enjoyed every moment of the monstrous seas. The experience took him back to his old destroyer, helming her across the stormy Atlantic in winter, trying to keep his convoy of slow merchant ships safe from U-boats.

Charles McMorris had taken command of the cruiser squadron in the Aleutians in January after his promotion to rear admiral. The commander had joined the crew of *Richmond* on March 20. He had hoped to stay aboard the *Salt Lake City* for the remainder of his time in the north, but Rear Admiral McMorris wanted him on his ship. The man was nicknamed "Soc" for Socrates because of his photographic memory and deep thinking. Twice in his career, he was assigned to the naval academy as an instructor, where Commander Allen, then in his third year, met him for the first time in 1925. The admiral received a message from Admiral Edwards concerning the man's temporary assignment and asked him to place him on his staff for any upcoming operations. McMorris was glad to have an experienced officer aboard, especially one who had experience in rough seas.

The light cruiser *Richmond* was not the perfect warship for these northern waters. The ship was old, obsolescent, and plagued by inadequate weaponry. The ship was commissioned in 1923 as one of the *Omaha* class "scouting" cruisers. On paper, it looked like a suitable warship for its mission, but it was designed in World War I and had ten six-inch guns, but six of them were in single mounts on the sides of the ship. Only two turrets, one aft and one forward, containing twin cannons, could fully rotate to meet threats. The single mounts were placed forward and aft on each side of the ship, which reduced the ship's ability to effectively fire heavy broadsides with all of its weaponry. The ship's antiaircraft weaponry was also inadequate, having only eight three-inch cannons and some recently added 40mm cannons, replacing old .50 caliber machine guns. The cruiser did have one powerful weapon system of two torpedo mounts, each containing three twenty-one-inch torpedoes. The ship was fast, capable of thirty-five knots but possessed only three inches of side armor protection. But like everything else in the Aleutians, the cruiser was all that was available. Task Group 16.6 departed Dutch Harbor on March 22 to patrol a line extending from the Bering Sea, west of the Aleutians to a few hundred miles south, looking for Japanese ships attempting to reinforce either Attu or Kiska.

Intelligence reached the American Task Group telling them several Japanese cargo vessels would soon be making their way to Kiska from bases in the Kuriles. The convoy's escorts were thought to be only destroyers, but it was still unknown. McMorris was ordered to intercept any enemy ships and ensure they did not make it to their destination. He was also ordered not to risk battle with superior forces. With the seas being in a tortured state, all the admiral could do was continue heading toward their patrol line and wait for the enemy to appear. Tomorrow, he would have to refuel a few of the destroyers from the heavy cruiser so they could remain at sea and be prepared for a running battle.

The *Richmond's* captain, Theodore Waldschmidt, was a quiet commander—the opposite of Admiral McMorris. The ship's captain was patient and would provide subtle criticism, but the admiral was known for dressing down subordinates and demanding top performance. This personality clash was already causing problems for the crew. Most of the ship's company had hoped the admiral would move his pennant to the much larger heavy cruiser, which was designed to be a command ship, but for some reason, McMorris decided to stay aboard the older and more cramped vessel. Now, every man aboard waited for any sign of the enemy and also the testy admiral.

Allen volunteered to stand watches, but McMorris told him to work with his minimal staff of four officers. The admiral wanted the commander to be everywhere, all at the same time. Allen worked with the ship's bridge crew on current positions and the ship's readiness, then was charged with checking incoming signals from the other ships and from high command. All of these activities kept him busy and happy. McMorris often quizzed his old student about how he would handle his ships if the enemy was sighted. *Would the commander rush his destroyers toward the convoy and let the cruisers battle the escorts? What course would he steer to place maximum firepower on an enemy if they were sighted at dusk? How would he evade Japanese torpedoes?* The admiral had seen combat as the captain of the heavy cruiser *San Francisco* at the battle of Cape Esperance in October and was now aware of the enemy's torpedo tactics.

The new member of the admiral's staff enjoyed the questions and sometimes the negative reaction to his answers. Yet, knowing McMorris from his days at Annapolis, he understood the reasons for the hypothetical situations. Responding quickly and correctly was not only essential but would save the lives of the crew. Allen had learned many lessons in the past few years, and this senior officer's methods were enlightening though fearsome.

The other members of the admiral's staff were glad to have a newcomer be the focus of the old man's rants but quickly saw the speed and clarity of the commander's responses. Allen made McMorris hesitate a few times and begrudgingly gave the staff officer from Washington high marks for good decisions. "Hopefully, Allen, we won't have to face many difficult decisions if we find the Japanese convoy."

Knowing that even with the advantage of radar, the ship could only see so far in the wind swept seas. Fog and mist came and went, allowing the vessels in the small American fleet to barely see each other, let alone find a group of enemy ships. Often the visibility dropped to less than a few hundred yards. Signal lights were used between ships to maintain correct station keeping as the ships moved along their course. Tomorrow, everyone hoped the sea conditions would lessen so they could fuel the destroyers, *Bailey* and *Coghlan*. The other destroyers *Dale* and *Monaghan*, would be refueled on March 28. The little ships would also receive fresh bread, sugar, eggs, and even ice cream from *Salt Lake City*. All of these were luxuries on a bouncing destroyer displacing a mere fifteen hundred tons with a length of three hundred forty-eight feet but only thirty-five feet in beam. Long and narrow equals a rolling and bouncing ride in the North Pacific.

The intelligence people at Pearl Harbor were a strange group. Former bandsmen from some sunken battleships, a few trained language experts, some mathematicians, radio experts, and probably a few voodoo priests made up the men in the dungeon. Working together in small groups and some working alone as what appeared to be a monk in prayer, all struggled to make sense of a long series of numbers, Japanese characters, words, and partial phrases. Intelligence was not a precise science, nor was it practiced by ordinary people. As enemy radio transmissions were intercepted, men transcribed the numbers or characters then passed them on to teams who would attempt to discern their meaning.

The Japanese merchant marine code was considered less important to the Japanese high command than the high-level codes of the Imperial Navy and Army. Yet, the merchant shipping code, JN-40, was of great interest to the Allied code breakers. At their Far Eastern Combined Bureau, the British had early success in breaking merchant and dockyard codes before the war. In September 1942, they successfully broke this fractionating transpositioning cipher based on a substitution table of one hundred groups of two figures, each followed by a columnar transposition. By November, the British and Americans knew the movements of individual Japanese merchant vessels and convoys, allowing the navy to position submarines in the paths of these ships, plus it allowed the Allies to examine other shipping movements that might indicate major Japanese operations.

Commander Layton had received summaries of this traffic for months and used it to interpret Japanese intentions. If a convoy was formed in Formosa to travel to the Philippines, it might mean routine resupply of the Japanese garrison. But if a convoy was moving toward a forward base in New Guinea or the Gilbert Islands, it might indicate a significant offensive or a bolstering of defenses. Subsequent interpretation of these signals would then be matched with corresponding traffic from the Imperial Navy code, JN-25. This code was changed monthly, forcing the men in the dungeon to work quickly to understand the nuances of the modifications. A Japanese destroyer might be assigned to escort a convoy known through the JN-40 merchant code, which could then be used to shed light on the changes in the new navy code.

Most of the time, the merchant code information would be funneled to the submarine force to help position their boats to interdict the convoys. This message would be communicated in a manner that provided only general direction to protect the source of the intelligence. A submarine skipper would only be given general directions without any specifics, saying a *"Possible enemy convoy was moving south to position X."* The same methodology was used in all aerial intercepts, such as what occurred at the Battle of the Bismarck Sea. Intelligence had determined the large troop convoy's size, scope, and destination and sent out a reconnaissance flight to locate the enemy vessels. This way, the Japanese didn't recognize their codes had been compromised. They believed the Americans just got lucky in finding the convoy from the air.

James was in the office with Lieutenant Waverly and Warrant Officer

Jones, talking about resupply operations needed in the Solomons. Brand had examined the plans for expanding the American air bases in the islands and was concerned about improving the number of sorties from Henderson Field and its new auxiliary air strips without improving fuel storage and local maintenance facilities. Over one hundred seventy-five aircraft were now based on Guadalcanal, with work going on in the Russell Islands to build new bases. James looked beyond the tactical bases on Guadalcanal to the bases in the New Hebrides, New Caledonia, Fiji, and Samoa. This pipeline of airfields kept pumping planes and their aircrews toward the combat zone, and each required the same level of logistical support.

A B-17 or B-24 consumed vast amounts of fuel compared to a P-40 or a Wildcat. The head of intelligence for CINCPAC looked at the impressive spreadsheet James handed him and saw the columns denoting aircraft, air crews, maintenance personnel, support forces, supply storage facilities, docks, fuel tanks, and most importantly, the types of aircraft at each base. The information was summed up by James in one paragraph, which concluded with the following:

> *The current supply of petroleum products, spare parts, experienced aircrews, and maintenance personnel precludes any significant offensive action until a logistics plan is formulated and adequately supported.*

Layton looked at the summary and agreed but knew the assessment would not go down well with Admiral Nimitz. The Pacific Ocean Area commander was being pressed to move forward with the Central Pacific offensive sooner rather than later. In addition, the admiral was committed to supporting MacArthur's push toward Rabaul, which would force his few major warships to remain in Halsey's South Pacific theater.

Putting the report down, Layton said, "James, I agree with your assessment, but the admiral is under a significant amount of pressure to move forward with the planned operations. Halsey is begging for more planes and men to support the move toward New Georgia, now planned for early summer. The same goes for the New Guinea push."

Thinking again about the increasing tempo of the war effort, Layton added, "You've seen the preliminary plans for Attu. This will require some of our ships to move north to support the invasion and then be held there until we can attack Kiska, probably in July or August. What do you think is possible based upon this assessment?"

"Commander, it's all possible but not very probable based upon the aggressive time frame set by Washington. We are woefully short of landing craft, support ships, escort vessels, and of course, aircraft carriers. The few escort carriers we received are helping, but for right now, most are being used to move planes to our land bases. The *Victorious* will be ready to move out in a few weeks to support Halsey and back up the *Saratoga* and the still wounded *Enterprise*. This ship has been kept at Noumea for emergencies but is slated to come back to Pearl Harbor in a few weeks to undergo major repairs."

Thinking a bit more on the situation, James added, "Sir, the majority of the army and Marine forces in the South Pacific area are green. The First Marine Division is rebuilding at Melbourne and won't be ready for combat for some time. The army air forces are adding new squadrons of fighters and bombers, but they are all new to the area and will require time to familiarize themselves with the environment. Lastly, the petroleum situation remains challenging. Last year, under the Emergency Shipbuilding Program, we only built thirty-three tankers. This year, the plan calls for one hundred-eighty-five. Until we can get these ships commissioned and moving, fuel will be a constraining factor on our ability to wage war."

As the men discussed the ramifications of the logistical needs of the growing American presence in the South Pacific, Layton's assistant, a lieutenant named Barkley, knocked on the door and entered the room. He quickly passed a note to the intelligence officer and then waited for a response. The commander examined the message and then asked his assistant, "Barkley, have they confirmed this information?"

"Commander, everyone in the dungeon vouches for the intelligence. The merchant code shows three vessels heading north from the port of Kataoka on the southwest coast of Shimushu island. We believe they are being escorted by a few destroyers, but we still have no confirmation."

"Any intelligence on what the ships are carrying?"

"Nothing definite. Probably supplies, food, ammunition, etc. Perhaps some men on one of the ships we have identified as the *Asaka Maru*. We know this ship has been outfitted as an auxiliary cruiser to carry personnel. The ship is fast and capable of making a quick transit to the Aleutians."

Layton stood and excused himself from his meeting without taking too long to think about the situation. "James, I need to take this to Admiral Spruance. We need to notify Kinkaid that a supply convoy is on its way to the Aleutians. I think Admiral McMorris is already at sea, so with some luck, we can find them and stop them from reinforcing Attu and Kiska."

As the man left, Gunny asked a simple question. "Lieutenant, isn't Commander Allen out there on the *Salt Lake City*?"

"Yes, Gunny, I think the commander will finally get his chance to see some action. If the intelligence is correct, his cruiser will have little difficulty in destroying the enemy convoy."

Waverly quietly commented, "Hope the intelligence is correct. I recall getting my ass kicked on Guadalcanal by Japanese ships that weren't supposed to be there."

James didn't reply but knew Bill Waverly was right. Even the best intelligence sometimes failed. He hoped things worked out well for Allen.

36

26 March 1943
USS *Richmond* (CL-9)
100 miles south of Komandorski Island, USSR

- North Pacific--Battle of Komandorski Islands is
  fought between a task group comprising two cruisers
  and four destroyers (Rear Adm. C. H. McMorris) and
  a Japanese force of four cruisers and four destroyers
  escorting reinforcements to Attu, Aleutian Islands.
  In this daylight action, one United States cruiser and
  one destroyer are damaged.
  - One Japanese cruiser damaged. Japanese
    reinforcements fail to reach Attu.
- Tunisia--British 8th Army having adopted new plan
  called SUPERCHARGE and abandoned original plan,
  renews assault on Mareth Line in the afternoon
  following destructive aerial bombardment that lasts
  for 2.5 hours.

Late in the night, the seas began to calm. The temperature ranged from twenty-eight degrees Fahrenheit to a balmy thirty-four degrees. The skies were overcast, but clouds no longer kissed the sea, with a ceiling of perhaps five thousand feet. As dawn approached, visibility increased to thirteen plus miles. The ships of Task Group 16.6 were located five hundred miles east of Adak and five hundred miles west of the Japanese base at Paramushiro. Placed into a six-mile-long scouting formation, the ships zigzagged on a northerly course at fifteen knots. The ships had gone to general quarters an hour before sunrise, and every vessel was ready for battle.

Commander Allen had hardly slept. As the ship ceased its incessant pitching and rolling, he became aware of the improving conditions. At 0400, he checked message traffic, but nothing new had come in from Admiral Kinkaid's command. Knowing the last situation report, Admiral McMorris expected to find three enemy transports heading toward Attu or Kiska with a covering force of perhaps two or three destroyers. The men of the *Richmond* were excited to finally engage the enemy. The cruiser had been under aerial assault before but never had they fought a battle against Japanese ships. The admiral was more cautious and introspective about the possibility. At the Battle of Cape Esperance in October, he commanded the heavy cruiser *San Francisco*, which escaped damage. During this battle, the *Boise* had been seriously damaged, as was *Salt Lake City*, with both ships requiring a significant amount of repair work.

The Task Group's ships were strung out on the patrol line searching for enemy ships that might be in the area. The lead ship, the destroyer *Coghlan*, was followed by *Richmond*, *Bailey*, *Dale*, *Salt Lake City*, and *Monaghan*. Radars were employed on each vessel but were often temperamental. As dawn broke, the ships were working their way north when the *Coghlan* made first contact. The destroyer's radar picked up three unidentified surface contacts. The *Richmond* was next to see something on its radar screen with two contacts quickly followed by a few more. Three to five contacts were confirmed, and the information was passed to all the ships. Admiral McMorris promptly ordered all of the ships to concentrate on his flagship, requiring every ship to bring every boiler on line in anticipation of top speed movements.

Allen took his place behind the admiral and watched as Captain Waldschmidt calmly gave orders to the men on the bridge and called the engineering officer for an update on the powerplant. Gunnery officers made last-minute adjustments and the crew prepared for a surface action.

The ships picked up speed. About the same time, the Japanese sighted ships heading toward them.

Using signal lights, the enemy ships misidentified the first two visible ships as Japanese vessels heading toward Attu. The Imperial convoy included a destroyer guarding a merchant vessel too slow to keep up with Vice Admiral Boshiro Hosogaya's Fifth Fleet. The small convoy had departed Japan two days earlier than the larger force now heading toward the Americans. The admiral commanded two heavy cruisers, two light cruisers, and four destroyers escorting two large transports. The Japanese admiral hoped he would not encounter American forces. Still, he was expected to destroy them if faced with the opportunity and continue his delivery of supplies and reinforcements to the Japanese garrisons in the Aleutians.

Both fleets increased speed. At 0824, the lookouts on the foretop of both American cruisers were alerted by the radar operators to four more ships. Swinging their binoculars to examine the new threat, the men confirmed the tall masts now coming over the horizon. These were not the masts of merchant ships but the tall foretops of heavy cruisers. The Americans now faced a totally different situation. A superior enemy task force now outnumbered them, two to one. The two heavy cruisers were quickly identified as the *Nachi* and the *Maya*. These ships had ten eight-inch guns, heavier armor than the American heavy cruiser, and superior speed. The two light cruisers, *Tama* and *Abukuma*, were smaller than the *Richmond* and armed with seven five-and-a-half inch guns, but also had twin torpedo mounts. These ships were also faster than the *Richmond*, making it difficult for the American warships to avoid action. The Japanese destroyers were slightly larger than their adversaries and similarly armed, but each was equipped with superior Japanese Long Lance torpedoes.

After receiving confirmation of the approaching enemy fleet, Admiral McMorris responded quickly. Knowing the situation had changed, he made his first decision, which would impact the course of the battle. With his ships still strung out behind the flagship, some five thousand yards astern, McMorris ordered a course change to three-three-zero degrees but not an immediate increase in speed. Looking at Allen, he calmly stated, "We need to keep out of their range. Allen, start plotting the enemy's course and our movements. We need to keep at extreme range for as long as possible."

Quickly confirming the order, Allen began working the plot board on the bridge, along with the junior navigator. The ship's navigator was below the bridge in a separate area, plotting the cruiser's course. More importantly, the commander would be doing the same, but keeping a plot on the enemy's ships as well. Radar operators kept the bridge updated on the current position and movements of the enemy's vessels and the American ships racing toward the flagship while observers in the foretop provided more details, soon detecting the enemy's gun turrets moving toward their ship. The observers could also see the white water churning around the bow of the enemy cruisers as they gained speed.

At 0830, the *Nachi* and *Maya* opened fire on the *Richmond* at a range of twenty-one thousand yards. Alerted by the foretop observers, the ship prepared for the arrival of eight-inch armor-piercing shells, each weighing three hundred pounds, which could do tremendous damage to the lightly armored cruiser. The effective range where the eight-inch cannon can reliably hit a target is perhaps twenty thousand yards, with a maximum range of nearly thirty thousand yards. The Japanese were within range of their targets. The first shells exploded about a thousand yards short of the light cruiser, but the enemy was already reloading and making corrections. The second round of shots straddled the ship, shaking it violently.

Allen stayed at his position as the ship rolled from the near-miss. He took the information from the observers and the radar updates and determined the enemy cruisers were closing to within twenty thousand yards, making their subsequent attacks more likely a direct hit on their target. Admiral McMorris ordered more speed, bringing the ships to twenty-five knots. The ships to the stern of the flagship were trying to catch up, which would allow them to concentrate return fire. The *Richmond* was not close enough to respond with her main armament, but *Salt Lake City* was now in effective range.

The Japanese commander realized this as well, and soon, the two Japanese heavy cruisers turned their attention to the larger American ship. Firing their main guns at more than twenty thousand yards, the two Japanese ships began to pinpoint the range of their opponent. At 0840 Captain Rogers, on the *Salt Lake City*, commenced firing on the Japanese. On the third salvo, hits were recorded on the *Nachi*, starting a fire, but it was soon controlled. Knowing he had no chance to reach the transports, McMorris ordered more speed and turned forty degrees to port to confuse the enemy. The Japanese ignored the bait. Ordering more speed, Admiral McMorris continued running in a southwesterly direction with the faster enemy cruisers creeping ever closer.

Commander Allen kept calling out course corrections and information on the enemy cruisers. The admiral wanted to keep his mind open to the unfolding game of naval chess, asking Allen to periodically brief him on any changes in the situation. Each course change by the enemy or perceived increase or decrease in speed was duly noted. Twice McMorris asked the commander about the position of the American destroyers to the heavy cruiser, wanting to move them further away to avoid accidental casualties as the big ships began slugging it out at long range.

As he picked up his binoculars to check the ship's heading and the locations of the enemy cruisers, he noticed *Salt Lake City* dancing on the waves at high speed. After every enemy salvo splashed near the cruiser, Captain Rogers made radical changes to the cruiser's course to throw off the enemy's aim. So far, he was doing an incredible job jumping between the splashes. The splashes were color-coded. The blue ones were from the *Maya*. The orange splashes were the work of the *Nachi*.

Throughout these opening moves by the big boys, the Japanese light cruisers and destroyers attempted to move within range for a torpedo attack, but as they closed, *Richmond* fired away at the maximum range of her six-inch guns, forcing them to break away. The *Maya* fusillade continued at an incredible rate of fire. *Salt Lake City* was doing the same, and around 0930 scored another hit on the *Nachi,* wiping out a five-inch turret and its crew. Smoking badly, the enemy cruiser turned away. The *Maya* and its enemy both checked fire but shortly the wounded *Nachi* regained strength and rejoined the battle. The ships were now engaged in a stern chase, reducing the firepower of both opponents—the American cruiser limited to its stern guns while the Japanese cruisers could only fire the eight-inch cannons on its forward turrets.

Allen kept up his running commentary on the positions of the American and the Japanese ships when he noticed the approach of an enemy light cruiser at eighteen thousand yards on the starboard quarter, allowing the ship to assist in spotting the fall of enemy cannon fire. McMorris confirmed this information, instructing the *Salt Lake City* to sheer out of position and fire complete broadsides at the interloper. The enemy's reaction was fast. The light cruiser made a violent turn to evade and fell back toward the larger cruisers.

Messages were being sent to and from Admiral Kinkaid to advise him of the situation. Kinkaid sent a message stating, "Suggest retiring action be considered." The statement added army bombers would be dispatched soon, but it would take five hours to reach their present position. The bridge crew and McMorris thought the message was humorous and at the same time foreboding. The army bombers or the PBYs near Amchitka were several hours away, and by that time, nothing would matter. The enemy was not backing down and continued their dogged pursuit. Admiral Hosogaya knew he had an excellent chance of damaging the Americans and perhaps stopping their plans to invade Attu or Kiska. All he had to do was close the enemy and destroy them, starting with the heavy cruiser.

The *Salt Lake City* had taken one hit, which penetrated the main deck and passed through the hull below the waterline. The damage parties sprang into action to stop the flow of freezing water into the ship, allowing the vessel to continue its current speed. Added to this problem, the steering system was limited to only ten degrees of movement. The ship creaked and groaned with each near miss, and more small cracks developed, allowing more water to enter the vessel. The conditions onboard the heavy cruiser were becoming serious. The admiral walked over to look at the plot Allen was updating and quietly asked, "What do you think of the situation, Allen?"

"Sir, the enemy holds all the cards. We need to protect the *Salt Lake City* and slow the enemy's advance. Maybe it's time to create a smokescreen."

"I was thinking just that. The winds are calm, so if we can make a big enough wall of smoke, perhaps we can gain some distance on them."

Turning back to the bridge, McMorris told his flag lieutenant to signal the destroyers to make maximum smoke in a line covering the *Salt Lake City* and prepare for a turn. The officer quickly went to the radio room to convey the message. Captain Rogers was asking for the same thing, and within a few minutes, two destroyers began a sweep around the ship, laying both chemical and funnel smoke to mask the whereabouts of the cruiser. Once the smoke wall existed, the admiral ordered a course correction to two hundred forty degrees to further confuse the enemy. Because of the windless day and high humidity, the smoke didn't dissipate, floating above the water and confusing the enemy as to where the Americans were headed. They fired their weapons whenever they saw a glimpse of their quarry, but the cannon fire was both inaccurate and sporadic.

The Japanese light cruisers and destroyers tried to move closer, but the *Richmond* and the covering destroyers quickly fired, pushing them away. This didn't stop the Japanese from launching torpedoes. The extreme range was too much even for the vaunted Long Lance weapons. None hit the American ships, nor were they spotted by the crews. The chase continued with the enemy cruisers trying to gain an advantage. *Richmond* and the other ships were now traveling at thirty knots, but the Japanese were going two knots faster, but could not gain as much ground because of their zigzag course, reducing their overall speed advantage. McMorris could not afford to do anything which might slow his movement and plowed straight ahead.

A little past 1100, *Salt Lake City* received another hit. This one was more serious, causing flooding in the after gyro room and engine room. Four feet of water was now in this most vital part of the ship. Damage control parties swarmed the area, patching leaks and using all available pumps to prevent the ice cold water from rising further. Another foot or so would douse the boilers, and the ship would cease to have any power. Speed dropped to twenty-five knots, and the enemy came closer. Things were looking bleak, but soon became dire.

Captain Rogers notified the flagship at 1155 that all power was lost. The ship started to drift and lost headway. Enemy cruisers were now nineteen thousand yards away on the port bow of the slowing ship. *Salt Lake City* kept firing as best she could but had already expended eighty-five percent of its ammunition. Commander Allen watched the heavy cruiser firing its main guns, knowing the enemy was closing in for the kill. Admiral McMorris glanced at the plot and then looked at the location of the wounded cruiser. Catching the commander's eye, the admiral asked, "Do you want to send in the destroyers?"

"Sir, I think we have only one chance, and that is to send our destroyers directly at the enemy and launch torpedoes. This might give us time for Rogers to get his ship moving."

Without a reply, McMorris barked his orders. "Send in three destroyers. Move the *Richmond* and one destroyer to cover *Salt Lake City*. If
they can't get it moving, we may have to evacuate its crew."

Immediately orders went out to the *Bailey, Coghlan,* and *Monaghan*
to reverse course and deliver a torpedo attack on the *Maya* and *Nachi,*
seventeen thousand yards away. *Richmond* and *Dale* closed on the heavy
cruiser, now dead in the water, making smoke as they moved into position to help shield it from enemy shelling. Commander Allen watched
the destroyers dig into the water, plowing great white waves as their
bows split open the sea and charged toward a vastly superior force. As a
destroyer skipper, he knew the little ships would travel quite a distance,
under fire, to get close enough to launch their torpedoes. Looking at
the plot, he knew it would take them maybe five minutes to get within range—some ten thousand yards—before they could launch. All the
while, the enemy would be trying to kill them. It would only take one
hit from an eight-inch shell to seriously damage or sink a destroyer, but
the officers and men of these valiant vessels knew they had to try to save
their fellow countrymen on board the *Salt Lake City.*

Five minutes passed when the enemy, for unknown reasons, turned
from a southerly to a westerly course, allowing the American destroyers
to get within range of their five-inch guns and pepper the *Nachi. Bailey,*
was quickly smothered in splashes from the enemy cruiser, but the destroyer's captain chased each of the enemy salvos, avoiding a direct hit.
Luck did not hold out for long, however, as an eight-inch shell exploded
on the starboard side of the ship. At once, the destroyer launched its five
torpedoes at the extreme range of ten thousand yards. A moment later,
the little destroyer was hit again, momentarily cutting all electric power.
Bailey and her two sisterships turned away and headed back toward the
Richmond. During the time it took for the valiant destroyers to charge the
larger Japanese ships, *Salt Lake City* was able to restore power and slowly
began to move. By 1215, the Japanese fleet was turning away from the
scene of the battle. The Americans were stunned. *Why did the enemy stop?*

Commander Allen continued to plot the situation and received
more reports on the exit of the Japanese fleet. Turning to the admiral,
Allen said, "Sir, the enemy is retiring. Shall we plot a course for Dutch
Harbor?"

McMorris looked through his binoculars and watched the last of the Japanese vessels fall beneath the horizon. Looking at the report from the *Salt Lake City*, he realized he needed to leave. The heavy cruiser could still make thirty knots, even with five feet of water in the after-engine room bilges. She was capable of fighting but had expended almost all of her ammunition. *Bailey* was now making good speed, and her damage control people successfully kept the destroyer dry, for now at least.

"Commander, set a course for Dutch Harbor. Send a message as to the last known position of the Japanese fleet. Maybe the air force can find them."

Acknowledging the command, Allen worked with the ship's navigator to establish the fastest course back to the safety of Dutch Harbor. After several hours of battle, only seven men had been killed, two on the *Salt Lake City* and five on the *Bailey*. Seven were considered to be seriously wounded, and some thirteen men received minor injuries. The commander finished the battle plot with the navigator and added his notes about the battle. Standing on the bridge of the old cruiser holding his first cup of coffee since early morning, Allen took a deep breath.

A few hours ago, he contemplated his death, either by explosion and sinking or by exposure in water with temperatures hovering twenty-eight degrees. Now, he was alive and thankful for his safety. It would take him a long time to comprehend today's action. This was the type of battle planned and practiced for decades by the navies of the world. After hours of shooting at each other, both sides exhausted their ammunition, suffered a few hits, and departed for safer waters. No aircraft or submarines were involved; only cannons and surface torpedoes, with few hits. Commander John Allen wondered if this was the end of an era.

37

1 April 1943
Office of Admiral Edwards
Washington, D.C.

- Aleutian Islands--CINCPAC issues directive for invasion of Attu on May 7. Adm. Kinkaid, as commander North Pacific Force (TF-16), will head the operation. Under him, Adm. Rockwell, Commander Amphibious Forces North Pacific, to conduct landing operations. Maj. Gen. Albert E. Brown's 7th Division, although trained for mechanized warfare in the desert, to make the assault.

- Solomon Islands--Japanese aircraft, whose attention during the preceding month has been largely devoted to Allied bases in New Guinea, attack Russell Islands.

- China--Infantry and artillery training centers open for Chinese Y-Force officers.

- Tunisia--In U.S. II Corps area, plan of attack is changed after another fruitless attempt by Task Force Benson of 1st Armored Division to break through enemy positions barring Gabes road. 1st Division continues efforts to clear southeast tip of

Djebel el Mcheltat. 9th Division is concentrating on
Hill 772, which must be cleared before operations
can continue against Hill 369.

Admiral Edwards was getting impatient. Not with anyone specifically, just the situation. He had been waiting on the final report from Admiral Hepburn concerning the Savo Island battle. The retired admiral had traveled far and wide to collect information and interview everyone associated with the debacle. Reconstructing a disaster, especially when four ships were sunk with many of their key personnel dead, was complicated. He had committed to having the report finished by the end of April but was now delaying it for a few more weeks. Evidently, additional information had been found in MacArthur's command concerning some of the ships assigned to the battle. No matter the reason, Admiral King would not be pleased.

A knock on his door disturbed his concentration. "Enter!" The admiral yelled. The timbre of command warning whoever entered to beware of an angry senior officer.

The commander came to attention in front of the chief of staff's desk and waited to be recognized. "What do you have for me, Tillman?"

"Admiral Edwards, a message from Admiral Kinkaid concerning Commander Allen." Handing the message to Edwards, the commander waited, still at attention.

As the admiral read the message, he grinned for the first time today. Looking up at the commander, he said, "At ease, Tillman. Good news about Commander Allen."

Not saying anything, the lieutenant commander waited for more information.

"Seems Allen is okay. The earlier reports on the battle were positive, and we lost only a few men. *Salt Lake City* needs a major overhaul, as does the destroyer *Bailey.* Allen was aboard the *Richmond* working alongside Admiral McMorris, who is singing the man's praises. Our ships were lucky as hell to get out of this battle with such little damage."

"Sir, that's good news, not just about Commander Allen but the entire task group."

"I agree with you, Tillman. The preliminary reports painted a hell of a situation. I'm surprised our ships were able to survive. I'm sure Admiral King will want a full report from Allen on what he saw, heard, and experienced. The poor guy will have to spend an hour in front of the old man answering a salvo of questions. Send a message to Kinkaid to put the commander on the first available aircraft to Washington. Tell him to confirm Allen's departure and ETA in Washington."

"Yes sir. Anything else, sir?"

Edwards thought about the question for a moment. He needed many things, but most of them involved answers to questions no one could answer. The war was moving forward in North Africa, but the escort problem was still not solved. The Atlantic convoys were still being attacked, and many ships had been lost in March. The Pacific theater was calm for the time being. The New Guinea campaign was moving forward, albeit slowly. The Solomons were quiet, except for continuous attacks on enemy positions from both sea and the air. Progress was finally being made on moving further up the chain of islands to encircle Rabaul. The Aleutian plans were being finalized, and Admiral Nimitz needed more of everything—ships, planes, men, fuel, food, ammunition, and significantly more construction battalions. Seabees were required to build the bases for the next series of attacks against the enemy. Looking up at the attentive and capable officer, Edwards said, "Nothing else for right now. Stay close. I expect another round of requests from the army on convoy support in the Mediterranean."

Coming to attention and knowing this would be another long day, Lieutenant Commander Jerry Tillman left the admiral's office and headed for the communications officer to send the admiral's order to get Commander Allen flown to Washington. Tillman thought the commander would be upset about leaving one war zone to return to another filled with boxes of files and piles of reports in Washington, but orders must be followed.

The newest challenge the admiral faced involved an upcoming conference, code-named TRIDENT, to be held in Washington beginning May 12 between Roosevelt and Churchill, and included the Combined Chiefs of Staff. The topics for discussion were being narrowed down to a manageable list. The prime minister would be driving for more action in the Mediterranean, plus more support for Russia. Admiral King and General Marshall were deep in discussion with their teams on developing plans for the conference, focusing on a cross-channel invasion and expanding operations against Japan.

Admiral Cooke was in charge of the navy's team working on the conference. He was asking for more support and was pushing the CNO to bring the professor back from Hawaii. So far, King wanted to leave Brand at Pearl in support of Nimitz, but Edwards saw the writing on the wall. Brand and the rest of the Science Team would have to be recalled. There were scores of issues on the table. After the American's poor performance at Casablanca, Admiral Leahy had challenged General Marshall and Admiral King to improve their planning capabilities and build stronger strategic arguments supporting the American position.

Another proposal for agenda consideration was the Azores. The recent U-boat battles in the Atlantic were causing even more concern. The ability of planes to adequately cover the central Atlantic needed to be solved and quickly. Escort carriers could help, but these new ships were just beginning to become available in larger numbers. Land-based aircraft were the solution to the problem, and that meant bases in the Portuguese islands were of paramount importance. As he thought about this issue, he remembered that Lieutenant Meyers was still in Lisbon. Perhaps he had some insights on the issue. He would have to contact General Donovan to find out about Meyers' assignment in Portugal.

Nighttime runs were tedious, boring, and sometimes frightening. Two boats were assigned to patrol the area between their base in the Russell Islands and New Georgia, some seventy miles northwest. Sometimes the boats formed a patrol line in the middle of the Slot, looking for Japanese destroyers, but most of the time, the mosquito boats searched the small islands to the south of New Georgia for Japanese barges or observation posts. Most of the time, they saw nothing but a dark ocean, squalls, and an occasional porpoise. But when they encountered the enemy, the action was fast and deadly.

Tonight's mission was different. The two boats worked in unison and approached the southern coast of Vangunu Island, near what was known as Wickham Anchorage, an area poorly charted and full of coral reefs. The operation was to rescue three American pilots who had crashed near the island and rescued by the local natives. The Coastwatcher working the south side of New Georgia had taken care of them for several weeks. The situation on the island was always tenuous for these brave Australians and their native supporters. Caring for three men unaccustomed to the harshness of the jungle was dangerous and affected the mission of the Coastwatcher. The pilots wanted out of the jungle as soon as possible, with one of the men suffering from a badly broken arm and other injuries.

The PT boats were to make contact at midnight, and a native boat would bring the pilots to their position. One boat would move in close to make the pickup, while the other boat stood guard further out to sea. Ensign Marcus Jameson's vessel had the guard duty, and every man aboard was armed with rifles and Thompsons, ready to repel all boarders if needed. Hopefully, the mission would be routine, and the pilots quickly found and rescued. By daybreak, the boats would be back at their base in the Russells and with the bearded and tired crews having coffee.

The two boats had operated in the area only a few times. A local guide came along for the mission to make sure contact was made at the correct location. There were no charts of the area, and local knowledge of the reefs and tiny sand spits was required. The guide was on the boat doing the pickup, and as the boats neared the chosen transfer point, Jameson's boat stood out in the channel to maintain security. It was nearing midnight when the boat's captain, Lieutenant Junior Grade Benjamin Holmes pointed in the direction of the Slot. Whispering to his executive officer, "Marcus, it looks like barges heading this way."

Straining his eyes and then looking through his binoculars to get a good mental picture of the situation, Marcus replied, "Two barges visible, heading toward us. Figure three miles out, but going slow. Probably feeling their way through the reefs."

Benjamin "Ben" Holmes was only two years older than Marcus and a graduate of Boston College. A born sailor, the man was in his element on a PT boat. He had been in the second group of PTs brought into Tulagi in November and had seen lots of action. His first exec had been wounded in an encounter with a Japanese destroyer in January. Jameson was proving a quick study, and Ben trusted the man completely. The situation unfolding to the north was difficult. Their orders were to rescue the downed aviators and avoid any confrontation with the enemy. Sensing the second part of his orders were about to be disobeyed, Ben told his radio operator to notify the rescue boat that trouble was coming. Within a few minutes, the other boat ordered Ben to stay in position and avoid contact. The message from the senior officer on board the rescue boat told him to fire only if fired upon.

Holmes acknowledged the message and ordered his men to prepare all weapons without taking any action unless ordered. The twin .50 caliber mounts swung toward the intruders. A 37mm antitank gun the crew had acquired from the Marines on Tulagi had been adapted in a Rube Goldberg manner to the vessel's bow, giving the ship considerably more firepower. New boats were being equipped with 40mm cannons and larger caliber antiaircraft weapons which helped make the small crafts formidable weapons, especially against the Japanese barges. The enemy also added weapons to their boats and often included heavy machine guns and even small mountain howitzers, potent but hard to aim at a moving target.

As the crew waited, half of the men watched the enemy barges slowly move toward their position. The other half watched the second PT boat slowly move toward the beach, waiting for the pilots to be brought out on native canoes. At 0014, the pilots were safe aboard the rescue boat, which was now slowly and carefully moving out to the main channel where Marcus and his boat were idling, making very little headway, and hoping the enemy didn't see them. Things were looking good, but suddenly, the Japanese barges picked up speed and headed toward their position. Within another minute, the enemy boats opened fire at less than half a mile with heavy machine guns. Each barge had two large-caliber weapons, with one of them seeming to have something more significant, like a 20mm cannon. Its slow but methodical shooting made everyone aboard duck down for protection, which was not to be found on a boat made of plywood and glue.

Ben ordered return fire and the machine guns opened up on the approaching enemy. Swinging the bow to face the enemy, Marcus moved forward to take command of the antitank gun. The gun crew was ready to fire but needed the boat to move just a bit more to starboard. Seeing the dilemma, Marcus gave the helmsman orders to steer the boat slowly to make the correction. Leaning down to check the sights on the small cannon, he ordered, "Fire!" The gun jumped, and another round was quickly thrown into the breech. The man yelled, "Ready!"

Marcus ordered another five degrees to starboard and depressed the barrel. "Fire!" As the shot flew out of the barrel, the crew quickly reloaded, and again, the cannon roared. Five times the gun barked, and suddenly one of the enemy barges was hit and on fire. Men could be seen jumping overboard. The other barge moved alongside, protected from the American's fire, and helped men jump to safety. All the time, the rescue boat had made progress into the deeper part of the channel, signaling Ben's boat to retire toward their base. Both PT boats turned away from the action and increased speed. The enemy barge was burning brightly, and the other barge had stopped firing.

For at least tonight, the Americans were victorious and accomplished their mission. The enemy had lost one barge and many men, plus what appeared to be a very volatile cargo. Marcus had experienced his first fight, which may have been similar to John Paul Jones or Blackbeard the Pirate. No injuries reported, and the boat received only a few new holes. Returning to base, Marcus took the helm and followed the rescue boat, happy in his accomplishment, but also in controlling his emotions. He didn't sense a lot of fear, but he knew it was not like fighting an enemy destroyer.

38

7 April 1943
CINCPAC Headquarters
Pearl Harbor, Territory of Hawaii

- Solomon Islands--Intensifying their aerial offensive
  against Allied shipping and aircraft, Japanese
  attack the Guadalcanal area in force, employing 71
  bombers and 117 fighters.
  - Three Allied merchant vessels are sunk.
  - Japanese plane losses in this action far outnumber
    Allied losses of 7 fighters.
- Tunisia--All available aircraft of XII Air Support
  Command and WDAF (Western Desert Air Force)
  attack the enemy, who is retreating in all sectors.
  British 8th Army pursues rapidly retreating enemy
  northward to general line Cekhira-Sedkret en
  Noual.

The message traffic intercepts increased with each passing day. Commander Layton and the men in the dungeon worked at maximum speed, but still, breaking the newest rendition of Japanese code was taking time. The enemy changed it each month, but for some reason, the newest revision occurred on April 5, not the usual first of the month. Something was up, but no one was sure what. The commander had spent most of the previous night working alongside Lieutenant Brand, but the codes were only halfway intelligible.

The professor believed the Japanese were about to launch a large air raid on either Guadalcanal or Port Moresby. James told Layton his gut feel was for the Solomons but was unsure. Two days ago, the intelligence officer alerted Admiral Nimitz to the probability of a significant Japanese raid on Guadalcanal, specifically any shipping in the area. Admiral Spruance thought Layton was right about the threat. Nimitz agreed and signaled Halsey to remove as many ships as possible until the danger was over. This morning the threat became real.

Coastwatchers, the guardian angels of all sailors and Marines, were the first to radio an alert. The enemy was sending a large number of bombers and escorting fighters south to attack American positions. The intended target was unknown, and about half the planes went undetected. The Japanese sent part of the attacking planes on a northerly route to come in a different direction than their previous bombings of Guadalcanal. The advanced warning gave the Americans a few precious hours to prepare for the onslaught. The fighters were made ready to intercept the incoming Japanese planes, and all other flyable aircraft were ordered to take off and stay to the south of the island and away from the battle.

The navy had a few remaining vessels in Lunga Roads, mainly landing craft, tenders, and barges. There were several larger ships at Tulagi, and these were immediately ordered to leave the harbor. The tanker *Kanawha*, was fueling other ships but soon left with the only destroyer in the harbor, *Taylor*. Several minesweepers and auxiliary craft also made for the open sea to find maneuvering room to avoid enemy bombers. The *Erskine Phelps*, the station tanker, was still fueling the corvette HMNZS *Moa*, which had not received the message to leave the harbor. The soldiers and Marines went into their defensive positions with all available antiaircraft weapons made ready. Radar systems searched the skies looking for the enemy as the first Wildcats, P-40s, and P-38s climbed to higher altitudes for the attack.

Commander Layton and James sat down in the communications room and monitored incoming radio traffic from the Solomons. Each man was aware of the danger facing the pilots in their planes and the men on the ground. Brand could feel the knot in his stomach as he relived his experience flying against the enemy in November. He recalled waiting for the first sighting of the enemy and hopefully, they not seeing you. Then the dive toward the bombers, for these were the planes that could hurt your countrymen the most. Other Americans would work on the Japanese Zeros to keep them occupied while your fellow pilots destroyed the bombers. Hopefully, this would be done before the enemy could even drop his deadly cargo.

The radio operators received signals from the Coastwatchers further down the chain of islands. As each one saw the enemy planes, from Bougainville in the north, then south to New Georgia, the reports indicated the number of planes and their course. Apparently, the enemy was heading for the base at Guadalcanal. None of the planes were heading for the Russells. James thought if he were the Japanese commander, he would undoubtedly go for the biggest prize, Henderson Field, or perhaps ships at the Tulagi anchorage. The plan apparently was designed to slow down the Allied advance up the Solomons and turn MacArthur away from any more conquests in New Guinea. Turning to Layton, James said, "I don't think the Japanese have enough planes to do the job. This may be our chance to hurt him much worse than he could hurt us."

Layton agreed and looked again at the newest report. American planes were now in a battle over the Slot and near Tulagi. Each message was open to different levels of interpretation, knowing that an overly excited pilot might report something which was not really happening. The intelligence officer had over a year of experience in, as he called it, "reality reports." The first blush of news was often tainted—planes reported as shot down were not even damaged; bombs hit targets but missed by hundreds of yards, if not miles. The number of enemy aircraft spotted, ships seen, or artillery positions found was often wrong or highly inflated. America was new at war, but as James had told him, even the war-weary British were known to over-report or miss-classify battle damage.

All this proved the fog of war truly existed. Only long after the battle, using their secret intelligence, was the truth to be found. The news the public saw was not the reality of the fighting going on in the South Pacific. James was learning truth really was the first victim of war. But for right now, the reality of war meant men were dying in the skies and the seas of the South Pacific. Far from their homes and loved ones, many a man would not come home, nor would his body be found to receive the tributes of the fallen. Each report told a new story. The enemy was being pummeled, and few found their targets. Yet, many men would perish this day, and ships, planes, and buildings would bear the brunt of the war.

The order to return to the United States was not what John Meyers expected. He and the OSS agent Robert Murdoch were hoping for a confirmation of a clandestine meeting with Admiral Canaris. For over a month, information was sent back and forth across the Atlantic seeking more details and confirmations about the German naval attaché, Gebhardt Wagener. Apparently, individuals in Washington were concerned about the man being a double agent or perhaps some nefarious plot to get intelligence from the Americans. Meyers had to arrange several more meetings to secure information about the Abwehr, which could be validated by other sources. All of this frustrated both the German and John Meyers.

The command to return came from Admiral Edwards, and a seat on the Pan American Clipper was arranged. Two nights ago, John had a brief meeting with Wagener to tell him he was leaving but would be returning. The last part was a lie since the American didn't know what he would or would not be doing in the future. He hoped he would come back to Lisbon if for no other reason than to secure more information from the German naval officer and possibly save the man from the Gestapo. Wagener was not a Nazi, and evidently, his boss, Admiral Canaris, was not one either. The opposite was true. Both men were patriots, but this also meant they were traitors to the current government.

Wagener was stoic about the news. Believing the American was telling the truth and being a man who followed orders, he understood the command to return. He was beginning to like Meyers, if for no other reason being his sense of humor. The two men had been seen in public on many occasions, which didn't turn many heads in Lisbon. Spies, counterspies, double agents, and the occasional independent operative were all familiar sights in neutral Portugal. This made their casual encounters easier and were used to establish clandestine meetings to discuss the war. Each meeting was in a different location, with Estoril being used on at least two occasions. Agent Murdoch had attended a few of these and would now handle contacts with the German.

The last casual meeting with Wagener had happened at the bar of the casino. The American was seated at the bar talking to Murdoch and the lovely Countess Christina when the German approached. Ordering a drink, Gebhardt said, "So, Lieutenant Meyers, I understand you are leaving us soon. I hope you have a good trip and don't run into any of our U-boats. I would hate to see you get wet."

Knowing the game, John replied, "Kapitanleutanant Wagener, as usual, your intelligence is correct. But I don't think I will have to worry about getting wet. I think the Allies are doing a good job of keeping your submarines in check. How about you? Are you staying in Lisbon for a while longer?"

"Yes, I will be here for some time. My country needs me to keep the Portuguese honest in all of its agreements." Looking at Murdoch, he continued, "And to ensure that you and the British keep theirs as well."

Christina, knowing both men, said, "Gebhardt, will you not miss Meyers, or do you think it will make it easier to get to know me?"

Both men laughed at the comment while Murdoch slowly sipped his drink. The German quickly replied. "Countess, I will not miss the lieutenant, but perhaps his removal will make my time with you more meaningful."

The countess smiled and sipped her drink. Knowing the woman played both sides of the street, Myers focused on the glass in his hand, swirling its contents. "Herr Wagener, please take good care of the countess in my absence." Then, looking directly at the German, he continued. "I don't think she wishes to be alone. I think she has a special place in her heart for you, and perhaps after the war, things will be better for both of you." Smiling, he raised his glass.

Most Spanish royal family members were not welcome to return to their homeland by Franco's government. Many had supported him, but since the king's removal before the civil war, the citizens were not disposed to welcome the royals back. So, for now, the countess was stateless and looking for support in the form of the right man. The injured German might be the right match, but who knows what would occur in Europe after the war. Vanquished and victor may play into each other's hands, and new unions might be made.

But for now, John Meyers needed to pass on one more piece of critical information. Passing a note would be dangerous, so John spilled a drink on his coat, which elicited the correct response from Wagener. The German grabbed a napkin and passed it to John, and as he did this, John whispered, "A new home for you is ready. Let Murdoch know if you need it."

Gebhardt was passing another napkin to Meyers, whispering, "Here, take another one to clean your coat. I think you will need to get a new one when you get home. Perhaps you can send me one as well in case I spill my drink while you are gone."

The men looked each other in the eye, signifying each man's understanding of the offer. Meyers offer had been accepted, but for now, the German would stay in Lisbon, but if he was compromised, he would quickly seek out the Americans to find refuge. His last message from Canaris provided more impetus for making plans to find safety with the Allies. The admiral's coded message told him the war situation was getting worse. Atrocities were now being committed on a grand scale. The message ended with a warning not to come back to Germany or travel to Spain for any reason. Wagener took this last piece of information to heart. Serious people were now planning a change in government, starting with Herr Hitler. Anyone with knowledge of this was in jeopardy of losing their life.

The other part of Meyers' mission involving the Azores question was moving along at a snail's pace. By necessity of their ancient treaty, the British mandated that the Americans do nothing on the diplomatic front without their knowledge. Playing second fiddle annoyed George Kennan, the *charge d' affaires* to Portugal. He disliked the slowness of his British ally and wanted to forcefully push Salazar's government to agree to American bases in the islands. He had been told to back off and let the British take the lead, which didn't make him happy.

The wolfram situation seemed to be working out as planned. Meyers had worked with the Portuguese government to secure more promises concerning the equal treatment of the warring party's access to the mineral. The OSS discovered several clandestine operations, which were then revealed to Salazar's government for action. With each month, the Portuguese saw the logic in being on the winning side of the war. They slowly closed down each of these mines and expanded their efforts to reduce illegal exports. These efforts were rewarded by allowing the Portuguese to increase imports of food, oil, and other supplies. Slowly, Portugal was moving closer to the Allied position. It was still a matter of time, but soon decisions far away from Lisbon would make things happen.

39

11 April 1943
Office of Admiral Edwards
Washington, D.C.

- New Guinea--Two Allied merchant ships are lost to enemy aircraft that attack Oro Bay in strength.
- Tunisia--In U.S. II Corps area, the 9th Division moves north to British 5 Corps zone. 1st Division, which is to follow 9th to the north flank of British 1st Army, moves to Morsott. 1st Armored Division remains in the Sbeitla-Faid region.

The admiral was busier than usual if anything in the navy's headquarters could be considered "usual." Paperwork was piled on both sides of his desk. Reports, updates, communications to various commands, and personnel requests from all over the world flowed into the man's office. Postings and promotions were reviewed at different levels within the command, but all major decisions concerning senior levels—captains and above—needed the approval of Edwards and Admiral King. If you were to be given command of a new cruiser or aircraft carrier, King wanted to know all about the individual under consideration. The CNO had an excellent memory for senior officers. Still, in the last few years, the intake of new officers was putting massive stress on everyone's ability to recall a man's name, let alone their experiences.

The navy's need for officers had overwhelmed their ability to find qualified candidates. Hundreds of landing ships like the small seagoing LSIs needed an officer in command, often a lieutenant junior grade or an ensign right out of Officer Candidate's School. Former destroyer officers were promoted to the rank of captain to take command of new cruisers, escort carriers, and squadrons of destroyers, submarines, and convoys. Land commands also begged for new leaders for stateside schools, air bases, ports, and enormous repair installations.

The navy was growing from two hundred eighty-four thousand officers and men in 1941 to 1.74 million by the end of 1943. The Marine Corps expanded just as rapidly from a 1941 total of fifty-four thousand men to a planned three hundred eight thousand by year's end. Planning for the future showed a total of 3.38 million in the navy by the end of 1945, with the Marines growing to four hundred seventy-five thousand officers and men. The navy started the war with less than eight hundred ships. The plan for the end of 1945 called for sixty-eight hundred ships of all kinds. This included twenty-five hundred amphibious warfare ships not even contemplated before the war began. This unparalleled growth tested the ability of the senior command to find the right man for every position. Most would learn on the job.

Edwards went down the list of commanders ready for promotion to captain. Most were products of Annapolis, but a few were products of ROTC programs created after World War I, while others held reserve commissions dating back to the Great War. He knew many of those up for promotion, having commanded them on various ships or shoreside assignments. The submarine skippers were well known to him, and the growth of the "silent service" required hundreds of technically astute officers to fill billets stateside and across the fleet. He smiled, thinking about his career, which started at Annapolis in 1903. It took him nearly thirty years serving on various ships, including submarines, to become a captain and finally command a major warship, the battleship *Colorado* in 1940. Now he was looking at a list of commanders who had graduated from Annapolis in the early '20s. He was envious, knowing these men would soon command great warships or lead complex installations vital to the success of the navy.

As he examined the list sent over by the Bureau of Personnel, several names jumped out at him. Several submarine commanders had shown great skill in the opening years of the war and were due promotions. But this also meant the combat veterans were often being replaced by far less experienced men. Hopefully, these men had been good understudies to the men on the list. Others were aviators who had survived the opening tumult of the war and learned the skills necessary to command large land-based operations or command the new carriers being launched. The destroyer officers were well suited to command the growing number of cruisers or lead brand new destroyer squadrons, DESRONs, consisting of two destroyer divisions numbering six to eight ships.

The skipper of a destroyer squadron was responsible for the training, equipping, and administration of the ships and operational command when the ships served with large fleet units or on specific missions. It was a demanding job requiring experience in commanding a destroyer, plus staff work and strategy. The squadron commander needed to allow each destroyer commander do his job running each ship, but when necessary, lead groups of ships into battle. Edwards knew a man who would be an excellent commanding officer, but he needed Admiral King's approval to release him from his current duties. Until then, the admiral couldn't tell Commander Allen about his promotion and new assignment.

As he continued his examination of the list, Edwards concentration was interrupted by Allen's replacement, Lieutenant Commander Tillman knocking on his door. Disgruntled but knowing something must be necessary, he thundered, "Enter!"

The commander entered the room, marched up to the desk, and stood at attention, holding a large file with TOP SECRET stamped in red across the front. "At ease, Tillman. What are you carrying which will make my day more difficult?"

"Sir, dispatch from Pearl Harbor. Commander Layton has updated the damage assessment from the Japanese attacks at Guadalcanal and New Guinea."

Holding his hand out to receive the file, Tillman passed the folder to his commanding officer and awaited instructions. Edwards looked at the top message from Layton and the battle report. Noticing a second message sent by the professor, the admiral put down the intelligence officer's report and started to read the one from Brand. It was the usual concise, no-nonsense report which made Professor Brand important to the senior leadership. As he read the five paragraphs, each one not mincing words, Edwards made several notes.

Re-reading the message then returning to Layton's report, the admiral looked up at the still-standing aide. "Sit down, Tillman. Have you read these messages from Pearl?"

"No sir. They were directed to you. I had the communications officer seal the report, and I signed for it per protocol."

"That is always the best policy, but from now on, I want you to take a look at these reports, especially from Lieutenant Brand, before you give them to me. The only exception is any eyes-only message to Admiral King or me."

"Yes sir. I will examine all messages in the future except those directed to you and Admiral King."

The chief of staff liked the man's approach to security and procedure. Must have learned this in pilot training. Handing the reports to Tillman, Edwards said, "Read these and tell me what you think."

Tillman quickly read each report. After he finished Brand's report, he re-read it to make sure he didn't miss anything.

"Okay, Tillman, What do you think?"

The commander tried to feel his way around the chief of staff and the nuances of top command. As a pilot, he had been taught to be specific in his approach to any problem. Every step in flying was based first on the approved procedure, then on practice, and finally gut instinct. Now was not the time for a gut reaction. "Admiral, it appears the lieutenant feels the enemy is losing steam. We have lost a dozen or so planes, while the Japanese are experiencing great losses in men and machines. The damage appears to be light, with only a few ships being sunk or damaged, and these are smaller vessels and merchant craft. Facilities have been lightly affected by the raids, and our operations are not in any way diminished."

The admiral thought this was a good, concise answer but lacked something. Looking directly at the officer, Edwards asked, "What do you think the enemy is going to do next, based upon Brand's concluding statements and Commander Layton's analysis?"

Seeing the intense stare coming from the admiral, the new aide wished he was flying a Wildcat or attacking an enemy base. Taking just a moment to collect his thoughts, Jerry told himself to answer the question. "Admiral, I think Commander Layton's assessment on losses is probably correct, plus or minus ten percentage points. Lieutenant Brand believes the Japanese losses are not quite as great as our pilots reported but significant enough to do long-term damage to their carrier operations. Evidently, the Japanese army bombers were not effective, but the IJN bombers gave us some problems. The significance of the attack, plus its duration, point to the enemy's desire to slow our advance. Brand feels they lost far more than they gained and will have difficulty recouping their losses. As Lieutenant Brand stated in his report, 'The enemy cannot sustain this tempo for more than another week, giving us a decided advantage for the coming months.' I would agree with his statement, and we should move up our plans for Rabaul and the Central Pacific."

The admiral looked at his aide and thought the young man was growing into the job, plus he showed a good sense of war strategy. He would be a suitable replacement for Allen. All he needed was some intense time with the professor to understand the other parts of war planning, including logistics, scientific advances, and war production. These were the elements that would make or break America's war strategy.

Turning to the piles of paper on his desk, Edwards gave Tillman an order. "Get a message to Layton asking for any confirmation on enemy activity or future intentions. Also, send a separate message to Admiral Nimitz asking if we can have Brand, and the team sent back to Washington within the next week. We are going to need these men briefed and ready for the Combined Chiefs of Staff conference starting in four weeks."

Tillman stood and went to attention. Asking if there was anything else and receiving a negative reply, the commander executed another perfect about-face and marched out the room. Edwards smiled at the man's actions and promised himself to tell the commander that these ceremonies were no longer needed in his presence. All the admiral wanted were men who could do their jobs quickly and without much guidance. He didn't have time to explain things, nor did his boss, who expected his staff to answer his questions before he asked them.

The meeting was led by Captain Charles J. Moore, Admiral Spruance's good friend, and principal aide, who would later serve as the Admiral's chief of staff. Captain Jameson and his officers sat in the meeting, listening to the plans for the push up the central Pacific. Admiral Cooke's war planning staff had provided the CINCPAC team a roadmap but not the details for a yearlong series of events leading to the conquest of the Gilbert and Marshall Islands. The plan called for selecting key islands that were to be captured from the enemy, coinciding with the neutralization of the other islands in each group by using air forces and sea blockade. The occupied islands would serve as stepping stones to the next island chain—the Marianas—and serve as a base of operations for the new B-29 bombers as well as advance bases for the navy and ground forces in subsequent attacks on the Japanese home islands. But first, the Gilberts and Marshalls had to be taken.

James listened carefully to Washington's most recent set of plans and how they were interpreted by the CINCPAC planning staff, led by Captain Lynde D. McCormick. The Chiefs of Staff had decided to move forward with two separate offensive campaigns in the Pacific. Operation CARTWHEEL, led by MacArthur, was designed to capture, or neutralize Rabaul on the island of New Britain. This operation required the SWPA forces to capture most of New Guinea, the Admiralty Islands, Treasury Islands, the remaining Solomon Islands, including New Georgia and Bougainville. The final act would be a direct assault on the island of New Britain to destroy the Japanese army garrison of nearly one hundred thousand men in Rabaul.

As the discussion moved from broad strategy to logistics, Major General Edmond H. Leavey addressed the manpower and supply situation. Working in close association with Vice Admiral William Calhoun, the commanding officer of Service Force Pacific Fleet, the man outlined the significant challenges of supporting the initial phases of the operation. The first operation, code-named GALVANIC, would require forces not yet available to Admiral Nimitz. A force of old battleships and supporting craft called Task Force 50, currently in Pearl Harbor, was the only force currently available for operations. Most of the modern warships and aircraft carriers supported Admiral Halsey in the Southwest Pacific, and in turn, these supported MacArthur's push up the Solomons. New ships were on the way, but for now, the United States Navy didn't possess the necessary forces to conduct new offensive actions.

The charts showed the anticipated manpower requirements for the planned operations against the Gilberts, including the islands of Tarawa and Makin, plus the island of Nauru, some three hundred eighty miles west of Tarawa. B-24 bombers moved to a new base at Funafuti Island and bombed and photographed the three islands. They discovered that on Betio Island, part of Tarawa, the Japanese had built an airbase, and on Makin, the enemy created a vital seaplane facility for long-range reconnaissance. Nauru had a large airbase, and when the Americans attacked the island, the enemy followed them back to the base on Funafuti and returned to bomb it the next day. With each passing day, these bases would become stronger and more heavily defended. The planners knew time was not on their side.

Information on the buildup of men, ships, aircraft, and supplies of all types was still non-existent. It would be a few more months before Washington could adequately address the number of men for any invasion as well as the transports available for both initial operations and ongoing support. James wrote more notes and started making calculations. Jameson saw the professor's face and knew his protégée was about to make a series of observations that would anger the CINCPAC staff.

Placing his hand on the piece of paper Brand was furiously making notations on, Jameson whispered a command. "James, now is not the time to start a war with these people. They have been dealt a difficult hand, and they have already acknowledged they don't have many answers."

The lieutenant looked at his boss and good friend and grinned. Whispering back to the captain, "Sir, I wasn't going to challenge their numbers. I have an idea or two about how to help them. May I continue?"

Major Flannigan recognized something was about to set off James Brand but saw the captain had already interceded. Nodding his head and hoping the professor wasn't off on a wild goose chase, the captain removed his hand. Waiting was now all he could do.

"Are there any questions?" Captain Moore looked around the room at the principal staff officers from the army, navy, and Marine Corps. He was about to end the discussion but saw a hand go up in the back of the room. He knew the man well and wondered what the "whiz kid professor" had to offer. "Lieutenant Brand, you have a question or perhaps an observation?"

"Sir, I would like to offer my help. It would appear that the planned Gilbert operation is not fully subscribed to by Washington. I would like to prepare an analysis for this staff and Admiral Spruance on the size and scope of the operations, starting with a detailed logistics plan based upon the assumptions in section one of the chief of staff's directive. The number of invasion troops, support troops, and garrison troops will require a substantial cargo capability, which we know does not exist. The number of large aircraft carriers is possible, but we need to look at the current commissioning plans for the new *Yorktown* and *Lexington* due out in July. Additional light carriers, *Independence, Belleau Wood,* and *Princeton,* should also be ready by the end of the summer. Air groups will have to be trained and ready to commence flight operations at the same time."

Checking his notes, the professor continued. "By the end of September, the newly constituted Fifth Fleet should be comprised of five new battleships, seven old ones, ten fast carriers, seven escort carriers, eight heavy and four light cruisers, sixty-six destroyers, twenty-seven attack transports, and cargo carriers, plus nine merchant ships suitable for transports. Units for the invasion will have to be selected soon and moved to training facilities. The majority of these men will be new to combat, requiring extensive preparation. The same goes for the naval support forces, including combat vessels assigned to soften up the enemy's beach defenses. Air units, including those aboard the fast carriers, will require training and must learn to support ground units in close contact with the enemy to avoid friendly fire incidents. All of this needs to be linked to the initial combat loading of ships and the ongoing support looking forward three months after these islands are taken."

Seeing the men around the room were now taking notes, James stood moving toward the front of the room. He held onto his one page of notes, and his incredible memory kicked into overdrive. "Consideration must be given to the number of Seabee units assigned to each island. Suppose the goal is to secure airfields for the next jump to the Marshalls. In that case, base building equipment must be ready on day one to start the process of rebuilding airstrips, building fuel storage areas, revetments for aircraft, bomb and ammunition bunkers, and the necessary facilities to support an operational air base. Monthly support estimates need to be created for all aspects of the occupying forces including food, ammunition, water, medical services, accommodations, electrical power facilities for radar and radio communications and for possible Japanese POWs."

The men around the room continued to take notes for fifteen more minutes as James provided details for each category and timeline from the beginning of fleet movement to three months after the successful occupation of the islands. Thousands of tons of supplies, thousands of men, hundreds of pieces of machinery, huge fuel storage tanks, and water tanks all needed to be sourced, transported, and then moved ashore. James knew that even with the best of plans, some things would go wrong, but if it wasn't planned for in the beginning, the smallest of things could thwart a major military campaign.

Later in the evening, Jameson and Flannigan gave James glowing reviews of his performance. The captain told Brand that General Leavey thanked him for allowing James to speak at the meeting. Everything the professor had said was important and critical to winning the war. As the supply officer for CINCPAC, his job was a constant battle of priorities and failures of communication. The general confirmed the lieutenant communicated the necessary elements of any logistics strategy. Without a well-thought-out plan of supply, even the most excellent military leader would fail. Flannigan agreed wholeheartedly.

Dr. Feldman told James not to get a big head with all of the flattery. "James, you did a good job, but be careful when you give a sermon like that. Sometimes people don't like listening to the message or the preacher."

Brand understood and recognized that he sometimes spoke down to his students in his zeal, even if those students had stars on their shoulders. Later in the evening, Brand pulled out the newest plan for the invasion of Attu and began his review. Admiral Spruance asked him to take one more look at the plan and make any recommendations. The troops had begun moving from California to advanced bases in the Aleutians. The navy was moving ships from California to provide fire support, including three old battleships. There were no large aircraft carriers available, but the force included one escort carrier. The cold, fog-bound island was far from any American airbase, and only bombers and long-range P-38s could make the roundtrip from their base at Adak to hit Attu. The Japanese had started building an airfield at Holtz Bay on the frigid island but progress was slow.

The more James read, the greater his level of concern. This would be only the third major seaborne invasion by the United States since the war began, and it appeared past experiences had yet to be learned. As he read the details for the logistics plan, the timetable for the invasion, and the expected date for securing the island, the professor knew the plan was in jeopardy. Only after he reviewed his notes did he come to a conclusion on how to help. It would involve some of his friends, but they were the only experienced people available to do the job.

40

14 April 1943
CINCPAC Headquarters
Pearl Harbor, Territory of Hawaii

- New Guinea--Japanese conclude series of heavy air strikes on New Guinea with strong attack on Milne Bay that causes little damage.
- Tunisia--In British 1st Army's 5th Corps area, U.S. 9th Division assumes command of 46th Division sector. 4th Division, in its first action, has been exerting pressure against the enemy north of Hund's Gap in conjunction with 78th Division's attack and has reached hills just southwest of Sidi Nsir.

The dungeon was always full of smoke, not from a fire, but from cigarettes, pipes, and the occasional cigar. The men listening and transcribing messages from the far reaches of the Japanese Empire sat silently in front of walls of hot black boxes with wires and tubes sprouting like weeds. The radio receivers were powerful and skipped about the ether searching different frequencies to capture and hopefully interpret the meaning of the messages. The men who worked the dials knew they had an important job but only transcribed the signals they heard. Some were just morse code, sets of numbers, but nothing they understood. Other men in the complex were charged with taking this raw information and hopefully making sense of it. Today started with the usual deluge of messages but ended with hushed voices and knowing glances. Something big had been discovered.

Two men entered Commander Layton's office and closed the door. The intelligence officers were sure of the message, but they could not do anything about its contents. Only Layton could make recommendations to the admiral. Reading the message, the intelligence officer asked for the raw information, which the men had brought with them. They knew how the commander operated and would want verification and examine every bit of evidence leading to the conclusions offered. Satisfied with the information, the two men were dismissed, knowing they had stumbled onto something that could change the war's direction.

The commander called a nearby conference room and asked one of its occupants to come to his office. The voice was calm, but the intonation gave him away. In a few minutes, Lieutenant James Brand, accompanied by the ever-watchful Gunny, entered the room. Quickly telling Warrant Jones to wait outside, Layton showed the message to Brand. The professor read it quickly then re-read it, slowly.

"Sir, is it possible to do an interception?"

The commander stood and walked to his large conference table and began sorting through nautical charts of the Pacific. Finding the chart of the Solomon Islands, he pointed to the various locations mentioned in the message.

"James, here's Rabaul, and I have marked the locations of the known airbases in the islands nearby."

Looking closely at the chart, Brand traced the flight path from Rabaul to the island of Bougainville and the Japanese base at Balalae. Quickly calculating the flight path from Guadalcanal to the interception point, James stated, "Sir, only a P-38 with drop tanks could make this flight. A straight line round trip would be over eight hundred miles, and with any fighting, the planes would be running on fumes. Drop tanks could help them make the trip, but I would see them taking a more circuitous route to the interception point, so call it one thousand miles. I would like to get with the air force boys to do some calculations on flight time, fuel loads, and the number of planes it would take."

"What do you think of the idea? We would be taking out the man who planned Pearl Harbor. Does it bother you that this could be viewed as an assassination?"

The last comment stopped Brand cold. He had not considered the problem at all. This was a time of total war. Innocents had been killed on both sides, and if a man in uniform was flying across the ocean, was he not a valid target for elimination? Commander Layton watched the lieutenant ponder the question. The commander had met Yamamoto once in Tokyo in the mid-1930s when he was an assistant attaché. He felt somewhat conflicted but knew this could help the war effort.

"Sir, the Japanese admiral is a valid target of war. If he was killed helming a ship, it would be the same thing as being a passenger on a ship or a plane. The man is a combatant, and therefore, if we can eliminate him, it could have a major impact on the enemy's plans and capabilities. From what we have seen of some of the other Japanese commanders, no one can replace Yamamoto from a strategic or tactical sense. We should move forward immediately with the planning while we get approvals from Admiral Nimitz and if need be, even the President."

Not having thought about the political repercussions, Layton thought this should be addressed first by Admiral Nimitz. Picking up the phone, he called the admiral for an immediate meeting. Getting a quick confirmation, Layton grabbed the message and the backup information and, with Brand in tow, headed for the admiral's office.

Nimitz reviewed the information and then looked at the chart Brand had marked showing the distances to and from the Japanese bases. Detailing his thoughts of an attack by P-38s on the planes carrying the enemy admiral, James stopped talking and waited for a decision. Feeling at ease about making this kind of life or death decision, Brand watched the admiral examine the message once more and then the chart. For a moment, the commanding officer of the Pacific Ocean Area appeared calm. Not one to make rash decisions but willing to make the necessary ones based upon solid intelligence and strategy, Nimitz questioned his intelligence officer.

"What will be the impact on the enemy?"

"Sir, Lieutenant Brand and I believe the enemy will be slow in recovering from the loss of their best admiral. We are aware of the political bickering between the army and the navy and losing their most famous leader will only increase their infighting. We doubt the Imperial Navy has anyone who could replace Yamamoto's capabilities or leadership qualities. Once the Japanese people learn about his loss, I expect increased distrust in the enemy's war efforts."

"What about the source of information. How do we keep this quiet?"

James spoke up first, "Admiral, we need to get other planes in the air for several days after the attack. We should get some attention in the news media about our Coastwatcher efforts and our increasing submarine attacks. This may keep them wondering how we found out it was Yamamoto. We should also not say anything about the attack, nor should we acknowledge whatever the enemy puts out on the loss of the admiral. We act like we don't know what we did."

"Put it down to dumb luck, Brand. I like it, and if we can keep a lid on this, we should be able to ride it out for several months. Layton, send a message to Halsey. Give him the particulars and get him planning the attack using Brand's idea on the P-38s. Make sure he understands the importance of a total information blackout before and after any attack. I need to get this to Admiral King and General Marshall, but I think they will agree."

As the two men were leaving the office, Nimitz called Brand back. Standing in front of the admiral's desk, Nimitz asked, "Lieutenant Brand, are you and the team ready to head back to Washington?"

"Yes sir. We have our travel plans set, and we'll leave tomorrow. I wish I could stay to watch what happens with the attack on Yamamoto."

"I would like to keep you, Mr. Brand, but Admiral King wants you back for the upcoming conference. You did a good job helping him at the Casablanca meeting, so now you are permanently tied to major conferences. I'm sure I'll see you and the rest of the team soon. By the way, Admiral Lockwood tells me you are helping him with the torpedo problems. Please keep me informed on any resolutions."

"Sir, thank you for the opportunity to be of service to you and Admiral Spruance. I do have a last request, which I think would be of great help in the upcoming Attu operation."

Nimitz looked up at the smiling young officer, knowing the man had another plan which might cause him a problem with the CNO. "All right, Lieutenant, what's on your mind?"

After a short five-minute overview of the idea and how it would help this operation and build for the future, Nimitz was sold. "I'll send a signal to Admiral King this afternoon with the request. I know you won't be coming along, but your idea will make a difference and, like you said, build our base of knowledge."

The two men, one young and one old, parted company. Nimitz smiled, thinking about how he had walked into the professor's trap, but agreed it made good sense and how it could help the field commanders who were new to amphibious warfare. As long as Brand was not involved, CINCPAC didn't think King would mind borrowing a few people for a cold boat ride.

The base was humming with activity. The addition of the carrier planes from Truk had more than doubled the available aircraft for the attacks on the Americans in New Guinea and Guadalcanal. Senior officers celebrated the operation's success, especially the number of Allied ships and planes destroyed. Every mechanic worked through the night to prepare the next day's mission, and none complained. Success was being won by the valiant aviators of the Japanese army and navy. Only one man doubted the success or anything positive about the operation.

The intelligence officer had flown south to support the admiral, and with each report, his doubts grew. The mathematics, he told his intelligence expert Petty Officer Second Class Shibuya Haruki, did not match up with the reports. As the mechanics worked on the planes in their hangers and revetments, Lieutenant Kaya Akihito examined reports from the pilots, then examined the daily loss report. *If the enemy was beaten so severely, where do they keep getting new planes to shoot down Japanese fighters and bombers?* Every returning flight contained fewer planes than went out. The bombers were being ravaged. On the last mission to New Guinea, over half of the army Mitsubishi Type 97 bombers failed to return. The ones that did were full of holes—many unrepairable. The runway was littered with aircraft of all types which could not fly.

The pilots told stories of great success, but Kaya had spoken privately with two returning Zero pilots who were drinking heavily. Both men initially kept up the success stories, but the pilots slowly told the other part of the story under the prince's glare. The last mission over New Guinea was a continuous battle against the Americans flying their new twin-engine fighter, which was much faster than their planes. While the P-38s kept the Zero's busy, American and Australian P-40s attacked the slow and highly flammable twin-engine army bombers and the IJN's Nakajima Type B5N bombers. Without adequate fighter support, the bombing force was devastated by the Allied warplanes. Neither man could confirm the glowing reports on the damage done to ships and airfields.

The veteran pilots also told Kaya about the replacement pilots that came along on this operation. Both men were veterans of many battles, and now they were the only two left from their original squadron. In the course of the Guadalcanal campaign, they had lost every friend they had. Most of the new men had less than two hundred hours and barely qualified to land on a carrier. Several of these new pilots tried to attack the Americans in the last two missions but were quickly destroyed. Each of the fallen Japanese pilots had failed to follow instructions and went into battle without support, nor would they stay with their assigned wingman. As one pilot told the intelligence officer, bravery will get you killed very quickly in the air.

Armed with the official reports and his own analysis, which excluded the Zero pilots' accounts, the prince went to see Admiral Yamamoto. His bungalow on the base was not as nice as his cabin aboard the *Yamato*. The commander in chief of the Combined Fleet wanted to be close to the action and be seen by his men. His staff had begged him not to go near the war zone, but the man was not to be dissuaded. Upon entering the conference room, next to the admiral's bedroom, Kaya came to attention and then bowed in his most respectful manner. The admiral was taken by the solemnity of the move and knew the prince had something important to say.

"Prince Akihito, please sit down and tell me what troubles you today. Did you not see the good reports from our attacks on the American bases?"

Seated next to Yamamoto was the chief of staff of the Combined Fleet, Vice Admiral Matome Ukagi. The man did not seem pleased about the interruption nor the implication that something was wrong. In 1941 Ukagi had agreed with his commanding officer about the problems and challenges of going to war with the Americans. After the initial successes, he quickly became resolute in his devotion to destroying the enemy. Kaya decided to start with a review of the reports.

"Admiral, the reports show a great amount of success with the attacks on the American positions in New Guinea. Today's bombing at Milne Bay appears to have been a success as well. However, we have no intelligence that these reports are accurate."

Ukagi exploded. "What do you mean, Lieutenant? Are you saying our brave pilots are lying about their great victories?"

The great admiral put up his hand to silence the chief of staff. Looking calmly at his intelligence officer, he asked, "What gives you the impression that our attacks are not successful?"

Short and to the point, just like Kaya expected. He had planned his reply for this situation, and kept the answer just as brief. "Sir, the numbers do not justify the success claimed. Our losses have been terrible. As each of the advanced bases on Bougainville, New Ireland, and Munda attest, we have lost between forty to fifty percent of our bombers and thirty percent of our fighters. Additionally, the returning planes are often damaged beyond repair. A walk down the flight line here at Rabaul will show you exactly what I mean. The losses of experienced air crews, especially our carrier pilots, are becoming untenable. We should stop using these resources immediately and return them to Truk."

The chief of staff was about to stand and hit the impertinent officer, even though he was a prince of the Imperial Household. Again, Yamamoto stopped him. As Admiral Ugaki sat back in his chair and fumed, the commander in chief exhaled. Looking up at the young man, who he both admired and respected, he said, "Kaya-san, show me what you have to support your analysis."

Pulling out his files and spreading them out in front of both admirals, he calmly went through the numbers. Each day's target was listed with the planes and crews assigned. Next was a column of the official damage report. Following this was Kaya's report on the number of returning planes and those damaged, along with a list of known losses, listing the squadrons, units, and personnel attached. The last item was the assessment from the prince's non-official sources. These included his interviews with flight crews, maintenance personnel, reports from American and Australian sources, and a correlation between what the Allies reported and what Japan reported. The discrepancies were apparent and glaring.

"Sir, if we consider the reports on our activities during the last nine months and then compare these to Allied claims, the enemy is increasing in strength and capability, and we are losing our best men and machines."

Even the chief of staff was impressed by the analysis. Admiral Ukagi began to wonder why his staff believed *every victory* report given by the pilots and ship captains. The losses being suffered could not be sustained, and the eagle-eyed lieutenant made all of this crystal clear. Yamamoto, knowing the quality of work the prince provided, agreed with the report. Yet, as the commanding officer of the Japanese Combined Fleet, he had to follow orders from Tokyo. Putting the information aside, he asked, "Kaya-san, this is good work, and I will study your conclusions. Based upon this information, should we pause our operation and reassess the situation?"

"Admiral, I think that would be wise. We need more intelligence about the enemy's capabilities and intentions. We need to increase our reconnaissance of enemy bases to understand the success of our operation and to pinpoint new targets."

"Sensible answer, Kaya-san. I will take this under advisement. I have decided to see our people in the field and ask them about their experiences. I know our remote operations could benefit by seeing me. What do you think?"

Akihito was shocked. "Admiral, please stay at Rabaul. I know the men would be honored by your appearance, but some of these bases are very close to American positions. Perhaps, we should send some of your staff instead?" Admiral Ugaki had already protested the idea, but the great admiral was adamant.

Yamamoto had already made up his mind. General Hitoshi Imamura, the Eighth Area Army commander, had also told him not to go because of the danger of American interlopers. "I have arranged a trip to some of the forward bases, and Admiral Ugaki will accompany me."

"Admiral, if you have to go, please take two planes. You and Admiral Ugaki should not be in the same plane just in case something happens."

"Kaya-san, the staff has made this recommendation already, but thank you for your suggestion. I will visit our bases in Rabaul first and then fly out, with a large escort of fighters, to the outlying bases. Do you want to come along?"

"Sir, it would be an honor to visit the men in the advanced bases."

Ugaki quickly interjected. "Admiral, I think it best if the lieutenant stays close to the intelligence people here at Rabaul. Something important might come up, and we may need his support here and not in some grass hut."

Yamamoto huffed a reply and then looked up at his intelligence expert. "Admiral Ugaki is correct. You will stay here and keep me updated on anything important about the enemy's movements. When I return, we will have a long conversation about your recommendations."

Knowing the audience was over, Akihito scooped up his papers then stood, bowed deeply, and left the room. The two admirals were discussing the intelligence report an hour later after consumption of several more drinks from Yamamoto's private selection of Scotch. The prince went back to his temporary office and found the information about the planned trip. As usual, it was efficient and detailed. Times, dates, locations, aircraft, pilots, everything was listed and communicated to the bases the admiral planned to visit. Kaya didn't like the idea of the admiral flying around so near the Americans. It appeared to him that the closest base to the American positions was probably out of range of any Allied aircraft, but it didn't matter. Admiral Yamamoto shouldn't be exposed to danger, but only the emperor could tell him no, and Akihito didn't have time to contact his cousin to make the request. Turning back to the newest reports, the lieutenant sat down and began reading about the success of Operation I.

41

18 April 1943
Office of Strategic Services Headquarters
Washington, D.C.

- Solomon Islands--Adm. Yamamoto is killed when P-38s from Guadalcanal shoot down a plane flying him from Rabaul to the Solomons for an inspection visit.

- Mediterranean--In Operation FLAX, Allied planes, conducting offensive to disrupt the flow of German air transports from Italy and Sicily since 5 April, destroy 50-70 of some 100 enemy transport planes and 16 escorts for loss of 6 P-40s and a Spitfire. Operation FLAX, while contributing materially to the success of Operation VULCAN--final ground offensive to clear Tunisia--had been planned originally for February, before VULCAN plans had been formulated. In preparation for VULCAN, other Allied planes intensify efforts against enemy airfields, beginning the night of 18-19.

The location was part of a complex of buildings in what was known as "Navy Hill." It was the former site of the old Naval Observatory dating to 1843. The old but stately building was not that much different from other buildings in the nation's capital, but the presence of guards gave the place an air of mystery. The man dressed in his naval uniform entered the building ten minutes before his appointment and was led down the hall to a large waiting room. Five other men in army uniforms waited. No one spoke. Every man gazed at the wall in front of them or read an old magazine from the pile on a nearby table. Occasionally, someone would glance at the others seated nearby. John Meyers enjoyed the setting, which reminded him of waiting to see the school principal for something he did wrong. He figured many of the men around him were waiting for job interviews because, based on his recent Lisbon experiences, they were not agents.

After fifteen more minutes and watching as one man was taken back to another room, a colonel entered. Every man, including Meyers, jumped to attention. Being the only navy man in the room, the colonel walked up to John and stuck out his hand, saying, "Lieutenant Meyers, my name is Goodwin. I'm proud to meet you."

The man had a broad southern accent and a row of ribbons that dated him to the First World War. Probably an old army buddy of Donovan's, but the man seemed genuinely happy to meet the logistics officer.

"Sir, pleasure to meet you as well."

"The general is looking forward to your report, as am I. You did a hell of a job for us, and I want to congratulate you on your success."

As the two men walked out of the room, the other officers began to sit down and stared at the colonel and the navy officer. Everyone wondered what the lieutenant had done to win such praise. They concluded the man must be fearless. Little did they know that John Meyers had been scared to death most of the time in Lisbon. After walking down a long hallway and across a small patio to another building, the two men entered a smokey conference room. Seated in the room were five other men—two in army uniforms, and three civilians in the employment of the OSS. Each man introduced himself to Meyers then offered John a cup of coffee and some pastry. Meyers had only been back in Washington for one day and was enjoying decent food. He had flown from Lisbon to Britain in a Coastal Command seaplane, spent two nights in Britain, and finally flew to America in a bomber, instead of the planned Boeing Clipper.

As the men watched Meyers devour a pastry, General Donovan walked in, along with Whitney Shepardson, the head of the Secret Intelligence Branch. Quickly standing, Myers attempted to lick the crumbs from his lips. "Well, Lieutenant Meyers, I guess we didn't do a good job of feeding you in Lisbon."

Quickly regaining his composure, John replied, "Sorry, sir, it was a long journey from Portugal, and this is the best food I have had since I left Lisbon."

"Sit down and keep eating. I guess you've met everyone except for Whitney, who runs the SI Branch."

Still unsure of what he should say or do, Meyers simply answered, "Yes sir, I have met everyone here except for this gentleman."

"Whitney Shepardson is my director for the Secret Intelligence Branch, the people charged with espionage and intelligence gathering activities. He's worked with me before in business and knows his way around the world quite well."

Not saying anything else about the man or his duties, the Director of the OSS continued his remarks. "Lieutenant, you did a hell of a job in Lisbon. So good that I asked Admiral King for you to be transferred to my command. He was not happy with my request, although I have been told that I can borrow you from time to time, but you are to stay with the Science Team."

Donovan glanced quickly at his notes then deferred to Shepardson. The cagey international lawyer and former secretary of the Council of Foreign Relations began asking questions about the situation in Lisbon.

"Lieutenant Meyers, I have reviewed the reports you filed from Lisbon along with other reports from our team in Portugal and wholeheartedly agree with General Donovan about the quality of work you performed. In particular, your intelligence on the German efforts to extract illicit wolfram will help us in our negotiations with the government of Salazar. The Azores intelligence is also helpful, but I want to narrow my focus to the German naval officer named Wagener. It appears he is leaning toward our way of thinking and apparently is being used as a conduit for information from other parties in Germany who wish us well. What do you think of this man? In particular, can he be trusted, and is he worth more investment?"

Sounding like the man was buying a railroad, which was also part of his previous business life, Meyers wondered about plans for Gebhardt. Was the OSS planning on leveraging the relationship for secrets or perhaps blackmailing him into more cooperation? Sensing the dilemma he was in, John responded cautiously.

"Sir, Wagener is to be trusted. I think he is conflicted by his religious beliefs, which counter what the Nazis preach. He talks of honor, and even though he was seriously wounded by British bombers, he appears to hold no long-term animosity. I'm unsure of his relationship with individuals higher up in the chain of the German command. Still, I sense he believes in a greater purpose, and evidently, so do others within this command arrangement. I cannot comment on the veracity of the information passed to you, but much of it appears to be valid."

Donovan nodded his head in agreement. Knowing the spot Meyers was now in and unable to add more factual information to the assembled men, the OSS director spoke. "Lieutenant, I can't go into our sources, but the information you passed meets our criteria. Murdoch has been given orders to go slowly on all contacts with the German officer, and we believe this relationship will be beneficial."

Meyers listened intently as Donovan provided more information on damaging the German ability to secure more wolfram. He didn't discuss the Azores airfields but knew the topic was to be discussed during the upcoming TRIDENT conference. Nothing was said about the man named Wilhelm, nor was anything offered concerning protecting Gebhardt Wagener. This concerned John greatly, but for the next three hours, he couldn't worry about it. The men around the table, led by Director Shepardson, pummeled the navy officer about everything he saw or did in Lisbon. They also asked about the men in the American consulate, relationships with the Portuguese government, especially the activities of the Portugal Secret Police known as the PVDE, and any contact he had with the British. Donovan was particularly interested in how, as he said, "our cousins" were behaving, specifically if they were sharing information.

After the meeting had ended, Shepardson escorted him to his office and asked about his experiences in North Africa. The Allies were closing in on the Germans, and the next step would be Sicily. The SI Branch director was looking for more men with credentials like Meyers. Intelligent, multi-cultural, and quick on their feet. Many men were being interviewed for the OSS. Still, this was America's first experience delving into the business of foreign intelligence with covert operators working around the globe, and no one fully understood what it took to build such an operation.

Donovan believed in finding people like Shepardson, who had great international business experience, which was fine for the top spots, but they needed young men and some young women with the skills to work in foreign lands. Not only language skills but also cultural awareness, all wrapped in courage and fortitude. Many applied, but few met muster. John Meyers had done it, at least fulfilling his role in Portugal. *What would happen if he were sent behind enemy lines?* The lawyer in him quickly told him to forget about it. But the patriotic young officer was interested.

Later that evening, Meyers spoke to Roger Stevens back at the Bethesda residence and confided in him his desire to do more work for the OSS. The logistics officer understood his friend's desire to face danger but told John he doubted Captain Jameson would release him for any mission behind enemy lines because he knew too much about the American war effort. John told Stevens that he would try to meet with Captain Jameson to discuss his situation and his feelings. Meeting with Jameson would have to wait because the captain and the rest of the team had returned late last night from Hawaii and had meetings planned with Admiral Edwards for most of the day.

Admiral Edwards had reviewed the report from the Science Team. The document covered the entire Pacific theater, with specific attention given to the planned invasion of Attu (Operation LANDCRAB) and the logistical needs for the planned Central Pacific offensive. To his credit, Captain Jameson had given the professor the central role in building the narrative, which included several pages of charts, spreadsheets, and lists of primary operational objectives. Each item had been blessed by Admiral Nimitz and his staff. The plans were a team effort and not just that of one man. The admiral smiled, knowing the whiz kid was growing into the job and no longer trying to do everything by himself.

As the admiral worked his way through the details on the Attu invasion, he recalled the request sent by Admiral Nimitz. The idea was solid, but Edwards knew the idea came from James Brand. King wanted the professor locked up, working exclusively on navy projects, but also needing the experiences from other members of the team wisely utilized, Edwards had voiced his approval to the CNO, who begrudgingly agreed. Knowing the team was waiting for an audience, the admiral picked up his phone and told his secretary to allow them to enter.

The Science Team, along with Commander Allen, entered the room in a perfectly ordered line. Captain Jameson was first, followed by Allen, then Major Flannigan, Lieutenant Commander Feldman, Lieutenant Brand, Lieutenant Clark, First Lieutenant Waverly, and Warrant Jones. Edwards knew Lieutenant Meyers was tied up briefing General Donovan, and would catch up with him later. As the men came to attention, he quickly ordered at ease, pointing the men to his conference table. There were just enough seats for the team officers and Edwards. Lieutenant Commander Tillman, already in the room, was directed to pull up a chair and sit alongside the admiral.

The admiral began by commending the team on their efforts in Hawaii. Edwards was glad to have the men back in Washington, "If," he said, "for no other reason but to be able to tell Admiral King the professor was in the building." Everyone laughed, aware of how much the CNO enjoyed Brand's insights. James failed to see the humor but went along with the group. After the bit of levity, the conversation turned serious.

"Gentlemen, Admiral King appreciates your efforts on behalf of CINCPAC and the men in the Pacific. Your contribution to the war effort has been well documented. I want to give you new orders which will cause some of you to have to depart soon for another mission."

The team had only returned the night before on a priority flight aboard an army C-54, which only required one refueling stop on the trip across the country from San Francisco. The men around the table were more than willing to do whatever was necessary, and if they had to leave again, so be it. The only man not wanting to go anywhere right now was James, who had a date with his fiancé tomorrow night. Since returning to Washington his only contact with Lady Margret was a brief phone call. James was having a hard time focusing on his job because of his emotions, or was it just lust? Whatever the case, the hormones were raging in the young professor, and things might get out of hand, playing into the desires of Lady Margret, who wanted to marry immediately. James wanted to have a private conversation with the captain about his feelings and what was the right thing to do—not what the good captain wanted. Jameson had enough on his plate with the team and a particular nurse in West Virginia. He also had a wife who didn't want to be married but refused a divorce.

Focusing on the conversation was challenging, but James managed to tune in to what the admiral was saying. "Operation LANDCRAB is only our third major amphibious landing in this war. This team has more experience in this kind of warfare than anyone in the country. Admiral Nimitz asked, and Admiral King agreed, to have members of this team serve as observers for the Attu invasion. Captain Jameson, you will be assigned to the staff of Admiral Rockwell, who is commanding the landing operation. Major Flannigan and Dr. Feldman will also assist you in these endeavors. Mr. Brand will stay in Washington to help prepare for the TRIDENT conference, which begins in early May. Any questions?"

Stunned by the announcement, Jameson quickly asked, "Admiral, when do we need to leave, and where exactly are we going?"

"Good question, Captain. You need to depart in two days. You will fly to Seattle and then on to Cold Bay, Alaska. There you will spend some time with Admiral Kinkaid, who will brief you on the overall strategy. After this meeting, you will join Admiral Rockwell's Task Force 51. The army is sending the new Seventh Infantry Division commanded by Major General Brown as the invasion force. General Marshall requested that Major Flannigan and Dr. Feldman be attached to the division. The invasion fleet sails from Cold Bay on May 3."

No one said a word as the admiral listed the ships in the task force and the support vessels for the invasion. Having seen most of the plans for the operation, the team understood the problems new men would face in their first encounter with the enemy. Feldman thought that at least the Imperial Navy wouldn't be a factor in the campaign. Before they departed from Pearl Harbor, Commander Layton had laid out the strategic situation for the Japanese navy in the north. After the battle near the Komandorski Islands last month, the enemy appeared to be in a state of confusion.

Intelligence showed that Admiral Hosogaya had been relieved of command of the Fifth Fleet and replaced by Vice Admiral Shiro Kawase.

They didn't possess many heavy cruisers, and their destroyer force was weak. The new IJN commander was given the task of reinforcing Attu, but he knew the Americans aggressively patrolled the seas between the Kuriles and the Aleutians. Until the new admiral could get more support, the Japanese navy could not help the men on Attu and Kiska. Feldman thought the naval part of the operation was well thought out but was concerned about the army. New men fighting a fanatical enemy was bad enough. But doing so in sub-zero weather on a treeless rocky island would test soldiers' physical strength and mental toughness. The doctor wondered if these soldiers were genuinely ready for what was to happen. Then again, he was not sure about his own readiness for another combat assignment.

The admiral provided more known details, based on their helping develop the plans at CINCPAC. A few minor changes were made, including adding the escort carrier *Nassau* to provide air support to the soldiers. Upon hearing this, the Royal Navy pilot's ears perked up. If there was an aircraft carrier going along on this invasion, he should get assigned to the mission. Clark would talk to Captain Jameson about this later, and there was a good chance he could be included. The only one who was lost in this conversation was Lieutenant Waverly. It appeared he would stay in Washington with Brand, bored to death while babysitting the professor. He decided to ask the captain about being assigned to the mission as well.

The meeting evolved into questions concerning the Central Pacific plans and the logistical needs for the operation. Incremental improvements were all that could be promised until later in the year. Ships were being commissioned, but new vessels needed to do shakedown cruises to find the bugs in the systems. Crews, most of which had never been on a ship in their lives, had to be trained, tested, and acclimated to life at sea. All of this took time, which the navy did not have. Realism was necessary, and the professor underscored the reality of building up forces for the offensive. Admiral Edwards agreed to the conclusions in the report and ended the meeting. But before anyone could leave the room, the admiral sent Commander Tillman on an errand, leaving the men to stand around sharing their experiences with the chief of staff.

A few minutes later, the door opened, and Tillman barked, "Attention on deck!"

As the door opened, in walked Admiral King accompanied by the wife of Commander Allen. The commander was shocked to see his wife, all dressed up in a conservative dark blue dress, with white gloves and wearing a smart hat. She looked radiant, and since he had been back from the Aleutians only a few days, he had not had much time to spend with his wife and children. King walked to the front of Admiral Edward's desk and turned around, still holding the arm of the commander's wife.

"At ease, gentlemen. I would like to introduce to you the wife of Commander Allen, Bonnie. She is here at my request to see her husband recognized for exemplary service to the nation."

Signaling Tillman, the lieutenant commander began reading from a piece of paper. "Attention to orders. On this eighteenth day of April 1943, Commander John Allen is awarded the Silver Star for distinguished service aboard the USS *Richmond* in action with enemy forces near the Aleutian Islands on March 26, 1943. Supporting the commander of the task force engaged with the enemy and providing accurate reports throughout the battle, he never left his post on the bridge even when he was exposed to constant enemy fire. Allen exemplifies the best of the service and traditions of the United States Navy."

Admiral King then pinned the medal on the commander. Stepping back to shake the man's hand, the CNO said, "Allen, Admiral McMorris reported that you were very important in saving Task Force 16. I have read his report on the engagement. Additional comments from the captain and other deck officers of the *Richmond* supported the commendation. You did a superb job in supporting McMorris, and both he and I are grateful. Well done, Commander."

Stunned by the award and not sure of what to say or do, Bonnie came to his aid. "Don't just stand there, John, say thank you to Admiral King."

Quickly recovering and not seeing the smiling officers standing behind him, he said, "Thank you, sir. I'm not deserving of this award, but I am humbled by it and the comments from Admiral McMorris."

"Well said, Commander. There is one more thing we need to do before we celebrate your award."

Upon a signal from the CNO, Edwards approached. "Commander Allen, I, for one, have appreciated your commitment to this office and the entire staff. But I know you want to go back to sea. Many new ships are being commissioned, but Admiral King doesn't want you on a new destroyer."

Allen's face could be read like a book. His wife was smiling, and the commander was confused. Quickly seeing the situation, Edwards continued. "Mr. Allen, we need officers with the experience to train new men and lead new ships into battle. But to do this, we need proven senior officers."

Looking over to Mrs. Allen, Edwards proceeded with his speech. "Commander, effective today, you are promoted to the rank of captain. You will be granted a two-week leave, and then you will proceed to San Diego to take command of a new destroyer squadron composed of eight ships. You will receive new orders from Admiral Tisdale, Commander, Destroyers Pacific Fleet upon your arrival. Congratulations, Captain Allen. Now, if your wife will assist me, I would like to pin these eagles on you."

As his wife pinned on one of the eagles, Admiral Edwards pinned on the other. Shaking the newly promoted officer's hand, Edwards backed away to allow his wife to give him a generous kiss as everyone in the room applauded followed by each man coming forward to shake his hand.

Taking a step away from the festivities, King pulled Brand aside and started a conversation about the upcoming TRIDENT conference. Things were moving quickly, and the CNO wanted James to take his work on the Central Pacific strategy and put it into context with the other plans coming from Admiral Cooke's department. Sensing the meeting was breaking up, King told James to come by his office at 1700 hours to review these ideas.

Walking over to Allen, King again congratulated the newly promoted captain. "Allen, now you will have to make even more decisions than you did here. Do a good job out there in the Pacific. I will follow your actions with great interest. Who knows, maybe I'll pull you back here in a few months to work on more staff projects."

Allen's smile immediately vanished until he noticed a slight grin on the admiral's face. The new captain quickly regained his footing, saying, "Admiral, I'll go anywhere and do anything necessary to help the war effort."

King moved closer to him and whispered, "Don't worry, Captain Allen, I'll let you have some fun chasing the enemy out in the Pacific for quite some time, but realize this, I need top officers in a host of new billets, so don't get too comfortable on your flagship."

Everyone came to attention as the CNO left the room. Then the men, along with Mrs. Allen, adjourned to a nearby conference room set up with refreshments and a big cake to celebrate the success of the newest captain in the United States Navy. Allen pulled James aside and thanked him for all of his support, especially in getting him the chance to join the North Pacific forces. He told Brand he would love to give him a ride in one of his new destroyers. James knew that might never be possible, but as his mother had told him countless times, never say never.

42

21 April 1943
Office of Admiral Edwards
Washington, D.C.

- Aleutian Islands--Adm. Kinkaid issues Operation Order I-43, providing an overall plan for the capture of Attu.
- Tunisia--18th Army Group completes preparations for main VULCAN assault. U.S. 34th Division, having trained vigorously in vicinity of Fondouk and Maktar, begins night marches, 21-22, to new zone in U.S. II Corps. British 8th Army concludes offensive operation in Tunisia. 10 Corps is so bitterly opposed at Takrouna that Gen. Montgomery decides late in day to confine the offensive to coastal region.

Being the chief of staff to the chief of Naval Operations was a twenty-four-hour-a-day responsibility. Having to always be ready to respond to a request or attend a meeting required Admiral Edwards to be, as he put it, flexible. This, in turn, made everyone on his staff act like they were made out of rubber. Twisting and turning in every possible direction was standard operating procedure for the staff at Main Navy. The upcoming conference was making the twists and turns even more pronounced. Still, Edwards needed to know everything else going on in the American military, not just the navy.

Going through the most essential reports on his desk, the top-secret message on the killing of Admiral Yamamoto was considered too hot to handle. Except for the successful army pilots and their commanders on Guadalcanal, few people in the high command were aware of the event. Less than a half-dozen knew about the intelligence that made the interception possible. Besides Admiral King and a few senior intelligence officers, only Edwards and James Brand knew what had happened. No announcements would be made now or in the future about the shootdown of the Japanese admiral. The army pilots were sworn to secrecy, and a press blackout was in full force about anything to do with any Japanese admiral. Until the enemy announced something, America would be silent.

The other topic of concern, besides the plans for the TRIDENT conference, was the impending release of Admiral Hepburn's report on Savo Island. The admiral provided a summary of the report to Edwards and King, but the full report would not be published until the middle of May. The report summary stressed how unprepared the navy was for war, especially with a highly trained opposing force skilled in nighttime attacks. Hepburn summed up his report by stating the failure at Savo was due primarily to surprise rather than negligence on the part of any officer. The enemy achieved this surprise due to an "inadequate condition of readiness on all ships to meet a sudden night attack," the "failure to recognize the implications of enemy planes in the vicinity previous to the attack," a "misplaced confidence in the capabilities of radar installations on the destroyers *Ralph Talbot* and *Blue*" and a "failure in communications which resulted in lack of timely receipt of vital enemy contact information."

The last item was most damning. Ships were sunk, and over a thousand men had perished because of poor communications. Commanders were taken by surprise, and whether through exhaustion from being at general quarters for most of the previous three days or sheer incompetence, there was no early warning given, nor was any signal sent once the enemy attacked. Reading the summary indicated that one man would probably bear the brunt of the criticism. Captain Howard D. Bode, the skipper of the heavy cruiser *Chicago*, failed to notify higher command or send out warning signals to the other Allied ships after his vessel was torpedoed. Hepburn determined that, unlike the soon-to-sink *Canberra*, *Chicago* was damaged but maintained headway, with all communication systems intact. Yet, no signal was sent to warn the other ships in the fleet the enemy was attacking.

As he read this summary, Edwards thought about Bode, a good man who knew his career was over when he was removed from command of his ship in December and sent to a shoreside billet in Panama. The officer saw himself as cursed because he had also commanded the battleship *Oklahoma*, which capsized at Pearl Harbor while he was ashore that Sunday morning. The admiral re-read the message, which reported that Captain Bode committed suicide last night, another victim of the tragedy of Savo Island. The admiral wondered how many more men would break during the war. Some would be relieved for lack of aggression or incompetence. Others would be sacked and demoted to some obscure posting until the end of the war and then quickly separated from the service. But many men would end their lives, either out of shame, stress, or fear. As Edwards pondered this twist of fate, Commander Tillman knocked on his door and entered the office.

"Sir, Admiral Cooke called and would like to speak with you whenever you have a moment."

"Does he have someone with him, or is he flying solo today?"

"Lieutenant Brand is with him as well as General Wedemeyer."

"Tell them to come over to the office now. I have a conference with BUPERS in another hour. Once they arrive, join us, I might need an alibi later," stated Edwards with a smile.

The aide left the room and phoned Cooke to come to the admiral's office. Within ten minutes Admiral Cooke, General Wedemeyer, and the professor walked in to begin a politically important discussion.

After the preliminary courtesies, Cooke began the discussion. "Admiral, the general and I, along with the professor, have been reviewing some of the preliminary ideas for TRIDENT. The British have already sent us some position papers concerning the war strategy for the remainder of the year and the first half of 1944. They align with the agreements reached at Casablanca, but I think more delays are coming concerning a full-scale European invasion. Mr. Brand, please tell Admiral Edwards about your meeting with Admiral Leahy this morning."

Edwards, not knowing about Brand meeting the president's chief of staff, was especially interested in the professor's comments.

"Admiral, I was called to Admiral Leahy's office early this morning and then, upon my return, went directly to Admiral Cooke's office, where he was in conference with General Wedemeyer. The admiral handed me recent communications from the prime minister and General Brooke. These were, as he said, 'Concepts for study.' In reviewing them, I agreed with the admiral about the direction we were being pulled."

Not knowing how political this was going to get, Edwards asked a question. "Mr. Brand, are our British cousins trying to drag us in a new direction or just asking for more delays?"

"Sir, it would appear to be both. First, the ideas being bandied about include driving more into the Mediterranean and on into Greece and the Dodecanese Islands. These subjects were discussed at Casablanca, but no firm decisions were made. It now appears the British want to go directly from the Sicily invasion to a full-scale invasion of Italy, plus an incursion further east to Greece. The ideas which are being outlined in their preliminary planning document include the establishment of forward bomber bases to attack the oil fields at Ploesti and moving up toward the Balkans. I believe General Wedemeyer has a comment on this plan."

Wedemeyer was a no-nonsense general who looked at global war strategy and not a series of set-piece diplomatic initiatives, which Churchill was so fond of. "Admiral, the professor is correct on our feelings. Airbases in the south of Italy would be all right with Hap Arnold, but going further east to Greece does nothing for the planned bomber campaign. The air force and RAF are in the same camp when looking at the strategic bombing campaign. They need masses of bombers to attack the industrial targets planned for the next year, and if the Allies march off to Greece, all it does is dilute the strength of the air force. Also, it would take another six to eight divisions to attack these targets, plus one or two infantry divisions to garrison them once they're occupied. The invasion of Europe needs a million men in Britain to start the cross channel attack, with another two or three million within the following twelve months. Any deviation from the center of effort by the Allies will diminish our ability to win quickly."

The chief of staff agreed wholeheartedly to the army general's words. If the Allies kept adding new objectives to their already stretched manpower, the war would linger for a year longer than planned, plus adding to the loss of life. "General, I agree with your view, and I can assure you that Admiral King concurs."

Cooke added his thoughts about the plans being formulated. "Admiral, I think we need to get in lockstep with the army and build a stronger plan than what we proposed at Casablanca. The conversation Brand had with Admiral Leahy gives us a starting point." Looking at Brand, Cooke said, "Mr. Brand, tell him about Leahy's ideas."

"Admiral Edwards, the gist of this is a comprehensive European strategy which is designed to be general in nature but allows us to keep extraneous objectives out of the conference. First, and I know Admiral King would agree, we must secure the lines of communications across the Atlantic. We need to eliminate the threat of German submarines, allowing the Allies to build up the forces for a cross channel invasion. Second, the Allies will invade the European continent in late Spring 1944. Third, we must conduct a vigorous air offensive against Nazi Germany to reduce its warfighting capability. Fourth, we proceed with the HUSKY operation and only selective ongoing operations to eliminate Italy from the war. Other operations will not be authorized which would diminish the effectiveness of the invasion of France."

Edwards mulled over what he heard, which was strategically sound but full of political risk. "What are the logical steps needed to make all of this happen?"

"Sir, securing the Atlantic lifeline and reducing the U-boat menace will require more effort in securing bases in the Azores as well as the continued buildup of our anti-submarine forces. We have made great progress in building destroyer escorts, and now several escort carriers are already at sea, making quite a difference. If we can secure bases in the Azores, we can close the air gap in the middle of the Atlantic. This will allow us to hasten the buildup of our forces in Britain. The other piece to the puzzle is expanding the bomber offensive, which was agreed to at Casablanca. Admiral Leahy outlined a six-part strategy for this as well."

Waiting for the next bit of information, Edwards glanced at Tillman, who took notes as rapidly as possible. Seeing the young aide was keeping up with the deluge of information coming from Brand, the admiral asked for the plan.

"Sir, the bomber offensive needs enough planes to make mass attacks. We currently plan for nine hundred forty-four heavy bombers and two hundred medium bombers to be in Great Britain by the end of June. This will expand to a total of twenty-seven hundred heavy bombers and eight hundred medium bombers by March 1944. General Arnold and the RAF expect a third of the bombers to be available for any single operation. This considers our losses, mechanical issues, and training of new crews in Britain prior to their first mission. The number of planes required to damage a target is based upon the assumption that it takes one hundred bombers to achieve success in what the air force calls target units, where these bombers will successfully hit and damage a target radius of one thousand feet from an altitude of twenty thousand feet."

Sensing something was troubling the lieutenant, Edwards asked, "Mr. Brand, I believe you gave us the air force numbers based upon what they plan to do. Am I correct?"

"Sir, the air force and RAF have made their calculations based upon perfect conditions, no antiaircraft fire, no enemy fighters, no high winds or frightened crews. Based upon what I have witnessed in the Pacific, it is more likely most bombs would fall within a mile or more of any target area."

General Wedemeyer had seen the successful claims by the bomber advocates but agreed with the professor. So far, it took a lot of bombs to hit one target, but if one hit a target of significance, perhaps the air force boys were correct. James disagreed, but could not disprove the theory until he could get on the ground with an assessment team. Moving on to the six-point air war plan, James summarized what Leahy had given him.

"The RAF and our air force people will be charged with an extensive campaign to hurt the enemy's war-making capability. The plan includes attacking submarine construction operations and bases. Next is destroying German aircraft production. This will be followed by eliminating the German ball-bearing industry, which amazingly is concentrated in just a few locations. Two of the target areas comprise seventy-six percent of all German production. The next item is the destruction of the German oil industry, staring at the Ploesti oil fields in Romania, which accounts for thirty-five percent of their output. Associated with this industry is the synthetic rubber industry, which requires oil as a feedstock. The final priority target is the military transport industry, including truck and tank factories. If these six major targets were successfully impaired and their output reduced by even thirty percentage points, our ability to win the war will be greatly enhanced."

The conversation went on for another thirty minutes with only a few thoughts on the Pacific campaign. The British didn't seem interested as long as India was safe from attack. At Casablanca, King had won his arguments, and now the British were letting the Yanks do as they saw fit.

The air plan seemed simple enough, but when Edwards took more time to think about it, it became evident the losses of men and machines would be heavy. Knowing the casualty count so far in the Pacific against a less concentrated enemy force, he wondered how many young men would die? Thousands or perhaps tens of thousands of the best and brightest would fly off into the frigid skies above Europe and never return. The thought of these losses sent a chill down his spine. As a submariner, he knew the danger of being in a steel tube hundreds of feet below the sea, with little hope of survival. Flying at twenty thousand feet in a paper-thin tube of aluminum might be worse. Some of the initial bombing runs over France had only a few losses, but with each new mission closer to Germany, the percentage of losses quickly rose to ten percent or more. Ten planes out of one hundred meant one hundred dead or hopefully captured men. Each of these men had been extensively trained at great expense, with the pilots, navigators, and bombardiers probably having over eighteen months of training. *War is an unforgiving mistress,* thought the admiral, *and she is about to claim a butcher's bill from this plan.*

Was it always wet in Seattle? The fog made things worse but waiting is what Marines do best. As the men of the Science Team waited an extra day for their flight north to Alaska, Jameson and Major Flannigan spent much of their time examining the latest plan for the invasion of Attu. Lieutenant Clark had nudged his way into the assignment by focusing on the need for an experienced aviator. He also expressed his desire to go along and help the pilots on board the escort carrier *Nassau*. The Royal Navy flyer was the only man in the operation who had been heavily engaged in combat in the far north. His 1940 experiences in Norway might be helpful, he told the captain, and his insights on flying in bad weather might help some poor pilot survive the battle.

Lieutenant Waverly was a last-minute addition. He was about to get on his knees to beg the captain to take him on the mission and was eventually rewarded when Lieutenant Meyers was required to support the TRIDENT conference. The logistics officer was the only experienced person in Washington who had actually spent time in Lisbon working with the Portuguese government. James told the captain to take Waverly along since he would be tied up working on the conference and didn't need a lot of security. Warrant Jones would be staying with him along with some of the Marine guards, plus he had the rest of Lieutenant Stevens' logistics team to help if needed.

Jameson would use Clark as his primary aide, along with the ever-resourceful Staff Sergeant McBride as security. Flannigan was accompanied by Sergeant Dean, and Waverly would be included in his activities. Dr. Feldman and Pharmacist Mate Hamlin stayed close to the major and hoped this operation wouldn't be like their last adventure in Tunisia. The captain also took Chief Schmidt to provide expert radio communications support needed onboard the task force's flagship, the battleship *Nevada*.

Nevada had survived the attack on Pearl Harbor and had undergone a major refit, which removed one of its topmasts and added additional antiaircraft weapons. The other two battleships slated for the operation were *Pennsylvania* and *Idaho*. The *Pennsylvania* had been seriously damaged as she sat in dry dock at Pearl Harbor. *Idaho* had been involved in the Neutrality Patrols in the Atlantic when the war broke out in the Pacific. It was soon transferred to California, where she conducted patrols up and down the coast.

As the men waited at the bar of a small hotel near downtown Seattle, a weary-looking Air Transport Command (ATC) pilot walked up to Captain Jameson and performed a semi-salute, the kind of casual army air force way of doing things, and introduced himself. "Captain Jameson, my name is Peoples, Charles Peoples, and I will be your pilot on your adventure to the cold climes of Alaska."

Jameson saw that the man was not one of the clear-eyed twenty-year-old pilots who were being added to the expanding ranks of the air force daily. This man was probably in his mid-thirties and looked like he knew what he was doing.

"Glad to meet you, Captain Peoples. This is my deputy, Major Flannigan."

Peering directly at Jameson, the pilot said, "Captain, you must have a hell of a priority or know the president well, cause I'm being pestered by ground control to get you up to Alaska as soon as possible. But that ain't going to happen today, and it may not tomorrow. The weather is bad here and worse up north."

Flannigan thought it prudent not to put his life in danger by making hasty decisions in flying a group of staff officers far to the arctic in lousy weather. "Captain Peoples, if you're not comfortable flying, we are ready to wait until you are. Sit down and tell us what you think."

Seeing the men having beers, he joined them at their table. "Captain, do you mind if I have a beer? I promise not to run off the runway unless there is a bear or a moose in the way."

Waverly heard the last comment, as did Dr. Feldman, who wondered where in the hell were they being sent. Only Clark thought the comment was appropriate and quickly introduced himself. "Flight Lieutenant Clark of the Royal Navy, Captain Peoples. Good to know some of you Yanks have had some bad weather experiences."

The ATC pilot replied, "Seems like you've done some bad weather flying yourself, Lieutenant. Was that in the sunny isles of England or perhaps further afield?"

"Several places in the far north, including Norway, where when you land on what some people might call an airstrip is often filled with reindeer. Bad to hit one of the big bastards on landing, wouldn't you agree?"

Smiling at the comment, Peoples began to enlighten the men. "You're going to be flying a lot over the next couple of days. My patched-up C-47 needs a lot of gas, and so we will have to make several stops along the way. We don't have a nice C-54 with lots of range and four shiny new engines. So we can't just jump across the Gulf of Alaska, but instead we will fly up the coastline to Anchorage with stops in Juneau or if we run into a lot of headwinds, Annette Island. Once we get to Elmendorf, we will head southwest and probably stop in Kodiak, then with luck, we'll find Fort Randall Airfield at Cold Bay. By my reckoning, this trip is a little over three thousand miles, and this old bucket of bolts with wings attached supposedly has a range of fourteen hundred miles, but I believe I can push it only eleven hundred miles and only with a small payload."

Dr. Feldman was doing the math and wasn't enjoying the story. Airfields in the far north were new and hastily constructed in the past year. If you flew off course, you would just fly until you ran out of fuel and crash somewhere in the frozen north or in the icy sea. "Captain Peoples, it sounds as if you have significant experience flying in Alaska. What did you do before the war?"

Taking a drink of his beer, which Waverly had secured, the ATC pilot gave the men at the table a short course in Alaskan aviation history. "Doctor, I started flying out of Sitka when I was sixteen. I finally got a license when I was nineteen or twenty after my third plane crash." Smiling, he continued. "Seems that when you land on water, and you don't have floats, the plane bounces really badly and sinks. But I've learned a lot since then, so you shouldn't have to worry much."

Seeing a captivated audience before him, Peoples gave them a brief outline of his experience. "I have a lot of hours in seaplanes, single-engine ski planes, and even more hours in multi-engine aircraft starting with an old Ford Trimotor back in 1934. I flew some of the old Boeing 247s for a while as well. Sweet little plane but starved for power in the higher mountains. Got my first ride in a DC-3 back in 1939, flying in Canada. The Canadians weren't as picky as the big American airlines and needed crazy people to fly their first routes across the Rockies, so I volunteered for a price. After the Germans invaded Poland, I was offered a full-time job teaching young pilot cadets how to fly. Worst job I ever had. I have never been so scared as I was sitting in the backseat of a biplane, watching some English kid who I could barely understand, bounce up and down on landing." Looking at Clark, he asked, "Were you part of the Commonwealth training plan in Canada, or did you get your wings in England?"

The Scot quickly replied, "No, Captain, I was taught by some dowdy Englishman who endured much of the same pain and displeasure as you did when I first tried to land in a Gypsy Moth."

Saluting the British pilot with his beer, Captain Peoples continued his saga. "After a full year of this, the Americans came north and offered me a job in the sunny climate of Arizona doing the same thing for less money. I decided to stay in the cold climate of Ontario, but in late 1941 I got a letter from one of my pilot friends asking if I wanted to stop training and do some real flying again. I jumped at the offer and ended up at the ATC. I know I would be a hell of a bomber pilot, but the colonel who interviewed me told me I was too old. Damn, I'm thirty-eight and know more about planes than most of these fools I work for. But the country needs pilots of all sorts, and at least they have me doing something I know how to do. I spend much of my time getting new pilots acclimated to flying in Alaskan conditions but sometimes that's not enough. I have attended a half-dozen funerals in the past year of young pilots who got lost, crashed in snowstorms, or ran out of fuel somewhere in the icy north or over the foggy sea. This is no place for a novice."

Jameson was well aware of how many operational casualties happened each day. New pilots with minimum experience were making mistakes that ended their lives. Often times it was not the pilot but the machine itself. Mechanical errors were daily occurrences, and James Brand pinpointed many of the problems about shoddy maintenance, bad fuel, and oxygen deprivation, which continued to take the lives of many men before they could face the enemy in combat. Captain Peoples knew the risks of flying in bad weather, and the captain was pleased to have an "old-timer" in charge of this flight.

Later that night, as Duncan Clark sat with Captain Peoples discussing flying in foggy conditions and landing on unimproved runways, the two Marine officers examined the battle plan for Attu. There were two separate landings, which they hoped would divide the enemy defenders. Only aerial observations were available, plus some sightings from submarines sent to scout the beaches. Not much was known on the enemy defenses, and with the foggy and cold conditions, anything was possible.

Reviewing the bombardment programs with Flannigan, Waverly spotted something of particular interest. "Major, it seems there is a plan to put men on the ground before the invasion."

"Bill, I saw something on it in the preliminary plan but wasn't sure if this was going to take place. What's the plan now?"

"Looks like a company of scouts will attempt a landing at 0300 on the day of the main invasion at a place called Beach Scarlett. A follow-up company of scouts will land later in the morning, and the combined unit will move to Holtz Bay, where a battalion will land later. The other major beach area is Massacre Bay, which will see the largest number of men deployed. Not too sure why the place is called Massacre Bay, but I don't like the sound of it. The Holtz Bay landings will focus on capturing the unfinished airfield nearby. I guess the southern force will then meet up with the northern forces at Holtz Bay and squeeze the Japs toward something called Chichagof Harbor."

The major looked at the island map and saw the different beaches charted in front of him and the total lack of civilization. There were no towns or villages, and locations of Japanese defenders were pure conjecture. The United States was going to take back one of its own islands and knew very little about the place. Sensing the lieutenant wanted something to do, which was also probably dangerous, Flannigan asked, "What do you want to do on Attu besides bask in the sunlight?"

Knowing the Marine major always looked out for his men, he replied. "Sir, I would like to land with the scouts. Sounds like something a Marine Raider would do, and maybe I could be of some help to these people. I doubt any of them have seen a Jap let alone had one shoot at them."

"Let me check with the captain first, but if that's what you want to do, I think it can be arranged. If you recall from your training, you will launch a small rubber boat from a large steel tube called a submarine, probably in the fog and pointed in the wrong direction. But if that's what you want, I'll check on it."

"Thank you, Major. This sounds like something right up my alley, and it might help those guys hitting the beach."

Flannigan would approach Captain Jameson with the idea, and it would be approved. Now, all that was needed was the approval of Admiral Kinkaid and to hitch a ride on the submarines *Narwhal* or *Nautilus* to the frigid beaches of the Aleutian island named Attu.

43

4 May 1943
Task Force 51
Cold Harbor, Alaskan Territory

- Aleutian Islands--Attu invasion convoy leaves Cold Harbor for target, a day behind schedule because of poor weather conditions. D-Day is consequently postponed to 8 May. As the convoy later approaches Attu, strong winds force a further postponement to 11 May.
- Burma--Continuing infiltration tactics, Japanese are now established on Buthidaung-Maungdaw road and resisting efforts of British Imperial forces to oust them.
- Tunisia--U.S. II Corps pushes forward in preparation for full-scale drive on Bizerte on 6 May.

Cold, dreary, foggy, miserable—words that represented the worst of war in the Aleutians. The ships of the invasion task force raised anchors and proceeded slowly through the mist and out of the large harbor. Thirty-four ships, including the three old battleships, slowly moved into the icy cold waters of the Bering Sea, heading west to Attu, the last island in the Aleutians. Captain Jameson, accompanied by Duncan Clark and Sergeant Mc-Bride, stood on the bridge of the flagship. The old ship looked good, not at all like the damaged old World War I dreadnought from the attack on Pearl Harbor. The ship had been modernized with new antiaircraft cannons, radar systems, new fire control systems, and updated crew accommodations. The crew had been extensively trained and were itching for a battle with the enemy. Similar conditions existed on every other ship heading toward the small island occupied by the enemy.

In overall command of Task Force 51 and the invasion forces, Admiral Rockwell was happy to see Jameson, who he knew as a student at Annapolis in 1921. The admiral was totally amazed when he saw Major Flannigan two days ago at the last planning meeting before leaving the anchorage. Rockwell had been the commander of the Sixteenth Naval District in the Philippines when the Japanese attacked. His office was at the Cavite Naval Base and was there on December 10, 1941, when the Japanese bombed the facility. The admiral had met Flannigan on several previous occasions when the Marine was serving as an aide to Admiral Hart. Rockwell had personally recommended Flannigan for the Navy Cross for his bravery and devotion to duty during the bombing. He also had visited the seriously wounded Marine in the hospital and helped arrange his evacuation to Java. But this was the first time the two men had seen each other since those dark days on Manila Bay.

Admiral Rockwell told Captain Jameson about that terrible day and the death and destruction. As he recalled the events of the day, Jameson saw how the story affected Flannigan. None of the Science Team, of course, had witnessed the man's bravery or knew exactly what had occurred on that tragic day. The major began reliving the carnage and held onto his hand. His senses heightened to the point of experiencing the burns and pain inflicted on his body that fateful day back in the Philippines.

Feldman quickly came to his aid by asking the admiral a question. "Admiral, how long were you in the Philippines before you were evacuated?"

"I went out with General MacArthur on the PT boats. I think that was March 11, 1942, and then we made our way to Mindanao. From there, we were able to get on a couple of worn-out B-17s and flew to Darwin on March 17. I have regretted the decision ever since. I should have stayed with the men on Corregidor."

Flannigan quickly intervened. "Admiral, there was nothing you could do for the men in the Philippines. Your best course of action was to get back to where you could fight another day. You're making a difference in the war, and in the next few days and weeks, you'll see what that means to the men of this command."

Jameson thought the impromptu speech was well said. "Admiral, the major is correct. It would do no good for you and other senior officers to become prisoners of the Japanese. Your evacuation, along with General MacArthur, serves a higher purpose and has already aided the war effort."

Rockwell appreciated the comments, especially from the wounded Marine. Extending his hand once more, the admiral said, "Flannigan, I look forward to serving with you in this battle and in future operations."

The two men held the handshake for what seemed to be a long time. For the two men who had survived the debacle of the Philippines, it was a homecoming of two warriors. But the war left little time for thinking about past events. The invasion force was aboard their transports, and the supplies were loaded. Major Flannigan, Lieutenant Waverly, and Sergeant Dean were now embedded with units of the army's Seventh Division and were coming to grips with the problems in the assault force.

But like most things in the army, plans go to hell when the need is great. The men of the Seventh Infantry Division had trained for many months, mastering the techniques of desert warfare. Being one of the few trained divisions on the West Coast, the army selected the division to be the force to invade Attu. With no previous amphibious instruction, the men were rapidly trained in March and early April near Camp Pendleton in Southern California. Marine Major General Holland "Howlin Mad" Smith, commanding general Amphibious Corps, Pacific Fleet, was put in charge and worked with the division's commanders to master the art of landing on an enemy-controlled beach.

The problem with the training was the men were not told where they were going. Most believed they were heading to Guadalcanal or some other tropical island. To keep the invasion location a secret, the medical team provided lectures on dealing with tropical diseases and mosquito control instead of preparing the men for frostbite and hypothermia. There was little thought about the actual conditions, including rocky and boulder-strewn beaches, no roads, towering mountains, and the below-freezing temperatures the men would face in the Aleutians.

Neither was the provision of proper cold-weather clothing, special boots for dealing with the Alaskan tundra, or for that matter, long underwear. Only once the men were at sea were they told their destination, and then the few items of cold-weather clothing that had been scraped together were passed out to the soldiers.

The only well-equipped unit was the Provisional Scout Battalion under the command of Captain William H. Willoughby. He had been informed early about the destination and headed a separate unit to conduct a risky operation before the main invasion. Knowing this, the enterprising officer found enough heavy clothing and special waterproof boots for his men. The next thing he had to do was plan a landing from submarines. This is where Lieutenant Waverly came to the rescue. Being a Marine Raider, the lieutenant had trained on rubber boat landings from submarines and all of the inherent risks of landing a fragile boat on a rocky coastline.

The moment the two officers met, there was a joining of minds. Both warriors were ready to do their duty. The men bonded and quickly made changes to the battle plan. The two large navy submarines, *Narwhal* and *Nautilus,* were to be supported by a navy destroyer carrying additional men, who would land later in the day at Austin Cove, the location of Beach Scarlett. Once ashore, the initial group of two hundred forty-four men would move up the mountain passes towering over four thousand feet and join up with the north force, landing later in the day at Holtz Bay. Eventually, these units would meet up with the southern force landing at Massacre Bay and push the enemy into the area around Chichagof Harbor. Once these forces joined together, the enemy would be pushed back into the sea and destroyed.

As Waverly looked at the final plan aboard the *Narwhal,* he asked the army captain a question. "Captain, what supplies are you taking ashore?"

The army officer laid out his plan to take minimal supplies, except for ammunition, relying on the other army units to have adequate supplies for his men. It sounded good, but the combat Marine provided a sense of reality to the plan.

"Captain, this sounds good, and having more ammunition than anything else is the right way to go. Yet, I wonder if you had thought about the terrain and possible enemy reaction to our wandering ashore in the dark?"

410

Captain Willoughby smiled at the comment and replied, "So, Bill, what's wrong with the plan?"

"I think the plan is good, but it doesn't take into consideration the probability that things will get screwed up. Start with the submarine and the rubber boats. Swamping a few of them is a definite possibility. How many supplies will be lost when this happens? What about the beach? If one or two boats get smashed up on the beach or out in the surf, what does this do to our supply situation? And one last thing, it's damn cold outside. How will this affect the men? I have been in the opposite climate, and when it was a hundred degrees outside with the same level of humidity, most men could only do half the work they could do otherwise, and with each day, the men lost more of their strength."

"Good point, Bill, but if we tried to take more, the men couldn't handle it all. Any ideas?"

"Start with the reserve units coming in later in the morning. If they are using landing craft, then pack them to the gunnels with supplies. Use the beach as a resupply point and think of every other man spending time as a pack mule. If we run into the Japs, all bets are off. If it's only a small group, squad size, or only a two-man patrol, they will try to pin us down and keep moving to stop us from finding them. All the time, they will get a message back to their commanders and call in support. When we run into the enemy, we must push right through them. Casualties may be hard to take, but if we let them take command of high ground or slow us down while we bring up support, we'll lose even more men, and the plan goes to hell."

The captain thought about these ideas, and knowing the Marine had combat experience and he did not, helped him make his decisions. Telling Waverly he would make some changes to the initial landing and the follow-up forces, he asked, "The skipper of the submarine tells me he doesn't have all day to let me set up my boats and then load. Any ideas to speed this up?"

"One of the things we tried was to inflate the boats quickly on deck and then get all of the supplies in the boat and then the men. This saved us the time and trouble of getting the boat in the water, dropping supplies over the side, and then loading the men. Once we were loaded, the signal was given, and the submarine slowly submerged until the deck was awash, and we floated free. I think it will make the sub captain happy."

411

"Great idea! I know the navy will appreciate us getting off their boat, and if we can load quicker and safer on deck, so much the better."

The two men wrote up the idea, added more information to their plan, and then met with the two submarine captains who agreed to the idea. The two large submarines, the only two of their kind in the navy, weren't as fast in submerging as the smaller *Gato* class boats, so the less time on the surface, the better for the submarines. Later in the day, the support company landing from the destroyer was given a shopping list of items to bring ashore as well as their final instructions. The submarines would sail a day earlier than the Task Force to get on station first and try to observe the enemy on land. A good idea, but fog and sea conditions made this impossible. Everyone aboard the submarines wondered if the seas would calm enough for them to land.

There was only one major combat unit in Alaska, the Fourth Infantry Regiment, that had trained for the battle in extreme conditions, but these men were placed in reserve for some reason. The other men of the Science Team had joined up with the Seventeenth Infantry Regiment under the command of Colonel Edward P. Earle. His regiment and supporting units would land at the southern part of Attu at the aptly named Massacre Bay. Flannigan and Dr. Feldman had several meetings with the colonel and his staff before embarking on the transports. Alaskan Scouts, many of them native Aleuts, knew the island and would be in the first wave. The Scouts were well prepared for battle and dressed accordingly.

Flannigan and Sergeant Dean would land with Colonel Earle, while Dr. Feldman and Pharmacist Mate Hamlin would come ashore with the field hospital on day two. The night before the ships left for the invasion, Flannigan and Feldman finished off Doc's Scotch and discussed the situation. Neither man was impressed with what they saw.

"Doc, the army thinks they will walk ashore, and the Japanese will bow down to them or run away." The major held his glass close to the table, swirling the golden liquid. His eyes echoing his fear for others. "These green recruits are unaware of what they're walking into, and, what's worse, a lot of the officers aren't much better prepared than their men."

The navy doctor agreed. "Robert, from what I've seen in the medical ranks, doctors are just now becoming aware of the probability of a large number of exposure cases. Combat wounds are one thing, but the men are not equipped with the proper cold-weather clothing, and their boots will get wet and freeze on the first day. I told Hamlin to find every pair of socks he can and stuff them in a big bag. They will be worth more than gold or good booze once we're ashore."

Mulling over the problem of clothing, Flannigan relayed what he had heard from the regimental staff. "Seems requests for cold-weather gear went out in February, but everything was on the east coast or over in Britain. There was no time to make additional coats or find the correct type of waterproof boots. The colonel is hopping mad and has the same concerns as you about exposure cases. How long does it take for a man's feet to freeze and lose mobility?"

Taking a slow sip of the warming whiskey, Feldman gave his friend the short answer. "It all depends on the core body temperature. Once the body drops below ninety-five degrees, things start happening. A man may become incoherent or delusional. Clumsy movements follow and often people become drowsy. If a man falls asleep in temperatures below freezing, he may never wake up."

He stared at the Scotch in his hand. "If you don't fall asleep and die, you will start having exposure problems such as frostbite. Initially, there is a burning sensation but no damage to the tissues." Feldman set down his glass. "If this continues, then second-degree sets in which blisters the skin. Third-degree occurs when all the top and middle layers of skin freeze. Then you have permanent damage, and things fall off, like toes, ears, and especially noses. Gangrene is often found in these cases because of the dead tissue. I have treated men who had fallen asleep drunk in the streets of New York and had their feet freeze to the extent that the only way to save them was to amputate the foot."

The comrades in arms sipped their Scotch, and then the Marine major said, "I talked to one of the men from the Alaskan Scouts who explained the Aleuts wear layers of Caribou and seal skin instead of socks, so they don't get moisture in their boots. Sounds like we're going to lose a lot of men to something besides the enemy."

The doctor added, "I think the Japanese will kill many of our men, but we could lose the same number from the cold. I hope we have enough stretchers."

The meeting with Admiral Leahy was scheduled for 0900, but when James arrived early, he was ushered into the White House without additional ceremony. James was accompanied by Lieutenant Meyers, Lieutenant Stevens, and Warrant Jones. Meyers and Stevens were nervous about meeting with the chief of staff to the president but were ready for questions the admiral might ask. James, on the other hand, was not concerned about anything. His numerous projects did not allow time for worry. Once the men were in the admiral's outer office, Gunny excused himself and told the officers he would wait near the kitchen and closer to the White House coffee and excellent pastries. All three men envied the old Marine, realizing their duty didn't link well with their appetites.

Once they entered Leahy's office, the men understood why they were brought in so quickly. Seated at the conference table was General Marshall, who stood to welcome the three junior officers. The men all stood at attention in the presence of the two senior officers and were quickly put at ease.

"Lieutenant Brand, good to see you again. Lieutenant Meyers, I hope you enjoyed your time in Portugal. I have also received glowing reports on your organization's work, Lieutenant Stevens, and their ability to make sense of all the conflicting reports on materials and construction contracts. The information gathered is of vital importance to the army, and we look forward to more of your support in the future."

Hearing the general's remarks, Stevens had never been so proud of what he and his small team accomplished in their little office piled with obscure reports and conflicting priorities. "Thank you, General. The team works very hard to make sense of the current logistical situation."

The admiral quickly took command of the meeting. "Gentlemen, the general and I, in concert with General Arnold and Admiral King, are working on the final recommendations to be presented at the upcoming conference. Your work has helped us immensely to focus on the priorities needed to create the war strategy. Lieutenant Brand has worked ceaselessly with the operations planning personnel of the army and navy to build a cohesive and unified plan to present to our British Allies. We realize our previous efforts in building operational and strategic plans were deficient. The president and the Chiefs of Staff of the armed forces will deliver a package of plans which will be well presented and backed up by hard facts, all linked to the current war situation."

The admiral told the men to sit down and immediately began asking questions. "Lieutenant Brand, I read your recommendations for the Central Pacific offensive. Since you returned from Hawaii, have you made any updates?"

"Sir, we are revising it in conjunction with Admiral Cooke and General Wedemeyer. The most significant change is in the timetable. Everything depends on shipping. The new carriers and other warships should be available for the planned October timeframe. The transports, cargo, and landing ships are the problem. As I pointed out in my memo of 5 April, the Sicilian invasion, HUSKY, will reduce the number of ships for the Gilbert landings. But suppose there are any delays in the Mediterranean operation. If that occurs, the effect will cascade downward to everything going on in the Pacific, including General MacArthur's operations along the New Guinea coast."

Marshall listened carefully to the professor then asked a hypothetical question. "Lieutenant, let's say the Sicily invasion went off on schedule, say middle of July. If there was a plan to do an immediate jump to southern Italy, would this have the same effect on Pacific operations?"

Not taking the time to even blink, James replied, "General, if we move toward Italy, the British will have to do most of the heavy lifting, and their transport situation is already under duress. They have expressed plans to make major advances on Burma, including an amphibious landing. If an Italian campaign of any significance—say four to six divisions—happens, the Pacific and Burma operations will have to be delayed or reduced in terms of objectives."

Thinking a bit more on the subject, James added, "If we went into Italy and ran into major resistance from the Germans, then we would have to reduce our tonnage available for the Pacific and for any offensive in northern France."

Marshall looked at Leahy, and neither said a word. The Science Team officers sat quiet and waited for someone to speak. Marshall asked, "If this situation were to occur, can you provide us estimates for shipping and landing craft which could be made available by July, October, and the end of the year?"

Stevens glanced at James and decided it was in his best interest to jump into the conversation, if for no other reason but to put a stake in the ground on what was possible. "General, these estimates are available now. The question becomes one of where these vessels will be deployed. If, for example, we need to get a dozen new LSTs to the Mediterranean by 1 October, then we have to take into consideration the entire supply and support situation happening in the continental United States and then move these calculations out to the location desired. As Lieutenant Brand stated, these numbers are available. We just need to get closure on where these resources are needed."

The admiral weighed in with guiding principles for the analysis. "Gentlemen, the professor has examined most of the long-range plans for the war, and if this team can use this as a guide, then let's proceed with what is currently planned. I would also recommend at least one backup plan based upon what we think our Allies may recommend. This way, we can quickly counter any abrupt changes in direction. The president wants to develop a consensus and closure in our upcoming meeting on the war strategy."

The men discussed the strategic assessments and how these things were to be handled. Leahy also had some pointed questions for Lieutenant Meyers about the ongoing debate concerning the Portuguese government. Everyone was pushing to establish bases in the Azores, whether from diplomacy or invasion. The lieutenant explained the situation in Lisbon and how the current government was still afraid of a Nazi invasion if they allowed the British access to the islands. Contingency plans were being made, including allocating several divisions to land near Lisbon to counter a German incursion. The diplomats from both Allied nations wanted more time to negotiate some sort of deal before resorting to force. General Marshall agreed because many of the men required to defend Portugal would be American, and right now, the army didn't have any spare divisions.

The meeting ended at 1100 hours with General Marshall asking James for an update on the Pacific strategy whenever it became available. Admiral Leahy asked James to stay for another discussion. Stevens and Meyers left to find Gunny and to see if the White House kitchen had any pastries left. The admiral, with Brand in tow, walked to the president's study for a short meeting. When the men arrived, the Secret Service agent opened the door, and the two men entered to find Roosevelt talking to an elegant Chinese woman.

"The admiral knows Lady Chiang, but professor, I don't think you've met the First Lady of China, Madame Chiang Kai-shek. Madame Chiang, this is the young man I told you about last night. Lieutenant James Brand is not only a heroic naval officer and pilot but also a professor of physics at Columbia."

"Madame Chiang, it is an honor to meet you."

"Professor Brand, the pleasure is all mine. The president has told me about his secret weapons, but he is reticent when speaking about you. Tell me, what do you think of the war in China?"

James' diplomacy skills were improving. Brand had heard many stories about the Chinese First Lady, who many saw as the real power in China. Knowing not to say anything which could be considered ill-advised, Brand replied, "Madame Chiang, China is fighting a total war with the enemy, and through its perseverance and dedication, China will emerge from this war a great power."

Smiling as she was oft to do, she replied, "Well said, Professor. Perfect political answer. You will go far in America, and I would welcome you to come to China and help us after the war is over. A man of your talents could do much to help lift our nation out of its backwardness."

"Now, Madame Chiang, don't think for one minute that I'm going to send the professor over to you and let him become your top science advisor. I need him here for the rest of the war and probably for some time after that."

The lady smiled again, and excused herself from the room. As she passed by the tall lieutenant, she whispered, "Please come to China soon. I could show you much of the great treasures of Asia, perhaps more."

When the door closed, Roosevelt was grinning, Admiral Leahy was frowning, and James was confused. Seeing the man's dilemma, the president provided some explanation. "James, the dragon lady is here on official business. She's staying at the White House and will have dinner with Eleanor and me tonight. Don't worry, I'm not sending you anywhere near China. The generalissimo would flatter you to death and steal every secret you possess. God knows what Madame Chiang would do to you, but I can only imagine."

As the president continued his grin, the admiral came to the rescue. "Mr. President, I know you have a meeting at 11:30, so if you allow me and the lieutenant to brief you on the Central Pacific plan and some of our suggestions for the TRIDENT conference, you'll be on time."

Turning serious, Roosevelt got down to business. He listened to an abridged version of the Pacific plan and other major initiatives to be put forward at the conference. The president was attentive and asked numerous questions about the Pacific campaign and then asked for several position papers for the conference. James informed him of Britain's numerous suggestions and their attempts to drive their agenda in the Mediterranean. Noting the different viewpoints between the Allies, the president wanted his top advisors to agree on what the American position would be in every major theater. He also wanted a few areas of negotiations to use as bargaining chips to keep Churchill happy, without changing critical strategies for a European invasion in 1944 and moving forward with the Central Pacific strategy.

Leahy and Brand left the president on time and returned to the admiral's office. They spent the next two hours working through the planned agenda for TRIDENT, determining where the British would push their agenda and how the Americans could build counter offers. Both men knew they couldn't win every battle at the conference table, but James believed the United States had learned the lessons from Casablanca and now had a sound strategy and battle plan to win the war.

44

11 May 1943
Attu Island, Territory of Alaska

- Aleutian Islands--U.S. 7th Division lands at widely separated points on Attu. Dense fog limits naval gunfire and air support but helps infantry achieve complete tactical surprise. Gen. Brown, 7th Division Commanding General, arrives on Massacre Bay beach and orders assault on Jarmin Pass for 12 May. The mud of Attu immobilizes trucks and tractors.
- CBI--Monsoon brings work on Ledo Road to a halt about 47 miles from Ledo.
- Tunisia--In British 1st Army's 9 Corps area, an uneventful sweep around Cap Bon Peninsula by 4th Division reveals that no important enemy forces are there.

The landing didn't start well. The men had a hard time getting their supplies up from the submarine and into the rubber boats. The sub captain became nervous about the situation in the pitch black night with low fog hanging above the frigid waters. Captain Willoughby knew he had to get the men ashore in darkness and stopped worrying about loading all the supplies. They had their ammunition and enough rations for a day of battle, so he signaled the captain to slowly submerge until the boats floated free. The men then paddled madly toward the coastline and Beach Scarlett, finally running aground at 0300 hours. The original date for the attack was May 7, but high seas, extreme winds and pea soup fog delayed the assault until May 11.

The weather was so bad two ships collided and had to return to base—one of them, *Sicard*, was to be the control ship for the landings. The crew had been trained to exact detail on the plans and the beaches and bays of the island. Now, these experts were heading to Adak. The rest of the Task Force had split with one group of ships near Holtz Bay on the north and the more significant force at Massacre Bay in the south. These men would land later in the morning, while the Scouts worked their way up from the beach and climbed the mountains above Austin Cove.

Waverly was in the second boat, behind the unit's commanding officer. He accompanied twelve men, armed with M-1 rifles and carrying an extra load of ammunition and hand grenades. As the boat touched the rocky beach and everyone scurried for the snow line, which was only a few feet from the beach, the Marine caught his breath from the exertion of rowing the boat ashore. The winds were calm, but the temperature was a chilly twenty-seven degrees Fahrenheit. His first steps in the snow quickly dispelled his hopes about making a quick dash up the ravine. Sinking halfway to his knees, Waverly knew this would be a tortuous journey.

Seeing Captain Willoughby nearby, the lieutenant moved toward him for orders on their next move. "Captain, good landing. Seems we didn't lose anybody on the boats."

"Damn lucky. We need to move up this ravine and try to get as high as possible before sunrise. Any ideas on where the Japs are?"

"No sir. I don't think they anticipated we would come ashore here. We might run into some of them along the ridge line. If I was the enemy commander, I would have small patrols moving across the high points looking out for ships and enemy landings."

The army officer checked his map then pointed at where they were and how he wanted to move. "Tell the other platoon leaders to follow me up. Also send some men along each flank to watch for the Japanese."

Waverly repeated the order, just like he had been taught as a Marine sergeant many years ago, and went back down the hill to help direct each platoon heading up the ravine. After he made sure the men were spread out, he clambered back up the hill so he could keep an eye on the captain. As he reached the superior officer, the sun began shining on the north side of Attu burning through the fog. For at least a few minutes, portions of blue sky were visible. The snow was blinding and the wind was picking up. As they climbed further up the ravine, the temperature fell below twenty degrees and felt even colder. Their destination was the top of the mountains overlooking Holtz Bay. There were no paths leading to their destination four thousand feet above the shoreline. The only thing in front of them was cold and snow and perhaps a hidden enemy.

The largest of the landing forces was in the south at Massacre Bay. Delays messed up meticulously planned timetables. The navy had fired at suspected enemy positions, and a few planes had flown from the aircraft carrier and dropped bombs and strafed positions further away from the two landing beaches. The landings had been set for 0740, but fog forced postponements, first to 1040 and then into the afternoon. Finally, Admiral Rockwell agreed with General Brown to land the troops. But it was nearly 1530 before boats moved toward the shoreline, with the first touching the beach at 1620. The only good news was the enemy didn't oppose the landing.

Even though the enemy failed to fight the Americans on the beach, there were sufficient casualties. Several boats capsized or ran aground on the rocks spilling their passengers into the freezing waters, with most of these men disappearing beneath the waves, carried to their deaths by heavy packs. The survivors moved quickly off the beach to secure their initial objectives. One unit occupied "Artillery Hill," which had a pair of Japanese 20mm antiaircraft cannons mounted in large holes, surrounded by boulders. The crews of these weapons had fled when the American battleships opened fire. The guns were well stocked with ammunition, a bad omen for the campaign ahead.

Major Flannigan and Sergeant Dean came ashore with the second wave and promptly attached themselves to an infantry company moving toward the hills on the north side of Massacre Valley. As they prepared to move out, the major watched as the first artillery pieces came ashore, including the 105mm howitzers pulled by tractors instead of trucks. The army knew trucks would quickly sink in the muskeg of the island. So they used tracked vehicles, pulling the guns on large sleds, which in theory would better distribute the weight of the five thousand pound weapon. As the two Marines watched, the tractors progressed about seventy-five feet off the rocky beach before they sank into the bog of Attu. One after another, the tractors sank deeper into the island. Several of the sleds also succumbed to the boggy conditions. Quickly artillery support of the invasion came into question. The artillerymen used brute strength to manhandle the weapons back to solid ground near the beach, where they set up four cannons and awaited orders. They could go no further.

Flannigan had met with some of the officers of the experienced Fourth Regiment while he was in Cold Bay, and had heard about the army's decision to bring in the 105s. They had urged the assault force to land with the smaller pack 75mm howitzers, which were much lighter at fifteen hundred pounds and designed for mountain warfare. Their comments were ignored, and now the men of the Seventh Division would pay the price for command stupidity. Until the engineers could build some sort of corduroy roads, nothing with wheels would move on the island. Even then, it was a question of where the engineers would come up with the lumber or steel plating to solve the problem.

The two Marines said nothing more about the artillery situation but calmly walked away to join the company now moving forward to occupy the high ground around the valley. So far, there was no sign of the enemy, except for the unoccupied antiaircraft weapons. As the men moved forward, they ran into the ground commander, Colonel Earle, who directed his men to occupy various pieces of terrain which could afford the artillery observers better fields of vision. Finally, at 1800 hours, as the fog became worse and men started to lose their bearing, the first artillery observers spotted the enemy and called in a fire support mission to the four howitzers. The guns promptly replied, ending the quiet of the island.

The soldiers of Baker Company were glad to have the two experienced Marines along for the landing and now listened to any suggestions the men made about their situation. Officers asked the major about setting out observation posts and dispersing the men for an enemy counterattack. Platoon sergeants had Dean inspect their positions and offer suggestions on keeping the men safe. The soldiers were doing well, and Flannigan told the company commander, Captain Hodges, that his men were well deployed, dug in, and adequately spaced out. By not having large clusters of men, enemy mortars might not attack these smaller positions. Flannigan's only concern was the forward observation posts. The enemy would crawl around looking for two-man positions and use their bayonets or grenades to kill them. He also warned the captain about the problems of frostbite and to make sure his men kept their feet as dry as possible, which was more of a problem than anyone had surmised. As the cold fog enveloped the area, the temperature hovered at twenty degrees and men were already experiencing the pain of being exposed to the elements.

The situation looked manageable, at least from the deck of the flagship. Admiral Rockwell conferred throughout the day with General Brown, who received reports from his commanders on the two main invasion beaches. Captain Willoughby's whereabouts were unknown, but evidently, they had been spotted by an air force bomber in the early morning moving up the ravines to the mountain tops overlooking Holtz Bay. Captain Jameson was not so sure about how "manageable" the battle really was. As reports came in from the beach regarding the inability to move artillery plus the cold weather, the captain became more concerned. The plan for the advance from Massacre Bay required the rapid movement of the ground forces, but so far, the units had moved only a part of the way up the valley. With only a few exceptions, the steep and snow-covered hillsides were still not occupied.

At Holtz Bay, the enemy reacted swiftly with artillery targeting the beach area. Luckily, the commander of the landing force had pushed his men off the beach, limiting the effect of the Japanese bombardment. The men pushed higher toward their goal of occupying a large hill overlooking the bay but failed to achieve it by nightfall. The Japanese, however, quickly seeing the strategic value of this high ground, moved in and set up strong defensive positions. For the next few days, the Americans would have to battle uphill and take many casualties to win this ground, further pushing back the timeline for the conquest of Attu. The plan had originally called for the battle to end on day three.

After the initial landings, Jameson read each report coming in from the island. The first and most important piece of news was the failure to move the artillery compounded by the buildup of trucks, tractors, and jeeps on the beach. With nowhere to go, the vehicles crowded the beach, slowing incoming landing craft and holding up reinforcements and supplies. As the captain had discovered in his meetings with the Alaskan Defense Commander, Major General Simon Buckner, many recommendations from Alaskan experts had been ignored. The problem of land transportation in the Aleutians had been discussed many times but dismissed by army headquarters in Washington at the expense of men sinking into the bogs of Attu.

As the evening progressed and some of the forward units ran into sporadic Japanese fire, supplies became paramount. The plan called for the army to move two miles up the valley, occupy the high ground on both sides and be ready to push on to Holtz Bay within the next forty-eight hours to link up with the northern force. As General Brown went ashore to take command of the attack, Jameson wondered about the number of men being used as human pack mules instead of combat soldiers. General Buckner had warned Brown about the slowness of moving men and materials around the island, with the additional caveat about the need to plan on using half of his force for transporting supplies. The Seventh Division was far from ready for the conditions they found, nor were the men prepared for meeting the fierce resistance the enemy was beginning to offer.

Already, a few casualties returned from the beach—many of them suffering from hypothermia. Some had battle wounds, which would increase significantly in the days to come. Thus far, Hiram Feldman and Jonathan Hamlin weren't very busy. They stood by in the makeshift hospital aboard the attack transport *Zeilin* talking to a few army doctors who would soon be going ashore to establish a forward aid station.

As the men waited for orders to leave the ship, a young army physician asked Feldman, "Commander, I understand you've seen some pretty bad cases in the navy, but what's the worst thing you've encountered so far?"

Seeing the young doctor, no more than twenty-seven or so, he replied in his best professional voice, "Doctor, every wound you'll see in this campaign is bad. Burns are a major challenge because we don't have many ways to successfully treat them. In a war zone, the options become even less."

Another doctor, a few years older but still younger than Hiram, heard the conversation and asked, "Commander, I take it you have been in a combat situation. If I may ask, where were you?"

Sensing the doctor was looking for confirmation about what he was about to see, Feldman became very serious. "Doctor, Pharmacist Hamlin and I have seen a lot of bad things in this war, most of which I would like to forget, but the brain does not easily allow such a gift. We had the honor of serving the Marines on Guadalcanal and aboard the cruiser *San Francisco* in a violent sea battle off the island back in November. We also spent time with the army in North Africa at Kasserine Pass as well as with our British cousins in Tunisia."

Both army doctors were amazed at the revelation. They moved closer to the physician and skilled front line medic. The older of the two said, "Commander, it's an honor to meet you and the Pharmacist Mate. I wish we had more time to talk and learn from your experiences. Is there one thing we should be looking out for once we're on the beach?"

The navy doctor looked at his younger medical colleagues and smiled. Taking his time to make sure he got his point across, he answered, "Stay low and out of the way of bullets. Once you accomplish this objective, use your medical training to save lives. Remember, a dead doctor saves no one."

The two doctors didn't know how to respond, but Hiram came to their rescue, saying, "You will know what to do when you see it. Expect the worse, and you'll be fine. The last thing you should do before going ashore is take as many extra socks and extra gloves as you can find. I think we're all going to need everything we can find to keep us warm."

As the youngest doctor was about to say something else, a sergeant approached the army physicians, ordering them to the main deck for transfer to the new aid station onshore. Feldman shook each man's hand then watched as they clumsily climbed the ladder to the deck and then descended the rope ladder to their waiting boat.

Hamlin watched as the men left and then whispered to Feldman, "Doc, you think those two will be all right?"

Without taking his eyes off the small craft headed for shore, Hiram told his friend and partner, "I think they'll do their duty like everyone else we've seen. Some men are braver than others, but I think they'll be okay."

Feldman didn't say any more but thought about how the doctors would fare when they ran into a mass casualty situation. He also wondered about the number of frostbite cases he would soon see and quickly added up the number of spare socks he had in his rucksack. Whatever the number, he was sure it would not be enough.

Lieutenant Clark was now aboard the *Nassau*, helping out as much as possible with the flight operations and coordination with forward observers on the island. Only a few planes were able to launch, and one of those crashed on landing. The skies were clear one moment and fogged in the next. The ceilings went from a few hundred feet to five thousand feet and back again, all within thirty minutes. The army bombers had the same problem, with most returning to their base on Adak without dropping their bomb load. One of the planes crashed in an attempt to locate the Scouts, probably because of the intermittent fog conditions.

The British pilot kept up with the reports coming from the army units on the island. Often these communications were garbled, or positions could not be accurately plotted on the map. Without this accuracy, the pilots could not with good conscience attack assigned targets without fearing fratricide. The last message sent to Jameson before ceasing flight operations was that only eight planes had launched in the afternoon—two attacked targets; one crashed into the sea upon a landing attempt; and the ship was awaiting new orders. If Clark could have spoken with Jameson, he would have expressed his anger at how the operation was going. Still, he did his job and worked on keeping up the morale of the Wildcat pilots, all of whom were new to combat operations, especially in the Arctic. Perhaps tomorrow would be a better day for flying, but the experienced Scotsman knew better. Things could and would get worse.

45

12 May 1943
Federal Reserve Building
Washington, D.C.

- United States--TRIDENT Conference, President Roosevelt, Prime Minister Churchill and Combined Chiefs of Staff, opens in Washington to reconsider strategy in the light of recent events in Tunisia, the Aleutians and the USSR.
- Aleutian Islands--On Attu, 7th Division, with naval gunfire and air support, continues 2-pronged thrusts toward Jarmin Pass. Frontal attacks from Massacre Bay beachhead fail to gain ground.
- Solomon Islands--Allied surface vessels bombard Vial and Munda, night 12-13.
- CBI--First Arakan campaign ends where it started as Indian 26th Division evacuates Maungdaw for defensive positions to the north. Cost in casualties has been heavy.
- Tunisia--Collapse of enemy resistance in the south is all but complete by nightfall. Enemy is surrendering en masse, among them Gen. von Arnim, General Officer CinC, Army Group Africa.

The senior officers had assembled and were ready to do battle. Not one involving hand-to-hand combat, but a battle of wits, strategy, and statesmanship, with an occasional verbal grenade thrown to spice up the meeting. The location for the TRIDENT conference was the Board of Governors Room at the Federal Reserve Building located on Constitution Avenue, looking out at the Lincoln Memorial Reflecting Pool and only a few blocks from the White House.

The building was completed in 1937, and the Board of Governors Room was one of the largest conference rooms in the city. The adjacent rooms were taken over by staffs of the British and American military leaders, and other men and women stood by in offices scattered across the Washington area if needed to find some obscure piece of information or create a new position paper. Hundreds of stenographers and typists waited to collect the notes from the various subcommittee meetings and create daily minutes for the participants. The conference was designed as another checkpoint for the ongoing war effort. Strategy dictates tactics, but it also demands logistics, manpower, realistic industrial production, and accurate intelligence. The meeting would help align strategy to capabilities, which often proved difficult or, sometimes, politically intolerable.

James Brand and John Meyers were in one of the small conference rooms with several of Admiral Cooke's navy planners. Another room contained the army and air force teams, plus staff from the War Production Board. Every decision being made required validating the amount of equipment, supplies, shipping, fuel, and available manpower. It was easy to tell a general that he would attack a particular spot on the map. The tricky part was providing the implements of war to do it successfully.

The Allies had many experiences with losing battles in the war, resulting from insufficient supplies, armaments, and trained personnel. General Alan Brooke was constantly reminding people of the British Expeditionary Force and the humiliation of the evacuation from Dunkirk. The men had fought bravely but were out maneuvered, overwhelmed by superior German tanks, communications, and aircraft. Without the sacrifices of the Royal Navy, the army would have suffered complete and utter defeat. Based upon his World War One experience as minister of munitions, the prime minister was always the first to ask about the supply situation and the ability to replace lost equipment and manpower.

Brand would be the first person to agree with Churchill on the need for sound logistics and linkage to realistic strategies.

The first day of the conference was like the opening of a bull fight. The matadors don't appear until the end of the event. The bull must be taunted by the picadors and the banderillas, plus the fancy cape work and stylized movements by the matador. Finally, the end comes, the *hora de verdad* (moment of truth), when the matador skillfully kills the bull. Sometimes, the bull wins and injures or kills the matador, so the outcome is never preordained. But unlike a bull fight, there were no trumpets signaling the entrance of conference participants. The British staff led by General Brooke and the American staff led by Admiral Leahy began deliberations. While the generals and admirals addressed their concerns, made rebuttals, offered compromises, and sometimes stonewalled their peers, the two ultimate decision-makers were at the White House looking at maps of the world.

The men meeting in the Governor's Room began their discussion with guidelines for the conference and the typical protocols for meeting agendas, minutes, and position papers. After lunch, the men headed to the White House for the "official" conference opening. James Brand was asked by Admiral Leahy to attend but not to interact with the participants. He wanted the professor to observe only. Later, the admiral and the other American military leaders would hold a separate meeting on the proceedings, including Brand's analysis.

As usual, the White House meeting was long on praise and short on decision-making. Both Roosevelt and Churchill seemed upbeat on the war's progress, with the prime minster referring to the last meeting he had held with the president at the White House in June 1942. Back then the news about the fall of Tobruk had taken a terrible toll on the British morale, and it was President Roosevelt who quickly provided solace by providing hundreds of Sherman tanks to bolster the defense of Egypt. Now, the Germans were near defeat in Tunisia, and Mr. Churchill was in an expansive mood.

Sitting quietly as instructed, James added Churchill's opening remarks for the TRIDENT Conference to his ever-growing notations. The statement concerned where the two Allied nations were in the war.

The prime minister told the Joint Chiefs that we had been able, by taking thought together, to produce a succession of brilliant events which had altered the whole course of the war. We had the authority and prestige of victory. It was our duty to redouble our efforts and to grasp the fruits of our success. The only questions outstanding between the two staffs were questions of emphasis and priority. He felt sure that these could be solved by mutual agreement.

The next hour was devoted to the expression of views by the president and the prime minister on subjects ranging from the impending HUSKY operation, the ongoing struggle in the Aleutians, the support of China, Russian convoys, the strategic bombing campaign against Germany, and the need to secure the bases in the Azores. Upon hearing the last item, James made a separate note to get with Lieutenant Meyers to check the latest intelligence concerning the attitude of the Portuguese government. After the meeting broke up and with a dinner planned for the senior participants, James went to Admiral Leahy's office to discuss his analysis of the remarks made by the president and prime minister.

Leahy sat down at this desk and pointed to the chair next to him. Before starting his session with the professor, Leahy placed a quick phone call to Vannevar Bush. As Brand listened to the admiral, it was apparent a meeting was being planned with Bush and Lord Cherwell and the two war leaders sometime later in the week. Once he put the phone down, the admiral looked at James, saying, "There will be an off-the-record meeting in the next week or so with the president, Churchill, and their respective scientific advisors. I think you will be invited as well, but I'm not sure yet. You can guess what the subject will be, but that's conjecture on my part."

James knew immediately the subject would be the Manhattan Project. Scientists collected from both countries were being deposited in a remote location near Los Alamos, New Mexico. The University of California had signed a contract on April 20, 1943, to operate the top-secret facility at the site of a former boys ranch in northern New Mexico. Dr. Robert Oppenheimer selected the location based upon its isolation, existing facilities, and because he had attended the school in his youth. General Groves approved of the site, in part because of its isolation, which would restrict access to the facility, making it easier for the army to maintain security.

Leahy then asked about the opening remarks from Roosevelt and Churchill. "Lieutenant Brand, what did you glean from the president and prime minister? Anything bothering you?"

James was ready for the question. "Admiral, it would appear the prime minister is pushing for more involvement in the Mediterranean. His approaches to Turkey to bring them into the Allied camp are continuing. This would allow the British to immediately push for more troops to attack the German forces in the Aegean Sea and Greece. The other point he repeatedly made was about post-HUSKY operations. He sees the Italians being on the brink of exhaustion and ready to capitulate, but his views on us jumping into the boot of Italy and quickly moving up past Rome are pipe dreams."

James quickly amended his last comment. "Sorry, sir, that was my editorial comment on the British intentions. I fear that if we go into Italy, we will be bogged down for a year or more. If the Germans meet us in any type of defensive operation in the mountains, we will have to slog through it like the last war."

"No apologies necessary, Brand. I concur with your analysis and have warned the president accordingly. General Marshall is dead set against any further incursions in the Mediterranean. If we were to move toward Italy, we and the British would tie up a dozen divisions, have a monumental supply problem, and probably have to take care of the Italian civilian population. Please be alert for any indications of Mr. Churchill moving us in that direction."

"Yes sir. I believe Admiral King agrees with General Marshall, and we can't afford to splinter our landing craft assets across two European fronts and support the Pacific at the same time. The other item mentioned by both the president and the prime minister was their general agreement to the buildup of our forces in Britain, BOLERO, and setting a date for a cross channel invasion for late spring of next year. If the president can move Mr. Churchill toward a joint statement on setting the month, it would help focus the entire production and training plan."

Examining his notes from the meeting, Leahy nodded his agreement. "Lieutenant, please sit in on as many meetings as you can. I will arrange this with Admiral King. General Marshall is in full agreement with having you observe the sessions. Have your team, Meyers and Stevens, stand by to help you over the next few weeks. If we can create a unified approach and get the president to back us up, I think we can set a date for the invasion by the end of this conference."

James had his marching orders. For the next few weeks, he would attend the Combined Chiefs of Staff meetings and provide a daily analysis of each session. His observations would be reviewed by the American leaders, and every morning, he would provide a short briefing on what to expect in the next meeting. This way, the American leadership would have a synopsis of what their Allies would recommend or want to table for future discussion. If the number of tabled items increased, the Americans would begin using their leverage points to regain control of the discussion. Above all else, Leahy told him, the Allies needed to come out of this conference agreeing to the prosecution of the war. An agreement was required to set the schedule for operations for the remainder of the year and into 1944.

"Damn, it's cold!" Waverly said, but no one in the platoon heard him, although they were all thinking the same thing. Soldiers' feet were freezing, their faces were wrapped to keep their ears and noses covered, making them look like extras in a movie about Egyptian mummies. But up the mountain they climbed, and by 0800 the Scouts crossed the mountain and looked down on Holtz Bay. A few hundred feet ahead of him, Waverly could see Captain Willoughby urging his men on, showing by sheer force of will what it would take to reach their objective. The men had been moving since 0400. The final uphill climb had taken a toll on the men, even though they were superbly conditioned. As the men started down the mountain, movement was easier but slowed by the ice, snow, slippery rocks, and boulders. There was no cover, but they were now behind the enemy's position.

The Japanese were established along a ridgeline above Holtz Bay. They were facing away from the Scouts, but someone saw movement in the mountains behind them, quickly forcing them to wheel around and fire at the Americans. It was a long-range affair from the enemy's artillery. The men took cover, and Waverly reacted quickly.

"Take that mortar and set it up behind those boulders. Get some men on the right and left of it, but spread out." The company commander quickly followed the Marine's suggestions. As they did, the artillery fire heading toward them fell short. Waverly put up his head, knowing that a sniper shot was not probable at this range—at least not yet. As he looked down toward the Japanese positions, he saw men moving up the hill toward their position. Doing a quick check of the range, he yelled to the mortar men, "Are you set up?"

The answer came back, "Not yet, need another few minutes."

Looking back down the hill at what looked like a platoon heading toward their position, Waverly didn't ask again. "Get that damn tube set. If you don't, you'll be speaking Japanese soon."

This had the desired effect. The men rapidly set up the mortar, attaching the rangefinder and pulling up their ammunition boxes. The 81mm mortar weighed about ninety pounds, and their high explosive rounds weighed another ten pounds each. The mortar teams had carried, dragged, manhandled, and pushed their weapons up, over and down the mountain, all the time making sure it was not damaged in the process. As the lieutenant looked down the mountain, he picked up a group of five or six men. Here was a proper target. Checking the distance and doing a quick calculation, he yelled back to the mortar crew where to find the target. The sergeant of the mortar team reacted quickly, taking a look at the area the Marine officer had given him and saw the enemy moving up the mountain. Working quickly with the sights of the mortar and making sure the round was ready to load, he set the deflection and elevation once more. He ordered, "Fire!" The round dropped and quickly exploded out of the tube, heading toward the target area. A second round was ready, and the mortar squad leader waited for impact.

"Up fifty," Waverly yelled. The sergeant looked at the impact site and saw what the lieutenant was seeing. The Japanese were moving quickly forward, not backwards. The last round was on a direct line but too far behind the attacking enemy soldiers. Making another adjustment came the order, "Fire!"

As the Marine looked, the explosion caught at least three men trying to move uphill in a standing posture. They were now down. The other two men seemed to be moving as well, but now both of them were moving back down the hill and farther apart. Waverly knew not to waste ammunition on two men, so he yelled back to the sergeant and his crew. "Good job. Three down and two heading south. Stand ready for another mission."

As he looked down the mountain, Captain Willoughby came trudging up to him and went to a prone position. "Good shooting, Waverly. Glad you saw that group heading up toward us. I think the enemy knows we're here. Any thoughts?"

"Captain, I think we better get situated and find some more boulders to hide behind. The Jap artillery will keep our heads down, and they will try to move to our flanks at the same time. I would beef up both ends of the line and hold a few squads in reserve downhill. It may be a long cold day."

Waverly no sooner finished his last word when another Japanese shell burst nearby. As Willoughby picked up his head, he noticed the Marine had not ducked at all. Pointing to the right, Waverly said, "Probably a 75mm mountain gun. I think it's down in that pocket and will fire at us every few minutes to keep our heads down. Tell your officers to be careful in their movements. The Jap gunners are really good with that piece, and can fire four or five rounds a minute if they see something interesting."

Taking note of the man's information and experience, the army captain asked, "What do you think they're going to do now?"

"Captain, they know where we are, but they don't know how many. They will continue to move toward us in small units. Get your machine guns set and keep everyone ready. If we get a lot of artillery fire, that means they are very close and will try to hit our flanks. I think they'll keep up harassing fire until dark and then move toward one end of our line. Keep the reserves warm and ready to fill gaps in the line."

"Thanks, Waverly. If you can inspect the lines and keep the men focused, it would be a great help." As he started to move back towards the mortar position, he had one more comment. "Tell the men to conserve their ammo. The reserve group brought up all they could, but until we can link up with the people at Holtz Bay, we're on our own, and it's going to be a cold and lonely night."

Acknowledging the command, Waverly was already cold, hungry, and thirsty. Eating snow, especially the dry snow on these islands, was barely helping his thirst. A few men were looking for ice formations to melt to get water for the canteens. If you could get some water in your canteen, you put it inside your coat to keep it from freezing. He never had thought that he would miss Guadalcanal until he landed on this God-forsaken island.

Flannigan and Dean, still working with Baker Company, moved into a front line position in the Jarmin Pass area. The Japanese had taken good defensive positions on all three sides of the slowly advancing Americans. They controlled the high ground, and any significant movement toward their positions was met with intense fire. The troops were new to combat and even newer to the horrible conditions. Food was in short supply and without any mode of transportation besides the backs of men, resupply of the forward units was difficult and in some cases, impossible. The company in front of Baker had experienced several combat casualties when trying to move toward the enemy's position. These attacks were uphill, requiring the infantry to trudge through the mud. Men were sinking into the muskeg up to their thighs, all the while trying to fight the Japanese. Many men were quickly wounded or killed by Japanese snipers, who waited patiently for men to slog out of the mud. The company commander was waiting for orders to advance when Colonel Earle loudly made his presence known.

"Captain, what the hell is going on? I've been on the radio trying to get a situation report from this battalion for the last hour. Where is the battalion commander?"

The man was agitated and covered with mud, just like his men. The colonel had trudged up the valley with an Aleut Scout, wanting to get his regiment moving, but nothing seemed to help. The radios were full of static—another problem not considered in the army's invasion plans. This far north, radio communications were erratic at best. The navy knew about this phenomenon for years and had worked hard to stabilize their shipboard systems, but even their powerful transmitters couldn't punch through the static. The army systems were much less powerful, and the colonel was unable to communicate with his field units or the navy for fire support missions.

The company commander replied, "Colonel, I haven't seen the battalion commander since early this morning. We were told to await orders to move up next to Charlie company, but so far, no orders have come through."

Colonel Earle turned red, or was it the cold? Flannigan stood next to the company sergeant going over a map, when the colonel spotted him. "Major Flannigan, is that you?"

"Yes sir, how can I be of service to the colonel?"

"I guess you haven't seen the battalion commander either?"

"No sir, I haven't seen anyone this morning, and like the captain said, no orders either."

Looking out toward the hills to the west, where the Japanese were dug in and keeping his regiment locked up tight in the valley, Earle asked for a moment of the major's time. Moving away from the company commander and an army lieutenant trying to make the radios work, the colonel pulled a map out of his coat pocket and spread it out on an empty ammunition box.

"Major, I would appreciate your thoughts on our situation." Pointing to their position in Massacre Valley and the landing beaches and then towards Holtz Bay and the unfinished airfield, the colonel gave the Marine his evaluation of what was happening.

"We have landed my regiment plus artillery. Everything with wheels or tracks is stuck on the beach. The 105s are doing good work, but we can't move them forward, so we must rely on the navy for fire support. General Brown is on the beach getting reports from my command and the men who landed at Holtz Bay. The north beaches ran into a lot of resistance today and are locked down. We are hemmed in on three sides and have not moved at all today. Supplies are being dragged forward, and I know most front line companies haven't received any food today. There are lots of supplies stacking up on the beach, but there are not enough men to move them forward. We're in a hell of a mess. What do you think of the situation, Major?"

The colonel had met the Marine officer at Cold Bay and had only a casual conversation with the man. He was late to realize the major had significant combat experience and was evidently closely tied to senior command. Now, he needed help and was not afraid to ask for it.

"Colonel, like you said, the situation is bad. Your men are new to combat, and I hear reports of frostbite, which will further impair unit effectiveness. We need to get the men moving forward, even though it may be costly. The Japanese will take their time and defend until the last, and the longer we wait to hit them, the more they'll dig in. I recommend some of your scouts move forward tonight to find the enemy lines. If we can get some decent intel on their positions, we can get the navy to punish them. Then we concentrate our forces and hit one weakened position. It would be too costly to attack everywhere, but if we can find a crack in their lines, we can turn their flanks."

The map spread before the colonel was a poor representation of what he was facing. The man was being pressed by division to open a hole in the enemy lines. So far, there had been no advance at all today. Folding his map, he said, "Major, I appreciate your advice. I agree with your idea, but I think we need to open a bigger hole in their lines. I need to find where our men are first, and then I'd like to get your help in creating a plan of attack."

The Aleut Scout joined the colonel and gazed at the hill in front of him. Earle stomped his feet to keep warm then moved toward the Baker Company commander. "I'm going to find the forward companies, and then I'll be back with the battalion commander to set up an operation for later tonight or tomorrow morning."

Flannigan moved up to the colonel and asked a question. "Sir, are you going to reconnoiter the front by yourself?"

"Hell, yes, Major. My scout and I will take a little hike up the hill to find out where the hell my battalion is. The radio isn't working, and we need to get moving now."

The Marine officer didn't hold back. It was good to see a senior officer leading from the front, but even the best officers back on Guadalcanal always went with at least a squad of men in case they ran into the enemy. "Sir, may I suggest you take a squad from this company to help you find the other units. It would help them to get the lay of the land for later."

"Good idea, Major, but I don't need to take these men away from getting prepared for the assault. My scout and I will be fine." With that last comment, the colonel and the Aleut scout trudged away, sinking into the muskeg with each step. The Aleut didn't sink as far because of his native boots, but every so often, he would stop to help the colonel pull his leg out of the mud, which sucked him deeper into the island of Attu.

Seeing the pair struggle, Sergeant Dean approached Flannigan. "Major, the weapons platoon needs more ammunition for their .30 caliber machine guns. Also, some more hand grenades. Any idea on getting more stuff up here?"

Flannigan watched the colonel and the scout move further and further away. Turning to his friend, he said, "Dean, I don't think the army knows when they're going to get any resupply on this cold-ass pile of mud. Double-check with each platoon for an inventory and let me know.

The captain is going to need a lot of help if the colonel moves forward with his plan."

The sergeant looked up the hill and saw two men slowly making their way. Dean asked, "Sir, what do those two idiots think they're doing? The Japs probably have them in their sights already."

The major didn't respond. He watched for another minute as the two men moved over the crest of a hill and disappeared. He had other things to worry about besides a colonel getting lost in the tundra. Moving to where the captain sat trying to get his radio working, Flannigan began doing his usual combat inventory—men, ammo, food, water, medical supplies, and, yes, the number of the enemy in front of him.

Holtz Bay was hotly contested by the Japanese, as were the hills around Massacre Valley. The battleships fired away at suspected targets and, on occasion, responded to calls from the army for a specific bombardment. Aircraft reconnaissance was limited to a few sorties from the ship's float planes, and the occasional call from a Wildcat launched from the escort carrier. The old four-stack destroyer *Williamson* served as a seaplane tender for Patrol Wing Four's PBYs, with three airplanes flying out of Massacre Bay. These planes had highly trained crews and served as anti-submarine aircraft and long-range scouts for the task force. Occasionally, they had the time to search Attu for enemy concentrations and radioed the locations to the nearest American ship for action. The army tried to send planes each day from the base at Adak, but the weather either canceled the mission or fog, clouds, or storms made their attacks impossible over the island.

The *Pennsylvania* and *Idaho* moved off the island and, in the afternoon, came in closer to Holtz Bay to provide shore bombardment at the request of the army. Hundreds of fourteen-inch and five-inch shells pounded suspected enemy positions. The ships were always underway because of reports of enemy submarines in the area. The escorting destroyers moved about in their search patterns, listening for traces of the Japanese subs, but the island's closeness confused the SONAR operators. Lookouts scanned the sea and overhead the PBYs flew about searching for periscopes. So far, nothing had been sighted, but Admiral Rockwell didn't want any of his ships, especially the battleships, encountering an enemy torpedo.

Captain Jameson was on the flag bridge with the admiral, reading the updates coming from the army commanders. Things were not going well. Both landings had been successful, but neither had made much progress. The Japanese held the high ground and had successfully repulsed every American advance. Sergeant McBride stood on the corner of the bridge, peering inland at the chaos of Massacre Beach. The chartered supply vessel *Perida,* had struck an uncharted rock and was taking on water. The captain of this merchant vessel was ordered to beach the ship before it sank, so it was now further down the beach, far away from where the army needed its supplies, attempting to make repairs.

Pointing to the location of the grounded vessel, McBride whispered, "Sir, it looks like we can't get a break on this damn island. That damn ship is too far away from the landing beach to unload any of its cargo, and now it's useless."

Jameson had watched the fiasco for the past few minutes, and after looking at the ship through his binoculars, he commented, "SNAFU is the word that comes to mind. Would you agree with that, Sergeant McBride?"

Smiling at the captain's statement, the Marine replied, "Sir, I believe the term is often overused, but today it fits the situation perfectly."

Admiral Rockwell walked up to the two men and asked, "Any suggestions on how to get the army moving?"

"Sir, I don't have anything to offer. I believe we are seeing the consequences of an overly ambitious plan meeting the harsh reality of the Aleutians."

Agreeing with the statement, he showed the captain a message he had received earlier. General Brown had wanted to know about the reinforcements he had asked about earlier in the day. Rockwell hadn't received the request until this evening because of the continuing radio problems. Another message from the commander at Holtz Bay reported his command had captured the high ground near the bay, but the enemy was counterattacking, and the combat was now hand to hand. The situation was serious.

The admiral took the messages from Jameson and said, "We have pounded the hell out of the enemy's positions at Holtz Bay which seems to have relieved the pressure on the army there. Supply issues continue at each location, but there seems to be little movement up the valley from the southern beaches. Any ideas?"

Knowing the challenges of communication in an active combat zone, Jameson could offer little solace. "Admiral, I haven't heard from Major Flannigan since last night. His report was similar in terms of lack of supplies getting to the front lines. Also, these men are new and have never been in combat. The leaders will have to push harder to get their men to build their self-confidence and advance. Perhaps tomorrow I can go ashore and talk to the major to gain a better understanding of the situation."

The admiral mulled the suggestion over and then approved. "Go ashore tomorrow and see if you can find your major. Don't take any chances, but see if you can get me some answers. Admiral Kinkaid is not happy with the army's progress and fears an attack from the Japanese navy while we are locked up helping the army. General Butler is also concerned and is providing help from the Fourth Regiment."

As the two officers discussed the navy's nighttime deployment, requiring the big ships to get further out to sea to gain room for maneuvering, a navy lieutenant commander came up holding a message.

"Admiral, this just came in from General Brown."

The admiral took the message and read it. Looking at the captain, he passed it to him. The message was simple and to the point. Colonel Earle was found dead a few hours ago. Apparent sniper attack. The Aleut scout was also found in serious condition and is now at a field hospital. Colonel Wayne Zimmerman was now regimental commander.

Handing the message back to the admiral, Jameson said, "Sir, the situation is perhaps more in doubt than we had originally thought. I will get ashore first thing in the morning and locate Major Flannigan. Anything else you want me to do or see while I'm ashore?"

Rockwell looked at the message again. He had met Earle on several occasions and liked the man's optimism about the coming battle. Now, the officer was dead, like many other men on the island. Optimism was quickly being replaced by reality and fear.

46

13 May 1943
Attu Island, Territory of Alaska

- United States--CCS, at TRIDENT Conference, approves final outline plan for the invasion of Sicily (HUSKY). British and U.S. forces are to land abreast between Syracuse on the southeast coast and Palma on 10 July.
- Aleutian Islands--On Attu, further efforts of Massacre Bay force to break into Jarmin Pass are repelled by enemy. Vicious and costly fighting occurs to north as enemy attempts to drive 7th Division troops from Hill X, but the crest is firmly in American hands by nightfall. Naval gunfire and air support of troops continues insofar as weather conditions permit.
- New Guinea--Japanese begin new series of heavy air attacks.
- Tunisia--With the surrender of Gen. Messe, Rommel's successor, who is notified of his promotion to marshal on this date, the Tunisia campaign ends.

Messages were sent to General Brown's headquarters during the night, ordering the general to locate Major Flannigan and have him report to his HQ in the morning. The messages told the general that Captain Jameson would be coming ashore early in the morning to meet with the major and the general. A landing boat took the captain and the ever vigilant Sergeant McBride ashore at 0830. Armed with only his pistol and looking like every other soldier on the island, the captain stepped ashore to the chaos of the beach. McBride was at his side carrying his trusty Thompson and scouring the area for Japanese snipers. Since the information about Colonel Earle's death, everyone on the island looked for the enemy under every rock and behind every boulder. The sergeant had urged the captain not to go ashore, but since he was going no matter what McBride said the Marine laid down the law to his commanding officer and friend. "No going to see the front lines. Don't try to get too far forward and never be by yourself, even in the latrine. And take off those damn eagles!"

The captain sheepishly took off the eagles and put them in his pocket. He wore a helmet with USN on the front and four bars in the back, indicating his rank. That was enough, McBride thought. The enemy wouldn't know what the bars meant, but they sure as hell knew what shiny birds looked like, especially when peering back at them through a telescopic sight.

After getting directions from a navy beachmaster as to where the HQ was, the two men trudged off the beach to their first education in the mud of Attu. Jameson was already feeling the intense cold as the moisture penetrated his boots and his pants. Quickly sinking almost to his knees, Jameson had to be helped out by McBride, who was also wallowing in the ice-cold muskeg. "Damn it!" The sergeant held his tongue but hoped the captain would quickly get his fill of beachcombing and head back to the relative safety of the flagship.

Struggling for a quarter of a mile, they finally found the division's HQ. Several radio antennas were arranged nearby, and a mess tent was thirty yards further to the north. A series of other tents were behind a large set of boulders, which had probably been blown out of some volcano millions of years ago, but now sat around like a child's toys scattered about his room. McBride wondered about the giant boulders and the rocky areas nearby. It appeared that the valley floor was muskeg, but the hills were hard soil or rock. Looking in the distance on some of the hill-sides under American control, he could make out jagged rocky outcrops, perfect for an ambush. Putting the thought out of his mind, he walked ahead of the captain and opened the flap of the first tent.

Inside the tent were the bedraggled communications people. A generator hummed nearby, but the messages were corrupted by static and poor atmospherics. Communicating across the bay to the support ships was proving harder and harder to accomplish. Instructions to the units on the other side of the island were similarly impacted. One of the lieutenants quickly told Captain Jameson that all messages for Admiral Kinkaid and General Buckner had to be sent to the ships first for re-transmission to Adak. The communications officer directed the captain to a nearby tent that served as the southern force's operations center. The man thought the general would be there this morning. When asked about Major Flannigan, the officer told Jameson a message had been sent, but no reply had been received. He explained to the navy officer it was common not to receive confirmation on messages sent or received. Things just did not work on the island.

Jameson and McBride slugged their way through the mud path to the operations tent and found two lieutenant colonels and a major up-dating maps. When Jameson walked in, he was ignored at first since he didn't have on any insignia. They thought the navy officer was some sort of new beachmaster and quickly asked, "Are you the new beach officer?"

Jameson took off his helmet, revealing the eagle insignia attached to his wool cap. The men knew they had made a mistake. "Sorry, Captain, we thought you were one of the beachmasters. Can we help you?"

"I'm Captain Jameson from Admiral Kinkaid's staff. I sent a message to General Brown to arrange for one of my officers to meet me at this HQ. His name is Major Flannigan."

"Sir, we know of the major, but we've not seen him since yesterday morning. General Brown is out with Colonel Zimmerman checking out the forward positions. Is there something we can do for you while you're waiting?"

Jameson looked at the men examining the maps and quickly re-plied, "Can you give me an update on the division's situation?"

Aware a member of Admiral Kinkaid's staff was watching them, they quickly agreed. The men gave a situation report on each of the invasion forces. "Sir, the north force is facing quite a bit of enemy resistance. This morning they are holding their own but have suffered more casualties. The navy is doing a good job hitting the enemy's positions on the hillsides, but there are more of the enemy than we assumed."

Jameson asked about supplies in the north and the whereabouts of Captain Willoughby's Provisional Scouts. A major who seemed to know exactly what he was doing answered for the colonels. "Captain, we have a few reports from the air force about spotting our men on the south side of the mountains overlooking the bay." Pointing at a location on the map marked in pencil the major traced their movements over the past two days from their landing point at Beach Scarlett. "Sir, we haven't been able to reach them, but from the last aircraft sighting, it appears they are fighting their way through enemy resistance, and I would think they should be able to break through in another day to link up with the north force."

McBride listened intently, knowing Waverly was with these men, totally on their own without means of resupply. Feeling if anyone could come out of this mess, it would be Bill Waverly, he stopped worrying. The army major worked his way through the known positions of the enemy in the north and then concentrated on the larger southern force. The battalions moved forward early in the morning and were beaten back with a significant number of casualties. Asking the major for his opinion on the battle, the major answered politically, befitting a staff officer. "Sir, I think we are behind schedule, but we're making progress in reducing the enemy's resolve to fight."

Not wanting to contradict the man, Jameson thanked the officers and told them he and the sergeant would be at the mess tent and to send Major Flannigan over if he showed up. Getting to the mess tent, which was only slightly warmer than outside but had duck boards in place to keep the men's feet dry and out of the wet, the two men got some coffee and sat down to watch and learn. McBride had told the captain that sometimes the best thing to do was just get some coffee and sit down to watch how the men behaved. Were they sullen, apprehensive, enthusiastic, fearful, proud, or were they looking for a way out of the fight? As they were getting a feel for the men in the tent, a muddy, unshaven, and cold-looking pair of Marines stumbled into the tent. Flannigan held onto his Thompson, while Dean carried an M-1 at the ready. Both men were glad to see Captain Jameson and Sergeant McBride, but first, they wanted hot coffee.

Sergeants Dean and McBride walked over to the chow line, poured four cups of coffee, and returned to the table. The officers talked in hushed tones, so McBride asked, "Sir, do you want me and Dean to step outside while you and the major talk?"

"No, Jimmy. I want you and Willie to listen to what we're saying and feel free to add anything you think we should know."

The two sergeants sat down and listened, but not before Dean downed the coffee like a man who had gone without water for a week. Seeing the major's cup almost empty, McBride got up and refilled their cups while the officers talked.

"So, from what you're saying, things couldn't get much more screwed up. Is that a correct assumption, Major?"

"Captain, the men, are willing but they aren't ready for this sort of combat. The number of men I found with frostbite was amazing. They could barely walk, so how the hell are they going to charge up some hillside? The junior officers are trying, but with little in terms of results. The colonel who was killed yesterday was a brave man, but he shouldn't have gone out on his own looking for his companies. I haven't met the replacement, but evidently, he gets good marks for leadership. The supply situation is critical. Every casualty requires a four-man team to carry him back to an aid station. Then they try to find supplies to take back. All the time they are gone, the unit suffers from lack of manpower, experience, or just waits for orders."

Jameson thought Flannigan's report perfectly described what he had witnessed since landing this morning. If half the men were now being used as stevedores carrying supplies, who the hell was doing the fighting? He asked Flannigan another question. "What do you make of the tactical leadership?"

The major knew this was a loaded question. Most of his time on the island was spent observing at the battalion and company levels and had only spent a few minutes with the regimental leadership. He had met General Brown twice since he landed, and the man issued orders without results. "Sir, I haven't had a chance to form an opinion on the division commander. He's moving around to check his units and get situation reports from the commanders, but I feel he's not leading his officers to do their jobs. Part of the problem could be coming from their selection for this assignment. The company commander told me this is nothing like what they trained for in California. Combined arms training, maneuver warfare, tank and artillery support had been hammered into them in the heat of the West Coast."

The major stopped for a moment as three officers walked into the mess tent looking for coffee and food. After they had passed, Flannigan lowered his voice. "Sir, I think they picked the wrong unit for this operation. They should have had mountain training in cold weather and learn not to rely on mobility, tanks, aircraft, and artillery barrages. This looks more and more like a Marine assault scenario requiring fast assaults, limited fire support, and strong fundamental infantry training." The major made his point and sat back to sip on the scalding coffee.

Jameson rolled the comments about in his brain and wondered what would happen in the coming days. He was about to ask more questions when a lieutenant colonel entered the tent. "Captain Jameson, the general just got back from the front lines and would like to meet with you. Please bring the major as well."

The men moved to the operations tent and sat down at a makeshift table covered with maps. The general went into a quick briefing about the battle. The north front was holding and making new advances on the high ground but taking more casualties. The southern force expected to advance this evening and attack toward Jarmin Pass, confident his men would break through and turn the enemy's flank. The biggest problem he had was with supply. The beaches were disasters filled with ammunition boxes, crates of food, piles of tents, oil drums, and every sort of extraneous supply imaginable. Except for the food and ammunition, everything else was useless. His men spent most of their time coming and going to retrieve supplies from the landing site. Everything was carried in, and the men were getting colder and needed more food to maintain body temperatures. Because of the lack of infrastructure to move men and supplies around the island, the general had requested reinforcements. He also stated the enemy was much stronger than he was told to expect. They were holding the high ground and making his men pay for every inch of advance.

The general thanked Flannigan for his support with the forward battalions then excused himself to meet with the new commander of the southern force. Abruptly departing before Jameson could ask questions, the Marine major knew his commanding officer was angry. After spending more than a year working for him, Flannigan knew how Jameson reacted to poor leadership. Not wanting to say anything more, the major turned his attention to the maps on the table top and waited.

About a minute went by before Jameson regained his composure enough to ask, "Have you seen Dr. Feldman since you've been on this mud pit?"

"No sir, but I heard he was ashore and working at the division hospital. Do you want to go see him?"

"Yes. I think the doctor could give me another set of reference points so I can discuss the situation with the admiral."

Noting the seriousness of the man's tone, Flannigan got up and asked one of the officers the location of the field hospital. Armed with the information and knowing it wasn't far away, the men made their way to the tents of the Seventh Division's field hospital. Inside, they saw lots of men with bandages on their feet and hands. This was a dead giveaway to men incapacitated by frostbite. Several more had white gauze wrappings on their heads, while a few were in red soaked bandages. Asking around, the men finally found Feldman and a lieutenant colonel examining a young man with black feet.

Upon seeing his friends, Feldman introduced the colonel to the officers. Then with the colonel's permission, Hiram walked to the nearby hospital kitchen to get some coffee and have a short conversation.

The officers sat down while McBride and Dean sat at another table with Pharmacist Mate Hamlin. Jameson's first question was simple. "How bad is the situation here?"

Taking a sip of hot coffee, Doc replied, "Sir, it's not as bad as the Kasserine Pass, but there are more non-combat injuries than anyplace I've seen so far in the war. The kid I was examining will probably lose at least one of his feet. I can't save it. In only a couple of days on this cold hell, I've seen toes fall off when a man pulled off his boot and I've watched a man with a black nose which is, now gangrene, requiring a major operation with years of reconstructive surgery. The combat wounds are like in Africa and Guadalcanal. At least we haven't had any burn casualties, but I'm sure something will happen soon. You can bet there will be a major outbreak of pneumonia within another week to ten days because these men have no place to take cover but a hole filled with ice water. Malnutrition may also become a factor unless we can get some hot food to the forward units. Do you want to hear anything more?"

Jameson shook his head no, realizing the doctor could go on another ten minutes on what is wrong on the island. "Doc, I think you have summed up the situation. Any remedies besides getting off this rock?"

"Sir, if we can get the ships to cook up some hot food and get it ashore, especially at Holtz Bay, that would be a good first step. Heavy tents and rubber tarps for the men to try to stay dry on the lines would help. I think we will be dealing with trench foot plus frostbite cases by the hundreds, perhaps more. One more thought, why did the Japanese want this hell hole to begin with? Let them have it and watch them starve or die of frostbite, not us."

Major Flannigan silently agreed. *Yes, it was American territory, but even the native Aleuts rarely came to this island, and few ever spent more than a few weeks on it. Was it pride that drove us to the decision, or was there some bigger picture?* He didn't quite understand.

Jameson took in all these ideas and worked with Flannigan and Feldman to update the maps he had brought along from the flagship. Upon his return, he would sit down with the admiral and give him a factual report on what was happening, and then he would tell Rockwell precisely what he thought about the battle and the piece of rock called Attu. He didn't blame the field commanders or General Brown. The plan was flawed from the beginning, starting with the intelligence estimates of the enemy's strength to insufficient winter clothing and failure to understand how the terrain would undermine American supply efforts.

47

16 May 1943
Presidential Retreat
"Shangri-La," Maryland

- Aleutian Islands--In an effort to speed operations
  on Attu, Maj. Gen. Eugene M. Landrum assumes
  command of assault force, relieving Gen. Brown.
  Holtz Bay force secures foothold on north end of
  Holtz Valley Ridge, thereby gaining control of the
  entire ridge. Most of Adm. Rockwell's naval force
  retires northward to safer waters. Gen. Landrum
  directs Capt. H. B. Knowles, USN, to assume control
  of remaining vessels; takes over air-ground control.
- Germany--RAF Lancasters, in highly successful
  night operation of 16-17, attack and breach Moehne
  and Eder dams, flooding large portions of the Ruhr
  and disrupting electric and transportation systems.

James had received a phone call from Admiral Leahy on Saturday night.
The president and prime minister wanted to see him on Sunday at the
presidential retreat, which Roosevelt had named Shangri-La after the
fictional Himalayan paradise described in the novel *Lost Horizon*. The

two leaders had driven up on Friday to have private discussions about the war and the numerous challenges facing the Allies.

Only Lord Beaverbrook, Harry Hopkins, and a few aides accompanied the war leaders. Beaverbrook headed the Anglo-American Combined Raw Materials Board and served as Churchill's primary advisor on war production. A staff car picked up James before dawn to drive up to the highly secretive and well-guarded complex. Gunny went with him as well as Sergeants Pride and Williams. A second car followed them, which included two army officers carrying dispatches for the president, driven by an armed Military Police sergeant, and the convoy of two vehicles was escorted by two motorcycles from the Maryland State Police. James thought the extra security was a bit too much, but he didn't know what might be in the dispatches.

Upon arrival at the camp, which was guarded by a company of Marines and what seemed to be half of the Secret Service officers in Washington, the men showed their authorizations, identification cards and had their vehicles searched for bombs. A big playful German shepherd dog sniffed every car entering the complex, and even though James wanted to pet the dog, he was warned off by Gunny. "Lieutenant, the dog might not like to be petted by anyone but its master. I would hate to have to take you to the doctor to get your hand stitched up."

Taking Gunny's sound advice, James declined the opportunity and waited for the search to end. An agent then directed them where to park and to enter the large building to the right of the parking area. In front of the building, the Marine guards saluted the navy officer and the Marine warrant officer, who gave both men a quick nod of approval. Inside, two navy stewards served coffee and breakfast. Both men declined the eggs and bacon but did sample the doughnuts, which went well with the strong coffee. Jones arranged to have coffee and doughnuts sent outside to his Marines and the state troopers, and then he sat down and waited. Looking around the rustic building, which looked like any hunting or fishing lodge found in the northern reaches of America, Gunny commented, "Nice place for a meeting. No distractions, and the forest makes everything quiet. Do you like this place?"

The professor hadn't noticed his surroundings, but looked about after Gunny expressed his opinion. He immediately thought this would be an excellent place for a honeymoon. No distractions except the one that seemed to be on his mind daily. Quickly erasing the erotic thoughts from his brain, he replied, "It's quite nice. I like the furniture and the big rock fireplace. Reminds me of a couple of places back in Flagstaff." Before he could continue the men were interrupted.

A tall Secret Service agent stood near the doorway. "Professor, the president and prime minister will see you now. If you come with me, I'll take you to their cabin."

Gunny knew not to follow but decided to accept the previous offer from the stewards about eggs and bacon. Perhaps a few pieces of toast would be good as well. Sipping his coffee, Warrant Jones wondered what the two leaders wanted to discuss with Brand.

The agent walked James down a long path. As he looked around, he noticed several agents patrolling the ground and even more Marines walking the perimeter line. He couldn't see heavy weapons, but was sure there were quite a few machine guns and perhaps some antiaircraft batteries nearby, probably hidden from sight. As they neared the cabin, two Marine guards came to attention and presented arms to the young lieutenant. Another Secret Service agent stood next to the Marines, who knew James. "Professor, good to see you. The president is inside with the prime minister."

The agent opened the door, announcing the Shangri-La visitor. "Mr. President, Lieutenant Brand."

Nothing else needed to be said. James walked in, came in front of the president, and saluted.

"Professor, you don't have to salute me every time you see me. The prime minister and I wanted to have a chat with you about what you've seen and heard in the meeting so far."

Churchill appeared pleasantly comfortable in an overstuffed chair, sipping what appeared to be brandy. It was early in the morning, but the old war horse apparently couldn't operate well without his morning libation. The British leader provided one of his cherubic grins before switching to his serious mood.

"Professor, it has come to the attention of His Majesty's government that you have failed in some of your duties."

Startled by the comment, James stammered. Roosevelt laughed and came to the young man's rescue. "James, Prime Minister Churchill is referring to your upcoming marriage to Lady Margret. Why have you not set a date for the wedding?"

James' exhaled a visible sigh of relief, bringing a loud chuckle from the prime minister. "Forgive me, Professor, but I was told to ask that question by your friend Lord Mountbatten. Evidently, he has been pressed by the family back in England about your intentions. I know they are honorable, but I do believe the lady is not going to wait forever."

Again, James couldn't collect the words. Much older and more worldly than the young officer, both men smiled. Roosevelt offered a suggestion. "If it is agreeable to the prime minister, perhaps we can determine a suitable wedding venue in Washington. Possibly, we can bring some extended family together for this purpose."

Churchill immediately agreed. "That would be most appropriate, Mr. President. I think Lord Mountbatten could arrange things on our side of the pond, and might I recommend the British Embassy as an appropriate venue for the festivities."

The president acknowledged the suggestion and turned to the prospective groom. "Well, Professor, what do you say? Are you capable of setting a date so that the planning can begin?"

Finally gathering his wits, James replied, "Mr. President, I would need to speak with Lady Margret to set a date, but I think it could be easily decided."

"Good. Now, if the prime minister will agree to these terms, perhaps we can get on with the war."

Picking up his glass of brandy, the prime minister saluted the president. "Mr. President, again, you have diplomatically come up with a solution. I shall await the decision of the fair bride-to-be and inform Lord Mountbatten to begin making suitable arrangements."

James was still flabbergasted. The two most powerful men in the world took the time to organize a wedding for him and his lady. He swallowed hard and clamped his teeth together to avoid making an emotional statement. "Thank you, Mr. President, Prime Minister. I will speak with Lady Margret tonight to gain her agreement on a date."

Both leaders smiled, and then the president said, "Sit down, James. We have a lot to talk about. First, I want you to attend a meeting with the prime minister and myself along with Lord Cherwell and a few others on May 24. We need to have a conversation about the Manhattan Project, so if you can make sure you are up to date on the progress of the various parts of this effort, that would be helpful."

Before Brand could say anything, Roosevelt continued. "Tell us about yesterday's session. We would like to get your impression on the progress the Combined Chiefs are making."

Speaking without notes, James outlined the decisions made to date and then discussed the Saturday meeting. General Brooke was the first to bring up the significance of building strategic plans for the cross-channel invasion. Admiral King added to this by outlining the need to establish the fundamentals for the destruction of Germany and then Japan. The admiral made a series of suggestions for the planners beginning with securing the lines of communications across the Atlantic and Pacific. Without the ability to ship large quantities of supplies and hundreds of thousands of men to staging areas, there would be no invasion.

King emphasized his agreement to focus the majority of Allied efforts on Germany while still keeping pressure on Japan. The admiral also asked about the necessity of keeping China supplied instead of other uses of shipping and aviation assets. Even though these principles had been discussed many times before, the American admiral believed it was in everyone's interest to create a new statement on the fundamental strategy going forward. Brand noted that General Brooke was the first to agree with the idea, followed by the remaining Combined Chiefs of Staff. A new statement and supporting documentation were expected by Tuesday's meeting. Additional detailed plans were also being created around the buildup in Great Britain for an invasion of Europe.

The last item James discussed from the Saturday meeting concerned the Azores. Admiral Leahy had pressed the Chiefs of Staff to come to an agreement on establishing bases on the Portuguese islands. General Ismay told the participants a recent series of suggestions had been created and submitted to the prime minister for comments. As James turned to look at Churchill for his reaction, another thought came to mind as the prime minister was about to speak.

"Excuse me, sir, but there was something else about the Azores, which was not discussed at the meeting that I believe has implications for our negotiations with Portugal and also with Spain."

Knowing how the professor worked, Roosevelt thought it odd the man would change course so fast in a discussion. He also knew the prime minister was vacillating on the subject of the Azores. The British government didn't want to pursue military action against their oldest treaty partner, nor did they want to support the Portuguese in a war with Germany. The president rescued his colleague, saying, "What's so important, James? Is there something we don't know?"

"Mr. President, a member of my team, Lieutenant Meyers, spent a couple of months in Portugal working primarily on the wolfram exports to Germany as well as the Azores problem. But his work expanded to include activities with the OSS. It appears he made an important contact with a member of the Abwehr, who has provided valuable intelligence. General Donovan agrees with the assessment and is working on this channel for more discoveries. Evidently, the contact in Lisbon informed our people of a growing effort by the German elite to expedite the movement of money, gold, and other valuables to Portugal and Spain. This includes the acquisition of companies and shipping assets. I believe the prime minister's intelligence agencies may be unaware of some of these transactions. Still, it would be an excellent idea to begin planning for isolating these activities before the close of hostilities."

Roosevelt looked at Churchill, whose hand remained rock steady as he held his morning brandy. If he knew anything about this, Churchill did not let on. "Professor, I will order our people to investigate this claim. If this is true, it would be best if our governments begin a joint operation to close these exit channels and isolate illicit funds trying to leave the Reich. It sounds quite plausible, and I would agree this is what the Nazi scum would do once they understand the war is going against them."

Brand waited for the president to speak. Roosevelt watched Churchill as the man spoke. Quietly picking up a notepad the president jotted down a few words. "James, thank you for that piece of intelligence. I believe both of our intelligence services will begin examining the possibility of rats leaving a sinking ship and trying to take their cheese with them." The president smiled at his little joke, Churchill did not.

"Mr. President, if what the professor says has any validity, it might also mean the Nazis may want to sneak away and start all over in some foreign land. With huge amounts of ill-gotten riches, it is quite possible they could reconstitute their movement. Let us agree on doing the research on this quickly, and if it is even partially true, we need to act."

James now saw the two leaders in a different light. Both were giants in their command of the strategy and politics of the war, but they now saw the possibility of the darkness they were fighting stealing away in the night to reestablish their "new order" in some other land. This could not be allowed to happen. Roosevelt looked at James and gave the officer an order.

"Lieutenant, you will not repeat any of this conversation to anyone without my direct approval. I will reach out to General Donovan today to inquire about what he knows. I am sure that your Lieutenant Meyers will be directed to work with the general, but you are to give him the same order I gave you. Do you have any questions?"

"No sir. I will await your instructions."

"If you hear from General Donovan, he will be working on my behalf. If you have any questions, call me direct. I will inform Admiral Leahy about this, but no one else on the Chiefs of Staff will be included in these conversations."

The president pulled his lighter from his jacket pocket. Bringing it up halfway, he paused briefly as if in thought, then relit his cigarette before asking James about the situation in the Pacific. It was like the previous conversation had never happened, especially about the issue of Nazi gold.

Only after speaking with Margret concerning a wedding date for June, did James stop long enough to consider what the president and prime minister had told him. *Were the Nazis trying to set up another location to continue their operations, or was this just a way for the high-ranking party members to try to leave Germany before it collapsed?*

The Japanese had finally been pushed off the high ground around Holtz Bay. Colonel Culin, who commanded the northern forces on Attu, had suffered many casualties but successfully drove the enemy out of the hills around the bay. As the Japanese pulled back, the enemy forces in front of Willoughby's Scouts withdrew. After three days of struggling against the entrenched enemy and horrid weather conditions, the Scouts made their way down the mountains and entered the American front lines. The three hundred twenty men who made it down the mountain were in a horrible state of health. Only eleven men had been killed, and another twenty seriously wounded in four days and nights of fighting, but of the remaining men, only a hundred sixty-five were still able to fight. The others had suffered horrible foot injuries, mostly from frostbite with gangrene, requiring the amputation of many feet. Many more had bleeding lesions on their knees because they had to crawl instead of walk. Even though covered with bandages and exposure burns from the cold, the ones who could still fight found hot food, warm clothes, and a dry place to lay down and sleep.

Lieutenant Waverly was one of the lucky ones. Dr. Feldman had chewed his ears off before the Marine left on the submarine and had packed four extra pairs of socks. He also gave the Marine another woolen scarf, which he started using on the first day of the hike across the mountains as a head covering. Waverly thought he looked like an old Russian peasant woman walking across the Steppes of Mother Russia instead of a U.S. Marine, but he had made it. He accompanied Willoughby as he reported to Colonel Culin, who had finally cleared the Holtz Valley of the enemy but were still pinned by the Japanese controlling the hills and a more significant force occupying Jarmin Pass. General Brown had ordered Culin to attack the enemy in the pass from his direction while Colonel Zimmerman made a similar attack from the southern direction. Both had failed, and now Culin wondered how to crack the Japanese front.

As the captain showed the colonel how his scouts had traversed the mountains and then worked their way down toward the colonel's position, Culin asked about the lieutenant standing behind him. "I don't think I've met this man before. One of your scouts?"

"Not exactly, sir. Lieutenant Waverly is a Marine Raider who volunteered to join our little walk across the alps of Attu. The man is a rock, and his suggestions have been worth a bucket of gold."

"Waverly? Do you work for a navy captain named Jameson?"

"Yes sir," was all Bill could get out. He was bone tired and as thirsty as a man in a desert.

"I have been receiving inquiries about you since the second day on the island. I'll let Captain Jameson know you're alive and in one piece. And thanks for helping out. Sounds like you did a hell of a job."

"Thank you, sir. Just providing help whenever the captain asked. These men are damn good, and I would serve with them anywhere—as long as it's warmer than this place."

The comment was met with laughter, which was rare on this cold hell of an island. "Lieutenant, let me show you and the captain our current positions and our plan to get the hell out of this valley."

456

The men examined the maps and the colonel's plan to isolate the locations of the Japanese in the hills around the valley. Willoughby reported how the enemy's positions were set up after they had pulled back from the hills. This told the colonel precisely what he wanted to hear. Not that the infantry commander liked the report, but at least it gave him a sense of his enemy and their defensive set up. He told the two officers to get some rest and check on their men. He would need them in the coming days.

The day before, General Brown had requested more reinforcements and additional naval gunfire support. The battleships had expended all of their high explosive munitions and only had armor-piercing ammunition left. They were coming in closer to shore and using their secondary five-inch cannons to bombard the enemy positions, but were now running low on these as well. Twice in the past few days, the *Pennsylvania* had to do a high-speed turn after spotting the track of a torpedo heading for them. The escorting destroyers attacked the Japanese submarine but failed to hit it. Intelligence had more reports of I-boats heading toward the support fleet, making Admiral Kinkaid, now on Adak, nervous. He could ill afford to lose one of the battleships, which were already slotted for the next series of island invasions.

Jameson's report to Admiral Rockwell had provided suggestions for the land campaign based upon the comments from Flannigan. The longer the men stayed in their foxholes and trenches, the more soldiers succumbed to frostbite, and now pneumonia was spreading. The captain's report wasn't trying to damage General Brown's career, but the continuing lack of communications and movement had begun to erode the confidence of senior leaders back in Adak. General John DeWitt, commanding general of the Fourth Army and Western Defense Command, along with Admiral Kinkaid and General Buckner were alarmed at the slow movement of the invasion forces. The recent intelligence estimate of perhaps twenty-five hundred Japanese troops on the island was vastly inferior to the eleven thousand men being used to subjugate the island. Conflicting information and requests for more reinforcements took their toll on the commanders at Adak. Finally, the senior officers decided a new leader would improve the situation on the island.

Major General Eugene Landrum, who had several years' experience in Alaska and had successfully occupied Adak and overseen the base development, was chosen to replace General Brown. Admiral Rockwell was given the unenviable task of informing the general of the decision to replace him. The admiral disagreed with the change, but the chain of command above him left him no option. Upon hearing he had been relieved of command, the general demanded a hearing, but Rockwell knew it would do no good. Reluctantly the general followed orders, and later in the day, Landrum flew in on a PBY. Jameson and Rockwell discussed the situation that evening. Neither man thought it was the correct decision, thinking the campaign was in trouble before the first landing, but knew they had no say in the matter.

While all of the political maneuverings were in motion on Adak and a new commanding general taking over, Flannigan was occupied with a battalion commander dealing with cold and demoralized troops. The men needed food, hot food preferably, but any rations would do. The soldiers desperately needed dry socks, dry boots, dry clothes, and above all, a dry place to sleep. He was also worried about Lieutenant Waverly. There were still no reports from the Scouts, then again, there were few reports about anything. The communications on the island were proving to be a significant obstacle to winning the battle.

The Japanese had spent nearly a year making preparations for an American attack. Many of their positions were connected by tunnels, which offered the enemy dry and, if not warm, at least temperate places to recuperate. Their food supplies were adequate, and their ammunitions supplies were ample. The island commander knew reinforcements couldn't make it to the island in time for any of his men to escape death. He had told his men this already and hoped if he could hold on long enough, the Imperial Navy would make an appearance and destroy the American fleet stranded off the coasts of Attu. All he had to do was hold on, for each additional day brought glory to the empire and the hope of ultimate victory.

48

25 May 1943
Office of Admiral Leahy
White House, Washington, D.C.

- United States --TRIDENT Conference in Washington
  ends. The conferees have selected 1 May 1944
  as target date for cross-channel invasion of
  Northwestern Europe (OVERLORD). In the
  Mediterranean, operations following capture of
  Sicily (HUSKY) are to be designed to knock Italy
  out of the war. Ploesti oil fields are to be bombed
  from Mediterranean bases. Material to China is to
  be increased, and communications with it opened.
  General approval is given U.S. "Strategic Plan for
  the Defeat of Japan," calling for the drive on Japan
  through Central Pacific.
- Aleutians--On Attu, Southern Force's 2nd Battalion,
  17th Infantry, gains toehold on crest of Fish Hook
  Ridge, breaking through elaborate tunnel system
  below the summit.
- Tunisia--Combined headquarters is established on
  Sousse by representatives of forces participating in
  Operation CORKSCREW (conquest of Pantelleria).

James had been in and out of meetings for the past week, assisting Admiral King and Admiral Leahy and sitting in meetings with various subcommittees thrashing out the many details. The Combined Chiefs of Staff had finally agreed to more than an outline for the war's successful conclusion. The British continued pushing for more action in the Mediterranean after the successful capture of Sicily. The Americans were adamant about not wasting more time in this theater of war but agreed to limited actions against Italy if the opportunity presented itself. But the American Chiefs of Staff demanded that additional operations in this theater would not delay the cross channel invasion of France. The American war leaders were also not happy with the large number of British divisions which would remain in places like Palestine, Syria, Egypt, Libya, Gibraltar, and Tunisia. It appeared the British were more interested in holding on to their empire than taking the war to the German homeland. Some of these divisions were considered garrison units, but the amount of required logistical support still weighed heavily on Allies' sealift capabilities.

The American air force was in lockstep with the RAF on the joint bombing campaign and agreed bases in southern Italy would allow their forces to attack critical manufacturing and communications facilities in Austria and Southern Germany. But General Arnold was focused on increasing the number of bombers in England first. This also coincided with the planned invasion of Northern France. A timeline had finally been set, and now every plan required adherence to the needs of this monumental undertaking. Admiral King had won his argument, which pushed for aligning the Royal Navy and the United States Navy in an unrelenting campaign to destroy the German U-boat forces in the Atlantic. This included increased pressure on the Portuguese to allow the British to operate airfields in the Azores, thereby eliminating the last gap in the air search capabilities of the Allies.

The Americans won their battle for the strategy against Japan. The Central Pacific plan had been approved, which allowed Admiral King the freedom of action he was craving. China would receive more support, even though the British did not believe this would help in the war against Japan. The other significant agreement supported the massive increase in landing craft construction. Everything possible would be done in both countries to ramp up production of all types of landing craft, but especially the LST. These unique vessels had proven essential in the Pacific. The upcoming landings in Sicily depended on their ability to bring in large numbers of tanks and other vehicles directly onto an enemy-held beach.

James noted how the message had finally gotten through to everyone, including the air force leaders of both nations. They saw the advantages of these slow lumbering craft in delivering large amounts of supplies for their forward bases and the equipment for building new airfields and facilities. The battle plan was now ready, and at last, the senior leadership agreed on the strategy, timeline, logistics, and major operations required to win the war.

As he waited to see Admiral Leahy on his conference analysis, he took out one of his note pads and scribbled a few notes on yesterday's meeting with the president and prime minister. Lord Cherwell, Churchill's science advisor, and Vice President Wallace, who served on the policy committee on Atomic Energy, and Harry Hopkins attended the meeting. The session concerned the financial needs of the program and the theoretical issues yet to be resolved. Cherwell was a physicist but not a specialist in atomic physics. The man disagreed with the leading American experts on if and how a bomb would work. The more the man spoke, the less James thought of his professional credentials and even less of the man. Hopkins had been watching the British boffin expound on his ideas and the diminished probability of a successful program. Finally, the president turned to Brand and asked a question.

"Lieutenant Brand, you've heard Lord Cherwell's arguments. Are you in agreement with his conclusions?"

Knowing things would not go well but watching Hopkins give him a signal to proceed, James made his statement. "Mr. President, the weapon will function as planned. It will take two years to achieve the final result, but I am supremely confident about the outcome."

Churchill, knowing how Brand worked and also realizing his own expert was becoming difficult in his dealings with others, provided a solution to the disagreement. "Professor Brand, I know you have spent many days in pursuit of a solution to this atomic mystery. You have also worked alongside some of the world's top scientists in this area of research. Do you feel we have the right people and the strong direction required to make this weapon possible?"

"Prime Minister, I continue to attend many of the planning meetings for the project and have assigned a member of my team to work with the engineers building the facilities in Tennessee. Everything is progressing according to schedule. Top people in several fields, including physics, metallurgy, electronics, ordnance, and electrical engineering, are being brought to a new facility to focus their talents on this challenge. I am sure they will accomplish the task within the time allotted."

Seeing a way to avoid conflict between the English science advisor and the young American professor, Harry Hopkins intervened. "Prime Minister, Mr. President, may I suggest that perhaps we set up a series of advisory conferences to provide updates on the progress of the project. This way, if there are major delays or technical problems, they can be addressed quickly."

Knowing Hopkins intention of reducing discord between the Allies, Roosevelt quickly agreed. "Splendid idea, Harry. Prime Minister, would this be a good solution and allow us to see if additional support is needed?"

Churchill, not wanting to cause any more problems at the end of the TRIDENT conference, thought the idea was valid. "Mr. President, I will establish a calendar for regular updates on the project and work with your advisory panel to communicate areas of interest."

Quickly winding up the discussion, Churchill noted the other activities for the day and how time worked against all the participants. "We need to get ready for the final conference dinner this evening, and perhaps Lord Cherwell will provide me his ideas for this meeting tomorrow."

Lord Cherwell, now on the defensive, quickly agreed, and the meeting adjourned. The British boffin and Vice President Wallace walked out of the room while James collected his papers. Harry pointed at the president, saying, "The boss and the prime minister want a word."

Moving closer to the two Allied leaders, the president said, "James, you held your own with Lord Cherwell. The prime minister and I aren't too sure about where he was going with his analysis, but I think we're both in your camp."

Churchill picked up the conversation adding, "Professor, you did well with my boffin. He is quite irritating at times, and you did not cause him any professional harm. Diplomatic of you to do so."

Before James could reply, Roosevelt asked, "James, we wanted to know the date of the big event?"

Not comprehending the meaning of the words, James replied, "Sir, I'm sorry. What event are you referring to?"

Churchill smiled and looked at his partner in the war effort. "Franklin, the young man needs to spend less time in a laboratory or stuffy meetings and more time with a certain young lady."

Finally grasping the meaning of the conversation, James turned a bit red in the face and apologized. "Sorry, sir. Lady Margret and I are looking at mid-June. We have been given a few dates from the British Embassy but need to see if they will work with our schedules."

"James, don't worry about your schedule. We can work around the wedding. Now, I'm sure the prime minister can influence scheduling things at the embassy, and I will arrange to have your family in attendance. Lord Mountbatten is working on Lady Margret's family to see if we can get them across the pond as well. Sir John is also heavily involved, and with the support you have from the military, I'm certain if we can invade North Africa from three thousand miles away, we can get you hitched!"

The two world leaders grinned like Cheshire cats while James stared in disbelief. How two men, facing terrible decisions, would have time to worry about two young people was beyond his comprehension.

Task Force 51 had moved about the reefs and rocks of Attu for many days. Japanese submarines had fired many torpedoes at both warships and transports but to no effect. The Imperial Japanese Navy had a cruiser force north of the Komandorski Islands, but it never moved toward the battle. Perhaps the intelligence from the submarines or the besieged troops on Attu regarding the American battleships moving about caused the Japanese admiral to be cautious of any approach. But on May 16, Admiral Kinkaid recalled most of the assault task force back to Adak.

The big battleships were out of high explosive shells and only had armor-piercing rounds left in their magazines. Most of the ammunition for their secondary five-inch guns had also been expended. The same situation was found on most of the destroyers in the covering force. The escort carrier *Nassau* needed refueling. New pilots were trying hard to make a difference, but the weather conditions were difficult. One hundred seventy-nine sorties had been launched by the carrier during the operation, and five planes had been lost. General Landrum was given control of the ships remaining to provide fire support to the army, including three destroyers and the newly arrived gunboat *Charleston,* armed with four six-inch cannons. The landing forces had lost ninety of its landing craft in all manners of collisions, groundings, and mechanical failures. The remaining navy ships were using lifeboats to take provisions ashore, and even one of the PBYs motored back and forth to the beach carrying food and medical supplies.

Captain Jameson sat in a heated Quonset hut drinking hot coffee with Lieutenant Clark. Sergeant McBride was on an errand to find Chief Schmidt, who was waiting at the communications shack for information on the whereabouts of Major Flannigan. The last message the captain received indicated the major was with the infantry as they closed in on the remaining Japanese positions. Evidently, Lieutenant Waverly was now with him as well, and everyone was doing all right. No word on Dr. Feldman, but his field hospital was near the beach, far from the fighting.

A series of coded messages had been sent and confirmations received from the captain concerning the situation on Attu. Admiral Edwards wanted the unvarnished truth, which is precisely what Jameson provided. Detailing a long list of problems encountered in the operation, the admiral wanted a complete report when Jameson and his team returned. The admiral's last message asked when their return to Washington was expected. Not knowing when he could pull his men off the island, Jameson left that question open to conjecture. Edwards could handle the information knowing the challenges being encountered in subduing the enemy on Attu.

The Scottish pilot had spent the last few days back on Adak talking to the army pilots who had flown missions to Attu. Most of them returned without ever seeing the island. When they did get a glimpse of it, they attacked, usually at a very low altitude. The B-25s successfully hit the ridgelines, and the P-38s had limited success with their strafing attacks. The navy Wildcats had some success as well but encountered difficulties in hitting the correct targets. One mission unknowingly attacked American forces, wounding some, but the pilots improved over time. As Clark told the captain, "The pilots are brand new. They have a hard time landing on the small carrier, have had no combat experience and very little training in ground support attacks."

Jameson added this information to his report and knew Clark would provide a tremendous amount of detail in his analysis. The Scot had flown four missions over three days and successfully attacked a Japanese troop concentration near Holtz Bay. He found many challenges supporting the invasion with only one small carrier but knew from his Royal Navy experience that you use what you have to accomplish the mission. Perhaps the next battle would be better supported. As the two men drank their coffee and enjoyed the warmth of the building, both thought about their comrades on the frigid island.

"Did you see that?"

"No, but next time, I'll be ready to shoot the bastard." Waverly looked out at the snow-covered mountain in front of him. Sergeant Dean was lying in the snow next to him, and both men were cold, wet, and miserable. The two Marines were trying to locate an enemy sniper who kept taking shots at the troops below. With a bit of luck, they would succeed before the Japanese sniper killed them.

The major had gone back down the hill to meet the battalion commander. This unit was part of the Fourth Regiment, which landed a few days after the main invasion and was experienced in dealing with the Alaskan weather. Older than a lot of the draftees comprising the Seventh Division, most had been in Alaska before the attack on Pearl Harbor and knew how the weather could break the human body and spirit. The men from the Seventh Division who had landed in the first days were being laid low by frostbite and other forms of exposure. Men were getting sick—colds, bronchial infections, and now pneumonia ripped through the American forces like a tidal wave.

Waverly spent three days receiving medical attention for lesions caused by crawling around in the rocky and icy mountains. His back was killing him, but he told no one of his discomforts. Lukewarm chow, dry clothes and new boots made the man feel well enough to fight the enemy. Flannigan had found him after the north and south forces made contact at Jarmin Pass. The major had to pull rank before Waverly left Willoughby's Scouts, but Flannigan wanted him close for the final push to take the island.

The new commanding general had extensive experience in Alaska, knew the Aleutian conditions, and acted accordingly. Knowing how the enemy would defend the high ridges and with their backs to the beaches of Chichagof Harbor, the Americans could now use their naval support and artillery to demolish the Japanese defenses. Engineers had been able to build a few hardened roads in the past week, and now artillery and transport could move close to the front lines. Pushing at numerous points in the enemy's lines, the Americans could move slowly toward the final defensive positions. It would not be long now before the enemy was defeated. In fact, two captured Japanese soldiers provided a good picture of the enemy's situation. It was desperate because of the number of casualties and the inability to move either supplies or reinforcements to meet American advances. The Japanese had built caves and tunnel systems which would require a great deal of effort on behalf of the advancing army troops to eliminate, but with each day, there were fewer defenders. The original twenty-five hundred men were now down to less than one thousand, with many of those men wounded. The end was near for both the Japanese and the Americans.

"What do you see in there?"

"I think it's ruptured, and if we can clamp the artery a bit further up, we might be able to suture it closed."

The two doctors worked feverishly on another young soldier. The man had been hit in the left shoulder about two hours ago, and the combat medic had been able to stuff a bandage in the wound and kept the pressure on it for the entire time it took to get the man down to the field hospital. Dr. Feldman partnered with a young army doctor who had been an obstetrician in civilian life but found himself getting a crash course in combat surgery.

"Doctor, do you think you can sew it up well enough to keep it from erupting again?"

Feldman looked closely with a pair of magnifying glasses he wore on his nose. His ability to do close work had earned him praise in New York City, and now it might save a nineteen-year-old's life. "Yes, I think we can. Keep the clamp tight and give me some more light." Pharmacist Mate Hamlin was assisting in the operation and moved the large field operating room light closer. He also had a flashlight at the ready in case the power went down again. The emergency generator had been nothing but problem-prone since the day they fired up the damn thing. Hiram had used some of his best curses to improve the recalcitrant machine's performance, but so far, everyone in the cold tent knew it would conk out any moment.

"Thanks, Jonathan. Keep it focused there, and be ready with some of the smallest sutures you have in the kit. I don't want to lose this kid."

The doctors worked on the soldier for another thirty minutes, and finally, as the clamp was relaxed, Feldman couldn't see any bleeders. Turning to the other doctor, he said, "Can you close for me? I need to check if we have any new chest cases waiting."

"Sure, Doc, I'll take care of him, and by the way, that was one hell of a job."

Hiram gave the man a sloppy salute and said, "Just another day at the office in this cold hell of an island."

As Feldman walked to the flap of the tent, he looked out and saw several men on stretchers being attended to by medics. Each man had a tag on his foot or around his neck listing specific injuries for the hospital personnel. From the look of the situation, most were frostbite cases. He saw men wearing boots caked in ice. The soldier's foot was more likely than not frozen. Cutting off the boot often revealed blackened toes or gangrene. This meant only one thing to medical personnel—amputation. Hiram had amputated more appendages in the last ten days than in his entire career. Perhaps a hundred men had lost a foot or fingers and toes.

As he looked around, he saw a stretcher being brought in, which needed immediate attention. The man's face was wrapped in blood-soaked gauze, with more bandaging across his neck. Fearing the worse, Feldman told the stretcher-bearers to bring the man into his tent for immediate attention. Perhaps, he thought, this might be the last case he would see. But he knew the truth. The Japanese would hold out until the end, and then, they would attack until they were all dead. The question then was how many more Americans would have to die or be horribly maimed before this battle ended.

49

30 May 1943
Office of Admiral Edwards
Washington, D.C.

• Aleutian Islands--After a weak counterattack,
  organized resistance collapses on Attu. 7th Division
  reaches the shore of Chichagof Harbor without
  incident. U.S. Army forces under Brig. Gen. John
  Copeland occupy Shemya Island without opposition.

As the admiral read the report summary, he sipped his coffee and occasionally wrote a note on a separate pad of paper. The full report, some four hundred pages long, was positioned next to him. After ten minutes, he put the summary down and looked at the four young men seated at the table. His new aide, Lieutenant Commander Tillman, was seated to his right. Lieutenant Brand was across the table from him with Lieutenant Meyers and Lieutenant Stevens on each side of the professor. The three men from the Science Team awaited the admiral's questions.

"Gentlemen, this is a good report summary. I take it that you have all of the backup detail in the full report?"

Brand replied for the others. "Sir, we have an appendix on each item, plus we can provide additional support materials for our conclusions if needed."

"I assumed you did, Lieutenant, but I had to ask. What about the update on the Central Pacific plan? Has Nimitz had a chance to review it yet?"

"Sir, we sent a draft of the full report via courier to Hawaii on 27 May. I have not had a confirmation of receipt, but will send another message today to confirm."

"What about the landing craft program? You made a good argument for increasing LST production by slowing down the destroyer escort program starting this fall. Did you get any comments from the construction committee?"

"Admiral, they weren't happy about the recommendation. I had to point out the major parts of each ship, such as the diesel engines are interchangeable and that it takes fewer hours to build an LST versus a DE. I think we need some additional push from Admiral King to ensure the changes are made."

Admiral Edwards put down his pencil and picked up his cup of coffee. He was pleased with this team of young men. Only his aide was a professional naval officer. The other three had different backgrounds, but under the tutelage of Captain Jameson, they had shown incredible creativity and dedication to duty. Smiling, at last, he took a sip of the now lukewarm coffee. "Plan to produce a bi-monthly report about the targeted levels of production versus delivered goods. That would include the finished product, like the LST, and the major components, engines, power winches, antiaircraft weapons, and other major subassemblies. We need to keep everyone focused on the end game."

After another couple of questions, Edwards dismissed the officers but told Brand to remain.

"Lieutenant, anything new from Jameson?"

"Nothing since yesterday morning. Chief Schmidt is still trying to get an update on Major Flannigan and Dr. Feldman. We know the doctor is with the division hospital and was keeping busy. The major is near the front with Lieutenant Waverly and Sergeant Dean. I believe they are with a unit of the Fourth Regiment. Nothing else to report, sir."

"I have ordered Jameson to pull his men off that damn island as soon as possible and return to Washington. We need to get organized for the next push in the Mediterranean and the Pacific." Seeing the professor listening intently to his every word, Edwards continued.

"Admiral King and I believe that using you and the team like we have these past six months pays extra dividends. The captain has developed a great sense of tactical knowledge on amphibious landings. We will need more of his expertise, so we want to continue using the team for new operations. The same goes for Major Flannigan and Dr. Feldman."

James knew the comment made sense, but he feared for his friends who were being sent into harm's way while he sat out the war in Washington. "Are there any new plans for my services?"

Expecting this would come up, Edwards was ready with an answer. "Admiral King and Admiral Leahy realize your significant contributions to the war effort and will continue to use your skills accordingly. I can't give you any other guarantees about what you will be doing, but I know that many of the projects you have worked on are extremely important to the Allied cause."

James accepted the information but wished he could get closer to the war, perhaps in the upcoming HUSKY operation. Edwards added one more item for the professor to consider.

"Lieutenant, the president wants you to continue with your special projects as well as new strategic initiatives as they evolve. I'm sure you will get a chance to get out of the country, but remember, you will not be allowed close to any combat zone."

The last comment didn't concern him. He just wanted to be near where the tactical decisions were being made. This caused him to immediately think about his friends in the Aleutians. At least they would be coming home soon.

The men were huddled around the cot. The injured man receiving their attention was bandaged above the eyes, and his heavily bandaged right arm rested in a sling. His lit cigarette was closely monitored by a sergeant. The medic offered food, but the man was not hungry. The doctor had been around twice in the last hour, checking on his patient and telling the sergeant not to give him any more cigarettes. The man's commanding officer was upset he wasn't there earlier to help his friend and comrade in arms. The man had been brought into the hospital late last night following a last gasp effort of the Japanese in defense of Attu.

The Japanese commander ordered his surviving soldiers to gather for a charge toward the American lines. At 0330 on May 29, the attack began. The timing was perfect because some of the American forward units were moving positions. The attack tore through small groups of men, a forward medical clearing station, a command position where a battalion commander was killed along with most of his officers, and they kept on moving toward their objective—an artillery emplacement. They nearly got there, but members of an engineer battalion formed up and fought back. The attack was broken, and the enemy pulled back. Later in the day, the remnants tried again, but the Americans were ready and well equipped to repulse and annihilate the enemy. Few got away. Some would hide for over three months on the island, but few surrendered.

Lieutenant Waverly had tried to sleep but heard the sounds of the distant battle and moved uphill to where he knew Captain Willoughby's men were holding a position. The captain's position had been overrun, and the senior officer was wounded but still fighting when the Marine found him. Working with a few other survivors, Waverly helped the engineers turn back the charge, and later in the day he was in for the final attack by the enemy. It was almost over when an enemy hand grenade landed near him. He hit the ground before it exploded, but the damage to his head was severe. His arm had been equally maimed by his attempt to protect his head. Luckily, he had been seen by other men who rendered first aid then carried him down to the forward hospital. From here, he was stabilized and moved down to the division hospital near Massacre Beach. Dr. Feldman found him among the other seriously wounded survivors from the Japanese banzai attack.

The Marine was in bad shape, but the medic who first treated him did an excellent job stopping the bleeding and keeping him from going into shock. The forward hospital doctors did their job keeping him stable and sending him to the field hospital, which was better equipped to handle head wounds. Hiram was lucky to have found him in the pile of injured humanity filling the hospital that evening. Finding Jonathan Hamlin, he told him to get a message to division HQ to locate Major Flannigan and have him report to the hospital.

Through the night, Feldman conducted major surgery on seven

men and performed minor procedures on another dozen. Bill Waverly was one of the significant cases. Luckily, an army doctor who had seen many head cases was able to assist. Bleeding in the brain was the biggest concern, and the two physicians worked for an hour to ease the pressure and then mend most of the damage caused by shrapnel. Hiram didn't know if the Marine would retain full function of his muscles or even of his ability to speak. The brain was still much of an unknown to medical science.

When Flannigan and Dean were finally located, the two men charged into the hospital like the place was on fire. Finding Hamlin first to get an update on Waverly's condition, they approached the man lying on a cot. He was sedated, and he had tubes and hoses stuck in him, some adding fluid, others draining fluid. Dean had seen many cases on Guadalcanal and wondered if all of this made sense. He had witnessed many men dying in the hospital, and most of them had tubes like Bill Waverly.

Flannigan got an update from Doc Feldman. "Bill is stable for now but the extent of his recovery is a guess. He may recover fully or be permanently incapacitated." Feldman looked the Marine in the eye and continued. "The passage of time is the only way we'll learn these answers."

Fortunately, by mid-morning, Waverly woke up and was at first thirsty as can be, and then he wanted a smoke. Dean quickly obliged both requests, which made the wounded man happy. Feldman quickly removed the cigarette, and told everyone within hearing distance the next man who gave the Marine a cigarette would be changed into a girl. No one laughed at the steely-eyed doctor who had gone thirty-six hours without sleep. Flannigan agreed to keep the smokes away and quickly knelt down to speak to the wounded man.

"Bill, how are you feeling?"

"Major, I'm really mad as hell for not moving faster."

"I heard you did a fine job with the engineers. Everybody said you were yelling and kicking ass to fight the Japs. Hell of a job, Bill."

Feldman walked over and took the man's pulse and then inserted a thermometer in the man's mouth so he couldn't speak. Telling everyone hovering around the man on the cot, he said, "Let Waverly sleep. We'll take good care of him, and I think he's going to be just fine." Looking at Flannigan, he whispered, "Bill is going to make it, but I'm not sure what long-term problems he's going to face. Keep him calm and stay positive."

The Marine major, a man of great courage and strength, wanted to go outside and scream at the top of his lungs. Another good man had been seriously injured in the war, and he knew things were going to get worse. *How many more men would die or be crippled?* Turning back to face Feldman, Hamlin, and Dean, the major said, "As soon as Bill is able to move, we have priority orders to head back to Washington. Admiral Edwards has plans for the team."

In proportion to the troops engaged, the Battle of Attu would rank as the second most costly in the Pacific Theater—second only to Iwo Jima.

U.S. Casualties
549 Dead
1,148 Wounded in Combat
1,200 Severe Cold Injuries
1,200 Exposure and Disease
614 Psychiatric Breakdowns
and Accidents

Japanese Casualties
2,300 Dead
28 Captured

Many lessons were learned from the battle on the frozen island. These were studied in great detail and helped improve cold-weather clothing, medical care, and the planning and execution for future amphibious operations.

Appendix

Historical Figures in Battle Plan
(Note: All officer ranks are as of June 1943)

American Civilian and Scientific Leadership

Franklin D. Roosevelt, President of the United States
Lee DuBridge, Director of the MIT Radiation Laboratory
Harry S. Truman, Senator from Missouri, Head of Truman Committee
James Wood, Financial Attaché, American Embassy Portugal
John von Neumann, Professor of Mathematics, Princeton University
George Kennan, *Charge d' Affaires,* American Embassy in Portugal
Allen Dulles, OSS Station Chief, Bern Switzerland
Whitney Shepardson, OSS Director, Secret Intelligence Branch
Donald Nelson, Director of the War Production Board
Henry Wallace, Vice President of the United States

United States Navy

Adm. Ernest King, Chief of Naval Operations
Adm. W. D. Leahy, Chairman, Joint Chiefs of Staff and Chief of Staff to the President of the United States
Rear Adm. Richard S. Edwards, Chief of Staff to Admiral King
Adm. A. J. Hepburn, Chairman of the General Board
Adm. Chester Nimitz, Commander in Chief, Pacific Fleet, (CINCPAC) and Pacific Ocean Area (POA)
Adm. William F. Halsey, Commander South Pacific (SOPAC)
Capt. Miles Browning, Chief of Staff to Admiral Halsey (SOPAC)
Vice Adm. R. L. Ghormley, Former Commander South Pacific (SOPAC)
Vice Adm. Raymond A. Spruance, Chief of Staff, CINCPAC
Comdr. Edward Layton, Intelligence Officer for CINCPAC
Capt. Howard D. Bode, Captain of the cruiser *Chicago* at Battle of Savo Island

Lt. Robert Oliver, Aide to Rear Adm. Spruance

Rear Adm. Charles M. Cooke, Head of War Planning for Chief of Naval Operations

Comdr. William "Deak" Parsons, Bureau of Ordnance and Staff for OSRD

Comdr. Samuel G. Mitchell, American Liaison for HMS *Victorious* mission to the Pacific

Capt. John L. McCrea, Naval Aide to President Roosevelt

Rear Adm. Ross T. McIntire, Personal Physician to President Roosevelt

Lt. Franklin D. Roosevelt, Jr., Naval Officer and Son of President Roosevelt

Rear Adm. Jesse B. Oldendorf, Commandant NOB Trinidad and Trinidad Sector, Caribbean Sea Frontier

Lt. Comdr. Harry Butcher, Naval Aide to General Eisenhower

Rear Adm. William R. Purnell, Navy Representative on the Military Policy Committee

Rear Adm. Harold C. Train, Director, Office of Naval Intelligence

Rear Adm. Robert H. English, Commander Submarine Force, Pacific Fleet (COMSUBPAC) until January 21, 1943, upon his death in airplane accident

Rear Adm. Charles A. Lockwood, Commander Submarine Force, Pacific Fleet (COMSUBPAC) effective February 14, 1943

Rear Adm. Thomas Kinkaid, North Pacific Area Commander

Rear Adm. Charles " Soc" McMorris, Commander Combat Task Group 16.6

Capt. Bertram J. Rogers, Commanding Officer, heavy cruiser *Salt Lake City*

Comdr. W. S. "Worthy" Bitler, Executive Officer, heavy cruiser *Salt Lake City*

Capt. Theodore Waldschmidt, Commanding Officer, light cruiser *Richmond*

Rear Adm. Rockwell Francis W. Rockwell, Commander, Amphibious Forces North Pacific

Rear Adm. Ben Moreell, Chief of Bureau, Yards and Docks

Capt. Charles J. Moore, Admiral Spruance's Principle Aide and Chief of Staff.

Capt. Lynde D. McCormick, CINCPAC Head of Plans (J-1)

Vice Adm. William Calhoun, Commanding Officer , Service Force Pacific Fleet

Rear Adm. Mahlon Tisdale, Commander, Destroyers Pacific Fleet

United States Army

Gen. George C. Marshall, Chief of Staff

Gen. Henry H. Arnold, Chief of Staff, Army Air Forces

Gen. Dwight D. Eisenhower, Supreme Commander, Allied Expeditionary Force of the North African Theater of Operations

Gen. Douglas MacArthur, Commanding General, Southwest Pacific Area (SWPA)

Lt. Gen. Brehon Somervell, Chief of Army Services of Supply

Brig. Gen. Albert C. Wedemeyer, Chief of Strategic and Policy Section, Operations Division

Maj. Gen. Claire Chennault, Commanding General, 14th Air Force

Maj. Gen. Clayton L. Bissell, Commanding General, 10th Air Force

Maj. Gen. Alexander Patch, Commander American Forces on Guadalcanal, after 9 December 1942

Maj. Gen. Henry C. Pratt, Commanding General, Trinidad Base Command

Lt. Gen. George Patton, Commanding General, Morocco, II Corps in Tunisia beginning March 1943

Maj. Gen. Lloyd Fredendall, Commanding General, II Corps in Tunisia until March 1943

Maj. Gen. Walter "Beetle" Smith, Chief of Staff to General Eisenhower

Maj. Gen. Ernest Harmon, Commanding General, 2nd Armored Division

Brig. Gen. William J. Donovan, Director, Office of Strategic Services (OSS)

Maj. Gen. Lucian Truscott, Commanding General, 3rd Infantry Division

Lt. Col. Elliott Roosevelt, Aerial Reconnaissance Officer and Son of President Roosevelt

Col. Benjamin Dickson, Intelligence Officer, II Corps

Maj. Gen. Orlando Ward, Commanding General, 1st Armored Division

Brig. Gen. Paul M. Robinett, Commanding Officer, Combat Command B, 1st Armored Division

Brig. Gen. Leslie Groves, Commanding Officer, Manhattan Project

Lt. Col. John Waters, Battalion Commander, 168th Regimental Combat Team, Lessoude Force

Lt. Col. Robert Moore, Battalion Commander, 168th Regimental Combat Team, Kassir Force

Lt. Gen. Delos C. Emmons, Army Commander Hawaii

Maj. Gen. Ralph Smith, Commanding General, 27th Infantry Division

Maj. Gen. Edmond H. Leavey, CINCPAC Logistics Officer (J-4)

Maj. Gen. A. E. Brown, Commanding General 7th Infantry Division

Capt. William H. Willoughby, Commanding Officer, Provisional Scout Battalion, 7th Infantry

Col. Edward P. Earle, Commanding Officer, 17th Infantry Regiment (KIA)

Col. Wayne Zimmerman, Commanding Officer, 17th Infantry Regiment, (replacing Earle)

Maj. Gen. Simon B. Buckner, Alaskan Defense Commander

Col. Frank Culin, Commanding Officer, 32nd Infantry Regiment

Lt. Gen. John DeWitt, Commanding General, 4th Army/Western Defense Command

Maj. Gen. Eugene Landrum, Commanding General 7th Infantry Division, effective 16 May 1943

United States Marine Corps

Brig. Gen. Allen H. Turnage, Assistant Commander, 3rd Marine Division

Maj. Gen. Barrett Charles Barrett, Commanding General, 3rd Marine Division

Maj. Gen. Holland Smith, Commanding General, Amphibious Corps, Pacific Fleet

United Kingdom
Winston Churchill, Prime Minister of Great Britain
Field Marshal, Sir John Dill, Former Chief of the Imperial Staff and British
    Military Representative in Washington
Capt. L. D. Mackintosh, Commanding officer HMS *Victorious*
Sir Ronald Campbell, British Ambassador to Portugal
Stewart Menzies, Director of British Intelligence
Sir Girija Bajpai, Agent-General for India
Sir Zafarullah Khan, India's Agent-General to China
Air Vice Marshal Arthur Tedder, Commander in Chief, Mediterranean Air Forces
Gen. Alan Brooke, Chief of the British Staff, Commander of the Army
Air Chief Marshal Sir Charles Portal, Commander in Chief, Royal Air Force
Adm. of the Fleet Sir Dudley Pound, Commander in Chief, Royal Navy
Maj. Gen. Sir Hasting Ismay, Military Advisor to the Prime Minister
Vice Adm. Lord Louis Mountbatten, Chief of Combined Operations Headquarters
Lt. Gen. Kenneth Anderson, Commanding General, British 1st Army
Gen. Harold Alexander, Commanding General, 18th Army Group
Gen. Bernard Montgomery, Commanding General, 8th Army
Brig. Gen. A. J. Dunphie, Commanding General, British 26th Armored Brigade
Lord Cherwell (Fredrick Lindemann), Scientific Advisor to the Prime Minister
Flight Lt. Roald Dahl, Assistant Air Attaché, British Embassy

France
Gen. Charles de Gaulle, Leader of the Free French Forces (French Committee of
    National Liberation)
Gen. Henri Giraud, Commander of Free French Forces in Africa
Gen. Juin, Commander of Eastern Sector, Tunisia

China
Chiang Kai-shek, Generalissimo and President, Nationalist Government of China
Madame Chiang Kai-shek (Soong Mei-ling), American educated and
    highly influential wife of the Chinese (Kuomintang) government leader,
    Generalissimo and President, Chiang Kai-shek

Germany
Baron Oswald von Hoyniger-Huene, German Ambassador to Portugal
Albert von Karsthof, Head of Abwehr (German Intelligence) in Portugal
Rear Adm. Wilhelm Canaris, Chief of German Intelligence (Abwehr)
Field Marshal Friedrich Paulus, Commanding General, German 6th Army
Field Marshal Erwin Rommel, Commanding General, Afrika Corps
Col. Gen. Jurgen von Arnim, Commanding General Army Group Africa
Field Marshal Albert Kesselring, Wehrmacht Commander in Chief-South

Portugal

Dr. Antonio de Oliveira Salazar, Acting President of Portugal
Captain Agostinho Lourenço, Head of Policia de Vigilancia e Defesa de Estado
  (PVDE)

Japan

Adm. Isoruku Yamamoto, Commander in Chief, Combined Fleet
Adm. Osami Nagano, Commander of Naval General Staff
Vice Adm. Boshiro Hosogaya, Commander 5th Fleet (relieved March 31, 1943)
Vice Adm. Matome Ukagi, Chief of Staff, Combined Fleet
Vice Adm. Shiro Kawase, Commander 5th Fleet (April 1943)
Vice Adm. Jisaburo Ozawa, Commanding Officer, 3rd Fleet
Rear Adm. Raizo Tanaka, Commander of Destroyer Squadron 2, "Tokyo Express"
Gen. Hideki Tojo, Prime Minister of Japan
Emperor Hirohito, 124th Emperor of Japan (also Known as Emperor Showa)
Empress Kojun, wife of Emperor Hirohito
Gen. Hitoshi Imamura, Commanding General, Japanese 8th Area Army

Terms, Aircraft, Abbreviations
Allied Forces

B-17 Flying Fortress Bomber: Boeing Aircraft four-engine, long-range bomber
B-29 Superfortress Bomber: Boeing Aircraft four-engine, long-range bomber
B-24 Liberator Bomber: Consolidated Aircraft four-engine, long-range bomber
BAR: Browning Automatic Rifle
Blackburn Skua: British Fleet Air Arm fighter/bomber
BOLERO: Buildup of forces in Great Britain for the invasion of France
BUPERS: Bureau of Personnel
BuOrd: Bureau of Ordinaces
CACTUS: Code name for Guadalcanal
CARTWHEEL: Operation to eliminate Japanese in the Bismack Archipelago
CBI: China-Burma-India command
CCS: Combined Chiefs of Staff, (United States and Great Britain)
Chance Voight Corsair: Carrier and land-based fighter/bomber
CINCPAC: Commander in Chief, Pacific Fleet, Admiral Nimitz
CNO: Chief of Naval Operations
CORKSCREW: Operation to invade Pantelleria Island off Sicily
Curtiss Wright P-40 Warhawk: Army fighter/bomber
De Haviland Gypsy Moth: British biplane trainer from the end of World War I
  until the 1940s

Douglas C-47 (Navy R4D): Twin-engine military version of the DC-3 passenger plane

Douglas C-54 (Navy R5D): four engine military version of the DC-4 passenger plane

Fairey Fulmar: British Fleet Air Arm reconnaissance/fighter/bomber

Fairey Albacore: British Fleet Air Arm biplane torpedo bomber

FLAX: Air operations in support of final Tunisia offensive

GALVANIC: Code name for occupation of Gilbert Islands

Gloster Sea Gladiator: Obsolete carrier biplane fighter

Grumman F4F Wildcat: Carrier-based fighter

Grumman Hellcat: Carrier-based fighter

Grumman TBF Avenger: Navy torpedo bomber

Hawker Hurricane: British single-engine fighter

HUSKY: Code name for invasion of Sicily, July 1943

LANDCRAB: Occupation of Attu

Liberty Ships: Standard design cargo vessel displacing 10,000 tons

LCVP: (Higgins boat) Landing craft vehicle personnel, capacity of 36 troops or 8,100 pounds of supplies

Lockheed Model 18 Lodestar: Twin-engine transport/military version used as a reconnaissance/bomber

Lockheed P-38: Twin-engine, high-speed fighter

LSD: Landing Ship Dock

LSI: Landing Ship Infantry

LST: Landing Ship Tank

M-1 Garand Rifle: standard issue semi-automatic Army and Marine rifle in WWII

M-3 Lee Tank: Early American medium tank in WWII, replaced by Sherman Tank

M-3 Stuart Tank: Standard American light tank in WWII

M-4 Sherman Tank: Standard American heavy tank in WWII

M-130: Martin Aircraft four-engine flying boat

M1911: 45 Caliber pistol

MAGIC: Code name for signal intelligence of Japanese communications

Manhattan Project: Secret project to design, develop and build the atomic bomb

Mark 14 Torpedo: Standard submarine launched torpedo of the U.S. Navy

Mark 24 Mine: American air dropped anti-submarine homing torpedo

Marston Mat: Perforated Steel Planking (PSP) used to build temporary airfields in remote locations

Model 317 Clipper: Boeing four-engine, long-range seaplane

North American T-6 Texan: Principle advanced training aircraft (known as the Harvard in Britain)

North American B-25 Mitchell bomber: Twin-engine medium bomber

ONI: Office of Naval Intelligence

OSRD: Office of Science, Research and Development, agency to coordinate scientific research for the American military

OVERLORD: Cross channel invasion of northwest Europe

PBY Catalina: Consolidated Aircraft Amphibious twin-engine patrol plane
POA: Pacific Ocean Area
PT Boat: Patrol Torpedo Boat, high-speed, torpedo carrying vessel, 80' long, crew of 12-15
Supermarine Spitfire: British single-engine fighter
Short S.25 Sunderland: British four-engine flying boat used by Coastal Command
SOPAC: South Pacific Area (sub command of Pacific Ocean Area)
SWPA: Southwest Pacific Area, General MacArthur's command
SYMBOL: Cover name for Casablanca Conference
Thompson: .45 Caliber Sub Machine Gun
TORCH: Code name for invasion of North Africa, November 1942
TRIDENT: Cover name for Washington conference, May 1943
ULTRA: Signals intelligence of German Enigma code
VULCAN: Final offensive to eliminate German defenses in Tunisia
WAVES: Women Accepted for Voluntary Emergency Service

Portugal

PVDE: Policia de Vigilancia E Defesa do Estado (Portuguese Secret Police)

Japanese Naval and Military

IJN: Imperial Japanese Navy
Kawanishi H6K "Mavis": Four-engine, long-range reconnaissance flying boat
Mitsubishi A6M "Zero": Japanese Type 0 carrier fighter
Mitsubishi Type 97: Twin-engine Japanese army bomber
Nakajima B5N "Kate": Single-engine, carrier-based torpedo bomber
Nakajima A6M2 "Rufe": Float plane fighter based on the Zero
Type 93 torpedo: "Long Lance" naval torpedo

German Aircraft

Dornier DO 17: Twin engine bomber/night fighter
Heinkel 111: Twin engine bomber
Junkers JU 52: Three engine transport
Junkers JU 87: Single engine dive bomber "Stuka"
Messerschmidt ME 109: Single engine fighter
Messerschmidt ME 323 (Gigant): Six engine heavy transport aircraft

Coming Soon from Author

J. EUGENE PORTER

Secret Surrender

Book VI in the Series
THE NAVAL ODYSSEY OF PROFESSOR JAMES BRAND

Made in United States
North Haven, CT
04 January 2023